THE LAST MERRY-GO-ROUND

C. L. CHARLESWORTH

Printed in the United States of America

ISBN 979-8-9924781-0-5 (sc)
ISBN 979-8-9924781-1-2 (hc)
ISBN 979-8-9924781-2-9 (e)

Library of Congress Control Number: 2025913245

RAVING REVIEWS FROM READERS:

"A dramatic, soul-rending tale... suspenseful and gripping from the first word to the last."
— Stephanie Kopetzky (Amazon)

"A real page-turner! Impossible not to be immersed in the story."
— Diego Gimar (Amazon)

"A beautifully written, clever, and intense exploration of toxic relationships."
— M.C.V. Egan, (Goodreads)

"A well-crafted, dark, and emotionally gripping story."
— Maria Catalina Egan (Amazon)

"A gripping novel that delves into the secrets of marriage."
— Ryan T (Amazon)

"Brutal and unflinching... a ride that takes you deep into dark places."
— DLP (Amazon)

"An important book that tackles difficult issues with skill and depth."
— Andrew (Amazon)

"A dark, intense, and unforgettable novel with twists you won't see coming."
— Jose Buenaventura Durruti (Amazon)

"A well-written book reminiscent of classics like The Awakening and The Age of Innocence."
— Julia Clem (Amazon)

"A fast-paced and emotional story that keeps you hooked until the last page."
— Christina W. (Amazon)

"A powerful and thought-provoking novel that holds a mirror to society."
— Mike Conner (Amazon)

"A book filled with dark secrets, gripping suspense, and raw realism."
— Sunshine Ink (Amazon)

"An ending that stays with you long after you turn the last page."
— Tamercindy (Amazon)

"A captivating read that exposes the harsh realities of power and control."
— Sedona Cave & Trail (Amazon)

"An emotional rollercoaster with strong characters and a gripping storyline."
— Jeff Jones (Goodreads)

I dedicate *The Last Merry Go Round* to all women
living between nowhere and somewhere, and to all men
lost between yesterday and tomorrow.

THE BEGINNING

The Normal Life

FIRST THOUGHT TODAY: the coffee is cold. And I can say with full honesty, sitting across the table from Richard, in our twenty-eight years of marriage, the word *yes* has brought me little happiness. I know and believe from all I've come to accept; the longer I stare at the kitchen's cracked plastered wall in need of repair; this image symbolizes our love and marriage. The light in a once romantic and naive sixteen-year-old falls dimmer and dimmer. Oblivion paints a foregone conclusion. If only Richard cared to listen. But this isn't the morning. He's too happy. His shaven face energizes and re-energizes the more he talks; the patient wife doesn't interrupt. A dutiful smile passes from her face to his. Richard is who I am, and what I am is lost between the beginning and the end of his sentences.

*

"All my time invested courting Jared Longview will finally pay off." My husband holds out his empty coffee cup—minus the word, *please,* a foreign word.

The obedient wife pushes away from the table; she moves unenthusiastically to the coffee maker. Silence is necessary while pouring his drink. She listens, trying to remember it all because a test will come. It always does.

"Father can no longer deny *my abilities.*" The husband's grin changes into broad laughter. "Damn. My portfolio will be quite substantial from this deal."

The refreshed coffee in front of him goes unnoticed. The wife wishes for *that,* thank you. She's a fool. Richard's consumption lay with Richard and money—lots of it. The *Wall Street Journal,* a preoccupation must, with breakfast, now has his attention. Fist pounds on the table means the stocks are up. Grunts and curses are losses.

The cussing appears minimal. "There's nothing crucial today. I get to keep the cars," chuckling in the wife's direction, "and *you,* my dear Diane . . . get to do what you do to look good for me."

*

My appropriate cue: cute upward turn of my mouth, plus several affectionate strokes to his arms. Yes. I'm a well-trained wife. A pinched smile and hot second-glances settle into my husband as he turns the paper's next page. Apple slices and black coffee satisfy the wife's mustn't-gain-weight-husband-rule. The wall clock says seven. Coffee cups clang on to saucers. Newspaper rustles. She sits expressionless. Hands fold into a neat lap rest. She sits watching time watch her. She hopes for love between them. Now, she imagines a lightning bolt crashing through the ceiling and killing him as it did to the priest in *The Omen.*

*

"Anyway," he clears his throat and stares at nothing in particular, "at last I've proven to the goddamn SOB I *am* the one with more damn balls than my two older brothers. *I'm* the one who brought in the multi- million dollar account any law firm would've killed to get. I deserve to be the fucking head managing partner. And he'd *better* realize that *or else.*" His happy face holds all my attention. "This deal goes to press in a few days. Can you imagine what this means, Diane? Can you?"

*

Thought of crowding: continuous talking leaves no space for me, nor does the onset of his abrupt silence. Emotions chase themselves. Anxiety intensifies the wife's sweaty palms. She tries to anticipate her husband's next move. He lights a cigarette. Deep, deliberate puffs accompany his eyes closing. A mischievous smile plasters his mouth as he leans back into his chair. His words *or else,* constitute a threat that is never without precise calculation. Would he dare hurt his father, Lloyd? Yes, stupid. Remember Richard's vile warnings when Lloyd reduced his son's bonus—and how things quickly resolved when Richard paid an unexpected night visit to his father's yacht.

*

"I must celebrate," he laughs in a wide-awake expression, "with something I've had my sights on. Damn stock market rallies high. Good luck fills my cup."

The wife dares not criticize or question the need for another possession. Already an acquired Maltese, Picasso, and rare first editions in his library give him huge bragging rights amongst his friends. The six-car garage houses only a fraction of his hobbies. Why doesn't he understand his wife wants to feel love, not material things?

"I need some damn reward. Jared Longview marks the biggest bore I know."

Does he not know I've not participated in this conversation? When will he leave? The clock reads seven-fifteen. He must know the time after checking his Italian gold wristwatch—*the one I didn't give him.* Why does he linger? What small comment requires no malice in agreement with my husband? I must converse something intelligent while he studies my face, or, as in the past, he'll accuse me of taking no interest in his career.

"Pay attention, Diane. Despite all his wealth, Jared and his frumpy old wife inhabit the very same four-bedroom brick house he has lived in since his birth. They don't entertain. They go to bed at eight o'clock. Drive used cars. Can you believe the old bitch clips coupons like they're on welfare? What do you think, or don't you care, Diane?" He leans closer, raising an eyebrow. "I guess *my money* holds more interest."

I'm stumbling over an answer, "Well, I . . ." because nerves steal my words. I do hate Richard's regular inquisition drills.

"Need I ask you again, Diane? *What* the hell *do* you think?"

Answer the damn question, or he'll call you stupid as he has many times before. Be careful. The intention must never be you're smarter than perceived, or Richard is wrong.

My response, "I guess you never can tell what happens behind closed doors," is quite rehearsed.

His nonchalant shrug may get me off the hook. "Yes, you never know. *Do you?* A house disguises many things. *Doesn't it?*"

The three-day-old bruises on my arms still haven't healed.

"You would know, Richard, because all our secrets have happened behind closed and locked doors.

Checkmate. I got you, Richard, returning no nasty comeback.

The unspoken truth punctures my heart. Tears hold back. Soon he'll leave.

We're unable to look at each other. The newspaper's financial section again occupies the husband. It's seven twenty-five. He must leave soon. They'll be overseeing details about Jared Longview. Why won't he go? His coffee must be lukewarm by now. Should I make more? No. He's going soon. He must.

"Take Jared's house, for example." He stops reading, still holding the paper within his hands. A sign to me he's not concerned about work. Why?

I fake interest, "What about Jared's house?"

"Piles and piles of old magazines and newspapers everywhere he claims are collectibles. Now, I *have* collectibles—not piles of dusty shit. Poof! One match, and I tell you the place would burn like a dry-ass weed." Watching Richard's arms fling about while making twisted funny faces, even at Jared Longview's expense, reminds me of the cheerful Richard, who first captured my love. But this Richard never remains. "Jared's fortune reaches millions, and he's too damn cheap to live. I suspect his dog-faced daughter will inherit everything. My father *better* appreciates what I *did,* securing fat-ass Jared's lucrative empire." Another cigarette lit. Deep inhaling and exhaling accentuate an elongated scowl seen more often than not.

The wife must diffuse his deposition before it spirals into something she'd instead not intake. Maybe he's working from home? It's seven-thirty. Hate the cigarette smoke, leave it be, read the signs, take another approach.

The wife extends her best smile. "Your father does respect you, Richard. He's proud of you."

*

Thoughts of certainty: my options are limited. The beast has a vicious bite and callous hands. Please, not today.

*

"You're squeezing my arm. Please, Richard, don't."

"You dumb bitch. Didn't you hear what I said about Jared?"

Now would be a good time for *Omen's* lightning bolt to plummet through Richard's heart.

"Why are you looking at the ceiling like some crazy-ass bat? Look at me." He pinches harder until the stinging shakes the arm already bruised. Don't cry. The husband hates weak tears.

"Are you going to cry? I let go of your arm. Are you crying, Diane?"

The wife is fully aware that his temper escalates with each fist pound onto the table. A whimper verbalizes, "No."

"I'm not talking about my fucking father? Know why I'm mad?" "No." The wife flinches back, positioning her hands like a sideways cross—protecting her face. "I don't know," she whines.

He laughs. "Pathetic little, Diane. Can you express one connecting thought? Get me some fresh coffee. And don't put it in the same damn stained cup I've been using."

The bully marks the territory. The wife bears the imprints. There won't be an apology as she refills his coffee, not the large dose of poison she imagines. Richard's rationalization—"*You drive me crazy, Diane, not knowing what I expect from you,*" stains my self-worth. God, forgive me. I ask for the courage to stab Richard's body beyond recognition.

"I'm sorry, Richard. I know you're under work pressure. Here's a fresh cup."

"Tell me, *what* do you know, Diane?" Sarcasm swims like sharks, the closer my husband pulls his chair. "*How* could you possibly understand *how* I feel? I compete for my father's approval within the firm he and my grandfather established. I graduated top of his law school. I've years of experience, but Father drags my ass behind my brothers, two mediocre attorneys. Why? Can you even tell me? I seriously doubt it."

"You're not fair, Richard. I try so hard to please you."

"*I try so hard to please you,*" he mimics me. "Fuck. Why do you have to whine?"

There isn't time to change my tune; the wife receives a slap, the back-handed one he likes, she takes another smack, then two more.

The bastard blurts out, "Sometimes, Diane, the level of your wifehood fits into a matchbox."

"Please don't, Richard. Don't hit me anymore."

Don't cry, don't cry, if you sob, Richard wins. He wins all the time. Doesn't he?

The bastard's breath fills my ears. "Your position in society holds either under me in bed, the mother of my children, and whatever means I provide, giving you the image of what I want. Now, *that's* fair to someone with only high school education. You can't take care of yourself. You depend on me for everything, *including* the toilet paper, to wipe your ass."

I can't shove away from his firm grip.

"Richard, please don't hit me again. *Why* do you say these things?"

"So, I ask you, Diane, tell me one thing about Jared Longview, you *think* you understand. I don't ever need your understanding of my father. Are we clear?"

I understand three words—*I hate you.* What news about Jared have I read? What to say? How many couples go through this shit? What to say? *'Just kill me.'*

"Richard, I *know* of him."

"By your weak reply, I don't believe you, Diane."

An index fingernail jab into my forehead emphasizes Richard's point. "Can't your brain produce intelligent conversation instead of them one-line-kid-answers? I've said a goddamn million times you're required to know clients whenever they come to dinner or meet us in other social gatherings. Can you comprehend my goddamn embarrassment when Robert Moore and his wife came here last month, and you continually called him Ronald?"

Unable to stop, like a chastised child—my head lowers, and tears fill my eyes. "I've never been inside Jared's home. You're fighting with me for no good reason. I've read about his daughter Amelia's engagement to a Boston surgeon, Andrew Hillman."

"Hell. I forgot your IQ is in line with the paper's society section or the latest fucking issue of *Vogue.*"

The quick kiss he places on my forehead solves nothing.

The wife's doubts sprout like weeds. "Richard, what do you expect me to say? Is Jared coming to dinner? I don't understand this whole manner of attack. What have I done wrong? Tell me."

"Conversations with you, Diane, are badly written comedies. You're as dumb as the blonde hair God gave you."

Annoyance accentuates Richard's forehead frown lines; his finger pokes my chest. The wife's ordeal isn't over. The time for him to leave has passed.

"This boy *had* to marry the pretty one. A damn weakness we Fletcher men share," He coughs up more chuckles and shakes head. *"Lord, give me strength."*

Pointless searching the air as if a cue card holds a formable self- defense answer. Are you there, God? Are you still, my protector? Fear of being hit again requires a necessary apology.

"Richard, I'm sorry."

No response. My prayer gets a reprieve. Without announcement, the husband's attention focuses on a notepad he brought to the breakfast table. Removing a pen from between the pages, he writes. What are his thoughts? The wife doesn't interrupt. She doesn't dare excuse herself until making sure there's nothing else he needs. I occupy myself with the society section that he doles out each morning. The wedding announcements drudge up the same question: will these future brides end up like this wife?

"Richard, did you want something?"

His persistent hand tapping on the table requires my attentiveness.

"Take a mental note, Diane, if you think I haven't been . . . the word you used *fair*? Yes, I believe that's correct. If you can shift your brain cells past the next fashion trend, I will tell you again about Jared, as I need you to be my *intelligent* partner."

I sit on my hands with believable, wide-eyed gratification for his crumbs of enlightenment.

"Jared fired his last incompetent attorneys." Richard lights a cigarette, blowing its smoke in my direction. "Our firm will now represent all his company's national and international mergers, acquisitions, manufacturing deals with China and Mexico, and real estate developments. I promised him undivided attention. The asshole demands treatment better than a king. His wealth staggers, even my mind." I follow his finger, pointing to the paper. "Since your brain cells devour the newspaper's society section, you should know aside from what I divulged, Jared's family holdings make them one of the richest in the state and the country."

So what? Money isn't critical. Disappointment in love is more valuable. A wife's intuition surfaces, "I'm proud of you, Richard."

"I suppose you are. But, Diane, I wonder how you can interpret my success or know the meaning of the words? I guess I'm to blame for not allowing you to attend college. On the other hand, you never asked me or indicated as much. Did you? So, we both bear guilt to your ignorance."

*

Quiet blankness: say nothing. Clear the dishes. You need the distraction. I want to scream and beat my feelings into your head, my dear husband. *'Our life's interpretations are miles apart. I've given you three healthy children, kept my figure and looks, and drowned my career aspirations. This choice is what small-town girls do when they fall in love with their Prince Charming. They marry young and carry on their mother's tradition, a sad label, one I wish wasn't mine.'*

*

"Come here, Diane."

*

Dark obedience: I *know* this wooing voice. God, why don't you help me? Those damn hands. Those severe hands open my robe. I allow the groping between my legs. Hands force down my shoulders. I assume the knee position, lower his zipper, and orally satisfy his needs. Straddle me over the chair. Squirm. Find a comfortable spot to rest my stomach. He bends my back to enter me from behind. It hurts. It hurts so much. The wife never wants it like this. She displays a plastic smile. Pretend the moans and movements are in sync satisfaction with his. Imagine another woman I wish to be. He's finished. My prize is a final grunt and several hard thank-you-slaps to my invaded ass. His coffee-breath-tongue seals our lovemaking with wet licks to my neck and ears. This time gentleness squeezes and squeezes my breasts like a romance written in those *Harlequin* romance novels. Not my life.

*

"You okay?" His whispers are as comforting as a glass blanket.

I turn around to face him. There's much to say but not about the cancer scare. My little smile approaches him. "Remember, the doctor said the lump is non-malignant."

His nothing kiss on my forehead means if we don't need to talk about it, then let's not.

9

"No matter how much you irritate, you're still my girl. The way you squirm in my arms makes me want you more, Diane. I'll never let you leave me."

"*Never*," the wife gives the politically correct answer.

The husband shells out a blunt smile, not the enduring flirtatious ones he gave when we first met and made love. I've settled and accepted so much.

His head buries into my chest while his fingers trace the small surgery scar, lifting and stuffing my sagging breasts to that of a much younger woman.

I close the mind to his lips, saturating my chest; I did it all for him.

The return value is worthless.

"I'm glad you had the procedure. Aren't you?"

The lie responds, knowing the bastard insisted. "I did it for you, Richard."

"My baby, *I know*," he expresses in a kinder voice than heard this morning while snuggling and fingering through my messy hair.

Once again, the cracks in the plaster distract me. Richard is happy. I can and will endure him this morning, snatching off my silk robe as if made of paper, and having his way with me, regardless of his hurtful words. I shield my solemn eyes. He doesn't care to listen yesterday, today, or tomorrow. When will he leave?

He zips up his pants.

"Did you call the contractor for the final kitchen estimate? Did you, Diane?"

The wife, at last, closes her robe. She is worn thin.

"The contractor will send the remodel estimate to your office by Friday after next."

"Good. I'll go up and change. You never disappoint me in *that* area, baby." He rushes upstairs.

Her time alone in the kitchen, no matter what transpired, gives some comfort that he's leaving. She'll be alone, breathing freedom, at least for a few hours.

*

"Diane. Here in the foyer. Hurry up."

"Coming, Richard." Fatigue accompanies the wife into the marble foyer, his design, she hates because of the ghosts of their arguments and fights.

He's leaving. Briefcase in hand is a handsome, developed physique, looking younger than his age. Trust? No. Women watch him enter a room, and he discreetly or indiscreetly follows their scent.

"Have a good day, Richard."

His flat cheek kiss concludes their business.

"Oh, I forgot," Richard stops before opening the door. His coyness gives the wife an uneasiness of what he's about to say. "I'm picking up Julie and Mark on the way to the office. I needed to wait until traffic died down. I'm glad because the morning kitchen sex pleases me. By the way, I'm taking your *BMW*. I need you to get my *Benz* washed today. And I won't be home for dinner. I've got a dinner meeting with my father and my brothers. What are your plans?"

His persistent sour cum is nothing in comparison to hearing Julie's name.

"I asked, *what are your plans?*" He demands.

My answer isn't easy. I stumble, "Camille will be here later this morning. Remember? We're planning her baby shower."

"You *know* how I feel about Camille." His disapproving eye roll repulses me. "You and I have discussed your family many times."

"Richard, she's my only sister, who didn't want your rich, alcoholic cousin. You and I have discussed *that* many times."

A lie would've been better. Richard is stepping closer. If he lunges, quickly raise your hands and cover your face.

"Diane, my family has wealth, power, and influence. Need I remind you of *that* fact, and not to use *that* tone of voice?"

"I'm sorry, Richard. I have to defend Camille, who caught Jeremy cheating. *How* could she marry him?"

His condescending laugh fills the foyer. I need him to leave despite my feelings about Julie. The more he paces back and forth, the harder my teeth grind.

"Camille spread her legs for some fucking nobody high school teacher. Jeremy could've given her the world. Alcohol is all about being an adult. You *don't* complain."

My heart beats faster. Richard doesn't mention infidelity. "I can change my plans. We can meet at Camille's house." "Your family thinks I'm a fucking bad guy. Don't they?" "No. I never say anything."

"You're a damn liar," And with those words, my stomach receives a hard punch.

I steady myself against the bottom step handrail. *"Please, Richard. Please stop."*

"Diane. I'm not a monster. You frustrate me. You need to take some or most of the damn responsibility."

Nod in agreement as he hovers over you. Tears are too close. He hates tears. Bite your lip to make them stop.

"Your plans are set without asking me. Don't let your sister be here when I come home. I'm not interested in her small talk. Are we clear?" "I understand."

"Good," the bastard snickers while swiping two slaps onto the wife's cheeks.

He turns, walking a cocky stride to the front door. "I'll see you tonight, Diane."

Despite the excruciating abdomen pain, that lovely send-off, *"Have a good day,"* camouflages well mental, physical, and emotional exhaustion. Screams will soon saturate my lungs, as you, my husband, the bastard, drives out the driveway, through the gate, and away from me.

*

Thoughts of what is: alone. Straight gin soothes the morning's agony. A hot shower drenches stench. Pour another stiff drink. Don't give a damn. The reason I stayed was for my children, assuring them Richard family's privilege and the best education. Now they're busy adults, coming home Christmas week then scatter before New Year's Eve. They don't anymore see the rose and perennial gardens, walk along the grassy pathways through the thick spruce trees, especially those planted celebrating their first birthdays, or row the canoes on the property's tranquil pond. What remains my purpose, dangling inside morbid loneliness occupying each room? A sprawling custom home within Thornton Hill's exclusive gated community, a closet resembling an expensive boutique store, jewels worth insuring, and a generous allowance all come with a price. Never ask prying questions. Never poke holes into his numerous business trips.

Never question his need for privacy behind locked home office doors.

Never wonder why he has an inaccessible phone number. Never challenge his control over the finances. Submit. Shut your mouth. Conceal the violence. Stop the shaking. Don't you dare bite your fingernails—impeccable appearance is essential. Don't start crying again. Dry yourself. Apply think make-up to hide Richard's handprint. Camille will be here. I need a pill. Get the bottle from the make-up drawer—one, two, four—not enough until your next appointment. You need to make *that* call. What about Camille? Cancel. She'll understand.

*

"Hello, this is Diane Fletcher. I need. No. I *have* to speak with Dr. Rose."

The nurse must make her come to the phone. "Mrs. Fletcher, Dr. Rose, is with a patient."

"I understand. Is Dr. Bishop available? I *must* see someone today." Damn. The nurse put me on hold. Finish the last of the Gin.

"Hello. Hello. Is anyone there? My name is Diane Fletcher."

"Mrs. Fletcher? Are you okay? You're breathing rather fast. Dr. Rose is with a patient."

"Dr. Bishop? Thank God. Can you or Dr. Rose squeeze me in?" I hate the dead quiet. What's taking so long?

"Dr. Rose had a cancellation for a one o'clock appointment this afternoon. Are you there, Mrs. Fletcher?"

Contact Camille. Stop the nervous head-scratching. More pills are on the way.

"Are you still there, Mrs. Fletcher?" "Sorry. Yes. One o'clock will be fine."

Now call Camille. My drive is sixty miles away.

*

"Hi, dear, this is your sister, Diane. Something has come up. Can we meet tomorrow? Call me back as soon as you get this message."

*

Third urgent thought: oh, no. Camille. I hear her downstairs. Richard will kill me if he finds out she has a key.

*

"Diane? Where are you?" Her pace quickens up the stairs, allowing minutes before she'll reach the bath and dressing room. "Diane? Are you up here?"

Grab your robe. Kill gin breath— swallow mouthwash. "Don't come up, Camille. I'll be right down."

I didn't stop her in time. Before I can spit three times, she reaches the top step. Animated, seven months pregnant, and looking way younger than her thirty-four years.

"Oh, there you are." All my rush to escape the house surrenders to her hug—a reminder of affection lacking between Richard and me.

Plant a kiss on her cheek. Thoughts of urgency pull me away. I can't be late for my appointment.

"You missed my message. Something has come up, Camille. Please don't give me *that* look."

Happiness falls into worry. The empty sideways gin bottle and high ball glass are in plain sight.

Her voice weaves into near tears. "What's wrong? Diane. I smell it. What about your promise to me?"

Add liar to my resume. Why did she have to come upstairs? "Only a small drink . . . *nothing.*"

Don't look at her, throw on this, throw on that, brush your hair. Finish with a touch of pink lipstick.

"I have to leave now. I left you a message. We can work on the baby shower tomorrow at your place. No need to drive way out here again."

"Stop jumping around, Diane. You're making me dizzy." Her pleas mean nothing. Sidestep her and turn off the light. "Come on, Camille. I need to go."

She's following me downstairs. Make her leave. Move toward the front door.

"Diane? Are you okay? You look thinner."

She's examining me. There's no time for talking. I have a long drive ahead. "And there's a black bruise on your shoulder. I don't care about a baby shower. Talk to me, Diane."

"You're going to have a beautiful child soon, Camille. Don't fret about me."

"You're diplomatically changing the subject," she points out.

Camille's serious clench to my wrists steals precious minutes from my travel time to make my appointment. No time to talk. I need to get out the door. I can't handle any more questions, don't want her feel- sorry-for-her-big sister-sermon. Walk her to her car.

"Am I crazy to worry about you, Diane? Richard's temper scares me. Please be careful."

Season our goodbye with a cooked lie, "Don't worry about me, Camille. He's been under work pressure for months with this new client. You know how he can be. I've been dieting to get into some clothes I haven't been able to wear."

"Okay. I'm leaving. But you know you can talk to me *if* you need to."

"I know. I love you, Camille. Soon we'll talk, but not today."

"*Is Richard,*" she whispers before entering her car, "beating you?" I heard her gasps when strands of hair brushed aside, revealing discolorations around my temple. "*Oh, Diane.*" She begins a long cry into my chest.

"I promise one day to tell you what you think you know and what you don't know. Not today, Camille. I have to leave."

Our arms bend around each other tight—and mine as if I hadn't seen Camille in years and didn't know when the next would be. Her belly pushing against me draws up a genuine fear, I won't live to see her child born.

"Call me. I love you, Diane. I worry about you."

"Camille, I promise to call. Don't worry about me. Get in your car. We'll talk soon."

Her terrified expression cements why I need the pills. I can't cope with my life. Give one more wave goodbye. Watching her drive away, and I wish I had wings to fly.

Time runs too fast. Get my purse. Go to the hidden stash for enough money to pay the doctor. Set the alarm. Don't forget to wash Richard's car and fix dinner. Breathe.

*

Non-consequential thoughts on the way to see the doctor: this necessary highway, a tourist route, despite the picturesque pitched and dipped mountain ridges and open blue skyline resembling an oil painting, makes an unappreciated ride of unforgettable arguments with Richard about the price of tea, and mascara tears stain some of the most photographed landscape of the state.

*

He pulled the car over into a remote rest station where a tirade of fists hit hard. No explanation was allowed, nor excuse accepted. My accidental fall spilled wine and broke his mother's Tiffany glass.

*

Let go of Richard. Just stop it. It's hard because I'm driving his car. Don't forget the damn thing needs washing before he comes home. Be the damn good wife. *Be* the damn good wife.

*

Soon I'll be there. I'll see the white wooden fence surrounding a yellow and white bungalow behind arched flowering lavender trellises. The sunflower metal sign on the railing: *A Woman's Health and Medical Care* will mean I'll soon be getting my pills.

*

The taste of Richard evaporates out the open windows with the turn-off from *this* highway. Wild daisies, Black-eyed-Susans, columbine flowers, and maples ease my thoughts driving along three miles of Meadows Ridge curving into Sage Miller Road following the lake. It's been years since we came here together. There you go again thinking about *him*.

*

People need to slow down. Memorial bouquets, scribbled goodbye messages on cardboard, wooden crosses, balloons, and stuffed animal memorials mark where loved ones crashed into the guard rail. Don't read the obituaries. Everyone I love is alive—mother, sister, and my three daughters Leah, Nina, and Sarah. But why do I laugh? His death is one exception.

*

Make a right turn on Thomas Road. Less than fifteen minutes for my little white pills. Crazy obsessing about time, but all wealthy housewives are six degrees of nuts at some point in between the gin and tonic.

*

"Hello. My name is Diane Fletcher. I have an appointment with Dr. Rose."

*

Observation: stop sweating. You're careful. Cash from your allowance pays for Dr. Rose's visits. Social appearances are important to him. The price of dependent imperfection will be severe if anyone we know discovers the clinic. Forgot to use her private patient entrance and wait in the hallway's alcove until the appointment. Instead, a perky receptionist escorts me into the general waiting room. My watch says Dr. Rose won't be too much longer. Peaceful walls, a bookcase full of books, and colorful pottery settle my eyes. Smart idea turning a 1930's house into a doctors' office situated within a neighborhood of coffee shops, quaint shops, and cafes. I wish I owned something. Alone, except for a woman vacating her chair to sit next to me.

*

"Can you make sure my doctor knows I'm here?" I remind the receptionist.

"Yes, Mrs. Fletcher. Please make yourself comfortable in the meantime."

Before I can move to another seat, an introduction from a gum-popping nuisance speaks, "My name is Ruby. It's your first time here?"

She must be the other doctor's patient. Mine doesn't schedule two patients. Want my own space. Her tug to my arm forces me down. How could I forget Dr. Rose's private entrance? Stay calm. Your appointment is soon.

"What's your name? We're neighbors until our appointment time.

Mine's Ruby," she repeats, getting closer to my face.

Her hold tenses my body.

"Please don't grab my arm," my voice can't help but rise. "What are you doing? Don't touch me."

She's strong—twisting my arm left—then right.

I'm more determined than Ruby. I yank away fast. "Stop." I'm pissed with her invasion of my space and privacy. "Are you crazy?"

The receptionist isn't at her desk. What to do? Sit nearest the door. Put the diamond watch into my handbag. Paranoia doesn't trust her gawking eyes.

"Please don't move away. Sorry. I don't mean any harm. I need someone to talk to besides Patty. I know she's sick of hearing my story. Hell, she's got demons stealing her mind." Ruby's pitiful plea mirrors my own when Clutching my purse as if Ruby has a gun on me, I'm frightened. I want to yell, *'I don't have anyone.'*

We're both here because of fear. Watching Ruby rocking back and forth says a lot. I decide to talk and listen.

"All nerves are raw today. Go ahead and talk, Ruby, until my doctor comes."

Ruby relaxes her shoulders, and to my gratitude, spits the gum into the wastebasket next to us.

"I admire your taste. My husband gave me expensive things. Jeff *is* a successful Wall Street investor," she begins short sentences after several quiet moments.

"Diane. My name is Diane," interrupting with tissues from my handbag. "I understand. Here, dry your eyes."

Between wild sobs and sniffles, Ruby talks, and I do what women do: I listen. "Emma, our only daughter, is a Boston surgeon. I drink too much. Emma doesn't talk to me since I got piss-ass-drunk at her wedding five years ago. The event destroyed me. Didn't Jeff and Emma know it would? Jeff came with *that* woman, Virginia Miller, my damn best friend."

"I'm sorry, Ruby. Life isn't always fair," I reply, visualizing Richard's grinding between Julie's legs. "Men will do what the hell they want."

"You can say that again." She licks her lips and slumps back. "Sure could use a drink."

I agree that a gin martini would be appreciated.

"Look," Ruby nudges my elbow. "Look," she repeats more directly while pushing up her dress's sleeve. I gasp. "I tried to commit suicide a few times. Such scars won't disappear. I drink too much. Jeff left me. Said he couldn't cope anymore. Bet no man ever said that to you."

Without warning, Ruby's fingers glide across my face and begin touching my lips.

"Ruby, stop," I demand, and pull back because her fingers won't stop touching my face. "It's good you've come here, Ruby," I extend myself.

My eyes stare down the empty hallway. Dr. Rose must soon rescue me from a depressive presence.

Heartache, the kind that's slapped me in the face, saturates her tissues. "What do I do now? I'm fifty-five years old. Who wants a size 18?"

I full well know her dilemma, but can't be cruel or honest. "You'll find someone."

She laughs then sobs. I feel caught in the middle of something out of my control. Extending my arm around her shoulders is all a person can do.

"I doubt it," she sniffles, showing the bleakest face next to mine. I know. "Jeff and his high-paid lawyer labeled me a dysfunctional-emotional alcoholic. Self-esteem and appearance flushed down the toilet. Fuck them! The court gave me a settlement—a fraction of his wealth. We had a prenup. I left it all behind—Long Island oceanfront home, designer clothes, except for some belongings in an airplane carry-on. Jeff took my pride. He stripped me of my life."

"You're brave, Ruby," I imply for misjudging her.

"Patty and I live in a cracker-box manufactured house I bought because the bank took my sister's house. Our place is on Denton Road. You know where that is?"

"I don't."

"*I guess not,*" Ruby's unexpected sarcasm and eye-rolling freeze my sympathy, "fancy shoes, fancy watch, and fancy clothes equal some fancy address . . . right? You *don't* know me. Tell the doctor your damn problems."

Irritation yanks my arms from around this ungrateful woman.

Thirstiness for a stiff drink is overtaking.

Ruby doesn't look at me; she's rocking back and forth; head tilts back, hands twist the ends of her hair, and despair runs down her cheeks. She exhales tiny huffs, and speaks, "Patty, my sister, recommended Dr.

Bishop. A truck's trailer killed Patty's husband. Left her broke from all his gambling addiction and bad investment debt. No insurance. Jack, her husband, canceled the damn policy. Patty didn't know because he paid all the bills. Dr. Bishop attends the same church. She helped Patty forgive a man who beat her most of their twenty-year marriage and left her two shakes from being homeless. My sister can't ever have kids from *that* fall."

Ruby's empty eyes turn into mine; my attention is hers; her story commands it, somberness draws my tears. I swipe them away, Ruby has, within five minutes, summarized her life into tidy sentences.

"*Life's a bitch when you marry an asshole,*" I'd say to a woman whose comfort, like mine, colors alcohol.

"Why are you here, Diane?"

Her straightforward question makes me angry and uneasy. I'm not telling her my damn story. I don't even want to think about it, myself.

Thank God. Dr. Rose steps into the waiting room.

"How are you, Diane?" My doctor's usual question and handshake relieve me of Ruby's presence.

Ruby's now erratic rocking back and forth intensifies my urgent escape into the hallway while Dr. Rose speaks with Ruby.

"It's good to see you, Doctor, finally." I clutch her hand when she rejoins me.

She studies my face. Her smooth fingertips stroke one side then another. "You look tired. We'll have a good talk."

"Goodbye, Diane. See you around," a monotone farewell and frazzled gaze call out.

"Good luck, Ruby," I say back, and by no means want to hear her life's soap opera again.

Taped piano concerto music fills the corridor. A few more steps closer to Dr. Rose's office and Ruby's encounter fades. Remember next time to use Dr. Rose's private patient entrance.

"Ruby seems to have quite a story."

"She's not my patient. Why are you drawing those conclusions?"

"No reason. You changed your hair?" Watching her fluff it out reminds me of how little time I spent this morning on my appearance.

"Cut off about six inches. Shoulder length now. Summer does a number on my curly hair. I do admire your straight hair in an elegant French twist." A pat on my shoulder eases the embarrassment of not well put together. "You're so Paris chic, Diane." She unlocks her office door. "But, you didn't drive all this way to discuss fashion and hair?" She points to our close forest green, velvet cushioned chairs facing each other.

"*No.*"

Erasing Ruby and Richard happens the second the doctor presses her hands into mine and awaiting tears run down my face. This time I'm the one needing a tissue from the box she hands me.

"I'm here, Diane."

Self-pity oozes from my eyes the more she taps my back.

*

Feeling sorry for myself, thoughts: Dr. Rose—perfumed model-figured woman. Well-chosen heels and form-fitting designer suit means a good lover or two. *Wasted Chances* will read on my tombstone, *not hers.*

*

"What's wrong?" Her standard opening line.

The answers are the same. Only the day and month have changed. I feel immature—unable to live without the help of a younger woman and those pills.

"Diane? Did you hear me? What's wrong?"

"Well . . ." the words trip over each other, "can't sleep, hot flashes, perpetually anxious, vomiting, headaches, constant, uncontrolled inner thoughts, and I don't want Richard to touch me. Sex with him continues to be nauseating."

"Are you keeping the journal as I suggested?"

This damn question makes me fidget, cross, and re-cross my legs. The answer, "I can't. Life is hard in writing all the-this-and-that of my day and what I feel."

She doesn't like the answer. A scowl seeps in her pulled together, made-up face. Nails tap on the table beside her. "We talked about the importance of not holding in emotions between our visits."

Studying my hand's lifelines distracts my truth. I mumble, "Writing it all down means facing my reality."

"I see." Dr. Rose's hands tilt my face. "Tell me about *your* reality." She won't let me lower my head. All this is for a handful of pills? "You know the home hasn't changed: hatred, crazy, insecure, mistrust, terror, and desperation for a new life."

She releases me. A smile comes but not from me. "Diane. A healthy dose of attitude adjustment can solve anything."

Worry lines harden my forehead.

"Can I have some water, please? You're not living with Richard. *A subject we've discussed numerous times,* enough to fill a thousand journals."

"Your husband's success means his wife's self-de-valuation. Decide on your path, Diane."

She hands me a full glass of water—I wish it were something more robust.

"Choosing my path sounds easy to a college graduate. Choices are thrown at you, *my dear*."

"Still drinking before bed? How much do you consume during the day?" She cocks her head, forms a tight lip, not even air can penetrate. I sense her anger around my spiteful comment. She's taking a seat at her desk on the other side of the room.

"Are you still drinking?" she repeats, and this time with a pen and paper begins writing.

Shrugging off the stupid question, I'll answer with intentional dry humor, "A couple of drinks . . . look at the French."

She'd also drink in reversed roles. I bet she's never cried a day in her life. Women with composure, education, and beauty are strong. I wonder what the next question will be the more she writes.

She looks up with arms folded. There's no give in her face. The distance between our seats, in my mind, accentuate our role of patient and doctor.

"What are you eating, Diane? You look thin."

A few well-placed tears will stop the questions. "Dr. Rose, please give me more sleeping pills *and* something stronger to pull myself together. We can talk about Richard and anything else another time."

"You're crying . . . *for you or me?*" She points a stiff finger in my direction.

Her frank remark intensifies my agony. "Can I have the pills?"

"What are *your interests*, Diane?" The questions and the writing continue without a break. "We talked a month ago. My answers are overdue. Next year will be the year 2000. How will *you* move forward? Do you understand?"

To my surprise, she sits next to me, placing her hand on my shoulder. "Please give me the pills." My hands shake like a fool. "Today isn't the day for talking. Too many words steal life. Richard's morning rant has left me shattered. Please, *no more* words today."

"No more sleeping pills or pills to cope with life. We need to talk.

You decide when Diane."

Maybe a few more sympathy tears will move her. I doubt it. She's again sitting behind the desk across the room.

"You know, Dr. Rose," humiliation lowers my head onto my chest, "I'm fourteen years older than you. I feel dumb, weak, and lost at forty-four years old. Coming here, talking to you for over five years has been difficult facing who I am. You'd think by now, after the thousands I've paid you, I could look myself in the mirror. What I see is someone who hates herself."

Her wooden statue faces down my beaten demeanor. "A decision comes with a price. You need to leave Richard. You need to leave all the wealth behind. *Are* you able? Most of my patients can't. They're trapped."

"Love, children, and marriage with Richard have been my goal. His family represented a social climb for any girl in the county. My family knew his grandparents, who banked when Daddy held the title Bank Manager. Richard, while on school break, brought them into the bank. We met in June. You know this story. Let me have the pills, *please.*"

"Love at first sight?"

A long breath drops before I can continue, "A sixteen-year-old impressed with fancy cars, money, and a country club membership. Did I know the difference? I thought I did. Daddy's fatal heart attack left us with a generous insurance policy. My part of the inheritance went on a must-have society wedding. Doesn't every girl want a fairy tale and Prince Charming?"

"When did your prince carry you off?"

"I became Mrs. Fletcher at seventeen, and within two months was expecting our first child."

"Happy?" She nudges.

Dr. Rose's question makes me remember the first time Richard hit me because I refused sex on my period. I release frustrating anxiety. "The pretty prom queen *blamed* herself and accepted his temper. She'd do anything for him because she wanted the handsome Harvard law graduate going places in his father's firm."

"Money colors life. Doesn't it?" The doctor's wisdom speaks. I know your story, Diane. I wanted you to hear it."

I don't stop. The words continue filling my chapters. "Fear of losing Richard kept my demands to a minimum. No college or skills made wifehood the chosen life. Rewards came from a prestigious family."

"Happy?" she says again

"You're smart enough to read between the lines." I pour the last of the water. "He took fucking care of me," the defensive voice raises, "showering me with everything. I took care of our house. I gave him three beautiful daughters. The price you mentioned earlier—I don't know where to start." The sobs drench the last of the tissues in my hand.

"You're unable to answer my question, Diane." Her relentlessness continues with more writing.

I want to smash her face with all its perfectness.

"Please just stop," I plead with the readiness to walk out.

"There are choices we all make. It doesn't mean they get buried with us, Diane."

"I don't understand," Uncertainty sobs.

I'll get my pills. Dr. Rose must feel my agony because she's sitting closer until our faces are in line.

"Diane, find something to do with your life now that your daughters are adults. What about the monster in the room, Julie Meyers?"

Julie's name conjures up the letters, the private detective's pictures of her and Richard in New York, Miami, and Paris, and his lies about client meetings. *Just give me the damn pills.*

"You're too quiet, Diane," a softness speaks, and her face openly welcomes a smile. "I'm here for you."

The wall clock says our time draws to a close

"Tell me, Dr. Rose, is there a paint-by-number-book to fix one's problems?"

She laughs on her way over to the desk and returns with what I desperately need.

"Here's a mild prescription to help you sleep."

Holding a paper, the one it took all this time to get, opens a long sigh. "*Why* did you change your mind?"

"If you can, eat a little more. Get out of the house," the doctor's response skirts around my question. "A change does a wonder. Can you visit your daughter, living in Chicago? I think you said the other two children are traveling together in Europe."

Medical suggestions appear easy. Life isn't. I give a smile of appreciation more for the prescription and not for her opinions.

I explain to probing ears, "Nina is still visiting Sarah in England. Leah, the attorney, and Nina's twin works for a Chicago law firm. I *could* visit her. Maybe Richard will approve."

I won't admit I'm not happy about an impending Leah visit, dependence on pills, or the doctor's well-intended lifeboat. My solace has to be my own doing.

"I think the trip will clear your mind. I'm sorry, Diane, but I need to leave now. I'll walk you to the corridor's end. I'll *see you next week*. We need to talk about the bruises on your face."

I will not end the visit in tears.

"Be careful, Diane. Call me at any time."

"Thank you for the prescriptions and for squeezing me in." "Don't worry, Diane."

*

Thought driving into my driveway: breathe now. You've gotten Richard's car washed and refilled the new prescription. The damn doctor peels me raw before she caves. Maybe I'll replace her. Don't be stupid. Your five-year relationship helps—even if the wife ignores the advice given on *the other* relationship, she walks on the shattered glass with— Richard Fletcher, who'll be late and late means past midnight *if he comes home.* Next remains the most challenging task. Get out of the car. Call Leah. Don't lock the keys inside the vehicle. Why am I so forgetful? Stepping on the brick-way leading to the stone, wood-burning fireplace the husband designed. Place a value on the opulent tour— worthless. Custom made this-imported that-art by whomever to impress his family, his clients, dinner party grandeur, charity auctions, or showcasing the newest toys to the cigar-smoking, womanizing men friends. Gated-million-dollar-shacks are sitting on prime mountain- valley view acres. Plastic smiling neighbors are giving jeweled hand waves from luxury cars. Entering the side entrance into the den's well- stocked bar, turn off the alarm. Make a tall Scotch with a water chaser. Alcohol numbs everything. It's four-thirty. Call Leah.

*

"Leah, this is your mother. Did I catch you at a bad time?"

"Mother, what's wrong? You sound funny. What's happened to Daddy? Are you alone? Can you hold on? I have another call I need to take? Please don't hang up."

*

The cell in hand, I'm walking from the den and standing in the kitchen— what a ridiculous waste. Richard and I claim the same two chairs at a table seating twelve. I can still feel his gifts from when he bent me over this morning: the knot in my stomach and the throbbing back pain. Turn left. Stand at the archway opening into the living room, more substantial than the three-bedroom guest house. Move through the French doors to the formal dining room, seating twenty without adding the two extra leaves. Past the next pair of French doors comes the enormous library, holding more first editions than a neighborhood one; rare coins, stamp and gun collections, oil paintings of past and present, race and riding horses, us and the children while in elementary school, and Richard's pride—this house. Through another set of French doors is his Majesty's office. The large hand-carved door Richard brought back from Spain stays closed. Never open unless he gives permission. Look to the right. See solarium. Tapestry furniture facing the gardens soothe when he's not here. Hate the media room to the left, storing his extensive collection of porn and violent action movies. Three additional guest rooms, a mud and laundry room down the hall. Make a right into the marble foyer. Look up the double winding staircase. Not a sound in all ten bedrooms. Yes. I am alone.

*

"My colleague George will call back. Hello. Hello. Are you still there? What's happening, Mother? I hear breathing. Your words are inaudible.

Are you on the cell? Did you forget to charge the battery again? What's wrong? Tell me why you're calling. Is Daddy there?"

"Leah. Stop the fifty questions. *Allow* me to answer you. Your father has gone to work. Don't keep asking. The cell doesn't need charging. Sometimes the hot flashes make breathing uneasy." I tell a lie instead of the truth. I'm lonely. "Give me a few more minutes."

Why did I call her? Return to the den. The Scotch needs refreshing. "Are you taking hormone pills? My neighbor's mother says estrogen balances her. Does Daddy know about your issues? He's the most understanding man I know. He constantly tells me he loves you."

I want to yell until I'm hoarse, '*Talk to Richard? What the hell do you think I've been doing all these years?*' Let the whiskey drown my words. How can I penetrate my daughter's blind admiration?

"Mother, what's wrong? I can't hear you."

"I'm . . . I'm fine, Leah. Attorneys are all alike. Conversations clocked in by billable hours. I'm sorry I called."

"Let's *not* argue this time. Didn't Daddy tell you about my big cases in two days? Don't you two talk? Can we make this quick? Things are time-sensitive right now."

"Don't talk to me in that *you're the adult, and I'm the child* tone. We haven't spoken in weeks. I don't like you favoring your father over me. I'm your damn mother."

"I need to take another call, Mother. I'll be right back."

Hang up. Scotch on an empty stomach works against me. Remember Leah's calculating questions emulate *Richard* giving you, the mother, little leverage. You do need a break from this house and him. Grovel and tell this one you're sorry.

"I'm back. What are you mumbling, Mother?"

"*Sorry* to bother you, Leah. Call you back later."

"Let's have this out since you've interrupted me. Something doesn't add up. *Are* you crying? You're evasive. Are you drunk? Tell me the truth. Daddy says, you drink too much. I must concur after last Christmas when you confused sugar and salt, ruining most of the meal. Tell me why you called. I can spare a few minutes. Please, for God's sake, don't make me feel guilty for my career because I don't call you."

On and on, her voice reaches an insulting annoyance. Drink some more.

"I'm *not* drunk. You call Richard because you think the two of you have more in common than the woman who brought you into this world. Career has *never* been my problem with you."

"Not going down that rabbit hole. Nothing changes with us. *What* do you want, Mother?"

"Are you eating? I hear crunching."

"Changing the subject? Okay. I'm finishing some chips." "Did you eat? I should call back another time."

"God damn . . . for the millionth time, *why* have you called? If you must know, stress takes away my appetite. This case is a huge career carrot."

She's still the child. Sit down. Finish the last alcohol. "Your mother wants to get away," I announce.

"I don't understand. Why are you getting away? Where? Are you and Daddy arguing? He says you don't understand how hard he works."

Dabbing away tears makes me feel desperate.

"Before you give me your valid excuses, I won't be in the way. I need to *get out* of this house for a week or so. Richard won't miss me. He's busy with some deal. Nothing is filling my time, Leah. *Please.*"

"You're crazy speaking of Daddy as if he's a monster, and the dream house he built for you is a prison."

Walk to the den and refill the Scotch.

"I can't hear you. Mother, what did you say?"

"Leah, *can* you give me your answer? I won't be in the way. Chicago is a big city. What are you typing? I hear typing."

"You're changing subjects. Okay. I'm finishing this brief. *Oh, Mother, our* conversations *do* wear me thin. But you *are* my mother, and for that, I'll let you visit."

Another stiff Scotch makes her flat invite more palatable. Damn you, Leah.

"Mother, I warn you, I'm busy with this trial and prepping for another one. When are you coming?"

"Next weekend, I'm helping your aunt, Camille, with her baby shower plans. The baby is due in seven weeks."

"How many kids *does* Camille have?"

"She has one. Michael, your three-year-old cousin."

"You must think me terrible for not knowing. I can't do kids with my life and career."

"You have your life, Leah."

"Yes, Mother, I do, and a *damn good* one."

She laughs. Don't bother asking why. The answer isn't worth hearing. "I've nothing in common with Camille. Nothing. Doubt she even votes or reads. She's married to some truck driver, isn't she?" "He's a high school teacher. His name is Alan. Alan Bolen."

"You're pissed, Mom. I imagine your eyes rolling up into such a state of disapproval by your sarcastic reply. I only speak the truth about your sister, Camille, way different from Daddy's side of the family."

The last sip of Scotch goes down like rocks. "Are you talking about the money, Leah?"

"Breeding. You're different. You married into a powerful family.

Poor Camille's shadow can't find the sun."

Awkward silence slices us. I need to end our call. Leah's points sink my heart.

"I can't wait to see you. I love you, Leah," I end.

"Call me when you make the reservation. Bye, Mother."

*

Maybe the last thought forever: the storm devours the forest. Legs can't move fast enough to find shelter from branches breaking, shredding my body—the wife with no identity.

*

"I demand you to answer my question." "Please, Richard. *Please. Don't anymore.*"

He punches. He reinforces two-three backhanded slaps across the wife's face—his preference for teaching the wife a lesson. He rips as if it were wet paper her silk blouse collar.

The husband crouches, hovering, commanding, *"Tell me why you called Leah. Damn you."*

Cuts deepen into the wife's cheeks, leaving their mark of blood dripping like water from swollen lips. Finding refuge would be possible if the legs could move fast down the hallway, reach the staircase, and get to the kitchen. The knives are there. This time I, the wife, would kill him.

"Come back here, you bitch," he hollers, filling demonstrative anger into the handsome face she first loved.

You'll never make it. Richard's quickness yanks your forearms. You know the marks will be scarlet red and ebony black. He shoves your 120-pound frame into the wall and readies another slap to your head. Your body surrenders to the floor. Thank God for its carpet.

'Damn you, Leah. Damn you', are my thoughts as I receive each of your father's kicks to my legs.

The wife's frightened sixth-sense shields her face. "Richard. Stop.

My mouth is bleeding. I didn't do anything wrong."

Knuckles tighten. Breathing intensifies. He's gone mad, landing punch after punch into my shoulders.

"Do you know how fucking disturbing it is to receive a hysterical emergency call from Leah? She phoned in the middle of my important dinner meeting with Jared, my father, and my brothers. How do I concentrate?"

My immense pain erases the question's legitimacy.

The wife looks into his angry eyes. "Richard, I have done nothing wrong."

"My daughter," the storm heightens pushing hard the wife's chest, asks fucking personal questions about us . . . about your damn mental state."

Full throttle terror sinks the wife's tailbone into the baseboard. She cries, "Don't *hit* me anymore."

Another cowardly backhanded slap—no one hears the wife's screams. The husband snatches her up by the shoulders. Deliberate hands enclose the wife's throat.

"Shut up, Diane."

Spit and blood garble my pleas, "I can't breathe, Richard. You're hurting my neck."

For a reason only God knows, the tornado subsides. The wife's legs collapse into a kneeling position, feel the cuts, feel the throat throbbing, choking for air. Look at the stairs. If only my legs could reach them.

"Why did I marry you? I could…" she hears and doesn't want to know the end of the sentence. His predictable fists rise. "I could smash your face, Diane. I could kill…"

Taking in Richard's inconceivable admission surfaces my insurmountable fear. How does he believe such vile things about me? At this hour, his erratic panting and thug vengeance spells pure hate. Can a life, a marriage, a woman count for so little?

"Kill me? You wish me dead over a phone call to your daughter. Am I forbidden calling my children?"

The animal's face comes within inches of mine.

I surrender. Tears burn the gash in the corner of my left eye. Hands shake wipe what wets the palm—red-colored water.

He shouts, "Damn you, Diane. Leah wants to know, and so do I, why her mother cries like a lost child needing comfort within her daughter's home. Damn you. Tell me what you told Leah."

"I . . . I just wanted to visit."

Cover your face. Richard's fists are ready again. Hard. Close and ready.

"Why do you all of a sudden want to go to Chicago? You plan on *leaving* me, bitch?"

The heart stomps my life into darkness, a lifesaving lie conjures instead, "No, of course not. You're busy. I just wanted to get away for a bit."

A part-chuckling,-part-grinning, and part-frowning madman pulls the wife to her feet. Maddened arms squeeze and shake the wife's shoulders. The bastard heaves the discarded trash onto the floor, allowing little protection from his Italian leather shoe soccer kicks.

"*Why* are you trying to turn our children against me, Diane?"

Sobs blur comprehension of his persistent fit saturating my ears. "I give you everything you want. I give you an enviable lifestyle. You show respect by going behind my back like some ridiculous second-class citizen. You're part of a prestigious family name. We never air our business to our children. We lead our children."

His speech accompanies another face slap.

Death would be freedom. Can you hear me, God?

"I didn't do anything wrong, Richard. I didn't do anything wrong." Choking on clumps of blood-soaked spit, I curl on my side with arms secured between my thighs. *Richard, please.* I hear my humiliation begging.

"Look at me, Diane."

The ability to see clouds his eyes. "I can't lift my head, Richard."

"Cancel the goddamn ticket."

A limp nod means I understand. No debate. Retaliation outweighs my significance.

"Leah told me she doesn't want you to come. Am I clear?" All the wife can do is a moan-nod.

"She's up for Partner if this case goes well. Your presence will warrant an ugly distraction."

"*I'm not welcome?*"

"Are you fucking deaf? Leah has a damn busy schedule."

I'll never think the way you do, Richard. No matter how many times your fingers poke my forehead.

"*She's my daughter.*"

"What? You're whispering, Diane. What about *our* daughter? What did you say?"

The wife must attempt to stand and brace against the banister. She can't run. He pushes her hard against the railing's edge. Turn around. Look down at the foyer's marble floor visible because the upstairs hall lights are still on. How long will it take me to hit bottom?

"Should I push you over and put you out of your misery? I'm smart. *Easy accident.*"

"*I'm your wife, Richard.*"

The husband's sinister, narrowed eyes leave little to a woman's imagination, beaten into a vulnerable state.

"I know who you are." a controlled voice talks, "children need their independence, *not smothering.* All the money I make, and you can't find a preoccupying hobby?" He edges closer. "Answer me."

My nerves are frail. I must watch Richard's hands. And if necessary, be ready to jump off the railing.

"You're right. I'm sorry I made you angry. I shouldn't have called Leah."

The bastard shrugs. "If you want to get away, Diane, I'll take you to our Maui condo next year. Stop crying. I didn't even hit you *that* hard or that much. Sometimes you jerk me off with your needy shitty crap. I'm the man of this house and won't let you undermine me."

The wife sucks it up. Reasoning with a fool calls for more stamina than she has. She straightens a crumbled body and pats back tangled hair.

"I know. I know. I should have discussed my trip first."

He smiles, kisses cover my palms. This storm makes way for another one.

"Enough. Do you understand what I mean? No more crying tonight." "Yes," she answers, patting dripping blood from her lips and her nose.

There's no other place to go except where he leads—the master bedroom entry. He stops. She stands beside him.

"Let's go." He tugs her tender wrist begging for ice packs. "Kiss me, Diane. Don't be a piece of deadwood. Make me glad I came home to you."

"I love you," I, the stupid wife, pretend while penetrating passionate kisses into his mouth.

A grin opens to his tongue, licking and smacking his lips together while stripping off his clothes and kicking away his shoes.

"I don't care about the blood. It tastes good. It arouses me." The wife watches his hands vibrate his penis.

Inserting the same fingers he used to beat her minutes ago, "Open your mouth," he orders. "Suck on them. Pretend it's my cock."

Their blood-flavor revolts the wife, wishing her teeth were knife sharp.

"Wait." He removes his sticky fingers. "Let me put tapes on. Which one do you want to watch?"

"You pick. I like the one we watched last time," passion lies.

He steps fast to the centerpiece of the master bedroom—the television cabinet. He presses the start button.

A smile says it all. A reach means more. "Come here, Diane,"

Her duty robotically shifts one-foot-in-front-of-the-other. Submission accepts him unbuttoning her torn blouse.

She withers into soulless isolation. Her eyes gridlock into misery.

Torn silk drops around her shoulders as he maneuvers the fabric through unemotional arms.

The garment falls to the floor.

He unhooks the lace bra and slides down its straps.

Revulsion anchors her mind when the material touches her bare feet.

Exposed breasts and tender nipples are cupped, and licked, and sucked until their wetness drags tears down her face.

The wife is invisible, listening to the bastard's monstrous, self-satisfying groans and moans, unaware of her silent weeping because she quickly swipes away the evidence.

"Take them off," he whispers while gyrating up and down against her body.

She knows what he means. Remove the skirt and panties. She must perform despite the painful memory of the husband's rage.

She is masterful. Kisses to her neck and ears draw desired images for anyone but this man, stroking her naked body. His movements say to her, he's forgotten the punches—and her permission, of this rape, says she has forgiven him. But you, the wife, would rather clean toilets with her tongue.

"Do it, Diane." His sleaze runs like shit into her ears. "Do what I ask."

He leads the wife to the bed.

"You know what I need. Put your hand here. Right there. Make me feel good, baby. Do it again." He mimics the porn movie and spreads his legs for her to massage his lower body.

The wife feels like a prostitute hearing her husband's commands. *"Again, slow down. Damn you. Take your time. Please me like I know you can. Move slower. Suck me, baby. You know what to do. Slower, bitch. I'm not ready yet. Get on top of the bed. Turn around. Put your ass in the air.*

Open your legs." His orders go on and on until the words become one big black nightmare. "Deeper and deeper. Feel my cock? I know you love my cock. Moan louder. Scream. I want your screams to show me you love me."

I scream loud, louder, and louder. It's not because I want it, but because I hate it so much.

"Love your ass, baby. Get me off, baby. Get me off. Turn around. Suck me. Suck my cock raw."

"Not too hard." He laughs. "Yes . . . Yes." The moans compete with a porn movie. "Fuck me on top. Fuck me. Yes, baby. Yes. I feel it. I can't hold back anymore. Goddamn. Love your ass."

Believe it doesn't hurt when he jams his fingers between your legs. Imagine you're deaf and blind when he grunts and grinds on top and behind you. Pretend he's not the man you fell in love with when a teenager. How can he explain why his hands touch you the way they do? Close your eyes. Pretend. Soon it'll be over.

*

The first morning thought in our bed after last night's hell: Richard's absent presence groping for morning sex. Good. No. Not good. Something's wrong. Why didn't he wake me as usual? *'Richard. Where are you?'* I want to call out. But it's too painful swallowing or forming words—*especially* his name. Leg movements take effort. Try and raise the left one. Slide it over the right one. Have to get out of bed no matter if your body feels as if a whole football team had their turn with you. Where's Richard? No shower water is running. I have to get out of bed. First, pull back the sheets. No need for a pity-party at your life's choices. Thick and thin irregular shapes of dried blood crease like veins into discolored bruises. Touch the swollen neck and arms. They're reminders of his and Leah's control over your pathetic life. Now what? His handwritten note on the end table is within reach. Prop yourself up on the pillow. Read what he's intended.

*

Diane, I left about five this morning. You are amazing. Spectacular sex. I know you love me. You proved your feelings last night. We BELONG to each other. Adults argue. All the years we've been together showing our battles mean we love each other. You must realize we'll ALWAYS live under the same roof. I FORGIVE YOU. Forgot to tell you, Father, my brothers, and I are flying to Jared Longview's Texas ranch. We're finalizing the deal. I'll be busy and have gone over the next few days. Don't forget to cancel THAT reservation. You'll see the children, as usual, come Christmas. They're busy, and so are we. Richard.

*

I've often felt, Richard, with all your money and Harvard education, cement fills your brain.

Ease out of bed, hobble to the closet, examine your body through the inside mirror's reflection. The nude's beauty shows caked blood about the swollen mouth; picking at these sores makes more blood; the face has two black eyes and significant puffiness. Neck abrasions make it hard turning the head. Shoulder blades, ankles, and forearms are discolored. I'm a sad assessment, at this exact moment, of a member of the wives' and girlfriends' club. I wonder whose injuries are worse. Who died? Maybe I'm the lucky one. Never forget—*we'll always be together.*

*

Significant thoughts for now: alone in the house, a new prescription bottle of sleeping pills retrieved from the purse feels good in my hand. Why can't Dr. Rose understand they're needed? Leah and Richard, I'll cancel the reservation. Nina and Sarah, my other daughters, love me. Don't bother showering because water will reopen the wounds. Slip-on fresh nightgown. Wrap robe tight. Painful walking. Ignore the hallway sections where he beat you. Brace your arm against the wall. Take slow steps down the staircase. Don't look at the railing where he threatened your life. Hate the foyer. Imagine my spattered body on the floor. Walk around through the other hall. Drink some coffee. No. Have Scotch with half a sleeping pill. Don't want Richard here. Do you? No. Get an extra blanket from one of the guest rooms' closet. Hobble to the den. Fix a stiff drink— more Scotch less water. The alcohol does burn the inside of my mouth. So what? Wrap yourself with the blanket. Sleep. Sleep. Stop thinking.

*

"Diane. Wake up. Wake up. It's mid-afternoon. What the *hell* is wrong with your face?"

A familiar voice thrusts open my coffin. Cover your body.

"How did you get in here, Mother? *Please leave.* I'm not feeling well."

I dread the lecture observing her reading the pill bottle's label.

"Don't give out copies of your keys if you don't expect people to use them. I rang the doorbell. Didn't you hear me? Are you retaking these? Why are you covered with a wool blanket with this heat? What's going on here? Don't answer. I can tell by your black eye. I assume the bastard is off to work because he'd never let me come in. *Someone should put him down.*"

Mother's words tumble out of my head after a torturous night. "What are you doing here, Mother?"

"I have a better question. What the hell is going on here? Why did Richard beat you? Don't answer. Don't give me another damn lie. I need a goddamn drink."

Her long exhaling shovels guilt. What can I say? I'll leave Richard. Where would I go?

"I fixed you one. Drink it." She hands me a drink—her favorite—rye whiskey.

What the hell. Alcohol numbs, we toast, the drink burns like acid. I say nothing as she situates on the sofa within eye range of her oldest daughter. The mother intends to have her say. After last night, I wonder if I'll live to be her age.

"Drink to forget, Diane. We have a few hours before the asshole comes home."

"Richard has gone out of town."

"Clara Hill and I went visiting her son, the Beverly Hills doctor. Do you remember him? I came by to see what help you needed with your sister's baby shower. My drink needs a refresher."

She has no comment on Richard. Her roving eyes over my body say more. Must cancel *that* reservation to visit Leah.

"Mother, I have a couple of calls to make." "You want me to leave?"

Not in the mood for shop talk or loneliness. Mother watches me tug the blanket close about my shoulders. Drink more alcohol. Get ready for the hard questions.

"Mother . . . I'm not in the mood."

"*Damn,* Richard. His presence has always been an inconvenience from my position all these years."

"Not today, Mother. *Please don't sit here.*"

She sits anyway with extracting scowls, surveying my face.

"Camille's shower can wait. Hell. Women have been having babies for centuries without showers."

"What are we going to do about this shit, Diane? Tell me what happened. I can call Dr. Morgan. He's patched you up before."

"I don't want anyone to see me. Don't ask me about Richard." "Where *is* the bastard?"

"Richard, his father, and brothers are on a business trip with a new client, Jared Longview."

Mother's cynical laughter draws a coarse sulk to my lips. "What's so funny, Mother? I know you think I'm a fool."

"Oh, don't be angry jackasses," she says grins, "The Longview family has more money than the law should allow. *I'm sure Richard will buy you something priceless.* Your grandfather knew Jared's grandfather. I don't know the whole story, but Grandfather said, '*You can drink with a Longview in the morning and prepare for killing him in the evening.*' His sister Jolene and I go to the same beautician. You'd never know the family's moneybags by her stingy tips and the used car, in need of paint, she drives."

The sunshine through the window makes squinting excruciating. "Since you're staying, please close the drapes, Mother."

"When are you going to wake up? You need to put something on those bruises," she subjects me to a continual sermon while darkening the room.

No matter the room's temperature, the blanket hides my disgrace. "Mother, don't. Please leave."

She won't stop. Her idea of sitting closer than close signifies that I will listen.

"We need to contact Dr. Morgan. Are you aware of what you look like, Diane?"

Her persistent, urgent concern worries me this time Richard went too far. Reality brings the drink to my mouth. I think Ruby, the abused woman I met in Dr. Rose's office, will understand. How do I contact her?

"Are you hearing me, Diane?"

Mother does something long escaping me in this house. Her arms enclose around me.

"I'm here. I'll never leave you," Mother's compassion whispers.

Uncontrolled, short, fast breaths embrace her presence and generate enough sympathy-sobs for two people.

I beg, *Help me, Mother. Help me.*

"First, where's the first-aid kit? All this crying doesn't help." She reaches to the table for a tissue. "I know from your past fights there's no going to the hospital or pressing charges because of his family's damn name. I suspect one day he'll kill you, Diane." Her head down. "You know I'm speaking the goddamn truth."

"I'm proud of Richard. I'm his wife. We have children together."

Touching my arms, I don't know another justification why I'm still here.

"I made a wife to your father for twenty-five years. He hit me once, and I gave him a threat he couldn't ignore. I woke him up with a pot full of boiling water, ready to burn off his balls. Your problem is that Richard doesn't fear you. Where's the damn first-aid kit? The way you two do battle, there should be one in every room."

"Check the kitchen's pantry," I say, believing Richard will one day kill me.

A quick finishing off of her drink and the nurse returns with enough of this and enough of that to mend at least three of me. "Take off the robe."

My hands pull tight. "No."

"You heard me." Mother's meddling agitation overpowers my swollen fingers. "I *want to see it all.*"

The daughter pleads, "I can't. Please. Don't ask this of me."

"I'm your damn mother," her defiance overpowers. "The cuts need to be cleaned and dressed if you won't bring in Dr. Morgan."

I curl tighter, shaking my head. "Mother, please stop." "Give me the goddamn robe," she commands.

We tug. Mother wins. Pulls and drags inch by inch without further discussion until my back, arms, and thighs are exposed. Shame forbids me to meet her eyes.

"My God," she struggles, "all your beauty and Richard disfigures you."

She weeps. I cry into her shoulders. Silence soaks the heat.

Our plastered melancholy chills the room.

She picks up the robe helping cover-up the unsightliness. "How can I help you?" Her voice quivers.

I sit, unable to respond.

"I can't force your decision, Diane. Right now, let me help you into the bathroom."

"Okay," I spit out.

Her arms become a crutch for us to the guest room nearest the den. "Sit on the bed. I'll run you a bath."

As the tub fills, we slip off my security armor. Mother's fingertips touch my indignity. "I hope the scars aren't permanent. *Why* did Richard do this? I must know."

Her question follows me as the water soaks into my skin. She sponges in soft circles.

"Your eyes read, Mother, I'm your biggest disappointment.

"You're wrong, Diane," her tenderness answers. "You need a fresh start. I'll stay tonight and make us an omelet for dinner."

How can I explain, making a fresh start is leaving behind my crutch, Richard? I haven't walked without him in twenty-eight years of marriage.

"I need the other pills from the medicine cabinet. Can you bring me one with a glass of water?"

She stops rubbing my back and sits on the chair, facing me.

"Pills aren't the goddamn solution, Diane. If I ever meet your doctor, I'd have no problem expressing my opinion. You took this shit for a long time. How many years? No more crying here. Screw the pills."

Mother's sublime reasoning carries no weight. Richard's face suffocates my thoughts. A pill takes care of everything.

"You know nothing," I snap.

"*Really?*" Mother's cutting remark hits a home run. "We'll talk during dinner. Do you have clothes down here?"

The daughter points. "Cotton pajamas are in the adjoining bedroom's dresser, and a terry cloth robe is on the back of the closet door. I'll get them."

"Don't be too long," Mother says on her way to the kitchen.

The wife swallows a pill from the cabinet. Happiness now can ignore evidence of Richard's anger.

Energy requires eating small bites of the cheese omelet; the hot honey-tea dilutes my mother's continual sermon. The daughter needs a soft landing. The last twenty-four hours have been a horror-show.

"Diane,' my name is spoken for the hundredth time, "*Richard* proves the biggest disappointment in my life and *yours*. I die examining your face. No wonder you've had plastic surgery. I wish you never met the son of a bitch. I need another damn drink."

Solitude assesses our gourmet kitchen, once featured years ago, in several national magazines—to reliving Richard's punches, throwing hot coffee on my leg, to calling me names from cunt to a bitch—all the reasons are unexplainable over a drink.

"You can use this." Mother interrupts the daydream with two Scotch and waters.

I accept, "Thank you," feeling the pill dissolving my reality.

"I tried to tell you, but no, you had to go behind my back and get pregnant right after school," she continues, not missing a beat. "You had a promise with fashion design."

The drink needs to hurry up and silence her voice.

"Mother, my time has passed. My mistakes are mine. They're not *yours or Camille's.*"

Grimness, hearing my opinions, sweeps her face. I know she's upset because her fingers tighten into each other.

My hands reach for hers.

"I shouldn't have said that. I'm sorry." She drinks.

I drink.

Mother's chatter will go on the more alcohol she drinks. I've heard it all before, but she here and I must listen. "The summer you turned sixteen after you two met, reasoning flushed down the damn toilet. Your demands for new dresses to attend country club dances drove me crazy. You had to ride in his *Mercedes* convertible instead of walking to school. You had to go sailing on a yacht and skiing in Telluride. You had to have a wealthy, good looking lawyer. You *sold* your soul, Diane, I saw the marks on your arms back then. You lied. I knew you didn't fall. I didn't protect you, and you didn't protect yourself either."

Her eyes turn muddy.

Stupidity rubs shit in my face. My mother's remorse is my fault.

"A mother and daughter are the same guilt and sin." Her fingers rub into mine. Our nods mean we understand. "The daughter learns from her mother how to be a woman. Diane, I blame myself for not protecting you more."

"Mother, I hope for a happy ending."

"Diane, Richard, is a con man." Her voice lowers with her head. "He came along when two strokes hit your father. I had my hands full of bills, his health, the doctors, and Camille chasing anything in trousers. I didn't shelter you. If your father had lived…"

I raise my voice, "You encouraged Richard, Mother. *Why* do we have to go over this? Life is over."

She looks away. Her words hit the floor, "I misjudged, I thought you'd be taken care of by an older man from a wealthy family. Richard claimed he loved you. *He promised your father on his deathbed and me that he'd never* hurt you. At least your father died the next day believing a damn lie."

"I remember all of Richard's promises, Mother." The Scotch goes down like lead. "His family did business with Father's bank for years. We *all* trusted the Fletcher name."

Mother's travels back in time-suckers her for another drink. She's drunk, looking into her empty glass. I'm a close second. Alcohol and the pill love each other.

My final assessment is full of self-examination as I pull the blanket around me. "Richard, isn't your fault, Mother. I got swept away. I loved him. I stayed because of the children. Isn't that *what* women do?"

*

Thoughts of solemn: accept my reasons. Dare I say what we both know— even though you, Mother, talk a happy, trusting marriage— Father drank and had another woman. She was the woman in the hospital parking lot you argued with after visiting Father three days before his death. The same subject woman I overheard outside his room—him begging your forgiveness of his ten-year affair. The same woman, your detective, followed—the same woman. You know you stayed because of me and Camille, but I'll let you die with a lie about Father and your marriage. We won't discuss your disappointments.

*

"I'll make us coffee, Diane. Whiskey has me out of sorts." "You don't have to serve me, Mother."

*

Coffee is drunk, and for a while, silence tastes good. My brain can rest.

"Can I stay until morning? Richard won't know. I'll leave early. We need to talk without drinking. I don't wear guilt and blame well."

Mother's intentions won't change. She talks, I listen. She'll stay whether I want her or not. I need to call Leah when I'm alone.

"Okay," I accept my houseguest.

*

"This is Leah. Did you make the reservations? I haven't heard from you. Tell me about the flight time."

"Leah, it's noisy. I can't hear you."

"Mother, I'm getting off the *L Train*. I'll go to a nearby, quiet coffee shop."

I don't want to talk to you, Leah. I've gone through enough shit with Richard because of you.

"Can you hear me now? Are you *still* coming this weekend?" Hearing a flat uninviting tone puts me off.

"I'm not. I intended to call."

"I see. Are you mad at me, Mother? You sound distant—*I'd like a non-fat latte*. I ordered some coffee. I'll be up late tonight. So, you're *not* coming?"

I mustn't give her a reason to call Richard. No calls to Richard. No calls.

"*Thank you*—I just paid. I see a seat I can grab."

"Leah, don't read into my words. I'm fine. After Richard and I spoke, a visit would be an inconvenience. I don't want to be a bother."

And while she slurps down her drink, the taste of highball fills my sore mouth.

"You sounded tragic. I called Daddy."

"You called your father because you're *concerned?* You should've stated you're busy."

"I did. But you kept pushing the issue. We're always at cross purposes, aren't we? Don't hang up. I have another call."

How well I remember your annoying teen years criticizing my judgment and parenting to Richard, and his agreeing with you. The smug, superior look you gave me set the tone for your authority over mine. Why didn't I put my foot down? Another sip of alcohol erases a lot.

"I'm back, Mother."

"Leah, we see things differently. But we're family. I miss my girls." Don't let your voice crack. Remember, Leah is the daughter.

"You need to be computer savvy since Nina and Sarah are away at college and my hectic schedule. Next year will be 2000. *No one* writes letters anymore."

I notice a stack of stationary on the kitchen's desk.

"Call me old, but I enjoy writing letters and telephoning."

She sighs in my ear. Yes, she knows more than I. How did I let myself fall down this rabbit hole? Don't show weakness. You know how Leah is.

"Speaking of which, Mother, Sarah's grades are spectacular at Oxford. I think she's leaning more toward law instead of pointless English Literature. What could she do with *that* major? Daddy and I think Sarah studying law makes a fine career choice."

The framed poem Sarah wrote is still in my bathroom. She dedicated it to me. I whisper the beginning verse: *'My mother shines through the rain.'*

"What did you say, Mother?"

"You and Richard have discussed Sarah? I thought all along she intended on teaching? We spoke three weeks ago."

"Don't you dare think Daddy and I are in cahoots against you as you've imagined all my childhood. I called him for a legal opinion. Sarah's name came up. I'm sure she'll soon inform you."

"I'm sure she will, Leah."

Leah's past tugs at my heart, *'I love you, Mommy. Can you help me, Mommy? What should I do, Mommy?'* Now, not even the slightest decision gets my first approval. "How did I lose the lifeline?"

"What did you say? I can't hear you, Mother." "Nothing. I'm walking to the den."

Another drink subdues anything.

"Now, there'll be Daddy, Sarah, and me (I imagine Leah's uncontained grin saying her idol's name—*Daddy)* and if you add Grandfather Fletcher and Uncles John and David, quite the collection of brilliant minds around the Christmas dinner table." The giggles make me sick because she and I rarely laugh anymore. "We'll all have something in common discussing law this and law that. Hold on. I have another call."

I'm picturing a formal dining room floor to ceiling tree, holiday china, polished silver, the best wine and catered food—one big blah-blah boring time. Can anything be more meaningful other than the damn law?

"I'm back. I do need to get home soon, Mother."

"You know, I recall you and your sisters in pajamas tearing downstairs, opening Santa's presents. Excitement filling the house means Christmas to me, Leah, not courtroom reviews."

"Mother, I'm an adult now. Speaking of which, Nina, my twin, needs to make some solid choices. She's got your genes for sketching and painting. How can she make a living? *But* she's pretty enough to snag some rich New York Wall Street broker. Hold on, Mother. I have another call."

Is my daughter labeling me and her twin sister useless? Shit. Drink more. You need it. I hate her. No. I didn't mean it. God, forgive me. Leah is my flesh and blood.

"Okay, I'm back, Mother. I'll speak to them soon. We won't be too much longer."

"I guess not, Leah. But know Nina's creativity will open doors. Do you think the world revolves around courtrooms? Don't answer. My sense of humor, you know. I'm not picking a fight. I'm proud of you, a junior associate on the rise. Your father can't stop bragging; you *can't* judge everyone by your standards, Leah. You lecture Nina. Make her cry. I doubt you apologize."

"Yes, I'm an outspoken bitch, Mother," she speaks in her—*I'm annoyed tone,* "one of the few brilliant female lawyers in an office of shit-head male attorneys. I work my ass off, proving I deserve a promotion. Hold on, Mother. I need to take this call."

End this conversation. Leah believes your lie about canceling the trip.

Her arrogance deserves no more of your time.

"I'm back. Our conversation left with *Nina, the subject at hand.*" "Nina being your twin and not in the same profession must be your disappointment?"

Her huffs are quite audible and more so annoying. End the call.

"Mother, she'll be thirty years old. How long does she expect Daddy to support her?"

I want to say much to this one living in a black and white world—not today. Leah's voice is grating too much. End the call.

"I'm thinking about coming home for a long weekend after things settle down."

"Your father will be happy."

"What about you, Mom? Wouldn't you be happy to see me, too? I *mean,* you did say you missed me."

Examining my wrists—missing you came with a price the night, Richard told me to cancel the trip. Touch my neck, feel inside my mouth; see the bruises. Think of a good response. You can't trust her.

"Yes, I would love to see you. Anytime you can get away."

"If I buckle down, I can surprise Daddy for his birthday next month."
"Yes. That would be nice."

"What are you going to do, Mother?" "About what?"

"Maybe for Daddy's birthday, Nina and Sarah can come too if their schedules allow. I'll find out. I need to go now. I'll talk to you soon."

"I love you, Leah. Goodbye. Have a good evening."

Drink alcohol, then pour another; the daughter cares, the wife doesn't.

*

Thoughts with the sunset: insecure shadows, a cigarette, and a gin and tonic keep me company. I'm more than drunk. The liquor still burns the cuts left from Richard's hands. He hasn't called. It's been two days. No reservation to see his daughter. Mother has long gone home. Should I call Richard's cell? No. He'll be furious. Say I'm checking up. Wait.

Just wait. The cigarette and tall gin go down well despite the cuts.

*

"How come it took you so long to answer?" "Richard. Where are you? I'm still in bed."

"I'm calling from Jared's Texas ranch, which is the second time this morning that I called."

"I didn't hear the phone. I'm sorry."

"*Whatever.* Anyway, I'll be home in a few days. Mother said you haven't even called to say *hello.*"

"I didn't think about it, Richard. I figured she'd be in Palm Beach or Palm Springs."

"Fuck, Diane. Remember, she and Father's plans changed until the deal completes."

You never told me. I'm not crazy.

"By your silence, I guess you don't give a damn about my family. Your sister's fucking baby shower and that nosey bitch of a mother you have is more important."

"Richard, that's not fair. I call your mother all the time." "Don't whine. Call my mother."

I hear his deep breathing. What can I say? "I will. Is there anything else?"

"I have to go, Diane. Just get off your ass and call my mother. Invite her to lunch. Be the grateful daughter-in-law."

"I will. Did you want anything else?"

"I need you to be more of a wife. Goodbye, Diane. Call me after you visit my mother, *and I hope you canceled that trip.*"

"Yes. I did."

What a mind fucker—not once asking how I feel. I could scream, I could die. I could kill Richard. I don't care.

*

I assume this one of many thoughts for today: the long arm of control extends miles away. The dutiful wife obeys her husband. She drives to her not-really-at-all-close-mother-in-law, Helen Fletcher's English Tudor home. Let's hope there'll be no conversation about the elephant in the room—her son's abuse.

*

Grant, her quite formal British butler, says to wait in the too-dark-for-my- taste wood-paneled entry. Until Helen arrives, my attention can absorb an oil painting seascape of a woman walking alone in the sand, which reminds me that my peace has been elusive. Wipe your eyes, reposition the sunglasses close to the face. High-heels on the wooden floor mean your host approaches. The smell of lilac perfume, half-empty martini glass, lit cigarette, precise make-up. French manicured nails, short-sleeved white cotton summer dress, large diamond wedding rings, not a hair out of place—fixed in her go-to ballerina bun—colors a lady swimming in leisure. Take a deep breath, absorb the Queen's reserved inspection. Accept her fake smile and rich lady's air kiss.

*

"Hello, Diane, so lovely to see you on a beautiful summer day. Aren't you quite warm wearing a long-sleeved, black cashmere sweater, black pants, and black closed-toe shoes?"

Flashbacks of Richard's cold hands tearing my body are still fresh.

The wife isn't ready for the grand reveal. She keeps on the sunglasses. "Hello, Helen. No. I'm fine."

"*Perfect.* I know you wanted to meet at your home, but, darling, I couldn't manage today with the temperatures and all."

Her still apparent English accent knocks for understanding as she winks.

I choose words Richard would like, "No. I didn't mind," spoken in my most phony, pleasant voice.

"Thank you, my dear Diane."

Politeness opens an arm pointing the way to follow.

"Let's retreat into my study. I call it my get-away-from-it all-room. We'll lunch there."

The woman's image in the painting lingers. I wonder what absolute calm feels like every day.

"I like the painting in the entry."

Helen's photogenic face elevates into a wide grin. "You have good taste. We purchased that from a San Francisco art gallery."

We go through two nearby doors into a recognizable *Laura Ashley* intricate and quite vivid yellow and blue different flowered wallpapered room. Scattered are blue and white striped patterned cushioned furniture, placed on top of a great pastel blue area rug embroidered with every kind of flower God created. Blue and white striped drapes tied back with black thick roped tassels complete her sanctuary.

Her fingers direct about the room.

"Is not too flashy? I hope not. You know Lloyd grants me total freedom," she laughs, "or I'll *leave* him. I'm joking, Diane, but we," she pauses, putting out her cigarette into a monogrammed crystal ashtray placed upon a Queen Anne side table cluttered with fashion magazines and a plate of half-eaten cheese, "wives need to rule somewhere. It's sure not in the boardroom. Right? Pardon the mess. Things go to squalor when Lloyd is on his so-called business trips."

Richard's perfection hates disorganization, and I'd sue the interior decorator for such a hideous room.

A lie smiles. "No. The room shows beauty. Richard focuses on his career, not the placement of a pillow."

"Yes. I see. Sit down, Diane."

My hostess strides, taking, I assume, her favorite spot, a large loveseat.

"Stretch out your legs on the ottoman. I do it all the time. Cost a bloody fortune to custom make. I think it's as comfortable as sin."

She lights another cigarette and gives me an open poker face.

Be careful. Make sure the pant legs cover evidence of Richard's kicking.

"What will you drink, my dear?" she asks, heading to the well- stocked bar. Her skills mean whatever I want.

"A Vodka Collins," I request and no sooner regret after the sweater's sleeves rise, revealing Richard's presents—still—black and blue wrist marks. I self-consciously tug on the sleeves attempting to cover the discolorations. "Don't bother . . . never mind."

"Oh, don't be so silly. Who sits on a hot day without something to drink? I prefer not tea, but a stiff one. Here, my dear." She hands the tumbler. "Good choice. I fixed me one too."

"Thank you." My unseasonal appearance hinders me from looking into her face. "I don't want to remove my glasses. *Okay?*"

No response. Helen's self-control opposite me translates into a silent microscope. She puffs on her cigarette. No questions. Am I to volunteer an explanation for my attire? She must suspect, knowing her son.

"I do miss England's countryside. My home in Surrey claims my heart."

Helen's unforeseen topic puzzles me, as she leans back and crosses her legs after a long silence. Sipping her drink in between long cigarette smokes stages a peculiar visit.

Why did she invite me after months? Mustn't fidget. I need to relax. "You go back each year, Helen," I add, thankful she's hasn't yet brought up Richard.

"I *insist* on it. I'm planning to visit my sister, Doreen, next spring. Why don't *you* come along?"

'In all my marriage, Helen, we've never traveled across the street together,' I want to remind her. I reply instead, "I'd *love* to. I *can't*. Richard needs me."

"*Interesting.*" That chuckle, the sarcastic one I've known for years, puts me on guard to tug down the sweater's sleeves Helen scrutinizes. Prying questions soon will begin. "My sons are quite the breed. Aren't they?"

Helen raised the bastards, an ignorant admission. "I don't understand the question," I bait her.

She pats the sides of not-a-strand-out-of-place styled-hair. "You *know*, Diane . . ." a prolonged pause accompanies extended cigarette smoking as she repositions her legs, "both my sons, John and David, are *long* divorced."

They're abusive women chasers, is a better picture. Common sense shuts my mouth.

Helen's uncharacteristic bleak disposition means what? Can she be begging for pity? Her sudden blue-mood makes me quite curious. "Are you okay?" I pretend to be concerned because we are anything but close. "Katrina, John's ex-wife, and his two sons live in Katrina's home in Brazil. David's ex-wife, Amy, and their three daughters move around internationally like gypsies. My husband drills, we don't owe anything to women divorcing our family. I can't argue on *some things*. Lloyd says they'll latch on to other men. Is it right accepting his *black and white judgment?*"

Am I witnessing a revelation of my stiff-upper-lip mother-in-law hinting at vulnerable loneliness? Is she patting away emotional tears?

Probe her. You may not get another chance. "Helen, how long has it been since you've seen your grandchildren?"

"Lloyd and I haven't spoken to Katrina for five years. Her sons are eighteen and nineteen. She hates us for not testifying against John on abuse claims. On the contrary, I never saw John hit her or those children."

"And Amy?"

"Amy, you know, plays the concert violin. I haven't seen those girls in about seven years. The last thing I heard from David is that she's in the Prague Symphony. His daughters are teenagers."

Is she going to ask about my daughters? I'll give the short version. "The wives get the checks. The kids get the best colleges. My sons get to screw girls in their twenties." Her voice cracks, "If you must know, Diane, *I blame myself.*"

"I'm sorry, Helen."

I know how a mother can blame herself—thinking of Leah. "Right," she says in a British matter-of-fact upright posture.

The air suspends into a low mood while we finish our drinks. Helen lights another cigarette.

Those back and forth glances centered on my sunglasses and sweater's sleeves push the release on the dreaded question. "How are you, Diane?"

Blink hard. Don't show cry-baby weakness for your long unhappiness list.

"Are you going to answer or mimic a sappy lost puppy, holding its head down?"

Her abruptness pushes my tear, ready to fall. "Richard did this," my announcement sounds embarrassed-angry.

Not even a flinch, a comment, or question at the black eyes and swollen cheekbones. If my mother-in-law doesn't care, why should I? A tear falls, I'm not ashamed. The sunglasses will remain off.

"Another one?" She shakes her empty glass.

"I haven't finished this one," I call out—too late—she mixes two more.

"Stay the night, Diane. Lloyd and the boys won't be home for several days."

Her invitation, never before given, plays out odd. Could it be a truce? I can't figure you out, Helen. Why this visit? Did Richard confess our fight? Does she want to hear my side because we're alone? Notice she's not returning to her position—instead kneeling—without asking permission—checks my wrists—turning them left-turning then right. Her fingers lift my chin, they touch my eyes, mouth, and throat, a raised eyebrow says it all. The daughter-in-law giving away her power says even more.

'Richard won't change,' I crave, yelling as my tongue rakes over the inside of my mouth. Glad she reads the signs returning to her seat.

She returns to her spot.

"Tell that son of mine to go to hell. Pack your damn bags." Directness startles me. "What's another family divorce mean? Lloyd," she continues precise and controlled, "and I have had rough patches. He hit me, but I got in my fair share. I damn sure did. Now we're just too old. I'd take him for everything he has, *and he knows it* if he hit me again. I don't give a God's prayer about the other women as long as the bastard remains discreet."

"You *want* me to leave your son?"

Confusion plasters my mind trying to process her frank and unapologetic stance.

"May I pry into a personal matter?"

She edges closer; her leg crosses over the knee. Eyes fixated. Steady cigarette smoke floats like small clouds. Gone is my chair's comfortableness.

"What is it, Helen?" I ask, petrified after hearing her question.

"*Why* do you stay with Richard? Do you love him *that* much? I have to know *why, why* do you love my son?"

"I married Richard because I loved him."

A flipped hand in the air translates that she's not buying the answer I've convinced myself of for years.

"I didn't *ask* you *why* you married Richard, my dear. I asked you, *why* do you love Richard? Can't you comprehend the difference?"

No matter how close she pulls a chair next to me, the complicated question remains unanswered.

"I've done a terrible job as my sons' mother." Softness? A sign perhaps she's not a hard bitch?

"None of their wives stayed around except you. I think I deserve your reasons, you're stalling. I understand. We're not close. Am I right?"

A gentle hand onto mine lures confessions. Can revealing secrets be done without the cruelest words?

"I ask you this question because you wear heavier make-up than at other times. You're quite pretty, Diane. He beats you. I know he does. *All my sons inherited the dirty trait from Lloyd, and I imagine he did from his father and so on. The reality mirror of life.*"

How do I know she'll not tell Lloyd? Fidgeting in my seat—pulling away—looking at the floor should say, *'I can't answer.'*

"Oh my, we're supposed to have a relaxing time together. I've spoiled it. Haven't I?" She returns to her seat. "Forget the questions."

"No, Helen. Don't think you've ruined anything."

"You lie well, my dear. I guess women pack lies in their survival kits."

My drink—the one I didn't want—helps reconcile much.

"My father owned a rather large textile mill in England." She starts on what I've heard before. Glad I accepted another drink. "My sister and I attended private boarding and finishing schools all our lives because Mum left with Father's best friend. The divorce and custody fight made society headlines. I never knew Mum's fate. The last post was twenty years back from New Zealand to my sister. I won't bother. She left. So be it."

Bits of her life force Helen's chain-smoking. I count five straight cigarettes.

"We enrolled my sons in boarding school. Lloyd and I built the business and the status we have now. Liken to my parents, and I didn't fancy motherhood either. Life's handed down the pipeline, you see."

"Richard said he loved being away at school, Helen." "Really?" She rises to refresh her drink. "Another?" "I'm okay, Helen."

"I will have another. My sons don't make for a cheery story."

*

She returns, reclining into the cushions. Shutting tight those well-made up eyes allowing water to soak her lashes.

"When Richard, John, and David came home, they witnessed Lloyd's drunkenness and our escalating physical fights over too many whores and his jealous control."

"And you stayed, Helen. Why? Why did you?"

There's no humor for me as she grins, wiping her mascara.

"My arranged marriage between our two families offered a wealth of goods in both the States and Britain. Obligation bound me to my father's family name; I doubt Lloyd loved me. A show card beauty captivated him, and I put up with his tramps. I gave up my desire to find out my dreams. I married early as a *sixteen-year-old virgin."*

Helen's admissions of lost ambitions and abuse shadows mine.

Maybe my heart's weight can be heard.

"Richard has been violent since we met. Nightmares, I want to forget. I stay because I have no other place to go. I've never worked. I've never had another lover. Do I love him? *No.* How many wives still love their husbands after being in a marriage as long as I have? If you tell Lloyd or Richard, I'm sure Richard will kill me," I warn her, giving a stern stare.

A knock at the room's door jolts Helen into a quick stand. She smooths back her hairline, swipes away traces of her crying, to flattening out wrinkles within her dress. Toes point. Shoulders erect. Head held model-runway high.

"Yes," the Queen answers.

Her British butler enters the room with a wheeled serving tray. "Lunch can be served per Madame's time."

"Thank you, Grant. Over there."

She indicates to the table facing a cluster of shade trees. Thank God because the bright sun still bothers my pupils.

We unfold starched white napkins, and Grant serves fresh salmon, rosemary vegetables, and rice pilaf. Zero conversation makes my portion tasteless. But smiles are given when our eyes meet.

"You know, dear, I have a wonderful Pinot Gris, Lloyd, and I bought in Napa. What do you think? Grant, would you please? Thank you. That'll be all," she finalizes her commands.

"Yes, Madame." Grant pours the wine before he exits the room. Silence waltzes a slow meal. The wine makes it tolerable.

"We don't have to discuss Richard anymore." She taps my fingers. "I know his capabilities. I wanted to know why you loved him. You should've had the sense to leave years ago." Helen sounds callous, sipping her precious Pinot Gris.

I want to slap her hard enough to feel my pain from Richard's fucking capabilities. Grateful wine neutralizes her coldness.

"I *stayed* for my children. Remember your grandchildren Leah, Nina, and Sarah?"

"Children need two parents. You've done more damage than you think, Diane. Children observe. My sons are an example."

"Are you saying I'm not a good parent, Helen?" I raise a vital question for my peace of mind and give her an unpleasant stare.

She holds a long, taut pause before answering, "Let's finish our meal and solve the world's problems later."

Damn-no filter-Helen is all pious drinking wine from her crystal glass. How dare she judge when her sons are worthless pieces of shit?

The English butler takes away the dishes. The wine bottle is empty.

Quiet waits for a word to replace it.

"Stay the night." Her invitation becomes more of an order.

Nailed to the chair, this family, and to my weakness, a reluctant acceptance gives in.

"Good," she replies, "we'll discuss my son later. Now take the dismal look off your face."

*

The next private thought hours since the last one: my mother-in-law insisted I spend the night after our yesterday visit. I awaken in one of her guest rooms. I hear knocking. Sit up. Awful pain felt raising my arm. The body abrasions are still visible. Damn you, Leah.

*

"Are you awake? May I come in?"

The doorknobs turn before I can answer. Sit up. The nightstand clock reads 10:00 a.m.

She must think I'm lazy. "Come in, Helen."

"Good morning, Diane. How did you sleep?"

"I slept longer than I should. I need to get going back home."

"You didn't answer me. How did you sleep?"

Why do she and I have this tug of war? No wonder we're not close. "I slept well. Thank you."

Her liberties sitting on the bed require my patience, letting her hold my hand.

"You haven't eaten breakfast. Besides, Richard won't be home when you get there. Remember?"

"I don't wish to intrude. You must have something else to do, Helen." "I'll see you downstairs in about half an hour? There are fresh clothes in the closet; I think your size. I dare say better suited for this hot weather. I keep some on hand," she laughs, "because I never know who'll be here in the morning."

I survey the room. "Where are my clothes?"

A proper manner answers, "You're not a prisoner, child. The garments are in a tidy bag. I can't stand wearing the same thing worn the day before. I'll see you downstairs. Take your time. No one has anything to do today." She winks with a brief smile before closing the door.

*

Time passes like a snail. I toss and turn, sit and sit, and toss and turn—in a four-poster-bed, and wonder how many guests have stayed in this room, resembling an English cottage-bed and breakfast. A woman of means, as Helen, must have many strays, running away from home. Between us, her authoritative pushiness, more than kindness, grates on my nerves. I wish I weren't one of her strays. Helen's decision is we eat together again. Oh, well, breathe a massive helping of her shit, and pick through the closet. Find something cotton. Maxi dress covers the legs.

Conceal my arms with a linen sweater. Rinse face. Brush teeth. Comb hair needing a trim. Make the bed.

Muscles are stiff. Hurry as best I can into a French chef's kitchen of intense white cabinetry, white painted walls, imported white marble tile, polished stainless-steel appliances, and brocade tapestry drapes. The sterile spotlessness accented with crystal table arrangements of white full bloom roses and bone-white china matches her ready-for-the- country-club appearance. I'm in the presence of the formidable Helen Fletcher, whose well-bred English stock gave her a stable life's station.

* "Are you full? Do you feel better?"

"Thank you, Helen. Eggs Benedict tasted good."

"My Grant and his wife, Stella, have been with me for nearly twenty years. Stella is a fabulous cook."

Our next course. Helen reads the business section of the *New York Times*. I read the fashion and theater parts. We're strangers in a coffee shop. She and Richard are identical. I understand the routine. Quiet.

"I have something for you," she announces after reading and folding the paper in its original state.

A cue. Do the same with my sections. "Yes." I hold waiting for her answer. "Advice."

Suspect of her control. My arms fold airtight, worry lines run through my forehead, and my face feels plastered with a million question marks.

"I don't understand, Helen."

Another cigarette and puffs of smoke saturate in little clouds about her face. She clears her throat.

The daughter-in-law waits for this grand must-be-said-wisdom.

"You know, my dear," she directs a stern finger my way, "you're not a good poker player. You wear your emotions like cheap clothes. A woman *should* have some mystery about her. Don't you think?"

Unable to uncross the damn arms, or relax your shoulders. Can't wait to leave. Helen's sour insults ruin a decent breakfast.

"What's your advice?" I bite back.

"I don't want to argue, Diane. Drop the attitude. I may be your lone ally."

She pours us more coffee from a sterling silver pot she bragged about bringing back from an over-priced London antique shop. The cigarette smoke is constant. Her quiet, I sense deliberate, accompanies barely blinking stares.

I'm getting annoyed spoken to like a child. My jaw tightens. '*I think I should go,*' I'm on the verge of saying, the more smoke comes to my direction.

"I'm not a good mother," she articulates what I've known. "So, my sons' wives put up with men who have no love. I never wanted children, you see. I missed the opportunity for a career. Married at such a young age. A mere child, I'd say."

'*It's all been said,*' thinking as she lady-like dabs the napkin about her mouth and primps the sides of her hair. '*Tell me something I don't know, Helen.*'

"How does this concern me?" I ask with mild restraint.

"Richard's deplorable behavior comes from Lloyd and me not setting limits on the spoiled child prone to fits of anger," Helen's out-of- character monotone dialog now has my attention. Tears come to a woman who doesn't push them aside. "Lloyd said his sons had to find their strength. Rules weren't for the privileged; they made their own. Boarding schools expelled Richard and his brothers. Lloyd said the teachers were wimps. I know my son beats you because he's bragged about putting you in your place." Her hands push up one of my sweater's sleeves. "I *know* his rage. *I've felt it before.*"

My head lowers until there's no space between my chin and chest. "I don't have any answers, Helen. Cruel as he stands, I've stood beside him because I love him," my dismal self mumbles peering into her eyes.

She wipes her face with the hand that shows its wedding diamond ring, and for the first time, I can appreciate Helen and my bond. We are unhappy.

"The other wives left. I don't blame them, Diane. My sons are a victim of their parents' irrelevant love."

This time, I don't mind her cigarette smoke.

"Richard and I are what we are. Some days we have a marriage.

Some days we swim in Hell."

"Your daughters are grown. I will tell you this. The love you seek from Richard doesn't fall from your reach. He doesn't . . ."

Her butler interrupts, "You have a telephone call, Madame." Thank God for servants. Space is more needed than a drink.

*

"Sorry." Helen quickens, with a present, two glasses of wine, and a bottle, that I will take.

"Helen, *what* do you want of me?"

"Nothing." She swallows half her wine. "I want you to do this *for yourself. And I suppose, to help my attainment. One has to ask forgiveness before the last breath.*"

On that note, all my wine flies down my throat.

"My son's unfaithful admission and his personality have, in my opinion, given you no chance for happiness."

"I . . ."

Sticking her hand in my face stops my thoughts.

"Listen, Diane; I don't care about your good reasons. I often speak to your daughters. I'm proud of them. I'm jealous. You've done an excellent job. One, I admit missing all the marks."

"Richard has told you he *doesn't* love me?"

"Don't be naïve insulting yours and my intelligence. A woman knows these things. Alright, since you want to act out this role, about five years ago, Lloyd and I went to Chicago. A close friend died. Out of all the cities in this country, Richard strolls out of the hotel across the street. He's kissing, as if a bloody fool teenager, a statuesque blonde woman."

I pour more wine. "*Julie,*" I speak her name with disdain. "So, you know? And so, my dear, we *are* on the same page." I don't answer. I can't.

"I asked my son about her," Helen continues while filling another wine. "He admitted their affair when I went to Palm Springs last year.

You remember my trip for my annual art charity event?" "Yes." Humiliated crying won't stop.

"I saw Richard again with *this, Julie.*"

"A private detective long ago informed me, Helen. I don't and can't talk about it anymore. *Please.*"

"Oh, stop these pity-for-me-tears. Have you not heard me? I'm your bloody damn ally." Her tone changes, opening a stern look. "Tears, yours, and mine are a waste."

"Ally?" I'm bewildered, wiping my face with her monogram napkin. "I will pay you a handsome, monthly allowance for twenty–eight years, the length of your ridiculous marriage. I have trust funds from Father's estate."

The-sorry-for-myself-crying lessens. Her offer can't be real.

"I don't understand, Helen. Money to leave Richard? Is this your purpose of my visit?"

"Contact me when you have the guts. My attorney will provide you with all the details. If I die, the funds will continue. I urge you. Consider it."

My hands clamp on the chair's armrests. Helen's unique proposition plummets all reason. Leave Richard? I can't. He's been in my life— more than half my life.

"My dear, you're sweating as if I've given you a death sentence. We won't speak of my plan *until you* come to me. I've no fear you'll be stupid enough to tell Richard of my intentions."

I have to inquire, "Did you extend such an offer to John and David's wives?"

She doesn't take time to answer. "Would it make a difference?" "I guess not."

Another sip of wine passes her lips before permitting an explanation. "No. My son's ex-wives strength outweighed yours. Act on my offer. My son has nothing to offer you. He doesn't love you, Diane."

Tension pounds my head.

"Why are you pushing me? If I leave, you and Lloyd will disown me as you've done Amy and Katrina . . . *and their children.* What about divorce?"

"Come on. You don't like Lloyd. I overheard you saying as much to Nina one Christmas. It didn't bother me because I respect what you've endured. I'll manage to see you and your daughters from time to time. Don't worry about divorce. Lloyd can be persuasive. Richard listens and wants to please his father."

"Can I have some more?" I place the glass in front of her. "I need it." "Of course." She pours a generous portion.

"I'm sorry, Diane. I made up my mind after seeing your face and receiving Richard's call about your recent fight. I don't know the reason.

I don't care. One day he'll kill you," a severe sigh comes out of out her mouth, "and it would kill me for my son to spend the rest of his life in prison. You see," a sneer captures her eyes' coldness, and I know she's thought out well her offer, "insanely the Fletchers *do* stick together. By the way, go ahead and keep those clothes. They're better fitting than the ones you wore here."

*

Terrified edge: visit with Richard's mother ends. I don't know what to do.

Pull into the gas station ahead to concentrate. Call Dr. Rose. No. Call Mother and Camille. No. Don't want their lectures. *Just think—okay— call Dr. Rose.* The office isn't far.

*

All her sophistication evaporates. Dr. Rose's pacing, cursing, and wild arms flinging rant shocks me. "How dare the son-of-a-bitch husband do this to you? Look at your face." Need to interrupt. Make the doctor listen.

"Dr. Rose, I'm here because there's nowhere else. Don't lecture."

"I apologize for unprofessionalism," she settles down. "I knew life with Richard tore through you. I had no idea how bad. We'll work this out together."

We sit. Our legs touching give a front row's views of my defined, black strangle marks.

"You don't deserve this shit. I'm glad you used the private entrance. My God, Diane." Her taps to my eyes, mouth, and shoulder blades should make an easy decision accepting Helen's money. It doesn't.

"Your face needs attention. Have you seen a doctor?" "I've *told* you about Richard's temper."

"But I *never* saw this type of evidence. Shit." "*I* will heal as in previous times."

The patient moans as if attending a funeral. To her surprise, she experiences the doctor's trembling hands, patting a tissue to the patient's agonized face.

"*Why* did Richard beat you? Tell me, *please.* There's no pen and paper. Talk to me because we are friends, also."

My hands tremble at her question conjuring horrid flashbacks of his backhand traveling too fast for escape.

"You can trust me," she consoles, rubbing all of her patient's broken nails. "Go on, Diane," she nudges.

Breathe. Let it out. Pondering over its graphic scenes takes a toll replaying them. A need to talk instead of digesting everyone else's opinion heaves out the patient's words, "The last days from the time Richard told me about *that* deal with Jared Longview . . . Damn. Life's complications . . ."

"Why did he beat you like a thug?" She thrusts into my face without giving me a chance to speak. "*Tell me,*" she insists.

I can't stand it. Between the heat, Helen's conversation, and the painting-me-in corner questions, it's all too much. I know everyone means well, but this is my fucking life.

"Did you hear me, Diane?" she prods again.

"Stop with the goddamn questions. Let me tell you in my own time. Can't you see I'm struggling to speak? I've *had enough* between my mother, sister, and Richard's mother."

"What are you talking about?" She throws perplexed daggers. "I'm dropped into someone's nightmare. You've come looking no less a battered woman. Am I supposed not to ask questions?"

Keep on the path; don't be confrontational. Get it out. The worst is over. "You told me to ask my daughter Leah if I can visit her—*a huge mistake.*"

The giving-advice-doctor pours a glass of water from a pitcher in front of us. I wish it were more substantial.

"Leah calls her father, "the story plays out to a quiet audience, "their closeness has remained my heart's dark spot. She informs Richard. He thinks two things: I'm leaving him, or I'm airing our or '*my*' problems to our children."

"What did you say, Diane?"

"I *can't* remember the exact conversation." Giving long strokes to my hair, I feel looks horrible in comparison to Miss Perfect Doctor.

"Something about—your father's business keeps him busy, and I want to spend some time away." Another long pause helps shovel this shit. "I've told you time and time again, Leah, and I can't talk to each more than a second."

"I don't understand. Richard beat you *because* you called your daughter?"

The wife squeezes together her legs. Can't forget. Will never forget the husband's fists pounding at will.

"Richard's creed is an outward appearance of a perfect marriage.

Status and privilege are symbols of success. "

"And so?" With big curious eyes, the doctor asks for more.

"Leah's pending promotion hedges on an important fucking case. She calls my visit a huge inconvenience. She assumes *marriage issues* are the reason for a hasty exit from our family home."

"Richard thinks you alluded to the problems you and he were having?"

Another gulp of water helps. "I won't go into all the graphic details. Richard demanded to know why I called Leah. My answer, *'Just to visit,'* because of his busy work didn't cut it."

The doctor shaking her head says a great deal. "It's pointless denying you're living in chaos, Diane."

"Richard demands I cancel my trip. Each time I ask *why* . . . well," slow moans punctuate the patient's unhappiness, "this is how Richard and I discuss things."

Stand. Slip off Helen's dress. Parade all the bashes. Endure another stunned examination. My sympathetic doctor is shocked. Sobs cover that perfect face.

"I say with absolute clarity. My husband *is* who he is."

Tissues take care of her face. "Put your clothes back on. We'll make a plan. You *have* to be safe."

While redressing, I inform her of my slightly different outlook, "I didn't think a rainbow could come after many storms. Richard's mother is an unexpected ally."

"I thought you two didn't get along?"

"Her lunch invitation turned into dinner, me sleeping over, and breakfast the next day. She divulged much about her and Richard. She knows he and his divorced brothers learned abusive behavior from their father. *She knows about Julie Meyers.*" Biting my lip hard to keep from letting it all go. "Do you have anything to drink?"

"We're off the clock." She pats my back. The softness feels foreign. "This should help both of us," she announces, pulling out of a drawer nearest her desk, a bottle of Jack Daniels and two glasses.

I can say, "Thank you," after a long swallow.

"Go on, Diane." She sits close again. "What *about your* mother-in- law?"

"Helen has offered me money to leave Richard. She confirms he loves Julie."

"How does she know?" "Richard said so."

"And you stayed all this time, even though I advised you otherwise?" "Educated women like you, careers in tack, no children, money in the bank with only your name on the account—have options. Women like me who have a noose around their neck called marriage have no options."

The drink and then another brings extreme quiet; Dr. Rose leans against the window. The patient sits alone.

"You *don't* know me." Her intrigue has my focus. "Why would you? I'm the doctor," downing another stiff drink, "and you *are* the patient. I've shown today my explosive side. Goddamn. Why I'm single stems from my fiancé beating the shit out of me. I've made bad choices. You see that even educated women are stupid."

*

Thought a long time coming: not alone.

*

"How can I help you?" My doctor's straightforwardness gives the wife a bit of a smile.

Summing-up my cause into a neat dirt pile, my answer is clear, "Be my friend. Listen to me. Help me map out the most important decision of my life."

What did I say wrong? There's a rush to finish her drink after putting away the bottle of whiskey.

"Have I offended you, Dr. Rose?" I ask, watching her swallow several breath mints.

"I have to go, Diane. I have another appointment. You've done or said nothing wrong. Is Richard home?" She proceeds to gather her briefcase, purse, and car keys. "Come, walk with me, to my car."

Unsure why she asked about Richard, I answer, "No."

A brisk pace to the sparse parking lot leaves me lost in my next step. "How long will he be away?" she inquires.

I know inside that the next time I see Richard, I won't be the same. How can I?

"He's away for several days. He's supposed to be in Texas with his father and brothers finalizing the Jared Longview deal."

"I know the name, Longview." She makes a peculiar sour pucker while writing on a piece of paper from her purse. "Here's my address. I won't be but an hour longer. Go to my house. Tell my sister Annette to let you in. I'll call her."

"I can't."

"*Yes*. You will. You asked for my help. Please do as I ask." The patient agrees with the reluctance of the unknown.

*

Annette, my host until the doctor, her sister, arrives home, listens to the ramblings of the shattered wife ending her babbling after an hour. "Richard is a monster. I'm sorry I've talked so much. I feel alone. Dr. Rose invited me because she understands my horrible life. Forgive me."

Her occasional calm exclamation, "It'll be fine," doesn't follow with those prying questions starting with how and why, and for that, Annette is a comfort.

Between my host and the minimalist Scandinavian décor, my mind exhales free thoughts. '*No. I'm not crazy, Richard.*' Peace falls within an unobstructed living room view of mountains in the distance. The relaxed houseguest no longer cares about showing her face.

"My sister will be home soon. Do you want another tea?" The running water breaks my meditation. "You must think me strange drinking, in the summer, hot tea. I find lemon chamomile soothing anytime. By the way, I'm glad you removed your glasses. The shame belongs not to you."

"Thank you for the tea *and for not judging me.*"

While she prepares our tea, Annette's relaxed manners and slender body reminds me of my dear Sarah, who's probably hooked on tea like all those uptight Brits.

"How old are you, Annette? I ask because you remind me of my daughter at Oxford."

"Samantha turned thirty. The next day I hit forty. We inherited our mother's genes. She's sixty but looks fifty. You'd like her."

Her kindness brings a full teacup.

"You'll be okay," she repeats, then takes a nearby seat.

How can a stranger be so sure? But that question has to wait; I hear the house key twisting in the door's lock, my doctor arrives home.

"Hello." A cheerful voice enters the room, "I see you found your way, Diane."

"Annette made me feel at home."

Dropping her belongings on the counter so that they could squeeze each other's shoulders shows evidence of their love.

"What did you do today?" Dr. Rose asks with a sweet kiss to Annette's forehead.

"Resting and thinking about the next phase." She bobs her head at me. "I'm going to my room to read. Nice meeting you, Diane."

Questions circle about Annette's history, but I don't interrupt the doctor sorting the mail.

There's a high-back soft leather chair calling my name. Drinking her tea—remembers Richard's training. Respect the quiet. *'Don't bother me.'* Insecurity whispers, *'Maybe I'm invading Dr. Rose's home.'* Watching her make a cup of tea—silence from my point of view makes me anxious — the decision to join her throws out Richard's rule.

"Am I intruding? I could go home because Richard isn't there yet."

Her answer—a soft hand glides over the tips of mine. "Give me a few minutes. Why don't you relax on the back porch?"

Time means nothing on a serene porch imagined from an issue of *Southern Living Magazine.* The wife soaks up wide spaces of grass and hears a nearby stream.

*

"Sorry, Diane, I took longer than expected." She joins the patient.

Beautiful without make-up in a sleeveless dress accentuating a toned body—I think the unthinkable—what does she look like naked? A full-lipped wide smile mirrors her sister's. Stop these thoughts. Affection starvation brings about incredible ideas.

Say something. The doctor is observing you. "Your home feels . . . tranquil, Doctor."

"Nothing special except avoidance of over cluttering objects. Operating a women's health clinic brings a multitude of headaches. No, not you, Diane," she clarifies.

"I *never* thought so, or you wouldn't have invited me."

"Please," I accept her touch to my arm. "Call me, Samantha. Are you hungry?"

"I hadn't thought about it. I ate late morning with Richard's mother." "Aw yes . . . the rich woman who'll pay you to leave her son." Her laughter sounds cynical.

Lack of confidence flops down my head. I detest being the brunt of everyone's point of view.

"I haven't decided." "*Why* not?"

"She made the offer today." The defensive patient feels awkward. The remaining tea slowly calms her. "I must discuss this with Richard . .

. at least give him an ultimatum."

What did I say wrong? Samantha's eyes begin to shut. Silence again. "I purchased," she sounds detached, breaking the quiet, "this land. I built this house after I got released from intensive care. You see, my fiancé broke my arm and cracked my ribs after he and his brother sodomized and raped me because I refused to co-sign and lend them money for a speculative business venture."

Did my situation make her confess a horrible secret? I "I'm sorry if me being here surfaces your past."

"No. Don't be, Diane. My life took a wrong turn a long time ago. I'm just explaining. Neighbors called the police, who broke down my apartment door." She stops for long breaths. "An officer shot one who wouldn't surrender. The other one was my fiancé, who got killed in prison."

"So, you pressed charges?"

"You have choices," she spurts out, entering the house. Let's eat. Annette. Is pizza okay?"

"Yes," Annette answers, joining us.

"Can you pick it up?" Samantha asks. "I want to continue my conversation with Diane."

"Sure. I'll go." Annette passes me a wink and then leaves through the front door.

Needing to explain while we're alone, "My children will be home next month for Richard's birthday. I don't know how, but a decision can't wait. I know this now. I must plot this out. I must. Can't you see?"

A tear, I thought long gone, surfaces.

"I do." Empathy comes in a tight hug—the kind of touch manufacturing a sense of protection. "I don't want anything to happen to you, Diane. I know a woman living in New York City. Her name is Cleo Miller."

Attitude slips into a scared zone because it sounds once again that someone else is making my decisions. "Why are you helping me? Do you do this for all your patients?"

'*When will I be free?*' These thoughts strangle me. Steps to the window's view I can take because it demands no answers.

"I'm grateful, Dr. Rose." I face her. "I have to know when I'll be able to stand on my own. All my adult life, Richard led me around like a trained dog."

"Diane. I'm still your doctor. Sure, I break the rules when it comes to assisting my patients. But women, like you, drowning in so much sludge, need a hand to pull them out. I want you to live, not like an animal. I want you to grow into a woman of purpose."

"I yearn for a teaspoon of happiness." I wipe my eyes and try hard to give a cheerful face, despite the body's pain, my marriage, and thoughts of Leah not wanting my visit.

"This is your chance to ask questions, Diane. Make decisions. I'm here."

Stress begins replacing weeping. I crave a drink. Maybe behind one of these modest doors is a cabinet full of happy juice.

"Hello." Annette comes in.

*

Plates, napkins, eating outside, and a glass of Chianti settle me. The sausage and feta cheese pizza with a Caesar salad isn't necessary.

"Are you going to stay the night?" Annette catches me off guard, pouring a wine.

"It's late," Samantha answers for me. "There aren't many street lights on. Yes. You'll stay."

Just like Helen, Samantha did the same annoying tapping on the back of my hand. She's made my decision.

The wife, the patient, the friend, the guest says nothing except, "Okay."

*

Thought at midnight: unanswered questions talk to me. What will the morning bring? Tonight the wife sleeps not at home again. She's at her therapist's house. The wife is out of place. Her norm is making love with Richard, no matter what he's done. Why? Her life has been with him all these years. Toss and turn. Don't know what the future promises. Richard has left messages. His last one said he'll be home tomorrow. Didn't say when—just tomorrow. Leah ignored messages. Have to face them. I have to face myself.

*

"Good morning, Diane." Thank God. Annette greets me with a much- needed strong cup of coffee. "I don't know what you take in it. Sugar and milk are on the counter. How did you sleep?"

Pull yourself together. Tighten the robe. Add a little milk and sugar. Lie, "I slept well."

"You can join me if you want." Her bare feet are leading to the back porch.

Our side-by-side seats make me envious of her skin's clarity. I can't but touch the side of my face. Feel a scab. Don't pull on it. Wonder what it'll look like when life comes back to me?

"Your soul heals everything," she speaks with wisdom. "I'd like to believe that, Annette. I'm forty-four."

"What's wrong, Diane? But not now," her voice lowers. "Tell me later. I hear my sister coming."

"Good morning," Samantha comes through, showering us with a huge grin.

Say something. Your host is standing next to you. "Good morning, Samantha. Thank you and Annette for letting me stay. I should get going soon. Don't you think?"

Annette's eyes wander into mine before she steps off to walk about the yard.

"No need rushing off on my account, Diane." She waves to me as her voice carries back to the porch.

"You don't have to leave," Samantha sounds put out. Dishes are rattling in the kitchen. I feel an edge in the air. "Samantha, let me say something."

"No." Her hands signal stop approaching. The patient does read messages well. She goes no further. "You don't owe me an explanation, Diane." Her stern expression says the opposite. "I know you need to attend to your house."

"Are you mad, Samantha? I should leave. I've intruded enough."

"Then do what you need to do," her raised voice catches me way off guard. "When you walk through the door, will you stay? Mark my word, Richard will beat you again and again. Think about his mother's offer. Don't trust him, a salesman, carrying a briefcase of torture."

The patient's hands tense up. She worries what to say. "I *will* make the right decision."

"*And she will*, Samantha," Annette comes into the kitchen. "Give *this one* credit." She pats my shoulder, then heats water for a teabag.

"You're right. I'm sorry, Diane," Samantha apologizes with a firm hug. "You've done nothing wrong. Call me. I'm here for you. *Please* be careful."

"I promise. I promise."

*

Thought running wild: driving home. Don't want to go, but have no other place except Camille's and Mother's. They'll insist on rehashing the shit. Go back. Face Richard. Fearful of another physical fight. Feel alone. Not far now. Slow down. Stop. Recognize a woman in a car at the four-way stop, down the hill from my house. Sunglasses hide my eyes. She can't see me, but I know her. She's Julie Meyers. Oh God, she and Richard were fucking in my bed. What do I do? Stop hysterics. You know what to do. Confront her. Drive to her house. You know the way. The detective showed you.

*

Watching from the same hidden and visible angle—the one detective and I once sat outside her townhouse—something the wife swore she wouldn't do again. It hurt too much seeing them kiss like newlyweds. Here still, the desperate wife hunts. And the prize emerges. Julie. Don't analyze her. Slide down deep into the car's seat. Peek over the dashboard. You observe three people. She and the two men you don't know. They laugh. Dear Lord—another man exits the door. Richard. Duck down quickly. The two men get into a truck. Back out the driveway. Richard and Julie arm-in-arm wave goodbye. Breathe. Don't open the door and call them every fucked-up name they deserve. What was Julie doing alone in our house? The bastard gave her a key. She's had one all along. How many times has she been in my place? Why try anymore? He's made Helen's offer easy. Go home and pack. No. You, the wife, will wait for him.

*

Thought since dark: drunk. The clock watches me. I watch the clock infuriated. Hurt. Alone. Jealous. I wait for him.

*

Thought the next day: the sun rises. Waiting. Morning. They must be done fucking. They must be. The beating Richard gave me should be enough to leave him. My heart locks hard into his. Why? His car's motor approaches the driveway. Noon; finish the cigarette. Need a drink. No. Need to be sober. Make more coffee. Pretend.

*

"I'm home, Diane."

Don't go to him. Stand at the sink with your back facing him, so you don't have to fake the first I-miss-you-glance.

"I'm in the kitchen, Richard."

"Hello, Diane," you hear him pull the chair away from the table. "Is there enough coffee for another cup?"

Turn around. My darling husband looks tired. Must've been up all night fucking her.

The angry wife plays sweet, filling an empty cup. "Your trip went well?"

"Yeah . . . better than planned."

The wife hands him his drink. Though she'd rather throw the cup into his face, she doesn't care about a *thank you*. The last time they sat together in this kitchen, he raped her. His arrogance belittled and labeled her an uneducated, stupid bitch on his business affairs. Those are his assessments, which no longer have meaning for the wife's improvement because this wife isn't as dumb as he thinks. She wants to scream at his hair stubbles needing shaving and the wrinkled shirt stained with not- my-shade-of-lipstick. *'I hate you, Richard. I know where you've been.'* Instead, the wife, with her hands folded, steadies for an opening to ask the unthinkable.

"We've signed paperwork. Our firm represents Jared's interests and .

. ."

Richard's peculiar stumbling for words hides what? "Your face is—*I'm sorry, Diane.*"

My husband's remorse colors an uncharitable characteristic.

"It will heal, or else you'll pay for me to go back to the surgeon. *'We fight and make-up.'* Aren't those your exact words?"

Bitchiness forbids weakness after witnessing him and Julie. "Previously in this room, I said things and . . . I hurt you, Diane."

Something's way off. Jittery hands swab sweat around his forehead and mouth. Apologizing twice falls short of his character.

"Richard?"

"*Please*—give me a moment, Diane. Please. I need a drink. You want one?"

"No."

"God. Diane." His breathing sounds as if he's been running uphill. "I *need* a drink."

"*What's* wrong, Richard? I demand to know before one of us has a stroke."

"Alright." He's mumbling.

Richard won't speak directly to me—an ominous sign of something awful lurks around the corner. Brace yourself, dear, dear wife. Your heart speeds into panic mode.

"Difficult, not at all easy . . . but I *must* tell you." Seconds pass like years. He clears his voice and lights a cigarette. "My flight came in two days ago."

"*It did?*" I calculate: *he's been with her all this time.* "Where were you?"

"Yes." Giving me the honest, unapologetic face I've seen on him. "Diane. I came home and didn't find you. Mother said, you spent the night. She had no idea where you'd gone. I assume to Camille's, planning the baby shower, it *doesn't* matter. I left you several voicemails. You never answered a trait I despise."

"I saw your mother. I got your car washed. I canceled the reservation. You told me the timeframe you'd be gone."

"Please be quiet and listen, Diane. Yes, you do everything I tell you like a puppet."

My hand bashes the table.

"I'm goddamn tired of your fucking name-calling."

"Yes. I suppose you are. I didn't want to be alone, Diane. I went to Julie's," he bursts out a confession spoken with no remorse.

The mention of her name breaks my heart. I can't subdue the rage and reality. His hands, his lips—vivid visions of them rolling around in bed kissing, touching, and saying those words, *Julie, I love you.'* Enormous-how-could-you-do-this-to-your-wife-tears build and drown into my rejected face.

Richard's repulsive fingers stroke my shoulders. They are neither desired nor needed. Pull away, erect my back straight into the chair. Show no weakness.

"I see," the attorney scrutinizes my heavy focus. "Alright, Diane. Let's not play games. I don't want to hurt you anymore. You *know* who she is."

"I *do,* Richard," a hostile answer states without hesitation. It's no longer matters. I saw Julie coming from this house's direction.

"I don't know how to say this except, to be honest, and straightforward, *but you and I can work this out, Diane.* Julie's pregnant."

To hear what I thought I heard and know what I've listened to are two different things. Pulse and heartbeat pushing, knotting acid from my stomach into my mouth, fists squash the air between them. Neurotic rage seeps to insanity.

"*What did* you say, Richard?"

"I can't believe it at my age," he answers, still not remorseful, "I never thought, at my age, I'd be a father. Julie's four months pregnant. A shock to me as much as you. You knew about her. I know you did."

My hands have control; I'm their messenger. One hand smashes my coffee cup onto the floor. I don't care about it being part of an antique French pattern. Goddamn, bastard.

"So this makes it right? You son-of-a-bitch." My storm grabs his shoulders. I'm forcing him to look at what his wife does best: cry the tears for ten wives. I plead like a wet rag, "Why? Tell me why, Richard." He touches my hand, but the shattered bond blasts insufferable hatred toward a man I've spent half my life bearing his last name.

"I can't answer, except at one point Julie and I . . . well, would have been married."

"Married? When the *fuck* did you want this to happen? I hate you, Richard. All the shit you put me through. Look at me." Jabbing my finger into his forehead, the exact way he did me. Years of pent-up anger holler, "See my scars? You beat them into me. Look at me, you son-of- a-bitch." I strip off my clothes. Stand naked Expose to the bastard, your new and old scars.

"Diane." His eyes blink too-late-for-him-tears.

Begging for sympathy infuriates the wife, picturing him and his bitch on one of those business trips making plans to marry.

"Why didn't you leave? You bastard. Damn you. Damn you." Such vile war within wages continuous unlimited powerful slaps to his face.

Richard's whimpering garners zero pity from his wife.

"I'll do the hell what I need to do. I don't give a damn. I'll gut you like the fucking pig you are if you ever, and I *do mean ever* hit me again, Richard. I'll never sleep in the same bed as you. My room will be in the spare room down here."

"I want to . . . I need to talk to you, Diane."

"Fuck you. I needed a lot of damn things. What I got is summarized in four words—a lifetime of misery."

"We'll talk later. I'm not leaving. I *do* love you, Diane." His announcement of commitment falls miles flat as he shuffles out of the kitchen. "Go ahead and sleep down here. I'll let you have your way *for now.*"

*

Thought in the middle of the day into the night: Richard has returned. I sleep, when I do, with a butcher knife from the pantry I stole while he was out. The sharp blade rests under my pillow. A chair props against the closed door. I sleep, but yet I don't.

THE MIDDLE

Absolute Gravity

A FRIGHTENING THOUGHT before dawn: Richard's relentless pacing and cursing continued most of the night downstairs. He breaks glasses and throws things against the walls. He stops too many times to count in front of my room, the guest room. His fists bang on the door; he won't stop. I'm beyond scared. I'm terrified. Both of my hands clench the knife; the more his body pushes against the door, the more the bureau and chairs come ajar as my blockade. I can't call the police without physical evidence of Richard's violence. I have the old scars, but the detectives will want new ones, or they'll say I committed an intentional act. A jury will wonder why I didn't leave long ago. If he breaks down the door, my evidence *will be* self-defense. I don't care if I take my last breath in prison. My cell phone and a knife are ready each time his feet stop in front of the bedroom door.

*

"I know you fucking hear me, Diane."

Trembling with eyes shut tight, the wife prays for Richard's Ivy League common sense to kick in. She begs for his respect. After all these years, she full well knows common sense and care are dead. Men like Richard should've never been born.

"I'm staying home today. *Please* open the door." He rattles the doorknob again. "We *need* to talk," his erratic instance devours the air.

"Go to hell, Richard."

The wife holds her ground. Her grip on the knife pointed at the door means business. She rechecks the bedroom windows. All bolted with security keys.

"Open the goddamn door, Diane."

My fingers shake, preparing to dial the police. "Go away, Richard. I'm fucking warning you." "What's blocking the door? I must talk to you."

His constant whinnying imitates me. A weak trait he hates by countless times, slapping my mouth. One day soon, I'll make him pay.

"Open this damn door, Diane. I'm through playing this game."

*

Thought of no resolve: air conditioner doesn't work. The windows are secure, and the curtains are closed. I feel strength jamming against the door until the furniture blocking begins sliding away. What to do? Can I kill him if he breaks in? He's pushing harder. Plead with him before one of you dies.

*

"Please stop, Richard. Please. Don't do this."

"I'm not going to leave you and our girls. Hear me? Just open the door."

Leah's name makes me spit when he mentions our children. She's responsible for Richard pounding my flesh less than two weeks ago. I'm way out of my element, Samantha. I've never gone this far over the cliff. What do I do but talk to him while we're under the same roof?

"Say what you're going to say, Richard." "I don't want barriers. Let me in, Diane." The knife is ready.

"No. You'll hit me. I don't want any trouble with you." "Please let me in, Diane."

Fear squeezes the blade's handle. Richard's deep breathing terrifies me. I know he'll beat me until blood covers my body. How can I trust him?

"I won't hurt you, Diane. I'm sorry. We need to speak to one another *face-to-face.*"

He thinks his wife's a fool.

"You got another woman, your lover, pregnant. How can you say you won't hurt me?"

Acknowledging my predicament ignites my ignorance, run to the medicine cabinet. Snatch the bottle of pink pills. Swallow two.

"*This* situation can be taken care of."

His remedy gives no comfort. Disregard for an intimate relationship, even though not with me, shows a lack of compassion when no longer convenient. Would he dare kill Julie? Don't entertain such a crazy thought.

"Go to hell, Richard. You think I'm the biggest fucking fool to accept what you've done as acceptable. Are you talking about abortion? Julie's four months pregnant. Or is there a more sinister idea you're planning?"

"I'll take her to Europe or Mexico. I *have* contacts."

Tears aren't for her. They're for me. The man I married will do anything to eliminate a problem. He's often bragged, *'When you have money, solutions are a phone call away.'*

"Julie will never go along with your plan. She loves you. What are you going to do?"

"I have no intention of marrying her. I'll get her an abortion. My marriage means more."

The wife, dumbfounded, asks a fundamental question, "Are you saying, Richard, that you'll kill your child for me, your wife, whom you've mentally and physically abused all our marriage? You *are* a useless human being."

He doesn't answer. "Richard?"

"Open the damn window, or I'm breaking it."

Oh, my God. The bastard is at the bathroom window. Can Richard break the triple-paned glass?

"No. Richard. Go away. I'll call the police."

No neighbor can hear me. The closest house sits two miles away. My hands shake too much even to dial 9-1-1. Goddamn. I dropped the phone.

"Open the damn door. I swear I'll take a brick and bash in the window."

"If you come near me, I'll kill you. Get the fuck away from me."

No noise. Where is the bastard? Hide in the closet, pick the phone off the floor. Call the police. Oh, God. He broke the window. I forgot to barricade the bathroom door. No one will get here in time to save me. Should I kill myself instead?

"Diane? Where *are* you?"

He's walking inside the room. Show him the knife as soon as he reaches for you. It's either you or him.

I hear Richard's eerie laugh. "I know you're hiding, *maybe* in the closet?"

The closet's doorknob turns to the left. It opens to a towering giant reaching down with his claws, ready to snatch my breath.

A formidable voice demands, "Get up. Put the knife down. I'm *not* going to hurt you. Put down the goddamn knife."

The wife crouches, shielding her head; her body leaves no space between her and the closet's corner. She's hysterical. "Go away," she screams for her life. She is holding up her lifeline—the butcher knife. "I'll kill you. I swear I'll kill you."

He stands still, pumping out fuming breaths. The petrified wife raises her head to a lamp light silhouetting the husband's shadow, molding a tight fist. He kneels. They're eye-to-eye. The knife's relevance vanishes as he squeezes her wrists together.

"Give –me-the-knife."

Richard's willpower pries open my hand, the knife falls. His reflexes catch its handle. Held to his side—out of reach—options are none. Control is lost.

"Get the fuck up," he commands.

My reality is either an emergency hospital visit or death.

The wife's wobbly legs stand. Her mind resigned. "Do your best and kill me, Richard."

"I want to talk to you, Diane," he unhinges a stern voice I'm accustomed to knowing I can't win.

The furniture blocking the door means nothing for him, shoving it aside.

"Dumb bitch. Come into the kitchen right now. This drama has gone on long enough. I'll put *this* back before someone gets hurt." He scratches his hair. "Shit . . . *like you have the guts to kill me.*"

The wife paces slow behind. Her mind rattles. What are her consequences for sleeping in the guest room? Her nearest escape door, in the kitchen, can't be reached unless she passes him.

"I'm waiting. Hurry up," Richard's impatience reaches a high pitch of frustration.

A child on the verge of a terrible chastising enters with caution into the kitchen.

Occupying the table's head chair, King Richard holds court with a tall glass of wine and two unopened bottles at his fingertip.

He watches her movements while he takes in one-slow sip after another. He's set another glass of wine to his right.

I reason another physical fight is looming. Concentration splits between Julie's pregnancy and Richard's steel pout while he rubs the side of his face's blistering handprints left by my ferocious strikes. Petrified—I stand.

"Sit." He offers an out-of-place gesture of pulling out my intended chair. "We *need* to discuss our future," the request digs more in the line of an order.

He takes his place; his smirk draws another long drink to his mouth.

He strokes his jaw. "I think you want to kill me, Diane. Don't you?"

The wife on the seat's edge forgoes the wine. Her fingers fold into each other. She is quiet, biting her inner lower lip the more Richard's eyebrows stiffen, accentuating lines stretching across his forehead.

The bastard grins, observing my wine. "Since *when, my dear,* did you give up drinking?"

The wife shuts out her husband's taxing voice. Contemplations drift out the open floor-to-ceiling kitchen window's view yielding blue skies, snowcapped mountains, overflowing wildflowers, maple trees, and her roses enough for several large weddings. She agonizes: *if she'll be in this house next year and Helen's offer.*

The sudden pounding of the table pulls her attention. "So, we're playing your silly ignore-Richard-fucking-game?

"You wanted to talk, Richard? Go ahead."

He laughs, scratching his head. "I'd thought a wife in your position, with *an unfaithful husband,* would seize the opportunity of nailing his ass with a million questions."

The cockiness, I detest, checkmates me.

Prying into my husband and his lover's bedroom won't be this ripe again.

Swallow curiosity, pride, and dignity. Helen's offer is worth the headlines.

"Tell me everything about Julie."

He pauses—drinks more, and lights a cigarette.

"*What do you want to know?*" He deals with a reserved question.

I call his dare, "I said e*verything.* I want to know *everything,* Richard, even the things you know will destroy me."

"Well, well, Diane. I give you a hell of a lot of credit. Do you even *want* to know the way she sucks my cock?"

Hate centers into a handsome face no longer existing for me.

"Your sarcasm can't belittle me anymore."

"You may well be right," Richard half-laughs while stroking where I struck him. "Okay. You want the fucking truth. I met Julie." He stops and gives a tilted head examination of not a speck of kindness in my eyes, fixated on his continual chain-smoking, I know his sign of discomfort.

"Better get another bottle." He uncorks the second bottle. His perfection tanks, he spills alcohol. "See how rattled I am?" He finds humor using a paper towel to clean up the wine.

I recognize the label; we bought it in Napa. I wonder if he took her also.

He shakes an empty glass in my direction. "You sure you don't want to join me? You might need it."

"No, Richard." I'm direct. "This isn't a happy hour at some bar. I want to know what I asked you. *Tell* me about Julie."

"I met her," he continues talking as he pulls some cheese and bread from the refrigerator, "when I took you to Santa Barbara for our tenth anniversary."

My bastard husband's unapologetic attitude while he chomps down on his snack and wine floors me.

"You're still not drinking with me? I thought for sure you'd be hungry."

He shoves a bit of bread into my face.

"No. Go on with your damn story, Richard."

He clears his lungs. The wife imagines either to cushion a lie or to be one-hundred percent honest.

"I recall *that* morning and our erotic lovemaking. Our passion, oh my God, set me on fire, Diane. While you were showering, I snuck to buy you a dozen of the reddest roses from that flower shop on the corner from the house."

"The house's ocean views," I reminisce too, as one of the happiest times of our relationship, "and on the porch talking about nothing in particular, to horseback riding on our private beach. I felt as if I were sixteen again. We *loved* each other. We said it. We meant it."

The wife's eyes water. Not once, Santa Barbara, in those two weeks, did they argue. Here they are today and can't hold a minute of civil conversation.

Richard's stroking of my hands doesn't move me. "I wish we could go back eighteen years ago, Diane."

The wife pulls back her hand.

The bastard wipes water from his eyes. The bastard consumes more wine.

The question looms. Hurt can't flush one subject down the toilet. "*What* does this have to do with Julie?"

His unhappiness finds the center of my eyes, and he says, "I met Julie that morning at the flower shop."

My heart breaks, consenting for tears, as Mother's when first seeing my black eye six months after my marriage.

The wife breaks her vow. She pours a tall glass and drinks as if it is water. The wife runs another before the wine glass's bottom is visible. The French Bordeaux, she and bastard husband, shared on their tenth anniversary, and after kept on hand, now tastes like shit in my mouth. The vow not to drink breaks, to comprehend the reason for Julie.

He reaches again for my hands.

"Don't."

"I understand." He gives in, Unable to look at me.

Coldness bears down, "Your touch, Richard, doesn't make hearing more tolerable."

Long breaths mix with a glazed expression. If there were love, the wife would hold the bastard.

"Julie's San Francisco husband and his parents died in a car crash," he begins. "A drunk driver killed them. She needed an attorney to protect her assets. Ed Moore, my father's friend, helped her with the estate. I helped myself to her bedroom."

The bone-exactness is so-like-an-attorney, who can fill in the details. The wife knows well her mate's preferences of oral, anal, and bondage sex.

"So, you two just started your affair at some damn flower shop?" "We struck up a conversation about flowers. I found out about Julie's family and circumstances in a manner of twenty minutes or so.

"Do you want me to continue?" he asks. "I say that because you're crying."

"Tears have been my accessory since we met. How should I take your concern, Richard? Don't let my sadness stop your confession, *my dear husband.*"

The wife wonders his thinking as he lights another cigarette. She feels no sympathy for the bastard whose tears drip down his face.

"I wanted to stop seeing her, Diane. I couldn't." He refills his glass. "I first slept with her two days after we met. You went shopping."

The unbearable insult visualizing them, making love accentuates my hand's tightness. I reach for the wine to fortify tolerance to listen and look at him.

"Go on, Richard."

"Julie's Swedish beauty and uninhibited sexual freedom became my cocaine. I'm *sorry*, Diane. How many times have you seen me cry?"

My mind can't take any more of a cheater's sniffling begging for forgiveness. More alcohol dilutes the picture.

"Richard, stop it. The tears are not for me. They are for you. I will be alright. I promise you."

"I don't want to lose you, *my wife*." "You loved her. Didn't you?"

"I won't lie. I love Julie. We spent years together. She carried our child. I thought marrying her would give me a chance to be happy because you and I stopped being in love."

"What do you mean *she carried your child*? What the hell are you saying?"

Shock and disbelief at the bastard's revelation have destroyed all the years of our marriage.

He drinks more. He cries even more.

Numbness hurls the wife into suicide contemplation, hearing her husband's raw confession, "Julie got pregnant before about eight years ago. You and I argued day and night. She gave me comfort. My easy solution would've been to marry Julie. I could've divorced you for alienation of affection."

Screams dump into his face. "Don't you fucking ever touch me." Reflexes yank my hand away because it's too many words too late.

"I *didn't* leave you, Diane. Love kept me here."

"Are you fucking sick? How do you validate this woman's child? I'm not talking about the one now, but the first fucking one? Where's the damn baby? I slept with you anytime you wanted, even after you beat the shit out of me. Alienation of affection? Go to hell with your lawyer bullshit."

Fuck the glass. I uncork the second bottle and hold it to my still not entirely healed lips. My skin crawls, remembering all the present and past punches.

An awkward long quiet tightens us; my fists clamp tight. Richard drinks the last drop of wine and opens the reaming bottle.

"She lost it." He mumbles. "What?" I demand.

"She lost it, Diane. I couldn't desert you anyway." The bastard's explanation comes just as the wife is about to return to her room.

An unremorseful attitude doesn't give a shit about her husband's distressful cries. The end of conversation means to the wife, return to her room.

The wife stops walking. The bastard looks into her face.

"Why not leave me when the scare was over? You loved someone else. Why didn't you leave me? Why did you stay?" I, the wife, demands.

He paces about the room—first to the sink—then to the counter—then to the window. His back and shoulders bend forward. The wife still feels no compassion.

"You got the cancer scare," he says. "I realized I loved you."

The wife places on the table the Tiffany diamond wedding rings, the ones she thought the most beautiful in the world. She studies with contempt for her husband.

"I don't want a divorce, Diane."

At the crossroads—can't go backward and afraid to go forward, the wife's mind chants over and over, *'I need you, Dr. Rose. I need you.'*

His kneeling forces the wife's hand in his before she can pull away.

He fixates on his wife's wedding rings.

"I fell in love with a woman I met at the wrong time. Forgive me," the husband pleads.

"You ask a lot—expect me to fuck you—expect me to love you all these years, you beat me. You killed my identity—now you expect me to ignore your lover is pregnant. Do you beat Julie as well? Look at me. See your goddamn handiwork from our last fight?"

"I can't look, Diane. I *know* what I did."

The wife unbuttons and lowers a blouse revealing the carved results of his tirade, "All this *because I wanted to visit Leah.*"

He weeps, "I'm sorry, Diane."

The wife exploded, "Stop. I can't take you, this house, anything, especially you and this farce of a marriage."

"I won't give up," he pleads. "I made a mistake."

He plants his unfinished wine bottle to his mouth. Its juices drip over the designer shirt I didn't buy. Glancing down, he remarks, "I don't care about the damn shirt," uncharacteristic to a man guarding their image. "What I do care about is saving our damn marriage," sounds even more ridiculous.

"I'm tired, Richard. Don't follow me into the guest room."

"I promise to leave you be, Diane. Promise me we'll talk later today."

*

A liberating thought: the wife leaves the kitchen to return to her room.

She has witnessed her husband's hands pasted to his head; she has heard his intense sobbing. Indifference padlocks the wife's feelings. The day has just begun.

*

"Are you cooking dinner for just you or the both of us?"

He joins me from somewhere in the house. His distance kept wide, noticing his wife's less than happy to see his face.

"I'm fixing an omelet, toast, and bacon," she answers.

The wife's appetite and weight are slipping, and clothes don't fit, nothing fits. She must eat protein. Cooking isn't a high priority.

Out of the corner of her eye, she notices his movements gathering plates, napkins, and utensils.

The thought of sitting with him is a temptation to toss the food in the garbage—Helen's offer makes anything possible.

"Will you make me one? I'll open another bottle. Shall we have the Oregon Pinot?"

"*Sure,* but no wine for me. By the way, how long will you be here? Will you be going to work in the morning?"

He ignores me—reaches for long-stem glasses. He places them, not at the table, but on the more intimate bistro table overlooking the garden. My proud bastard shines, pointing to the table setting that we rarely sit at together. Too bad the sunset is a waste.

"Father gave me a week off for my hard work," he says in between forks of the egg I wish I laced with rat poison.

I'm annoyed he'll be here all fucking week. "I see," I reply.

"Several years back, Diane," he sits, waiting for me to join him, "I lost my keys. I recall you made an extra set in the pantry. You *were* careless."

"What are you talking about, Richard?"

He opens the wine and pours himself a generous glass. "Don't have time to let it breathe. By the way, I *found* the files the detective you hired had on my relationship with Julie," he exposes with staggering directness.

I ponder a justified explanation but say nothing until Richard plays another card.

"*And* you never said anything all this time? I ask because of my heightened curiosity."

"No." His slight laughter changes to a weepy weakness. "I figured all this time you *knew*. So *the secret* couldn't be a secret because my wife knew. You kept quiet. *Why, Diane?*"

"Hell. I don't know, Richard," the wife's hostile answer hurts because *she loved him*, "yesterday when I said tell me everything, I guess I didn't want to hear what I knew placed inside legal-size envelopes. I would've left had I known about the previous pregnancy. My stupidity hired the wrong detective."

"I paid the detective more, Diane, *not* to tell you certain things." My self-respect sinks. Nerves push out sweat.

"I can't win with you, Richard. I'm your wife, and it is a goddamn game."

"The detective was tailing me, Diane. I traced his license plate. The rest was a matter of outbidding your fee. Look. You have pictures. You have the dates. You have a whole file on me, but you played dumb and said nothing. Why?"

I shake my head. "Our relationship is a joke."

He pours another glass of wine and shoves it in my direction. "Drink with me. Alcohol cushions the pain."

A sunset preoccupies wondering the next page of my saga. The bastard is right—wine absorbs the shocks.

"Diane, I saw you spying on Julie and me."

Not a minute passes before knowing the conversation's direction. I replay the image of Richard and Julie kissing as if their day belonged to them. My days and nights have been a blur of unhappiness.

"When I called Mother inquiring about your visit, she told me you two discussed Julie. Mother didn't go into details, but again, I assumed you knew everything."

His poker face does me no good with tears waiting to exit my eyes. "You see, Diane, I'm not sure where we go next with the Julie-subject because you know everything."

The wife sits. Wine trickling down her throat is a band-aide. "I *hate* you, Richard."

"*I know you do*, Diane."

A rush to escape forces down my glass and leave uneaten food my weight desperately needs.

"Wait," he speaks with odd urgency, "your detective won't have known this. My father has an illegitimate daughter in London. My parents moved from England after the child was born, the same time, Mother was pregnant with my oldest brother. I'd hear them whisper- arguing at night the way you and I did when our girls were here. I admire my father providing for the woman and her child from day one."

"*Why* are you telling me this, Richard?"

"Mother forgave Father. You can be mad. Get it all out of your system. Men are men. I'll *handle* the Julie *situation*. I need to confess what my life was like from day one. We can move past this. You can forgive me. I *can* and *will* change."

A picture of him and her makes pound the table. "What do you mean *handle*, Richard?"

He braces my hands. "Listen to me, Diane. I've given this matter careful consideration for not further tarnishing my family and reputation.

My brothers' circus divorces did enough of that. *I'm going to* make her an offer to go away."

I tug under his hands. "Let go of me, Richard, and aren't you afraid our girls will find out?"

"They won't because you or Julie wouldn't be *that* stupid. Julie fears what *would* happen to her, *and you,* and what our children would think of their father."

I need the wine to cope with this bastard's reasoning. "You've thought of everything, have you? You'd hurt Julie?"

"My influence can make her life hell with tax audits and identity theft," he chuckles, "but you can't prove a damn thing by this conversation, Diane. Don't even try it."

I nod because he speaks the truth.

"I know you, Richard," admitting it. "I hate you, and hate what I've become."

"Diane," he shrugs, "A husband confesses adultery and his mistakes. What else can there be? How many millionaires have more than these skeletons?"

The wife sitting across from an absolute nothing for a human being can't fathom another year in this house. Her eyes glimpse at the roses outside; her joy and emptiness make her sad, beyond sad. "Who besides your parents know of Julie?"

"Father and my brothers won't talk. Their hands are deep in the cookie jar too. Guess the old man still can't keep his dick in his pants."

"Tell me more about Julie," I ask while eating the cold toast and bacon because the wine needs a companion.

"After my secretary went on medical leave, I hired Julie three months ago so we could be together. Jared Longview stole too much of my damn my time." His voice fades, "*No. I'm not proud of it.* She didn't need the money and wasn't even proficient. The truth is I *had* to be near her. God, what a fucking mess I've made, Diane."

Unfazed by his remorse, another question comes forth. "Julie never pushed for marriage?"

"Julie understands life. A ring isn't important. She had my love, financial support, and the townhouse you know of, and looks bending any man to eat her pussy. Marriage meant a symbol of what we already shared."

As he takes his empty plate to the sink, the wife can't believe his lover never wanted any legal claims.

"Will you sleep with me tonight, Diane?"

The bastard touches her shoulder when he rejoins the table. Lifeless desire shows on her face. "I'm serious. No. I'm sleeping down here Richard."

Grimness inches over the bastard's face while he shrugs and nods. "We'll talk more in the morning, Diane. I'll wash the dishes."

A clean custom kitchen ceases mattering. I can't reach a knife, Richard is standing between me and the counter. I walk toward my room. The mission concentrates on barricading the door with a chair and dresser to securing all bathroom and bedroom windows. Sleep will be a hit or miss.

"Good night, Richard." "Good night, Diane.

*

The husband's footsteps stop outside the locked door. She pushes hard against her makeshift barricade.

"Good morning. Are you awake in there?" "Yes. Why?"

"Your mother called. And I wanted to let you know I'm going out for a while."

"All right, Richard."

"Don't say it like that. It's not to Julie's. I need to drive and clear my head, which is nothing new when I've got a lot on my mind. Will you be here when I get back?"

"Sure. *Where* can I go, Richard?"

"Please don't feel that way, Diane. Will you tell your mother about us?"

"Why do you ask?"

She hears his breathing as if standing behind her.

"Don't tell her anything. We'll survive this challenge. We always do."

The wife sits on the bed and chuckles at the bastard's rationale. "You won't say anything, will you, Diane?"

The wife answers, hoping he will leave, "Richard, our union is a *long* twenty-eight-year marriage. *Julie,* my humiliation and your abuse isn't an organized box tied with fancy forgive-me ribbons."

"We have children. I do love you, and you love me, Diane."

A mystified wife analyzes, "Do you think, Richard all this shit can disappear with your *'I'm sorry?'*"

"Diane. I love you." He attempts to enter.

The wife presses against the dresser and chair, blocking the door. "Go away. Leave me alone."

She listens for his next word.

His shouts from the hallway, "Goodbye. I'll see you later. I love you."

She doesn't answer. She waits until the car exits the driveway. Hunger and craving for a drink hasten pushing aside the chair and dresser. She'll need a full stomach and strong alcohol for another conversation with her mother, who'll shred all logic to stay with Richard once she knows about Helen's proposition and the Julie disaster. My mother will help. I'll drive over. She'll help me sort out Helen's offer and all the rest of the crap.

*

Shock plows into giant sobs. My timing is off. "Are you sure?" I ask, hoping the truth is wrong. "Yes."

"When did you find out, Mother?"

"Remember I went to California with Clara Hill? Her son, the doctor, had me tested at Cedar Sinai hospital. I wanted to tell you when we last visited, but it was the day after Richard beat you."

"You *must* get a second opinion."

She almost laughs.

"My dear daughter, I've seen *four counting* Cedar Sinai. Treatments vary, but the verdict remains the same. Cancer has come back. Let's sit. We've been standing in the front entry long enough."

The meeting of all meeting rooms—our washed-out wallpapered dining room, the hub for family discussions, decisions, every kind of meal served—celebratory or sad, as when my father passed. She today, sitting in Father's chair, she has his same quiet stillness with folded hands.

"Can I get you anything, Mother?"

"*Sometimes* you need to accept the cards dealt, Diane, especially when you've been through the whole damn deck. You need a new style. A lazy French Roll gets passé." Her reply isn't appreciated.

"Why are you so mean, Mother? I'm here for you because of your cancer," I lie because now I can't burden her with my issues. Her health has to take priority.

"Have you been to the doctor to see about those scars?"

I lose it, "Mother, I don't give a damn about these scars. The cuts are healing with the cream my dermatologist gave me last year. You're calm as if nothing matters. You're going to die if you don't do something other than worry about what my hair looks like."

Her hard laugh infuriates. How dare she die when I need her now? "Your watery eyes say you're upset. Looking at your beauty torn in pieces is far more potent than my damn cancer. I'll be dead one day, but you'll still be with Richard. Mark my words, Diane, one day, he'll kill you."

Her frankness won't allow my crying to stop even if my life depended on it.

"Don't worry about me, Mother. Please let me help you. We'll see the doctor in Switzerland, Richard's mother knows." I feel my pleas can't penetrate her stone face.

"Dry those eyes, Diane," seriousness deepens her voice as she flips on the light switch, "I know you love me. But we've much to talk about before Camille arrives in an hour. Better see about those cuts."

"Why does everything have to be black or white, Mother?"

"Life's either black, white, *or variations of gray.* I've told you this time and time again."

She points at the corner bureau full of her best dishes, and her thin fingers touch mine when we fix to each other's face mirroring lines and dark circles. "Your father and I bought this at *Milton's Used Furniture* on our second wedding anniversary. I'm leaving Nina the cabinet because she appreciates antiques. Hope a small New York apartment can accommodate, or maybe she can sell it for its value." Mother's morbid conversation continues tightening the rope. "Pour us a glass of Sherry from the kitchen cabinet, Diane. My time will come soon enough. Your running tears don't help my situation, Diane."

"I'll get Sherry," the daughter sniffles.

Standing Mother's kitchen conjures memories of learning to cook and bake, and planning my wedding. How foolish to leave home into the arms of someone I've hated most of my life. I won't tell her about my problems. She has enough on her mind. Her head bows as if in prayer. We both have a plate of shit. Can I still believe God hears us?

*

"Here are our drinks, Mother. I also brought in chicken and apple slices."

She looks around, giving back a hollow glum face. "We never stripped the wallpaper or removed the carpet. Do you think Nina will sell the bureau, Diane?"

"No," I answer, handing her a glass of Sherry. "I'll make sure of it. Don't worry."

She smiles a bit, yet my outlook doesn't change, seeing a contemplative stare devour her face.

"I recall you and Camille dragging me to the hardware store some five years back. I still have, in your father's toolbox, under the sink, the paint chip, and the swatch of carpet we chose. It's too damn late now . . . waiting for the right time in one's life is a waste of living."

"Camille will be here soon. Tell me about Richard." She leans in. "I know you, Diane."

The necessity of avoiding the *weary Richard* question is challenging.

I mustn't aggravate her stress. The daughter has to grow up. "I'm okay."

Glances swing between my poker face and her motherly-raised eyebrows. I won't break and tell her about Richard and Julie's baby.

"I want you to fly in your dreams," she lectures what I've heard. "You deserve better than Richard's fists."

I don't like her hisses, but that's okay.

"Please concentrate on getting better, Mother. Richard is my damn problem."

I listen to her coughs and wish she'd rest.

"Since you want to talk about me, Diane," another cough interrupts, "I'm *not* going through anymore damn chemo or radiation."

"What are you saying? You *want* to die?"

I pour more Sherry to understand her stupid abstinence.

"My cancer has been in remission three times. I've had eight years of on-off treatments, this and that drug. Lord, the procedures are one big funeral. I've been to doctors here, New York, Canada, and even Mexico. I'm sixty-four and goddamn tired."

"You can't just give up."

"Were you listening to me when you first got here?" her voice changes to the color of anger. "Do I have to spell it out? I'm going to fucking die on my terms."

"Why, Mother?"

The daughter sobbing can't be consoled even by her mother's hold. "The cancer is spreading." Mother throws a persistent matter-of-fact into my dire face. "I'm not going to hang around one second longer than I want to, my dear daughter."

"Where is cancer?"

"Lymphoid. I should've gone a while ago to the doctor, but I didn't." "We'll go to the best doctors. You can't give up."

Her exhausted breathing, I know, means drop the subject. I can't and won't as I wipe my eyes.

"I'm not changing my mind." Her fingers squeeze into my wrists. "If you won't tell me about you and Richard—let's move on. Other than me asking you here about cancer, I want you to contact my grandchildren," she requests, looking firm into my face.

My tongue taps the roof of my mouth. I replay Richard beating me and have to swallow hard at the thought of seeing Leah.

"I'll get them here. Does Camille know?"

"Yes, I told her last night the same as I'm telling you." "How'd she take it?"

"Shocked like you. But Camille promises not to push me to get treatment." She grins into her glass. "We'll see if my daughters can keep their words."

"Get whatever treatment available. I think you're expecting a lot from Camille."

"Damn you, Diane. Stop it," she orders.

Her straight-up posture leaves little doubt she's on her terms.

"You know, Mother, what I love about this house, the one I grew up in?"

She pulls her silver and black waist-length ponytail through bobby- pins.

"No idea," she answers.

"It's home on the same street with most of the same neighbors. What will I do without you?"

I hear her deep breathing through her nose. I wonder if she's in pain. "We'll make the most of each minute we're together. I *want* to know about Richard."

"It's not important. I *promise* to tell you."

Her eyes well. "*Time*," she speaks low in her glass of Sherry, *is relative*."

"Yes, I know, Mother," is all I say with emotionally draining tears.

Our trance breaks with Camille's car approaching the driveway. The minutes before she reaches the door, an awful sense of abandonment enters me. I wipe my face and allow my arms to hold Mother. Her smaller frame emphasizes the time left between us; I close my eyes, the loss can't be written, spoken, or understood. I want to scream until hoarse.

"I love you, Mother."

"I'm here for you, Diane. Even after death, my spirit will watch over you."

"Camille's coming," I announce, hearing the car's door shut. "I'll leave now. See you tomorrow."

"I'm a little tired, Diane," Mother's breathing intensifies. "But I promised your sister."

Outside, Camille's happy-to-see-me-face lightens my mood.

I feel her belly. "A baby will do wonders for our family," I beam, forgetting for a moment, Mother and the bastard husband.

Her dimples vanish into a sullen face. She starts sobbing, "What are we going to do about our mother? I assume she told you her cancer has returned?"

"Don't let Mother see you cry like this. You know her mind is satisfied with not getting any treatment."

She dabs her soaked lashes. "We'll find a way, Camille."

"I better go in. Are you coming here every day?" Richard can go to hell.

"I'll be here tomorrow."

"Good. We'll come after Alan, and I see my doctor for my regular checkup."

"I'm sorry for Richard's rudeness toward Alan," I try to soothe over a bitter subject. Another reason to accept Helen's offer is the uninhibited freedom to see my family.

"Alan hates Richard for calling us poor trash because his school board salary doesn't pay well. So what if our neighborhood has fast-food chains, too many strip malls, *Wal-Mart,* and a *Costco*?"

We laugh as if we were kids again on Mother's porch.

"Remember, Camille, counting over forty *Mercedes* and *BMWs* at Walmart?"

"I guess that's how you, rich, stay rich." I catch her sneer. "Richard mocks my Alan to his face, a loser, since five years ago when we asked for your help paying our property taxes and mortgage during a teachers' strike."

"His rudeness to my own family hurt me too, Camille. I'll tell you one day."

It's hard forgetting Camille, and Alan told, to call before they come over in case we're busy entertaining his wealthy clients or neighbors. He didn't want them parking a used Honda in the driveway.

"The only reason Richard didn't get punched hard is because of Alan's arthritis. Richard never forgave me for not marrying his beat- you-24-7-alcoholic cousin. Not everyone on this planet needs to make millions to feel worth living. Changing the subject," she pulls my attention to the house, "I do need to ask you something. I can't now because of Mom."

"I see her, Camille, pulling back the curtains."

"I'll try to talk tomorrow when you're here, Diane. I need to go now. She's still at the window."

I hold on to her hand. It feels like a family. "Camille, remember how Mother used barge outside into our conversation."

She clings firmly with watery eyes. "I wish we were kids again. Don't you, Diane? We'd sure make every second count with Mom and Dad." "Children think their parents will live forever, Camille. Life has a plan. Goodbye. We'll talk later."

*

Thought of unhappiness: Mother has cancer. She won't seek treatment. I'd trade places with her. Can you hear me, God? Damn you. Take me, not her. What is happiness now? Richard left a voicemail: *'I'll fix dinner tonight.'* His message doesn't force me racing home to my hilltop-gated community with scenic views I've long stopped appreciating. Which entrance should I use to avoid him? Try the sunroom side entrance. Maybe he's in another part of the house.

*

"There you are. I watched you from the kitchen window." "Hello, Richard. I wasn't expecting you."

Full happiness and his famous martinis shed a hint of what to expect this evening.

"Remember the first time I fixed you one, baby? It was a week after your sixteenth birthday. We fucked in a room at the *Hilton*."

He's more than slap-happy escorting the wife into the dining room, a once showplace, now its grandeur feels cold, dead, and a waste of money.

"Are you hungry?"

I remain standing, trying to take it all in. Richard's gone overboard with this, asking for forgiveness—enough candles to light the whole room, the opera of La Boheme playing through the speakers, vases of red roses scattered throughout, our hardly ever used wedding china, silverware, lace tablecloth we purchased in Paris, and the smell of something worth eating flowing from the kitchen.

"Here, sit." He hustles, pulling out my intended chair. "I cooked your favorite." He's remaining too long. "Remember when I took you to Milan's La Scala Opera House to see La Boheme?"

The word *favorite* is not even in my vocabulary. Out of politeness, and not desiring bookends of drama—his—and my mother's, I compliment, "It smells good."

"I made shrimp scampi. I'm trying, Diane. Give me some goddamn credit. Will you?"

The wife's box closes. Force down the evening. It will pass. Your mother is far more important than any candlelit dinner with this bastard.

"I'll be right back. I forgot, Chianti."

The wife's quiet composure allows the millionth tear to slide down. How and why are things the way they are? For an average couple, love holds them together. She wipes her eyes before the husband returns with two warm plates.

He pours the drink, and before they drink, he takes hold of the wife's hand.

"We'll get through this, Diane. I'll change it. I promise." She says and does nothing except tip a nod.

"Let's eat before it gets cold. I bought some tiramisu from the bakery we pass on Clover Street. Dylan just baked it today. I special ordered it for you, baby."

'How can I enjoy this meal, this house, Richard, or my marriage?' I think, and I'm afraid the answer is easy.

"How's the food?" "Fine, Richard."

"I love you, Diane. Do you believe me?"

"I saw my mother today, Richard. She's dying," I blurt out because I feel so alone in the same room as him, and don't want the love stuff-talk.

"I'm sorry. Is it the cancer returning?" Richard asks.

His concern for my mother sounds out of place. Their closeness is like oil and water.

"Yes," I say to keep the subject on Mother and not us. "Has Ester gone to the doctor?"

"She's been to several. They all say the same."

I watch him place his elbows on the table, hands under his chin as if he were trying to figure out the next sentence. I can't read his thoughts. The wait comes and goes as the opera aria plays in the background.

"How long have they given her?"

"Mother didn't say. I don't think any doctor can predict the exact time and day, Richard."

"Well, this makes for a sad ending. I'm assuming Ester's affairs are in order. Probate will be a bitch if she doesn't have a WILL."

"My mother has taken care of *everything*."

"Good," he says in a flat tone and starts on his dinner. "We'd better eat before the food gets cold. We can talk about Ester later. Nothing can be solved now."

"Richard, I'm going to either bring my mother here or stay with her." The sudden decision gets his attention. He turns into my face.

"Yes, of course, you should bring her here. I was just wondering how we could help."

"Really?"

"Diane, I *do* care about your mother. Why are you taking this attitude?"

"You're full of shit, Richard. You loved calling her a nosey bitch." "Oh hell," he raises his voice, but I don't back down. "I *said* I'm trying to change. Can't you fucking believe in me?"

God holds my hands. I can absorb Richard's anger. Mother's death is giving me the strength to accept and take anything.

"Now you're giving me the damn silent treatment. You know, Diane, I'm here tonight because I fucking want to be."

In a shitty huff, he pours more wine and takes a pack of cigarettes from his pocket. "I wanted to give these up, but I guess now's not the damn right time if you're bent on making this evening a total failure."

A determined wife anchors her mind. "I'm tired of arguing with you, Richard. We both know you never liked my mother. The reasons are no longer important. She's coming here, or I'm going there. Taking care of her is *my priority,* whether you like it or not."

"I don't care if she comes here, Diane," his voice raises louder than mine. "I want us to get back to where we were *and . . .*"

The wife shuts him off with her tirade, "What is your damn fairytale? We read more like a horror story, and you kick my ass, fuck around on me and belittle me, *come on* Richard, do you think a cheap dinner, wax candles, and soon-to-be-dead flowers can make up for all the hurt you've done?"

"I'm sorry," his voice drops, "I know I've hurt you."

"I don't even care about *why* anymore, Richard. My priority *has* to be my mother."

"Please let me try to make things better, Diane."

The chair anchors my back. No matter the ambiance, the imperfection of two people, makes for a not happily-ever-after ending to their fairytale.

*

Thought left on the plate: La Boheme ends. The dinner comes and goes; candles melt, conversation bares nothing to normal; the husband and wife say nothing. His beckoning glimpses back and forth hold for her no love, our seats are next to each other, but the space measures miles apart.

*

"Good night, Richard." "Good night, Diane."

*

Morning thoughts: did he say *'goodbye?'* Between all the wine and a half-sleeping pill, fog floats inside my head. Be quiet. Listen for movements outside the door. I can do nothing but wait. Quiet. He must've gone. The time says 8:30 am. He took the week off. Where has he gone? I can't trust Richard. Still, barricade the door. Keep the knife under the pillow that I stole from the kitchen. What to do? First, call Mother. I need to tell her I can help. I need to talk to Dr. Rose. I need to decide about Helen's offer. I have to contact the children.

*

"Leah. Please call me. Your grandmother's cancer has returned."
"Hello, Sarah. I hope studies at Oxford are going well. I imagine you're asleep or out. Call me. Your grandmother's cancer has come back. She's asked to see you."

"I hope all's well in New York, Nina. I need to speak with you. Your grandmother's cancer has returned. Please call me."

*

Resolution thought: life would be alright if curing Mother's cancer could be as easy as purchasing a plane ticket. Our visit has so too many shades of black.

*

"You're not able to take care of yourself. Your breathing sounds as if you're in pain."

"My mind won't be changed, Diane, I'm *not* living with you. And you're *not* moving in here. Hospice will come when it's time. I appreciate you and Camille's concern. She suggested the same thing."

Stubborn woman. Make her comfortable. Prop up her bed's pillow. Fight back despair, the more I stare at a dresser's picture of Camille, her, and me, which Alan took last summer on the front porch. Our mother was so vibrant. Now significantly thinner; how long will she be around?

"Are you hungry?"

"I want a piece of toast with orange juice later. Now can we talk about Richard?"

Put distance between her. She'll read your worried face.

"Richard and I are trying to make things work. I'll fix some coffee."

Shaking her head, Mother knows me well. "Is this why you can't look me straight in my face? I don't want any damn coffee. I want to know what's going on between you and Richard. Convince me, my intuition is wrong."

I don't have the temper to go ten rounds with her on my marriage, after doing twenty with him. Not in the mood for the grill, even if this were the last time I'd see her. I am keeping my promise never to tell her what a mess I made of my life.

"I told him your cancer came back. I also phoned the girls."

"I don't think my cancer," she grunts, "has anything to do with your marriage *working out.* If so, then dying has a whole new purpose. I'm losing my appetite on your bullshit, Diane. Fine. Change the subject. When will the girls come?"

"I don't know. I left messages," is my powerless response.

Displeasure coats her eyes. "Leah's got Richard and his mother's damn uppity attitude. I can count the times on one hand with fingers left over, how often in the past year she's picked up the phone. Sarah and Nina are better because they call every month. They're busy. Still, I'd like to see them. I got final things to say and personal items I want them to have—*even* for Leah."

"I'll be back with your toast and apple slices." My mood isn't anything but happy. I know the value of my children. I feel the same way.

"Diane," she calls me before I can leave.

Her hand passes over mine; we don't need to say anything. It's all understood.

"I love you, Mother." "I know, Diane."

*

The daughter returns with a bed tray minus coffee.

She finds her mother's preoccupation rummaging through papers in a shoe size metal box on her lap. She holds out three law envelopes.

"Sit. These are for you, Diane."

"Can I open them?" I ask permission after placing her tray on a table.

Her nod gives permission.

I read her handwritten numbers. My hands shake, opening the first one.

She interrupts, "The deed to the house."

"*The deed,*" I repeat, tasting the finalization of its meaning. The second one opened.

She's calm to my sadness, "*The WILL*. I leave everything to you and Camille with a few exceptions." She points at the folded document, "Camille has a copy. My attorney, Ned Hollis, has the original. I put his card in the envelope you're holding."

Finality draws bleakness. How can this be?

"Now open the *last* one, Diane." Her determination doesn't waver. "Go on."

Emptying the contents into my palm is critical. My curiosity jumps all over the map. "I don't understand."

Her softened bright eyes are the opposite of the red of her daughter's from excessive crying.

"It's to a safe deposit box. Camille has one, too. When I die, Ned Hollis will provide its location and passcode."

Stress lines within my face weigh a ton.

"I don't understand. Mother, why the mystery?"

"I'll tell you the part and the rest you'll have to wait on. I left you and Camille two-hundred and fifty thousand dollars each. Your father had four insurance policies when he died. I lived off one policy and paid for you and Camille's wedding with the other."

A calm woman closes the box.

"*The rest* . . . here is my birth certificate, passport, and papers paying for my funeral and miscellaneous papers like my marriage license and your father's death certificate."

Absolute torment can't stop my sobbing. Her hands cradle my face.

"I love you, Diane." "*Oh, Mother . . .*"

"I think we need a brandy from the kitchen cabinet. It'll go well with toast," she giggles, handing me the closed box. "My bedroom has served its purpose. Set the box in the top drawer of my dresser. Let's set the food and drink in the dining room. Stay until Camille arrives. I want to talk to you both."

As we pace arm-in-arm out of her room—the sum of Mother's wishes, dignity for her resolve has given me the courage to make my most challenging decision. Our time in the dining room is a closeness I've taken for granted.

Knocking on the front door and a little girl's voice indicates Camille forgot her key.

"Hello. Hello."

"I'll get the door. Camille. Where's your key?"

"I left it on the counter. The chain broke. I need to get another one. How are you, sis?"

With a returned hug, I answer, "Fine. I haven't been here long. We don't want to exhaust Mother because she looks a bit washed out."

"Yes." Camille nods, watching over my shoulder, "I understand. She's not the same. How are you feeling, Mom?"

"Fine," Mother answers. "Would you like some tea? No alcohol until you have the baby," her motherly advice perks a twinkle in her face.

"I'll get water," Camille replies and waves me to stay while she steps toward the kitchen.

Helping Mother prop up straighter, I worry about her lack of energy. "Are you sure you want to talk now? You look tired."

"Yes, Diane. I won't take long."

We sit around the dining table, and my problems stagger in and out of my mind. Our time together would be an opportune time to tell the two people meaning the most to me what's going on with me. But Mother's drooping facial muscles and breathing indicate the time for my issues won't be today.

"I want to make this clear," she starts after a few sips of brandy, "when the time comes, hospice will take care of me."

Containing my distant tears as the eldest, listening to Camille's sniffling, has got to be the hardest thing I've done. Years living with Richard have trained me to control crying, and this is one of them.

Camille's fingers fill into mine. "I'm trying to be brave. This dying thing isn't fair. What are we going to do without you, Mom?"

"Listen to you two; I'm not dying tomorrow. Diane, refill my glass." Her voice has a tinge of anger. "Don't you *think* I want to live?"

"Then get the damn treatments," I interject pent-up frustration. "You're not going to get treatment?" Camille screams.

Mother grabs Camille's flapping arms and calmly speaks, "Camille, child, I thought you understood my wish. You said you understood."

My sister's hysteria unnerves me. I can't be a hero for both us, not with what's going on with Richard and me. I take hold of her arm. "Camille, stop."

She pushes away my hands. "Diane, can't you talk sense into her since you've had a breast cancer scare? You're the oldest. I don't understand either of you."

"Camille. Please be quiet." Mother speaks with control, "I don't want any damn more treatments. The decision falls to me, Diane *has* tried to convince me. You have to respect my wishes. We talked about this when my cancer returned a few years ago. It's called borrowing time, you must understand. You have each other and your families. We three will have memories *forever*."

I swallow the wad of milky spit, waiting to purge. My life is fucked. Camille's emotional state and pregnancy and Mother's cancer convince me my support system can't be them. Dr. Rose will be there for me as she always has.

"Why else did you want us to be here, Mom? Don't you see *anything* wrong with her position?" She vents in my direction. "I'm trying to wrap my head around all of this."

"Enough," Mother intercedes, tapping her nail on the table. "You each have a copy of my WILL. I've given much thought to the content. My lawyer, Ned Hollis, will help when the time comes."

"He's an honest man. My mother-in-law uses him." Camille shakes off a few more tears. "*I hate this*," she whispers.

"One more thing," Mother interjects, "before my pill, and rest. I'd like to see more of you than before. You don't have to come every day but at least several times a week. I have help with June Roberts, my cleaning lady. There's a nurse from hospice and the women's aide members from the church, plus a few old friends like Leslie Peters, Irene Stubbs, and my dear Clara Hill, all living not that far."

*

We watch her fall asleep in her bedroom.

"I'll stay with her, Diane. Miss Peters will come and spend the night.

All her friends take turns helping out as they can, which I imagine until hospice, or she agrees to live with either of us." Tugging my arm, she continues, "We still must break her stubborn ideas about treatments."

Squinting back the damn tears, I wonder if our mother will die alone. "I'll do my best, Camille."

She wraps her arms tight around my waist. "I know," she chokes down her answer.

"Are you sure you can stay?" I ask.

"Alan gets off work soon. He'll pick up our son from Alan's parents. I'm just glad we live close to Mom. I'll walk you to your car.

Words are understood within our solemn expressions as we approach my car.

"I have a *question*." She catches me, with the oddest puzzling glaze, before I open the door. "I don't know how to say this. I suppose yelling out would be the best."

My sister's evasiveness equates—I don't want to answer her question. "Wait." She rushes, giving a glance back to the house.

"Hurry up, Camille, in case Mother awakens."

"*Okay*. I saw, now I wasn't spying." Camille rattles those hands. I know her habit when she's lost for words. "But, Diane, I must have some answers."

My impatience brings about more sweat with the rising humidity. "You're not making any sense. Fuck. Tell me, Camille," I shout at her.

Within seconds I'm sorry because of her continual scratching her neck. Whatever is on her mind is essential. Her flustered composure fiddles with the ends of the ponytail cascading down her chest. What's tormenting her?

I need to let her speak by rubbing her shoulder. "Take your time. I'm not in a hurry."

"I saw this pregnant woman, Diane, leaving one of the pediatrician's offices located in the same building as my doctor."

I knew the rest of her story. "And what does this have to do with me?" I say with my head held high for dignity's sake.

She sucks in her lips. Her hold my arm means prepare for a slam against the wall. "Sister, your husband kissed this woman in the underground parking lot. I watched them, Diane. I followed them. He couldn't recognize me because of my sunglasses; this woman pushed the garage's elevator button for the 6th floor. I looked in the directory. Nothing but pediatricians occupy the floor."

"We don't have time to discuss this, Camille." I point to the house. "You have to go."

Her tight yank on my arm stops me from opening the car. "Tell me *what's* happening. I'm concerned. I love you, Diane. What is going on with you and your husband?"

"I will, *but* not now," are whispers into her face.

"Are you okay? Just tell me that." A frantic question consumes space between us.

"Don't worry about me," I lie. "See you soon."

*

Driving nowhere thought: need to find my footing. I need to call my doctor; I need to hear from my children. Don't want to go back to *that* house. I think the neighborhood Ruby lives in is less than an hour from here. Crazy thinking, I can locate her without an address. Would the doctor give me the street number since Ruby's not her patient? Maybe I'll drive around. I might see Ruby walking down one of the streets. Why am I doing this? She doesn't know me. I don't even know her last name. Then again, talking to a neutral person might be the solution.

*

"Excuse me. Are you ordering?" A rude woman talking on her cell sounds way too pushy for a sunny day in a relaxing coffee café decorated in hanging plants and jazz background music.

Ignoring her impatient hisses, I order a large hibiscus ice tea.

*

Thought of adventure: where to sit? Seats come with choices. An open window by a sapphire blue table cloth near a bookcase full of art books calls me. In a broad view of a street sign with pink tea-roses growing up its wooden pole, reads *Bend Road Vista: 2 miles,* means I'm near where Ruby lives. Exploring the calm of this picket fence surrounding a bungalow house neighborhood, scattered with fifties-style counter seat diners, cottage antiques, and vintage clothing stores, community markets, to seeing used parked cars, bicyclists, and families walking with children or pushing them in strollers eludes an appropriate rich woman's lifestyle. Don't think of what I can't do. Helen's money will give me unforeseen freedoms.

*

"Excuse me. Are you using this chair?" Excitement jumps face.

"Ruby," I cry out, not caring about disturbing others, "I can't believe you're standing here. Sit down with me."

Giddy laughter fills her face, unlike the last time when tears and depression consumed her.

"My, my, my . . . what the hell are you doing in my neck of the woods, Miss Diane?" "My mother doesn't live far from here."

"*I see,*" she says, looking puzzled, taking the seat across from me in full sight of blackness about my eyes and cheeks.

"We probably shouldn't talk too loud." My heartbeat slows down, allowing a familiar voice, which I think close by patrons appreciate. They're no longer gawking at our table. "How have you been, Ruby?"

She takes my cue leaning within a short reach. "You know as they say—one day at a time."

Examining my face, she squints into a definite frown. "How *have you* been, Miss Diane?"

My comfort zone drops. What can I explain, not leading to a thousand questions in a public place? I swallow a cold cup of embarrassment.

"You *can* tell by my face."

My brief reply gets me to the head of the class. Her hands touch my forearm the way someone who cares about you does. Can my outlook be lightened with so few words because she's been with a terrible husband too?

"*Why* are you in *this* neighborhood, Miss Diane? Aren't there any cafes near your mother's?"

"I was looking for *you*, Ruby."

"Well, I'll be goddamned. I know what you've been through, lady. You'll be just fine, Miss Diane. Let me order us a chef's salad and a slice of apple pie a la mode. Do you have time? I recommend both dishes."

The wall clock reads 2:00. "Yes."

Ruby, since we last met, has traveled miles beyond me. A slimmer woman strides to the counter. She catches men's attention. Flattering auburn layered hair cut above her shoulders makes me feel outdated—ugly—even if my face didn't hold traces of Richard's rage. *'Your French Roll gets a little passé after years,'* Mother's nasty comment rings true, in comparison to someone I thought worse off than me.

"You look different. I mean, you look so much better than when we first met," I compliment, noticing a younger man fixating on her silhouette.

"I saw me for the first time, a gutter mess. My ex-husband doesn't give a shit. He's remarried to my ex-best friend. Once you let go, *you're fucking free*."

"*Letting go*," somber words I repeat into my tea. The term 'free' reminds me of the landscape painting in Helen's entryway of the woman walking alone in the sand.

"He did this to you? Didn't he?" Ruby pushes by tapping the table. Don't start crying. Tell the truth to the guardian angel God sent. Yes,"

I admit straight into her angry face.

"*What's your plan?*" Ruby dumps my future into a neat pile of three words.

Correct answers between two women mean a lifetime of friendship. And I need that. "Don't have one, Ruby. Who has a plan, anyway?" I laugh, feeling my cut lip.

"I love the way they make salads here. You know why? It reminds me of what our cook prepared. Damn. The rich bitch, *me,* who had a cook and no fucking plan either. None of my friends did. You know the people with so much money they wear an outfit once, then give it to the Goodwill, or shred it for the trash. Yep. We know those types."

I look around. Lots of women are talking, and I wonder what's their plan.

"My point is, Miss Diane, rich women never have a plan. Why would they? They're *fucking* rich." She laughs and laughs. "Do they need to worry about tomorrow? Hell no."

"I don't have a list of the next steps. I'm one of those *rich bitches* you describe. But now, I need one friend, Ruby. You guessed right when we met. I need to talk to someone who has walked in my shoes."

"My husband beat me. He cheated. Are we on the same page?" Ruby drills without blinking, surveying my facial marks. "You can tell me." Her will power pulls me in. "We'll talk about your plan, or *help* you make one."

Exaggerated breathing pumps my chest up and down. I had to talk to someone, or I'd go mad.

"You want my story? Here's the short version," I start after a big gulp of lukewarm tea wishing it was something giving me a buzz. "Richard, my husband, has a longtime lover. I know because of his admission and a detective's finding. The other woman is expecting Richard's child."

"You're fucking kidding?"Ruby's voice carries so far that customers turn in our direction.

I feel embarrassed. "Keep your voice down. The world doesn't need to know my business."

She stretches so close her make-up-free skin shows no blemishes. "You're beautiful, and the bastard sleeps around? Sorry." She looks about the room. "Sometimes class ain't anything but a four-letter word. Go on."

"I have a way out. Richard's wealthy mother has offered me money to leave her son."

"Shit. Why?"

"It's too complicated." In a rush to leave, the wife pulls out a fifty-dollar bill. "Pay the tab. I've got to go."

But I don't go. Not with Ruby's stronghold on my wrist.

"Sit the fuck down," she demands as a couple shakes their heads, walking past our table. "You drove here to find me. Sit down."

I don't want to imagine what their thoughts are as I return to my chair.

"It's hard exposing my life, Ruby."

"I know," she gives a small smile, "but getting it out is important. Didn't *your doctor* tell you that?"

I've time—no damn Richard errands. Home is the downstairs guest room. Remember why I drove here was to find Ruby and talk to her.

"Richard does beat me . . . for years," I reveal. "The scars, in the beginning, were on hidden parts of my body. As the marriage went on, I've learned make-up tricks to hide his work. Plastic surgery for a broken nose and cheekbone and an expensive Paris dermatologist are my saviors."

"Aside from all the drama and goddamn shit, *what do you want to do,* Miss Diane?"

Wiping my wet lashes is my answer.

"Hey, don't," Ruby says while stroking my neck. "Do you know why I call you, *Miss Diane?*"

I shake my head.

"I give you the respect you don't have. You've been discarded and unloved. Your clothes hang off you, and your hair shows no style. Your face needs attention, or the scars will go with you to the grave. Bags and lines under your eyes have aged you since we first met, Miss Diane."

My appetite aligns more with a child picking at the generous salad and pie crust. My mother's cancer absorbs my thoughts. The fullness of my state draws tears.

"Don't be sad. I'm here," Ruby says and leans closer.

Her scent of nothing but vanilla soap draws my concentration to the blackest colored eyes I've seen and olive skin as if she'd been in the sun. There's something about her hair—its coarseness now visible with a stylish haircut. I think Ruby is part black.

"I can't tell you anything you don't already know, Miss Diane. I will say if it were me, I'd leave your husband. Life brings a shorter ribbon, the older you get each Christmas." She chuckles with an odd puckering of her lips, "*Unless you want me to have him killed?*"

Startled at her honesty, I look quick to see if anyone heard such an absurd suggestion.

"Don't joke like that, Ruby."

The server comes to the table because Ruby's signaled. "I'll have this to go." She points at her pie.

"You're *kidding* about my husband. Aren't you?" She looks serious.

"Now, why would I want to get involved with a murder? I'm kidding. Do you have a pen and paper in *that Chanel bag*?" I open my purse.

"Yes. Miss Diane. I know *Chanel, Gucci,* and *Dior*—all of those high-priced designers. I had tickets to all the fashion shows. Now I can't even afford to window shop." Sadness moves water into her expressive eyes, the more she gapes at my purse. "Call me when you're ready. I have a friend in New York, a realtor who helps women relocate to New York."

"I have a daughter living there, Ruby."

"My friend, Anna, was married to one of Washington's big-time Congressmen. Her real estate company gives back to abused and discarded women. She is a great contact. I never used her because I hate New York for obvious reasons."

I want to reach for the number. But I don't. All I give back is a bitten lip smile.

"I'll get the number when I call you, Ruby. I can't rush any decision. I hope you understand?"

"Miss Diane, life *will* turn around if you dare to accept the path it shows." Her bit of kindness shows with a good-earth hug.

"Thank you, Ruby, for your time, it means . . ." Unhappiness takes my words.

"We met for a reason, Miss Diane. Mine was to help you."

I pat her knee and throw in another hug for good measure. My voice cracks, "I agree."

She hums, putting the pie in its to-go box inside a bag made of colorful fabric patches with a thick black rope for handles.

"My story lays down these tracks, Miss Diane. I was born in New Orleans. Our family tree mixed with a little of this and a little of that. Grandma made a point to seed into her only daughter, my mamma, *'We all never know when we got to walk through the same door.'* If I help you, then you'll help the next *Miss Diane*. I should go now." The new friend ends our visit. "I have a session with Dr. Bishop. Let's have a big."

Affection isn't phony Country Club air kisses. Its sister kisses we exchange, with wrapped-tight holding around our shoulders and waists.

"Women are strong. You *don't* need your head doctor pulling your strings or me. You already have the answers," she makes sense when she releases me.

"I know that you're right. My mother says the same thing." "Take care of yourself, Miss Diane."

We walk out onto the sidewalk; I go to the left. Ruby walks to the right. The sun hurts my eyes, and for a moment, I can feel Richard's hand slapping me. The stupid wife turns to wave goodbye to her guardian angel. But she's gone.

*

Thought pulling up to the driveway: calculating time won't be easy. Should I wait until Mother dies before I leave Richard? Will he bend and give me a divorce? Curb the questions. Patience will reveal the answers. I see his car in the rear-view mirror. Why did I come back? We emerge from our vehicles at the same time. Outside in the driveway, joy disappears, surveying a house worth millions. We spoiled it, allowing him to mold my life into an iron pretzel—unable to form my own identity. The sound of his movements on the gravel twists the wife's nerves until her breathing breaks into long anxious puffs as if yanked from her lungs.

*

I hear his toxic voice. "How was your day, Diane? How's your mother?"

The wife turns with no emotion. He asks about her day, a rare question.

He hands me a bouquet of sweet-smelling roses, which will never- ever mean the same after his admission of meeting Julie at that Santa Barbara flower shop to buy me, of all flowers—damn roses.

"Mother is fine."

"I had several calls today." He walks beside me with the gall to put his arm around my shoulder to walk together. "Leah and Sarah wanted you to call them about your mother."

Why would my children contact him and not me?

"Don't look like you lost your best friend, Diane. They called here. I answered the phone."

His humble-pie face almost has a dot of sincerity; I look at the roses wrapped in a white French silk bow. I won't fall for his magic. I want to shake the flowers until their gorgeous petals fall, then take the thorns and stems and stab out the bastard husband's eyes.

He unlocks the knob at the side entrance sunroom door. We enter.

What's next? My watch reads 5:30.

Bastard heads to the bar.

"I feel like a nice gin and tonic . . . you?"

"Better put these roses in water, first," I answer back to avoid as long as I can his company.

Saliva swims like garbage inside my mouth on the way to the kitchen cabinet where I keep the crystal vases. Why am I making a big thing about the girls not calling me back?

"Our drinks are ready," his voice crawls into my ears. "You've put them in the vase I gave you last Valentine's Day. They're as beautiful as you, Diane."

His compliment and charisma, which I loved when we first met, now carries as much weight as air.

"Let's sit in your favorite room," he suggests.

His liberty walking hand in hand does me in. We stand before the same sofa I sat with Mother, the day after the bastard beat me for asking Leah if it'd be okay if I came to visit. He finds his place then pats on the empty cushion, an understood signal to sit beside him.

"You know you've done a nice job decorating this house."

His words don't resonate because Richard's final approval sealed every purchase and placement of furniture, accessories, and art. I am objecting to the ones I wanted.

"Thank you." My non-caring response mixes well with the highball, drowning the sour taste inside my mouth.

"How is your mother?" he asks again.

Are his questions about a woman he didn't care for, for the sake of conversation? Get up before he rambles on about whatever's too late to hear.

"My mother is fine. Richard. *You asked before.* I need to call Nina."

"Don't bother, Diane. I called her myself. She said you called, but it was late. She'll be here in two days." His in-control arrogance gives the details. "I've taken care of everything as I've always done for you. No matter what you think of me, you've never wanted for anything. All necessary arrangements are bringing our children home within twenty- four hours."

A terrible thought wishing Mother were dead so I could start a new life, pushes the wife to say, "Thank you."

The bastard scoots closer and places his hand on her leg. He smells more of gin than tonic.

He shows remorseful eyes looking into his wife's willful stone face. "Are you ready to forgive me?" He sounds pathetic, begging.

The wife can't shake his violence. She conceals her fear by finishing off her drink. She answers from her heart, "No. I can't."

He wipes his brow, giving an open remorseful face. "I think I'll have another." He shakes the empty glass. "You want one? Diane, are you going to cook dinner for us?"

If I refused, he'd remind me he cooked dinner last night. The conversation isn't worth it. I answer, "Sure."

"But you *can't* forgive me, right?" He stops mixing the drink to face me.

Arms folded across my chest. "Why should I, Richard? Give me five good reasons to stay with you. Let me believe in something. Make me feel I'm worth it." My real answer sounds like little steps toward freedom, even though inside, I'm dying because I still love him.

He finds the furthest chair after handing me the drink. The distance between us, his agonized face to my unapproachable one, to me, epitomizes our marriage now.

"Diane, I made a damn mistake," Richard suddenly belts out, "I'm sorry. I'll give you five reasons to stay with me. The one meaning more than anything—I love you."

My humiliation won't step aside. Tears fall, his, not mine. I don't know how long he'll allow this wall. At any rate, I must continue fortifying my mind. Keep my distance; don't cry. Repeat over and over to him, my anger. I must do this until I have a solid plan.

"Let's look at the picture, not with romantic, rose-colored-glasses, Richard. You beat me. Is that love? Let's not forget *your Julie. I won't and can't forgive her and the pregnancy* with three fucking words, *I love you.*"

"I won't marry her." He pushes forward to the chair's edge. His hands shake. His voice rises, "I told her to expect my financial support for the baby because it's the right thing to do, but no marriage."

I want to vomit hearing the word *baby.*

"And *when* did you tell her?" I press him.

"I called her from my car phone this morning. We met for lunch. She doesn't work at the office anymore for a few weeks. Oh, God, Diane, I've been a fool." His tears run as mine has for the better part of our twenty-eight-year marriage.

The wife's cross-examination doesn't break. "I thought you weren't going to see her. Isn't that what you said, Richard?" Now my voice peaks a higher volume into a vicious scream. My fists tear into the side table. "You damn bastard. You damn liar. How many lies are in that little pinhead? The morning you told me about Jared Longview, you said you were picking up Julie on the way to work. I'm *not* stupid, Richard." I lunge at him with disdain. Pure hate slaps the hell out of him until his drink tumbles.

The bastard weeps into his hands, "I'm sorry, Diane."

I'm beyond angry. "Talk to me. I want the damn truth," I blast louder into the bastard's face.

"Alright, Diane, I fucking lied. Okay?" His sorry-ass voice shakes. "Julie arrived home from visiting her sister in San Diego. I timed, leaving here in time to pick her up from the airport. Yes. I'm the dirty bastard."

A question free-falls inside my head — '*Where do I, not we, go from here?*'

The bastard husband removes a pack of cigarettes from his pocket. The methodical lighting of the cigarette follows long exhaling. His stiff demeanor extenuating worry lines scares me because he's rarely without words.

Intuition alerts—race to the guest room before he hurts you. Too late, his speed blocks the hall entry. Take full account of his strength, jamming me into a corner.

"You can do what you want, Richard." My words are a false shield. I'm terrified. "I can't deal with Julie and you. My mother has cancer. She *has* to be my priority."

"I've been with another woman for more than half our marriage. Fuck. I never left you, Diane." His grip doesn't yield the more he cries out. "I could've left you anytime. Julie made no demands because we were as man and wife."

"Let go of me, Richard. Am I supposed to be happy with an analysis of your lover?"

"I've made arrangements," he continues without regard to the more I twist to be free.

A ready fist conjures the *old Richard* with calculating, narrowing severe stares. The wife knows her vantage point falls, watching his mouth grind his teeth, she braces for an altercation, fear can no longer hold its line, mercy tears drip down her face, she doesn't move, she's reflective, alert, on guard, and petrified. Breathing accelerates, pain becomes unbearable.

"You're hurting me," I scream. "You haven't changed at all. Look at my arm."

He looks, I look, the bastard husband, one-by-one, opens his fingers. "No, I won't hit you. I've changed."

The wife rubs her skin. Red coloring soreness stiffens into the muscle. How can she help her mother out of a chair or to bed?

"You're the same, Richard, a bully until the end."

"Listen to me," he hollers, "Julie will join her sister and brother-in-law in Switzerland. His family owns several large hotels in Geneva. I've changed, Diane," the bastard husband repeats, stepping back.

"You can't change, Richard," I yell.

"I love you, Diane. The children will be home soon." He offers no apology for the past minutes. And the wife's stupidity wants one. "We must put on a brave front. We *don't* put our problems in front of the children." He shakes my arm. "Are we in agreement?"

"*We agree*," I mimic him.

Still holding my arm, his fingers begin to squeeze and squeeze. "You'll sleep in our bedroom, then?"

The apprehension of what he'll do if not agreeing lowers the wife's head to give the nod, a hated symbol of surrendering—*yes*.

The husband gloats victory. The wife doesn't.

"Sleep in the guest room tonight as my treat to you." "Good night, Richard."

Discontent kicks the incapable wife.

The bastard returns to the sunroom. Assumption thinks he'll mix more alcohol and get drunk.

"Don't bother cooking, Diane," he calls out.

In the kitchen, the wife carries a couple of apples and a half-drunken bottle of Chianti. She steps downs the hallway into her cave, locks the door, barricades it with the bureau and chair. She hears the opera La Boheme music filling the downstairs; she turns off the light and sits on top of the bed. Her tears build. There is no hope of stopping them in her lifetime.

*

Morning thought after less than five hours of sleep: dressed. Mother's right, I need a new style. Skip make-up. Rain changes the mood, and dampness permeates into layers of utter loneliness. Richard didn't wake me. Stepping into the hallway, I find a note taped to the guest room door. He decides to check on things at work even though Lloyd gave him the week off. He's a damn liar. My bastard husband right now is sucking on Julie's pregnant breasts to saturating his tongue over her skin as if it layers his favorite—chocolate. Richard left me a note. How kind of him.

*

Diane, I didn't want to wake you. I need to check on the Longview deal even though I have the week off. I'll be home late from the office because of the girls' staggering flight arrival times. I love you.

*

Coffee sits cold. I know he's with Julie. I've missed three messages: Dr. Rose, Camille, and again Dr. Rose. Call Dr. Rose first.

*

"I haven't forgotten about our appointment. There's much happening now. I must see you. *Now* isn't a good time."

*

I can't talk too long to Camille. Need to make the bedrooms ready for the children. Need to force me to enter *that* bedroom. The room the wife hasn't been in since he beat her over Leah.

*

"Am I assuming your nervous stretch of this phone conversation revolves around Richard?" Dr. Rose, I hope she is still my friend, starts with a base hit question.

"Things are in a direction I never dreamt they'd be."

"What has happened, Diane? Are you still living with him? Where are you?" She rushes one question then another.

Our role as a doctor versus a patient wears thin. Little does she realize with each question; the gun jams further and further into my temple.

"I'm home. It isn't a good time. I'm sorry about our canceled appointment."

Her silence lasts more than I like. There're too many demands dragging me to the edge. I want to tell her all about Richard and Julie. I want to talk about Ruby. I want. I need. Lord, please help me.

"I'll make time for you, Diane. If you can't drive this far, I can meet you wherever you want."

I see the rainbow in the distance. Maybe it's a sign God heard my prayer. Compassion offers an olive branch.

"You've been my doctor for a long time, Samantha. The patient will tell you everything quite soon."

"Okay. Goodbye. Take care of yourself, Diane. *Please* call me."

*

Forbidding selfish thoughts unable to die: put down the cell phone.

Don't forget to leave it on in case someone tries to reach you. I am processing hard decisions about my marriage, mother, and my children, who haven't stepped foot in this house for over a year. Call Camille. First, make a martini before hearing her relentless questions. The wife must sleep with the bastard husband tonight. The ritual will start when the girls walk through the door—hugs and kisses. Why didn't they call *me* back? And I must be kind to *that* bitch, Leah. Let it go. At least they're coming to see their grandmother. Children are clueless. All the years, sacrificing my dreams give me little consolation. As my mother often preaches, *'one has to accept the cards dealt.'* God kill me now.

*

"Camille, sorry I didn't call earlier. I should call Mother and tell her I won't be there today. I need to get things ready for Sarah, Nina, and Leah, who are coming to see her."

"I'll explain to Mom. She'll understand. Right now, I have something more pressing. Is Richard home? Can you talk?" She erases one subject for another.

"No, he's not here."

Glad I made that well-fortified drink, but it goes down too fast. "Diane, please tell me what's going on."

Reflux acid swirls inside my throat. An ordeal of explaining something quite personal to my happily married sister constructs an intolerable conversation.

"Diane? Diane? Are you still there?"

Fix another drink to douse the acid. Mix a good bomb cocktail that annihilates Camille's non-stop concerns. Sit on the floor. Feel the imported Italian tile under your butt. The flooring you hate, your husband thinks you love because you've done a fantastic job decorating this fucking house.

"I'm here."

"Tell me, Diane. I *won't* say anything."

Spill your guts, in your case, slit your wrist. Take a deep breath. Put it all on the line. And pray, the little sister doesn't say a goddamn word. "The woman you saw my husband with has a name. She's Julie Meyers, Richard's lover, mistress, or a class-ass homewrecker. Take your pick. Their relationship has gone on for years. Julie carries Richard's child. This version stamps the approved abbreviated version."

"I thought as much, Diane. I saw them together. I thought as much. I hate Richard. I hate him. You two were supposed to be married forever."

If I listen hard and I don't want to, but I do, whimpering comes from the other end of the line. Little sister's innocence and love for one man prints a bestselling romance novel.

The rain starts again. Thunder darkens the skies.

My sister's weeping for me forces a conclusion to my confession. "Camille. I have to hang up. My girls will be here tonight. I have to get things ready for them." "I *want* to help, Diane."

"Help me by taking care of yourself and your baby. My life won't always be shitty."

Another rainbow appears to the east, I see from the foyer. God must be listening.

"I have a way out, Camille. I have a way out." "You do? What is it?"

A brighter rainbow appears. Hope fills my eyes.

"The details aren't worked out yet. Please believe me. I *do* have a way out."

"Will you tell me, Diane?"

"When the time comes . . . I will. I promise."

"I guess there's nothing else to say, except I'm glad you told me about Richard. You've kept a lot from me, Diane. I hope one day we'll have a real conversation."

The sun breaks. I feel the angels are lighting a path.

"I love you, Camille. I'll bring the girls to Mother's tomorrow. Will you be there?"

"I have a doctor's appointment in the morning. I'll be over after that. I'm bringing Alan with me." "Where's my nephew Michael?"

"He's with Alan's mother. How long are *my nieces* staying?"

Sarcasm sounds foreign coming from Camille. They all don't know each other—especially Leah.

"I'm not sure because Richard spoke to them when he made the reservations."

"We'll see you tomorrow, Diane. Please be careful. Richard has a bad temper."

"Goodbye. Camille. I'll see you tomorrow."

The sun's rays open the dark clouds; God's given me a sign.

Everything will be fine.

*

Thought before the appointed hour: a call comes from the airport. Richard is with Leah and Nina. Sarah's London delayed flight will bring them home at about 11:00 pm. Anticipation delivers anxiousness seeing Leah. Call Ruby. No, it's late. She'll think it's an emergency. No one calls anyone at nine in the evening unless they're desperate. I need to eat. Open a can of soup. Mix a drink. How long will my daughters stay? Imagine a different life without him, Mother's dead, and you live anywhere but this house.

*

"Mum, where are you?"

I hear my Sarah's transformed English accent bouncing throughout the foyer. Move fast from the kitchen table. A nap wasn't long enough to gather my wits for the uncertain hours, days, and nights ahead.

"It's you. Oh my God, Sarah, you're here."The mother holds her child as if she's been missing for an eternity while silent joyful crying consumes us.

I shouldn't be upset with her talking to Richard instead of me. She's here, and that's all that matters.

"Let me look at you, Sarah."

She twirls around, giggling as if a little girl. My youngest is thinner and taller since last year.

"How are you still growing?"

"I don't know. It must be the English tea," Sarah giggles. "And you cut and dyed your hair?"

Flipping hands through her now red hair cut into a feathered bang-pixie cut resembling a Parisian, she asks, "Do you like it? Oh, please say you like it, Mum."

"It accentuates those inherited high cheekbones and *those* dimples. I've missed you. Thank you for coming to see your grandmother. I know with school and all, your time is precious."

Pointing to one oversized shoulder bag, "I have better clothes packed." She smiles, revealing baggy sweats under her trench coat. "Who would've thought the rains in Denver mirror that of London? I'm glad to be here. I love her and hate that the bloody cancer is killing her."

"I love you, Sarah. There'll be time for us to have a real chat."

The door opens, and my Nina bustles in, opening and hurrying to shut the door. "Man, the rains are coming down hard." Nina drops her two suitcases. Her arms are clasped around my shoulders, intensifying my happiness. "I'm so glad I came home, Mom. I think you need us."

"Does it have to be a bloody family emergency to get us together?" Sarah's giggles widen her face as she ecstatic jumps Nina and me.

For a few minutes, the mother is transported back to when Nina and Sarah were children, and the home was a happy place despite Richard's and my secrets. The sisters are—holding, hugging, jumping, and laughing about as if in their world. The mother observes in awe at one of the few miracles with the bastard husband, and a selfish wish for him and Leah not to join us penetrates my heart.

"I can't believe you live in England." Nina's enthusiastic gushing reminds me of Camille's energy. "You sound like a real Brit. I love your hair. It fits you, Sarah."

I pledge when things settle into a healthier life, my daughters and Camille will know each other better. My mother would approve.

"Dear sister," Sarah adds, "you look amazing. Are you modeling in New York these days? If not, you *should* come to London. I know people who'd delight in meeting you."

"No. I wish." Nina sways damp, waist-length eye-catching black wavy hair, layered over a maxi coat showing a jean's hemline—agreed she is a potential *Vogue* cover model. "I exercise a lot. I'm a dog-walker. The job pays well for school books and sharing a Village studio with a fabulous Julliard student ballet dancer."

"Really," a curious mother says, "and *when* did all this happen?"

She signals me to come closer, so just three of us can hear. "Please don't say anything to Daddy or Leah. They see things a lot differently from me. To them, I'm irresponsible."

Sarah, in her funny way, uses her fingers, pretending to turn a lock on her lips and throw away the key. The mother crosses her heart in the delight of still playful bonding with her grown children. A bonding she misses.

"I won't tell," I promise. "Except that we do need to talk. I want to talk to you both. By the way, where *are* Leah and your father?" Noticing by now, they should've been in the house.

Nina rolls her eyes. "She's in the garage with Daddy. What else but talking law?"

"Let's not discuss them," Sarah says with a somewhat frown. "You know how they are—lawyer talk day and night."

"Mom," Nina looks about the foyer and then takes a few steps a bit into the lit hallway, "w*hy* do you and Daddy *still* live in this too-big-for-two-people-house? I can't stand a space like this. *It feels so damn empty,*" Nina states, in her known for, outspoken opinion.

Sarah catches my solemn moment. She looks puzzled.

"Your father *loves* this house," I respond, "this is also your home." My face changes into a small smile. "Your father loves you, Nina."

"Yes. I *guess*. Daddy does," Nina answers back in an ugly tone. "When do we see Grandmother? Sad the way life changes *yet remain the same.*" Nina takes hold of Sarah's fingers. "We're family."

"I know," Sarah nods at both of us. "Family and home are comforting. I'm glad we're here. Mum."

I want to tell them both just how life has changed, but can't.

"I wish I'd spent more time with Grandmum. My whole flat near Oxford can fit in the full entry. I'm with you, Nina. I can't live in a beast like this. Mum? Are you happy here?"

When the mother looks up at the well-lit stairs and upstairs—the ghosts of she and their father's last fight are ever-present. "I'm happy with *my dream house*. We see your grandmother tomorrow. I know it's late, but are you girls hungry?" I figure it best to change the subject. Leah and Richard should be coming through the door straight away.

"I'm jet-lagged," Sarah proves with a series of long yawns. "Can I just go up to my room?" She looks up the steps. "Let's chatter in the morning. Can you not wake me too early?"

There's comfort in giving her a firm hug. I've missed everything about her, my baby.

"Not too early. Sleep well. I'm glad you're here, Sarah."

"Good night, Mom. I'm tired too," Nina follows. She glances at the door before leaving for her bedroom. *"I guess Leah and Dad have a lot of legal stuff to discuss."*

I don't like her brash tone. "Nina, stop. Sleep well. I'm glad you're home."

At the top of the stairs, she waves with a thrown kiss. Happiness, sadness, isolation, and tears fill my eyes. Everything has changed.

The front door remains closed. Questions spin. Why are they taking so long? A drink may be needed to meet her two favorite people. No sooner than a martini gets mixed, poured, and ready to sip—a mood descends. A familiar voice enters the house; the drink can wait. Her guest has arrived.

*

"Hello, Mother."

I hear a sterile greeting and replay our last conversation while my tongue rubs a remaining mouth's soreness from Richard's hand. Her indifferent expression reduces her time here as a formality.

"Leah. How are you?" the mother asks as if her daughter were an acquaintance.

Chanel No. 5, the same Richard gave me, accompanies her power-red lipstick air kiss. "You *finally* get a chance to see me, Mother. I'm sorry this can't be under better circumstances. How has Aunt Camille taken the news?"

"Where's your father?" I'm thinking by now he'd be inside because of the heavy rains.

My daughter cuts a quick look at the door, then back to her mother. "He's coming. We were talking. I hate this rain."

She removes her leather mid-knee coat, revealing a black *Dior* pencil skirt with a double-breasted jacket. Her pose begs for comment; I study her blonde, past the shoulder, side-parted full straight hair. Her beauty at one time was my twin.

"Are you hungry?" I offer food and not the ego-stroking compliment. "No. Aren't you going to answer my question?" Her expensive well-heeled shoe taps her self-importance.

Uncomfortable sensation bites. *'Take a deep breath. Leah is the child. You're the adult,'* I reason inside my head.

"Camille and I are coping. Your grandmother will be happy to see you, Leah."

A brisk returned nod the daughter gives before strolling up the stairs. "It's late. I'm tired. My day and flight *were* too long," she announces without bothering to turn back. "I know my way. Good night." "Where are your bags?"

"I have them," her father answers rushing into the foyer. "I had to wait until the rains eased up." He shakes off the wet and closes the door. "My gorgeous daughter, the over-packer, *has* to look the fashion plate." Richard beams carrying three suitcases like a bellhop.

Leah stares down from the railing. I see two things: her small wave and my ghost clinging to the banister, that her father beat me against for calling her.

"Here's your luggage, your majesty," the bastard husband bows his head when he reaches our daughter.

The wife gives her husband a failing grade; his humor stinks, a martini calls. The night hasn't ended. She still must sleep in the master bedroom.

*

"How are you doing?" He peeks out the window. "Damn. What a mess. But we needed the rain. What are you thinking? Good to have the girls back home?" He asks questions I don't want to converse about, as he pours a tumbler of Scotch and water. He drinks it fast and pours another.

I sit not worrying, the rains, our daughters at this moment, or even to offer Richard a glimpse of my thoughts. I don't have to answer anything.

He fills a spot closer to me than I want.

"Well, tomorrow is the big day. Have you called your mother? I mean, to let her know they're here."

The visible lightning show has my attention. I ignore Richard's small talk until he places his hand on my shoulder.

The wife shoots away a few inches. She hopes he gets the message. "She's asleep. I talked to Camille today. My sister informed Mother.

I'll ring in the morning, Richard."

My drink needs refreshing—an opportunity to distance myself as Richard's tight-lipped pout could mean any number of things. When the wife rejoins him, she sits opposite, accessing the brooding husband's disposition.

"We should talk, Richard."

He squints, which isn't a good sign.

"Yeah . . . I've been *trying* to fucking talk to you for the past few days, Diane."

Heightened agitation can't end well for me. Would Richard have the gall to hit me while our children are here? I struggle thinking a response to survive through this whole ordeal of Mother's illness and all the rest.

"Our babies are here, Richard."

"I know *that*, bitch. I'm not fucking stupid, Diane. Tell me, my wife," my heart thumps faster as he stands to hover over my head. One hand holds his glass. The other remains rigid against his pants leg, "Are you going to make love to me tonight or piss on about Julie? The more I think about how I've been begging you, the madder I get."

The wife's disgusting choice smashes words into mush.

A towering shadow over her head means prepare—if she can, for a fight.

"Damn you, bitch," he leans down into my face. He squeezes my arm until my drink spills into my lap. He gives one. He lands two. He enforces three slaps to the side of the wife's head. "You'll be damn sorry if you cry and wake our girls. You'll be damn sorry. Now answer my goddamn question."

The discomfort of his questions, head throbs, and clothes saturated with the smell of a wasted martini forbid any sounds waking the girls despite dreadful sobs oozing down my face.

His alcohol-soaked breath, dripping spit, and bulging neck veins infest my nightmare, trembling as if naked in freezing weather.

"I . . . I will make love to you, Richard." "Do you want to, or is this a damn lie?" "No. I'm telling the truth."

"Prove it, Diane."

Concern rattles me. "The girls *are* upstairs, Richard." He looks over his shoulder.

"Get over there."

I follow his instructions, moving to a corner in a sizeable room that can hide us.

He pulls a side chair, the one with an uncomfortable wooden back. "Sit down. *Don't have me tell you twice.*"

I obey.

He stands in front of me. He straddles his legs into a bent position.

The sound of his zipper makes the most degenerate sound.

He gives me his glass.

"Drink so you'll be in the mood." "I *am* in the mood," I mumble.

"Alright, as I said, prove it, bitch."

I watch him pull out his limp penis. He shoves my head into his crotch.

"Suck my cock. Suck my cock until I cum, over and over into your throat. You stop when I tell you. You're going to do whatever I want tonight in that fucking guest room chosen over our bedroom."

*

The rage of night thoughts: and so the night of ravage sex starts. Uncaring hands push my face into his legs. I suck. I lick. I do it over and over until his dick and fetish of urinating on my breasts are satisfied. And my mouth, tongue, lips, and throat are contaminated with his vile stench. We then tiptoe into my cave, the guest room. The wife swallows his sperm. Her mouth can't taste anything but him. She spreads her legs to receive his dick into her ass. The pain doesn't matter. His hands squeeze her breasts until her nipples feel as if they'll break off. Yank. Pull her pubic hairs. He commands her to assume a dog position on the bare floor while he rams his fingers and dick into her ass. She stands against the wall. She lies in bed. She lies on the floor. She sits in a chair. He fucks her in every position he remembers from his porno movie collection. This wife doesn't cry. She doesn't make a sound. Her children are in the house. His French kisses rape her mouth. He sleeps. His naked body, entangled in the bed linen she got from Ireland and France, is stained with yellow, red, and white body fluids. The rains stop. But the storm remains. Her time will come. Not now—her daughters are in the house.

*

"Mum, are you okay?"

"You startled me. Go back to bed. I'm fine."

I hoped for solitude before dawn after Richard. Smile. I can't do anything.

"I wanted a glass of water. My London time clock says to get up. Sorry if I scared you."

An urgent need straightens matted hair and wipes mascara stained face.

"Please leave the light off, Sarah."

"Moonlight comes through enough to see. Shall I pour you a glass of water, Mum?"

"Sure, dear."

Not even filtered water kills Richard's fluids free-falling in my mouth and lungs.

"Funny, Mum, things remain constant. These glasses are in the same cabinet for years."

She's right in more ways than she'll ever know.

"I remember when we all sat at this same table. You'd make sure there were fresh flowers." She giggles a bit. "Some things about this house I've missed . . . most of all *you.*"

"Funny, Sarah, even though you think of our home as a beast?"

"I didn't mean it. My shoe-box can fit inside your pantry. Home is relative to you, Mum."

"I'm the same . . . *in many ways,*" I confess in self-pity for my last hours with Richard, her father.

Rains start again. My attention turns into the darkened hallway. I hope Richard won't bring another kind of storm.

"The bloody rain is as depressing as seeing Grandmum. I'm sorry for being crude."

Sarah's cries compound my helplessness to console her because my life hinges in devastation.

"Your grandmother knows about your studies. Don't beat yourself up," is about all I can say.

"I've disappointed you, haven't I, Mum?" "I don't understand."

"We need to talk later about my school. I thought law a better career choice. Leah told you. She said she did. I was going to . . . "

A mothering gesture pinches her lips to stop. "We can discuss this later. Try and get some more sleep."

"Mum?"

"Yes."

"Are you alright?" My daughter mimics Camille's persistent concern. "*Please* tell me the truth."

What does she know, and *why* is she asking an intrusive question in a face scrunching into a million wrinkles? Now I'm worried.

"I don't know what you mean. Sarah, I'm fine."

"I ask, Mum, because I hovered on the stairs. I overheard you and Dad in the sunroom. I don't think you're honest. You can trust me. Come back with me if you're unhappy."

Sweat comes, an obvious clue. "What did you hear?"

Her muffled cries into her palms mean she's heard arguing. "I heard Dad raping you and saying the vilest things a loving husband should never utter. I heard him slap you, Mum. Why? Tell me, are you in danger? You can stay with me."

Sarah's crying into my arms passes into me, raging grief. I can't tell the truth. God, give me the right words to quiet and reassure my child.

"Your father and I have issues. We're not unlike any married couple. Sex for husbands holds more value than for their wives. Your father's drunken behavior means nothing in the morning."

Sarah steps closer and peers into my face. She knows me as well as I know her. "I *don't* believe you, Mum. I can't. You're hiding something. I fear for you. *Why* do you have scars on the side of your face? I noticed bruises on your neck."

"Well—well, what's going on?"

"I thought you were asleep, Richard."

His answer is stretching his arms around my chest; the wife feels his kiss on her ear. Sarah is here. I mustn't show the least discomfort, returning Richard's kiss.

"Dad, I woke up and wanted some water," Sarah answers. "You must still have jet lag."

"I'm going back upstairs. I came to get some water. Mum was here, and we were chatting a bit."

I give her a great hug. "Get some more sleep, Sarah."

"I will, Mum." She slowly turns around before leaving us and studies our arm-in-arm position. *"It's good to be home."*

"Her thick accent cracks me up," Richard comments when she's gone. "It's almost as if she'd rather not be a part of this family. Fuck, as long as I'm paying her tuition, she'd better not think about divorcing us."

"Sarah's a good girl,' I add, pouring a glass of needed for my mouth's crud.

Richard interrupts with moans and groans grinding my ass with fingers, "You like it?" He whispers, sucking my neck.

A lie covers the discomfort. *"Yes, Richard."*

"You amuse me, my dear wife." The bastard pushes my head. "You can tell me later about your and Sarah's early morning fireside chat. Right now, I'm going up to bed. Come on." He smacks my ass. "We have at least another hour of fun ahead."

I watch the rain subside. *"I'm coming."*

Up the staircase into the bedroom, he closes the door behind us.

"Tomorrow will be a long day. Better get some sleep after you suck me off." He strips off clothes and climbs into bed. "When do you want to go to your mother's?"

The wife assumes her place in the bed. "I think noon is a good time, Richard."

"Fine," he agrees with legs spread open. "

*

Nina's more excited than I can handle having gotten barely four hours of sleep.

Her camera phone ready, she says, "Smile."

My position between Sarah and Leah gives breathing room away from him. Nina notices my long face.

"Smile, Mom. Christmas was the last time we were all in this house." "I'm just tired, but promise a decent picture after a shower and more coffee."

"Come on, Mother. Act like this is your wedding day, *and you're happy,*" Leah snips.

Nina and Sarah observe their mother's instant eye roll.

"Jesus, Diane, can't you give us a precious smile?" Richard barks. "I need more coffee. Thank you, girls, for fixing breakfast."

I smile a quick one for Nina's damn picture. Breathing into my coffee while Richard at the counter refills his cup, I imagine a gun with a precise aim to the back of his head. In one second, my misery is over.

"Sarah prepared the eggs, bacon, toast, and I cut the melon." Nina happily states while sharing the family photo with Sarah, before passing around the phone camera phone.

Leah, in an intense stare, targets me sitting across from her.

I won't look away, no matter how nervous her presence makes me. "Nina *and I* set the table, Mother," she boasts in my direction and winks at Richard.

"Well, it's all good," the bastard compliments while refilling everyone's cup.

When he reaches his wife, a grin passes from him to her expressionless face.

"You need more coffee, Diane, to get with the program," he pushes. "When do we leave?" Leah asks. "I have some work calls to make."

Tapping on the table with her nails draws Nina's attention. "Something wrong, twin sister?" Leah folds her arms across one another.

"Oh, get off it, Leah, with your self-importance. Everyone knows you're this big-time lawyer. Can't you turn off the success? We're here to see our grandmother, not hear about your job." Nina holds back no sentiment about her twin, giving Leah the *middle-finger*.

Sarah slides back to her seat.

Richard watches. I wonder how long he'll allow the bickering.

"Well, fuck you," Leah lashes back before shoving away from the table.

"Leah," Richard's uncharacteristic soft voice begs, "let's not argue." "Don't," she answers back with her hands held up. "I'm taking my shower now. My plane leaves tomorrow."

"You brought enough clothes for a week," Nina shouts. "So, you're cutting this trip short?"

Leah's deliberate stomps out the room and up the stairs explode redness into Nina's face.

"*You just have to love my dear twin,*" Nina's harsh words cut to me. "Sorry for ruining our breakfast. Leah doesn't deserve my apology," Nina's firm as she gathers up her dishes.

"Why do you and Leah argue? So what if she has to make work calls?" Sarah tosses on the table her napkin. "We're supposed to be here for the family, not some sister-brawl."

"Sarah, my little sister," Nina sounds not sympatric to Sarah's sullen face, "believe me, there's much you don't know about Leah. I'm going to take my shower now."

Left are the three of us. Richard fixates on the rain—Sarah removes the dishes—and the mother wonders where she failed.

"I'm taking my shower while you and Sarah get dishes," Richard announces on his way out of the kitchen.

Before Sarah can fix her lips to ask me more questions, I head off the inquisition when she takes away the last plate. *"Enough talk."*

"Okay, Mum, as you wish," she responds in a gruff voice.

"We'll talk later, I promise." I hope to eliminate any misunderstanding. "Your grandmother is looking forward to your visit."

*

One by one, we gather at the bottom of the steps. Sarah wears blue flats. Her plain dress, a front button-down power blue, hitting her knee, looks beautiful. Nina chooses a mint green shift with sandals, and me, in my usual black—this time, a maxi dress and light blue sweater for comfort concealing the healing bruises. Our best doesn't measure up to Leah's.

"I didn't know we had to dress up." Sarah nudges into my side.

Leah checks her cell for messages. "I want to ride with Father," the career child dabs her lipstick after putting her phone into a *Dior* handbag. She stands as model straight, head up, and three-inch heels pointed. I recognize the design - *Dior*-skirt, with a cropped, thin lapel jacket; the outfit—her taste—rings money. Her make-up and hair mean perfect.

"I want to discuss some work cases," our impeccable Leah lays out her plan.

I hope my daughter's snotty daggers thrown at her twin won't set the tone while we're at Mother's. I'm not in the mood.

"Who cares?" Nina grinds. "Mom, can I *please* ride with you?" Since their father and I spoke a handful of words getting ready—

Leah's demands are a clear decision. The wife is grateful for separate bathrooms and dressing rooms. The bastard gathers his car keys from the office, giving me a few more minutes of not having to see his face.

"Yes. You and I can ride together."

"And me?" Sarah wiggles in a don't-leave-me-behind sulk.

Before I can speak, Nina latches her arm inside her sister's. "You ride with us."

"Alright then," Sarah says playfully. "Sorry, dear Leah. Perhaps we can talk about the price of tea later?"

The off-handed joke brings out her and Nina's chuckles. "Are we *ready,* Father?" Leah grounds her hands on her hips.

"Leah. I didn't mean any harm," Sarah apologizes, extending a handshake.

A stiff-lipped Leah answers, *"Forget it."*

Nina shrugs her off.

I don't like Leah's quick dismissal of Sarah's apology, but the time isn't right for a mother lecture.

"Glad she's going with Dad," Sarah lowers her voice as Leah pushes toward Richard's study.

"Are you ready, Father?"

Richard's custom-made business suit emerges before Leah reaches his precious study.

"Let's go. You look quite beautiful, Leah."

"Thank you, Father, I tried," my daughter's snide answer slings towards her sisters and me.

Richard's once-over-no-compliment for the rest of us allows Leah's gloating. He checks the diamond watch, another one I didn't buy. "Didn't you say your mother expects us about noon?"

"Yes," I answered, trying not to give too much attention to his damn watch.

"I doubt she'll serve lunch. We can stop at the Club after our visit. Leah and Sarah, I have a couple of judges I want you to meet. You don't have time to change clothes." Richard scrutinizes Sarah's casual attire to Leah's. "Next time, pick a better outfit."

Sarah's tense face shows as her father fixates on her wrinkled dress. "Sorry I didn't know."

"It doesn't matter. You need to use Leah as an example of how an attorney dresses. Let's get going." Richard's lashing colors, no doubt of displeasure.

Leah and her idol walk past us without a *'goodbye* or *drive safe.'*

"Don't forget to lock the door, Diane," he bosses before stepping off the porch.

"I won't forget."

"*Why* is Leah need to be *the one*? I mean Dad's favorite," Sarah draws a crisp picture of Leah and Richard chit-chatting, arm-in-arm.

"*Because*," Nina interrupts, sticking out her tongue at Richard and Leah entering the garage, "*the world has always been round.*"

*

An observation: Sarah and Nina's childish snickers irritate me as much as Richard and Leah's closeness. Today he chooses the two-seater, black *Porsche* to drive her to the Club.

*

"Enough. Okay? Stop," the mother orders when they reach her car. They settle into the car—Sarah in the back—and Nina beside me. "Are you okay?" Sarah taps her sister's shoulder.

A quiet covers Nina, resting back into the seat. I wait and listen.

"Leah's damn importance bugs me. How, as twins, can we be so different?"

"*They're close.*" Sarah scoots up until her head props between us. "*I won't be a lawyer like her,*" Sarah's defiance turns angry. "Don't know if I even *want* to be a goddamn lawyer at all."

Sarah isn't one to cuss. Concentration into the rear-view mirror gives a view of worry moving into her face.

"He and Leah *talked* you into selling your soul," Nina lashes out. "You were set on English Literature, Sarah."

*

Thought of surfacing fear: my daughter and their father referred to as *she and him* stiffen my posture. Hands refuse to put the key into the ignition. The steering wheel's *Mercedes'* insignia memorizes my focus.

*

"Mom, did you hear me? Sarah and I have *something* to tell you."

The tips of her nails tap on my shoulder. I'm back on earth. "*What* do you have to say, Nina?"

*

Thought of suspicion: the word '*something*' scares me, but not in as much as the way it's spoken. Why now? The mirror reveals Sarah's downward head as she fiddles with her hair. What is going on? Nina wringing hands together to wiping her wet cheeks is an out of place trait.

*

"We're not going anywhere until I know what's going on. One of you better talk."

And Nina does with sharp clarity while taking hold of my arm. "Mom, listen to me, Leah talks disgraceful about you. She calls you a damn fool. She says she despises you."

My daughter's absolute stone seriousness opens sweat into my make-up. I'm mortified over her well-chosen words, that in seconds, destroy my life—the main reason I stayed with Richard—to be a good mother to *all* my children.

Sarah bears down into her sister. "*Why* did you have to say anything? We said we wouldn't."

I unlock the door. Remove my seat belt. I'm determined to take control. "Both of you get out of the car. Go back inside the house. My mother can wait. There are too many secrets running like ghosts around me. Get out of the car *right now*. I'm *not* your father. You can tell me anything," I remind them as we enter the kitchen door. "Talk to me."

We take our seats.

A pretense of calm conceals my agitation for not on our way yet to see my mother, and interact with Richard and Leah, my least favorite people right now.

Sarah nudges Nina. Both are fidgeting, clamming up, unable, or unwilling to talk.

"We have to leave," my impatience shortens, "the time is 12:45."

"*Okay. Okay.*" Sarah stands and bunches her dress's hem. Sweat and tears mix into a running mess. "Leah hates you, Mum. She told me as much. The reason she insisted on me becoming a solicitor or lawyer as she calls it, is so that I don't turn out to be as useless as you."

My daughter's truth nails Leah's feelings about my lack of education when we last spoke on the phone. I want to crawl into a corner forever. But today, right now, I can't show a spineless mother to my girls struggling from harboring this secret about their sister.

"Leah's words don't define me," I give a convincing speech. Sarah and Nina must never know I fear and don't trust Leah. She and her father are alike.

"Leah told me Daddy should've married someone like her. She calls you weak," Nina now begins adding a lousy season to Sarah's story. "All your marriage, you've asked for money to buy toilet paper to wipe your ass."

The simple sentence from Richard's mouth plunges the knife deeper. "Go on. *Tell me everything—even those things that will hurt*. I need to hear."

*

A lost thought as I endure another horrible minute of my life: alcohol salivates. I mustn't crumple into desperation for the rest of the pink pills the doctor gave me.

*

Sarah's presence covers the upper part of my body. Nina's hands grasp mine tight. Our collapsing emotions hold us together.

"We love you, Mum."

"What else do you girls have?" I ask, praying for no more, and not wanting it.

"If she found out we told you . . ." Sarah's voice vanishes into her palms.

I huddle my children. Right now, feeling as if we're all we've got. "Leah feels she is better than any of us . . . *except for Daddy*," Nina says with a bite to her tone. "What makes her so fucking special?"

"An attorney's ego comes with the territory. I attest from living with your father."

"We're twins, but I'm *nothing* like her symbolizing money and power."

"*I know,* Nina. Don't cry. Have you two told me everything?" I repeat.

Sarah's strained worry grows as if she's raking over details. Shall I push her? "What else is there, Sarah?" I pry a little but pull back, seeing the tension in her face. "We can talk about it later if you wish, or now. Don't worry about my mother. We'll see her soon enough."

"I do have one more thing, Mum. I've wrestled with for about a year. Please forgive me for never telling you, or *you,* Nina. But this time, with the three of us alone, may not be more opportune."

"Go on, Sarah," I coax her by standing beside her with my arm around her waist. "Take your time."

"What is it, Sarah? I don't like your hesitation." Nina rises to stand with us.

Her chest accentuates long breaths as she wrings the hem of her dress. We're an hour late. Should I call Mother? Not with Nina's nails digging deep into the back of my hand. Something terrible has happened to my child.

"Take your time, Sarah. Tell me," I coach her with gentle rubs on her back that won't stop her eyes from crying.

"What happened to you, Sarah? I swear if Leah hurt you, I'll make her pay," Nina impatience paces her back and forth. "Damn bitch," she repeats over and over.

Sarah's deep swallowing and trembling as she dishevels her styled hair presents me with a million dark questions.

"I need a glass of wine, Mum." "We all do," I respond.

Opening a bottle of Napa Pinot and bringing three glasses from the sunroom's bar gives me a mental break of whatever information is sickening Sarah. A slow walk, rejoining in the kitchen, Nina's nail- biting to Sarah clenching her fists to wringing her hands together, does little to calm my battered nerves.

The three of us drink. Time isn't our friend. I wait until Sarah finishes, witnessing her grim demeanor.

"What do you need to tell us, Sarah?" Nina asks with a rub to Sarah's back.

"Please, Sarah, tell me," I lean in. "Why are you afraid?"

"I saw them when Dad came to visit me last year," Sarah mutters.

"*What* did you see? *What* did you say?" I probe more. "Repeat it, Sarah."

Sarah's target is her mother's arms. The tension frightens me because Sarah's character is the calm one.

Trembling, she delivers, "Oh my God . . . help me." Sarah's profound weeping mixes with hesitation.

I take her into my arms and cradle her. "Sarah," I whisper, "*tell* me what you saw."

"I'm sorry, Mum. Forgive me. I didn't say it before." "What? What?" Nina asks.

Between pauses and biting lip, Sarah begins talking, "Last year when Dad visited me in London—Leah came with him. Their mission was to convince me to change my major to law. Dad treated us to the *Savoy Hotel.*"

Sarah's story interrupts with constant wiping her face and deep out of breath breathing. An annoyance right now that I don't need.

"Sarah, *please* . . . tell me."

"I retired to my room," she continues after more long breaths, "because of a head cold. Several hours later, I felt better to meet Dad and Leah in the hotel's restaurant as planned. They weren't there. Of course, this took me by surprise because Leah expressed all day she wanted the lamb special."

My child presses her fingers together to her lips.

I don't interrupt seeing it's a most painful recollection.

Nina's anger flares into overdrive, "So *where* the hell did you find them?"

"*Oh, God,*" Sarah's staggering trepidation stumbles, searching the air for words.

My nerves are raw. Thoughts swirl, unable to put one word in front of the other. "Sarah. *Please. Please tell me,*" I beg on the verge of screaming.

"Sarah, say it. Go it out." Nina yanks her sister's shoulders, shaking them hard. "Say what the fuck you have to say."

Sarah's continual tears are my instinct. Something will forever change my life.

"I—I— saw when I got off the elevator," her story moves but not fast enough.

"Goddamn. *Who* did you see?" Nina's short fuse resembles her father's animated bulging eyes.

I gather my wits, grabbing Nina, whose temper moves to uncontrolled.

"Nina. Calm down right now."

"Sorry, Mom, but this *is crazy*, Sarah. What the fuck did you see?"

"Stop," I forbade another one of Nina's interruptions.

"Sarah," I look into her misery and feel every tear she's shedding, "tell me. Pretend it's just you and me. Just say it. We can work it out. I can set things right. I give you my word."

"Mum," I can barely hear her.

"Speak up, Sarah," I render all my empathy. "I," she stops and begins rubbing her head hard.

I've never seen her words stuck like this. I offer her my wine.

"I don't need it," she shakes her head, "to say what I'm struggling with."

"Sarah. Continue. *I'm right here.*"

"I was on my way to Dad's suite," her head down as she muffles the words.

With gentle strokes, I run the base of her neck. We should be driving into Mother's driveway now. But I can't rush Sarah's distraught, struggling to say what's tormenting her. "

Speak up, Sarah," Nina lends support. "I'm here. Mom's here. "I saw him and Leah."

"Who did you see Leah with, Sarah?" a protective mother asks with careful attention to what her daughter will reveal.

"Mum. I saw *them* in a private alcove leading to Dad's penthouse suite. They didn't see me. I saw them fucking bloody kissing as if in love."

"Did you see Leah's boyfriend or one of your father's law partners?" I delve for more information."

"They were fucking kissing," her red-tired eyes bulge into shock. "Nina and Mum . . . I *saw* them. I heard their passionate groans. I saw his hand crawl down her blouse. I saw him ravage her exposed breasts and nipples. I saw his hand reach under Leah's dress until she moaned and said, '*I love you.*'"

The silence excels; I look at the clock. We're two hours late. It doesn't matter.

"Sarah," I take her palm into mine. The mother's eyes well, "Sarah, *who was with Leah?*"

"I saw *Dad.*" Her precise answer crashes her into my arms. Nina's wails as she lays her head on the table.

My cell, on mute, indicates four missed messages, all from Richard. The wife, numb, can't think with clarity right now.

"Mom," Nina looks at me, "what are you going to do?"

"Mum, I'm sorry," Sarah sobs and sobs. "I wish it weren't true. I swear to God what I saw has taken all my willpower never to say anything to Leah and Dad."

"This is *not* your fault. Both of you go upstairs. Freshen up. We need to leave. I don't want any mention of this conversation. Are we clear? I have to think. I love you more than anything in the world." My arms can't begin to hold them long enough.

"Your grandmother has asked to see you. Goddamn—what a fucking mess. Sarah, did you question your sister?" I must know," my containment sounds as strong as a one-year-old.

"How could I ask Leah such a bad thing?—*Are in love with our father?* Oh God, Mum, tell me you're going to leave Dad. *You must,*" she hollers in my face as if I'm deaf.

"I will get to the bottom of this, Sarah. Please calm down. I promise this to you and Nina."

She distances herself, shaking her head.

"You'll stay. I know you'll stay." Her hysterics dump more powerless guilt into my heart.

"Don't say that. Don't think that. I'm not stupid. I have to plan this. How could I forgive your father?" I plead for her understanding, feeling my heartache speeding, taking me a place of no-return.

As if I can swallow another ounce of this poison, Nina's screams gyrate her into the corner. I can't hold her, not even for a second. She's too strong.

"Nina, calm down. I said I *would* handle your father, to make sure this never happens again. Trust me."

She screams as if I'm deaf as she leaves the kitchen, "I wish I didn't come here. I wish Leah were dead. I hate her and my father. I shall never forgive them as long as I live. I promise I'll never step foot in this damn house. I'm leaving as soon as I see my grandmother."

Sarah and I hear Nina slam her bedroom door.

"This is my fault, Mum. I shouldn't have said anything. I'm sorry." "Go upstairs and freshen up. Bring Nina downstairs. We need to go." "I'm sorry," she whimpers, apologizing again before she leaves me alone.

The wife and mother's mind lowers her into a pine box. Willpower empties on to the floor. On her knees, she sobs into her hands, cursing Richard and their daughter, Leah's secret, hurling the family into an unforgiving disgraceful scandal.

*

An impossible thought in the car: my daughter and my husband are lovers. Gather all your strength to do what you must.

*

"Do you think they'll be there?"

"I think so," I recall reading Richard's last text. "Don't worry, Sarah."

*

Another shitty thought: my two babies huddle in the back seat. The thirty-minute drive curdles my stomach; the closer we reach Mother's. I never suspected or saw anything. But then, don't women whose husbands abuse their children say the same thing? I swear on my mother's dying soul, I never suspected anything. Will Nina and Sarah believe me? Suppose Richard touched them, too.

* "We're almost there. Are you two okay?" "Fine," Nina snaps.

"Tell me and *be* honest, did your father ever . . ." "No."

"No."

Their interrupted answers could be believable. I have to ask again. "Why are you pulling over, Mom?"

I stop the car off the side road. We're a few blocks away. I must step inside their minds as only a mother can. Turning around, I ask, "I want the truth. *Did your father ever once, anytime, ever touch you?*"

"Fuck no. I'd kill Father." Nina's tightening frown confirms in her no-nonsense honesty.

"Sarah. Tell me the truth."

I get a clear view of her face. Clenching Nina's hand, Sarah struggles by biting her lips. I could kill the bastard husband with the gun I've hidden under the seat for protection.

"That evening, after I saw Dad and Leah together, I hadn't slept. I hadn't cried. I was in shock. Midnight and there's a knock to my door. I thought it'd be Leah wanting to talk. I don't know; I just thought it'd be her. When I opened the door, Dad stood there. He asked to come in."

"You said the asshole didn't touch you. Why did you lie? Are you protecting the prick?" Nina blurts out as mad as I am appalled.

"I didn't lie," Sarah mumbles, wiping her mouth.

"Go on, Sarah," I coax with intentions of staying parked until I hear what she has to say.

She touches the car window and almost smiles, then starts to speak, "I *wish* I were home. Dad never did anything to me, except destroy my admiration and love."

Nina intercedes, shouting, pounding her fists into her thighs. "Did the bastard leave?"

With hollow eyes, Sarah bends her legs tight onto the seat. She glances at me before turning toward her hands, entangled inside each other.

I dread what she'll say. I can't look at her. I face forward, watching the rain splash the window.

"Dad," she clears her voice, "didn't listen when I told him I wanted to sleep. He pushed me, smelling full of alcohol. From his wallet, he handed me a gift of ten-one-thousand dollars for anything I wanted. I took the money because I was quite afraid of his insistence caressing my hands. I didn't say anything. I prayed he'd leave me be. His face softens, leaning in as if to kiss me. My heart raced. Was he going to rape me? What could I do? Scream? I didn't want a scene. He is my father. I pulled back as he stroked my hair. He called me his baby girl and appeared bewildered the further I stepped away. He suddenly bid me a good night. I locked the door. I cried, feeling sorry for him and angry at the same time."

Rain pours as Sarah's story ends. The storm swells inside.

"Things will be different," I swear, looking at each of my children's anguish.

"We better get going, Mum. We're quite late," Sarah points out as she wipes her eyes for the hundredth time.

"I hope they're gone," Nina growls, "I hate them both. Can't he be arrested?"

Nina resonates I've married a sick man.

"I need to process it all. Let me take care of it. *Please.*"

I see them through the rear-view mirror peering pensively out each window. I don't have a plan. I have to soon not just for daughters, but also for myself.

*

Catching all the red lights adds another ten minutes.

*

"We're here, Nina and Sarah. It's stopped raining." I announce, subdued, observing Richard and Leah, laughing and touching each other's arms.

Well, that's two good things, no rain, and they're leaving." Nina points to Leah and Richard exiting with Camille, from Mother's porch, to reach Richard's car in the driveway. "Thank God, because I don't have a damn thing to say. They are no longer my father and sister."

"I don't want a scene, Nina," I warn her. "You and Sarah get into the house. Your father sees us and is coming. Act normal. Get out of the car, and at least wave goodbye."

"Fuck them. Sarah, let's go," Nina snaps back.

"I'm right behind you, Nina. I don't want a scene, either." Sarah opens the car door. "Let's get this over with."

*

Thought of needing a plan: as instructed, they dash to Camille, wave to Leah and Richard, and enter the house. I must have it out with Richard, but not now. His fists are too ready. I need a plan and quick.

*

"Where the hell have you been?" The bastard opens the car door. "Get out of the fucking car, Diane."

There's no time to think.

"Get the fuck out of the car. Diane."

"Sorry, I'm late," I apologize, hoping his fists won't take a jab at my head as he leans into me.

"I had to entertain your mother all by myself." His breath soaks my ears. "What took you so damn long? And why didn't those ungrateful girls even speak to me? You're intentionally pissing me off, Diane. "

"Stop it, Richard." I square into the center of his flaming eyes. "I'm tired of your bullying me. I apologized. Now, move out of my way, I want to see my mother."

"So, when did you grow a dick?" He chuckles, patting the side of my face. "We'll discuss *your* attitude later. Today *won't end* well for you, Diane. I'm taking Leah to the Club for lunch. You deal with your mother and Camille. You *will* regret this disrespect."

"Sure, Richard, whatever you say," I shove past him, hearing my favorite pet name, '*Bitch.*'

"You made it. Are you okay, sis?" Camille's hug breaks my concentration from Richard's angry face.

"I'm sorry, Camille. How is our mother?"

"She's having some tea. What's wrong? Are you crying?"

Before I can answer, Richard waves back, opening his car's door, but stops short of entering. "*See you later*, Diane," he calls out, ignoring Camille, standing by my side.

"Well, whatever is wrong," Camille, shaking her head, looks like a worried mess, "I'm glad Richard is leaving. Both of you, in the same room, haven't worked for years. Leah and I don't speak the same language. I guess because I'm a boring housewife, and she's a career woman. Dear sister, what will become of us all?"

"Camille, we'll speak later. *Leah is approaching.*"

"We'll talk, Diane. Right now, Mom is the priority. I'll see you when you come in." Camille moves, giving Leah a slight smile, nothing more.

"Hello, Leah." Raw torment steals any motherly-desire to converse more with her.

"I'm glad you made it before I left." Leah's sincerely is as sincere as a stranger's.

At this point, Leah's manners aren't my concern. Sarah's story won't stop replaying.

"Mother," Leah extends an open sun-tanned arm, "I see you got here just in time for me to leave. Wonderful timing you and I have."

I'm hurt, mad, and vindictive, for the uncommon tears, in both of our eyes. What is the cost? Could this be the last time I decide to see my daughter?

"So you're leaving tonight, Leah?"

"She has a trial to prepare for," Richard interjects.

"I'll get my suitcases before Father, and I stop at the Club for a quick cocktail with Grandfather Lloyd." Her disposition transforms from executive to almost human-daughter as she places her palm into mine. "I wish the visit were longer. We . . ." Her face turns away. "I have to go." "Another time," I end. "Have a safe flight. You had a good visit?" Bleak questions flood my thoughts as we stare into our faces.

"Come on, Leah," Richard butts in. She ignores him. "I did."

Her surprise embrace produces an insurmountable sadness. "I love you, Mother." She kisses my ear. "*Goodbye.*"

I want to say something—anything. But the time between us runs out.

Richard drives away until the car disappears around the corner.

A chill comes. The thunder starts again.

The front door unlatches. A cane balances her. "Mother, the rain is starting. Go Back inside."

"I'm on the damn porch. You better step up here. Why don't you talk to me, Diane? There's something horrible going on in your life. I can't help you when you don't tell me."

Her slowly-losing-weight-frame implies time won't wait on me. I have to get things in order before I dump all my crap.

"Can the girls stay here with you? I have to take care of an urgent matter," I ask, hoping she doesn't want details.

Her pause takes its time. A hard stare, I won't deny, is an unappreciated trait.

"I have to leave, Mother. I promise not to be gone long."

"Go. I tell you, child, we better talk soon. I'm not in the mood for your and Richard's shit. My gut tells me *this* has to do with him."

A kiss to her cheeks seals my gratitude.

"Don't bother telling Sarah and Nina," she calls out as I hurry to my car, "I'll do it myself. Take care of this so-called urgent business."

"I won't be long, Mother." "Where are you going?"

Nina catches up with me before I can open the car's door. "Stay here. I'll be back soon."

Her stubbornness won't move.

"Are you going to see Daddy? Let me go with you." "No. Go back inside," I insist.

"*Be careful,*" her warnings sound like a threat. "Please let me go with you. I sensed when we came home, and something wasn't right. Not once did you two speak more than a couple of short sentences."

"I can't explain my life in a short-pitch, Nina." Glimpsing toward the house, Mother peers out from the window. "Go inside. Talk to your grandmother. This time may be the last as her health…"

"She's dying?"

My voice sinks, "It's her reason for seeing you."

"And she won't take any medication or treatment? I know she won't. She mentioned as much the last time. I think about two years ago. Now with this, Leah and Dad stuff, *how* are we going to get through it?"

Her small pats to my back don't soothe my troubles. Looking up at the sky, we see a rainbow.

"Maybe, Nina, we'll get our happy ending."

*

Loss of thoughts: fear of change. Fear of the unknown. Fear of no concrete plans. Fear of revealing everything to my mother. The first turn available away from Mother's street gives privacy into *Shelton's Park.* Shaky hands remove the cell from my purse — the first call—Richard's mother.

*

"Hello, Helen."

"How's your mother? Richard tells me the bloody cancer is back. I'm sorry. The good thing is your girls are here."

She sounds drunk. I should end the call. Helen? Do you want me to call back?"

"Goddamn, Diane. Don't be an accommodating ass. Jesus, this family hasn't been an inch of polite to you. I'm fine. I'd say so if I weren't."

Ask for the money. Get off the phone. "You made me an offer to help. Remember?"

I wonder if her face shows agitation with me begging, sounding desperate.

"I want to see them before they leave, Diane. Sarah's Oxford days bring full circle my dreams of attending there."

"I'll try and get them over. But I'm not calling about *that,*" I answer, holding my ground.

The clouds cover the sun. I've no place to go—nowhere at all. "Diane, *why did you call?*" Her impatience is quite clear. "I'm interrupting. I'll call back."

"Damn, silly girl. Speak your mind. I have time. Lloyd left to meet Richard and Leah."

An emergency cigarette helps cope, begging a drunken rich bitch for money.

"Damn. Are you still there, Diane?" Her crisp crack means get on with it.

"I want to take you up on your offer." The wife doesn't sound any more confident than a child asking to go to the movies. She centers her mind and sucks in her haven't-exercised-in-weeks-belly. *I want. No. I need Helen's offer.*

A long silence gives reason my mother-in-law never meant her support. The grinding of my teeth deposits shame for at my age, begging for help.

"Never mind," I say, "I'll think of something else."

"You assume by my non-response the offer folds because of your desperation. How I wish we'd known each other better, Diane. Don't be so naive. I heard you the first time. But your insecurity wouldn't shut up."

I'm sorry, Helen."

Oh, God, the child, don't fucking grovel. Listen. I'm going to give you my best goddamn advice." She stops to sip something. I hear the ice cubes. "Fuck the children. They have their life. And long after you're dead, their lives will be moving along. If you can't whip your husband into livable shape, then leave. Your problem amounts that you're too bloody nice. You lack a backbone."

Her straightforward, brutal logic pisses me off. I say with contempt, "You're right, Helen."

"Decisions like yours aren't easy. You've been wallowing in shit for a long time. I know of Richard's indiscretions. He's a bastard. You *know* that."

A headache threatens.

"So, Richard has told you?"

Helen's catty laughter is her known cat-and-mouse game. With minimal options for free money without Richard's attachment, I have to prostitute my ass.

"Dear Diane, my son confides in me. I know when he takes a shit. I know when he's hit you. You see, Richard, my youngest, lacks leadership and maturity. Lloyd will never make him a partner."

I puff more on the cigarette. Recalling *that* morning when Richard bragged, it was him, not his brothers, who brought the firm Jared's lucrative business. "But Richard counted on the partnership from Jared Longview's deal."

"Why do you care anyway, Diane? Don't be a sap. If you must know—my husband knew Jared for years. As cruel as it sounds, Richard's eagerness to please took the load off Lloyd, who is no spring chicken as you Americans say."

"He *still* is my husband, Helen."

"Oh dear," she snickers, "I know all about *Julie's pregnancy*. And you still give a rat's ass about what Richard thinks. I'll give you the money. I need to do one good deed before I kick this goddamn world. Call me after your daughters leave. I won't make time to see them. There'll be other times. Good night."

"Thank you, Helen," I'm trying not to sounding as lost as she thinks I am.

*

Thoughts, torpedoing into the sea: craving runs through my mouth for straight alcohol. Gnawing my lips until the taste of blood occurs. Hands shake as if on fire. Sweating as if wearing a winter coat running a marathon—all means the wife's brink closes in. I thought if and when I could leave, freedom wouldn't taste so bitter.

*

"Hello. Helen?"

Why is she calling back? Am I ungrateful to want her money but not her in my life?

"Did you hear me, Diane?" "No. What did you say?"

"Child, where are you taking my call from, a cave? Never-you-mind, I guess you're in shock about Julie. *Get over* the cow. I paid for her first-class ticket back to Sweden. You know she's been pregnant before? Richard confessed that little horror to me also."

I refrain from sounding any weaker to her.

"Anyway, when my dimwit son informs me about this new dilemma, I threaten to tell Lloyd, who'll disinherit him because of the *one more* scandal to the Fletcher family name. Richard's news counts as a double whammy. Because of Lloyd's shit of an illegitimate grown daughter child back in London, it makes for a hell of an ironic must-see movie, I dare say."

Spotting another rainbow dissolves Helen's rattling on and on about her family's skeletons because I can checkmate better with what Sarah disclosed.

"Is there something else, Helen? *I do know all about Julie.*"

"Yes, I know you do. Richard told me about that detective you hired. I've often wondered why you didn't act on his findings."

"I stayed for my children, Helen. I know you consider me a fool for that."

"Diane. We must meet not here or at your house. A neutral location, I know."

I say anything to get her help. "I'll call you as you suggest."

"Lloyd told me at breakfast; the Longview deal has some new projects. I gather all my sons' occupation will be placed more to law and not fucking around." Her sarcasm ends with what I hear are sips from a glass.

"Helen, I can't thank you enough."

"No, I guess you can't. By the way, I won't be annoyed at the slightest if Sarah and Nina don't stop by. Your mother's priority comes first. I did call her and sent a dozen roses. Next week, I'll make an effort to visit."

"She'll like that."

"I have to go now, dear. Call anytime. Do try until you leave, keeping my son on a tight chain, but then Richard is way too quick for a leash."

*

Thoughts sitting alone in the park: Helen will help. Why didn't I mention the *other* awful truth about her son? Could my reason be that I *refuse* to believe my child, or am I afraid of Helen's seasoning the truth with her own horror stories? Who has the formula for happiness? Marriage, and despite three miscarriages, I gave him beautiful children. I put my family first despite everything from the plastic surgery, other women, and those beatings. I consider Helen's offer a reward for my marriage, her son, and, most of all, my stupidity. I'll stuff the money she gives me down my throat and plant kisses on her ass every chance I get. Will I ever speak to her about Richard? I don't know. As revolting and twisted as it is to admit, I still love Richard. The rain starts again. The next call I dial is Dr. Rose.

*

"Diane, how are you?"

"I want to talk to you."

"I hear the urgency in your voice. You didn't keep our last appointment. Today my time belongs to my sister Annette, whose flight leaves in the morning. Can you see me tomorrow afternoon?"

Press your forehead into the steering wheel because a headache pounds. You have to talk to someone.

"I may have time tomorrow, Samantha. *I don't know.*"

"Diane. I can't hear you. Listen. Do you want to talk now? I'm heading home. I'll put you on speaker. Diane. Diane. Do you hear me? Say something."

I say, replaying Sarah's story, "I can't go into much detail because I have to get back."

"Back to where Diane? What's happening?"

Painful, exhausting crying coincides with the rain. Tell Samantha a few sentences, unload, in a few sentences. Don't do this to yourself.

"My mother has cancer. My daughters are visiting her..." "Diane. I can't hear you. Are you crying?"

"Never mind, I'll call you tomorrow . . . *at least try.*"

"Diane. Diane. Diane. Don't hang up. Hello—hello. Damn. She hung up." I heard you, dear Doctor Samantha, but I didn't reply. I'm tired of the damn questions. I'm tired of people thinking they're superior because of my mistakes. This stupid wife does enough self-examination. I have to make my decisions and no one else."

*

Two more calls. Next is Ruby.

*

"Hello. May I speak with Ruby?"

"She ain't here."

"Are you her sister, Patty?" "I am. Who the hell are you?"

"I met your sister, who said to call when I needed to talk." "I'm hanging up if you don't tell me your damn name."

"I'm sorry. My day has been horrible. My name is Diane Fletcher." "Ruby went to New York to see her no-good ex-husband. I don't know why. She just left me a scribbled note on the table. *'I'm in New York. Call you later. Need to get things straight with Jeff'.*"

"Did Ruby leave a number?"

"No. When my sister gets a notion up her ass, not even a common-sense-enema can flush out common sense."

"I'll call another time. Wait. Do you know the number for a woman named I believe—Anna? Ruby told me Anna helps women find a place to live in New York."

"I don't have a damn number. Ruby made mention of her a few times from a letter Anna sent. I don't like New York, and neither does Ruby."

"Do you remember her name? Do you remember her last name, Patty?"

"*I think Walker.* I can't be sure. Why?"

"Can I hold on the phone if you look and see if Ruby left the letter?" "She tore it up. I don't know why. Sometimes my sister gets a notion.

Do want anything else?" she winds down the call real quick. "Please tell Ruby I called. Can I give you my cell number?" "I don't have any paper handy. Call back."

"Okay. Sure. Thank you, Patty. Sorry to disturb you."

No goodbye. Instead, I get a dial-tone.

*

The last call is to him.

*

My message to his voicemail: "Richard, I'm staying with my mother tonight. Nina and Sarah are with me."

THE END

Calculated Risks

SHE COULD NEVER sleep past sunrise. She opens the closet and throws my robe on the bed.

"Are you going to sleep all day? Call him, or go home and settle this mess."

A daughter's defiance can't ignore her presence. Sliding curtain hooks across their rods allows the sun to peel open my rather-not- wished-to-be-awaken-eyes, to my old room as a teenager, now my residence for over a week. Implicit obedience gives me little choice.

"The weatherman says no rain. Get up, Diane." "I need some coffee, Mother."

"A pot's ready. It's *not* free. I want to talk to you. Don't keep me waiting."

The daughter gathers the robe. She knows her mother's impatience, feeling its sting when the door slams.

Alone in a room painted peach, a white canopy bed matches the dresser. Two thrift shop Irish countryside landscape pictures her father bought in Ashville, and her grandmother's handmade, rainbow areal hook rug, are familiarities of carefree youth and not trapped, complicated adulthood.

"Are you getting up?"

"Don't yell. I'm here," I answer and pour the coffee Mother brewed and butter the toast on the saucer.

I remember Camille and me doing dishes, or Father talking nothing to everything of importance in the kitchen. I wish for those days; I won't be here long, I got plans.

She gives a bitter squint. Our talk won't be something I want to hear. "I know there's something foul when Camille's husband Alan, not you, drives your daughters back to your house so they can pack to try and leave on two standby flights after one day here. What the hell is going on, Diane?"

Thank God for hot coffee.

"They weren't here long enough for a damn decent bottle of wine between us. Sarah loves London. Nina loves New York. Leah loves the law. We could've talked over the damn phone."

"I'm sorry, Mother. Plans do change."

"I've something to ask you, Diane, after a few ladies from the church take me to breakfast. I want you here when I get back."

"What time?" "One o'clock."

"I'll be here, Mother."

*

Thoughts of envy: Samantha Rose pushes I'm losing weight. I'm aware not because of exercise. Right now, alcohol and prescription pills sustain me in between what food I can force down. We sit not in her office, but the park; a convenience for me and consideration on her day off. Samantha drinks bottled water, my habit when exercise mattered. She's quiet watching joggers and bicyclists. Our ages spread not in years, but her brilliance is recovering from life's catastrophes. I, the envious patient, sink without a lifeboat; she tightens her lip; crosses toned legs beneath a simple short sleeve summer dress.

*

I'm a bundle of no-confidence, bearing down a serious palm- dabbing-fix to my sweaty face.

She hands me a tissue and an extra bottle of water from her bag "Shall we end this session? You appear uncomfortable."

"No. One minute." I'm relieved and grateful for her emergency kit. "I've gotten away from water since not going to the gym. Thank you for seeing me."

"I don't have another appointment." Her hand rests on my forearm. "I *want* you to be okay. Do you understand?"

She doesn't have the usual pen and paper scribbling down her patient's ramblings. I decide not to ask. Figuring on her day off and our informal session is more for my benefit than hers.

"I guess I should tell you I'm not living at home."

The beginning of my B-rated movie comes out as natural as I can say my name.

"Why?" she responds without a blink of surprise.

Laughing and squirming for a comfortable position on a fucking metal park bench. A small three-letter-word, *that* three-letter word, I've asked myself all my life: '*Why,*' amuses me. I wish her water gift were straight, Gin.

"*What's funny?*" She leans in, removing her sunglasses. "Why are you not at home?"

The sweat wouldn't stop.

"Do you want to go to my office?"

My watch gives me not enough time to drive there. "No. I have to get back to my mother."

"It's ten now. How long can you give me?"

Just as I'm about to answer, a couple holding hands, about Richard's and my age pass. A clear view of my downward glance minus laughing sets the mood for her close up.

"*What's* happened, Diane, since we last spoke?"

"I've about two hours," I start the story, the one the doctor should have brought a pen and paper to record as I don't want to repeat it—not for a long while. "I've been with my mother for about a week after my daughters came to visit her. She has cancer."

"How is your mother? I remember you said your daughters were coming. Cancer took my parents. It's my sister and me as with you. So I do understand."

"Richard and I are living apart."

She looks neither bewildered nor surprised.

"Do you want to tell me the reason? I gather your decision has little to do with your mother's heath."

"I should've left long ago, but *I still love Richard.*"

Stupid admission hunches my shoulders into a visible slouch. Desperation needs a stiff drink, on a hunch that more challenging questions are ahead.

"Your scars are healing, yet your soul has no light. *What* are you willing to admit, Diane?"

Children and couples around us accentuate loneliness shouting inside my heart.

"Richard informed me Julie, his lover, and I can say for certain most of our marriage has been his mistress, is now pregnant." Thankful sunglasses shield my eyes. "I imagine close to six months now. *She lost the first child.*"

This time Samantha, with her mouth agape, is the one who can't settle into a comfortable spot.

"Diane, go on."

"Ironic, you'd say '*go on*' as is my full intention to go on with my life."

"Where is Julie?"

"It's laughable. Richard won't marry her. She's living with her family in Sweden. He wants a second chance with me. *In his case, it's a million-and-one second-chances.*"

More profound puzzlement crunches Samantha's face. "Will he support them?"

"I suppose."

"All this happens in a week, Diane?" "Yes."

She looks at the cloudless sky. "God creates miracles. Be grateful, Diane," she assures, by rubbing my back.

"Samantha, I've been through so much. Where's the damn finish line?"

"It's right in front of you. You must believe."

Doubts on that point keep me quiet. Richard's other darkness must remain my secret.

"Is there anything else, Diane?"

"I'm meeting Richard's mother and an attorney next week." "She's still going to help you?"

"Yes."

"Are you going to stay here?"

"I want to leave, which brings me to the next point. I've been in contact with Ruby, the woman I met at your office."

She shakes her head. "I don't know, Ruby."

I refresh her memory, "She's Dr. Bishop's patient. You saw us in the patient waiting room."

"*Now, I know.* Be careful, Diane. Dr. Bishop stopped treating Ruby for threatening my colleague with a gun. There's a warrant out for her arrest."

"I wondered why I couldn't reach her."

"What do you mean, *reach her*? Do you know where Ruby is?"

A long drink of water helps reshuffle our last conversation. "Ruby's sister says that Ruby is in New York visiting her ex-husband. I called because she knows a woman—a real estate agent, who helps women resettle in New York after abusive relationships. We had lunch once."

"Stay clear of her. Dr. Bishop calls Ruby a paranoid-schizophrenic. If you're moving to New York, I have contacts to help you." Her fingers squeeze her point. "Promise me you'll leave Ruby alone?"

"You're right. Don't worry," I change the subject with no intention of not contacting Ruby. We share the same history. And I know madness comes with the territory.

"Good. You don't need more problems," Samantha's smile tells me she's pleased she's won this battle. "How are your children? Do they know about the separation?"

Sarah's story and Nina's rage, still fresh, nails a final stroke to my marriage and devastating ruin to my and Leah's fractured relationship. Samantha's question brings me to the brink of crying, which I don't want to in a public place. Given a sad ending, I choke out the answer, "Some things they know, others they don't. Sarah goes to Oxford. Nina's finding her way in New York."

"You didn't mention Leah. We've never dug into that subject after all this time."

"*Leah,*" I barely can say her name straight, "my daughter still does her Chicago law spin. We can discuss her another time."

"Is there anything else? Have you told your mother Julie is pregnant? You said your mother has known about Julie and Richard's affair.

"I couldn't add to Mother's stress. I didn't tell her Julie is pregnant. *My sister,* Camille, suspects after noticing Julie and Richard leaving an obstetrician's office."

Guzzling down the water doesn't put a dent in my dry throat, craving hard alcohol.

"You can't carry this alone," Samantha speaks what I know. Lost fills my eyes. The tissue comes in handy.

"I know, *but* . . ."

"Diane, I see you're having a hard time talking. I can help." She does the reassuring shoulder patting thing. "Call me day or night." She peeks at her watch. "You have to go. We'll talk soon. I sense something else. Please eat. You'll need all your strength."

*

Thoughts driving back to my new home: what's happened to Ruby, how can I tell Mother about Julie, what do I say to Leah, and where will I go once this is all over?

*

"I'm home, Mother."

"We're in here having tea." Helen's accent wags from the dining room.

Caution scolds me for not returning her messages. A survey in the hallway's archway presents Helen with Grandmother's bone china, eating French chocolate truffles she bought in a box labeled *Café Dumont* and sipping tea from *Oliver's London Tea Shop*, another one of her decadent imported pleasures.

Mother, five years younger, in better days, would conceal blemishes, red blotches, and natural wrinkles. White nightgown visible under an untied ugly blue cotton bathrobe, bobby-pins keep straggling hair strains isn't the way she'd choose entertaining Helen's high notch eloquence.

"Well, don't just stand in the doorway." My mother-in-law's British accent demands way too much from me.

I don't dance, in Mother's home, to Helen's common trait of grating my nerves, despite her offer of help. Stubbornness waits for another invitation.

"Please join us." Mother requests me to sit beside her.

The daughter enters not because of her mother-in-law's commands; it's her mother's tea and favorite sweets calling for an end to Helen's visit.

"Are you okay, Mother?"

She manages a slow, *"Fine."* Her hands pull tighter the robe's strings. I sense by Mother's glances; there's a woman-woman- embarrassment, comparing herself to Helen.

Helen, unmoved, continues sipping tea.

"I hadn't a chance to call you, Helen," I rush into my part. "Have you finished visiting? Mother should rest."

"Unable to reach you," Helen sounds put off, ignoring my question, "Richard informed me you're staying with Ester. That's why I'm here."

"Mother, *not* Richard, is my priority, Helen."

"Ester," those fingers with diamonds a celebrity wears, taps Mother's hand, "we just have to get you better."

"I smell shit in the air. What's going on, Diane?"

"We've all been the other woman at one point or another, Diane. I told you, Julie and *that* baby are out of the picture."

Helen's bomb annihilates. My mother's fists feel like steel.

"What the hell *is* this woman saying?" Her loud voice pitches into a furious battle.

Helen's callous coldness in her face is a picture I'll never forget. Her tortuous death can't even give me satisfaction. Have I sold my soul accepting your money?

"Oh dear, I thought *everyone* knew." Fucking bitch twists the blade deeper. "Aren't you here because of refusing to forgive my son?"

"Everyone *but* me, Helen . . . I've been asking for days what the hell is going on."

Not slitting Helen's sanctimonious throat takes willpower. "I wanted to tell you, Mother, but you got sick."

"I informed you, Diane," Helen butts in, "Julie is home with her family in Sweden. Richard will assume his responsibility. Lloyd and I insist he sells the house, worth millions according to our real estate confidante George Miller, to pay monthly settlement payments to Julie and the child."

The gall after all he's put me through heaves disbelief punching my gut. "*What* are you saying, Helen?"

"You'll agree with me, Ester; Richard and Diane's marriage is over."

"He needs my goddamn signature. My name is on all the fucking property papers."

"Helen," Mother's anger rallies, "this is between my daughter and your damn son."

Helen re-shifts her body for a clear view of my mother. "Listen to both of you," her voice and face are unbending. "I've offered Diane money if she leaves Richard. Did you tell your mother *that*? We Fletchers stick together. We handle our shit, and at the end of the day, sit at the table as a family."

My fire explodes, "I've been through hell with your damn son, Helen."

"So tell me," she doesn't back down, "what woman in the world hasn't cried your same tears? He beat you before you two married. Stupid creature accepting his proposal. No woman can change a man." Bitch laughs, finishing her tea as if time is hers. "*We're all fools.*"

"I'm a joke wanting an abusive husband's love?" I scream. Out of the corner of my eye, Mother's silent tears kill me. "You hid so much," she whispers.

"When will you speak to Richard to put this all behind you?" Helen rams.

"Are you his mouthpiece?" I spill not giving a damn about her help. Mother clearing her throat, speaks, "Take me to my room, Diane."

*

Tension piles thick inside Mother's room. Her stiff hand waves me back from helping her to bed. Before you say a word, Diane, I want you to stay in a hotel for a couple of days. See Richard. Be a woman and handle your damn business. I have to process all this shit."

Her conclusiveness shatters me. "*Mother, please.* Camille is on bed rest until the baby comes," I say, hoping to jog her memory that she needs me.

"Clara Hill can come over. Leave tonight," she's adamant, "get Helen out of my goddamn house, and close the door behind you."

*

Helen's quiet composure watches me sit across from her. "Diane. *I'm sorry.*" She sounds insincere.

"I'll never forgive you for hurting my mother on purpose," I engage my frustrations, "I would've called you."

"Aren't you considering my offer?"

My will won't falter. "I'm your slave now? Why did you come here, anyway?"

"I wanted to tell you about Richard selling the house." "Richard should've told me, *not* you."

I hate that annoying laugh as she folds her napkin, placing it next to the teacup. She leans in and settles a hard stare. "My son is your husband, is irrelevant, my dear. I never meant to upset Ester. The words came and snowballed. I hope my offer makes up for my discourteous manners and rudeness."

Thinking of a stiff drink soon in my hands, I speak nothing to apologize for, "I'll take your damn money. I'll keep the appointment with you and your attorney next week. I want this done. Tell your son the next time he'll see me will be in the attorney's office. Draw up the papers relinquishing my share of the sale and all its contents, including my clothes, jewelry, and personal effects. I'll keep my car and my cell phone until this over. I don't want any of our savings either. Nothing."

"Are you sure, Diane?" "Please leave this house."

She gathers her things, a cue to walk her out. We stand on the porch.

Dusk ends one drama for another—finding a place to stay tonight.

She tightens my arm. "Honestly. Would you have been accommodating if I hadn't offered to help you out financially?"

I snatch her grip.

"Honest. Yes. Julie Myers came between us. Your son's behavior came between us," I replay my secret. Sarah's distraught, witnessing her sister and father together. "*Yes. Your son's behavior came between us.*"

"Goodbye, Diane. I'll see you next week." "Goodbye, Helen."

*

Thought in my mother's house before I find a hotel: her door closed. No sound. She must be asleep. Need courage solving problems from A to Z. Have four-hundred dollars in my purse. Need. Need. Need.

*

"Goodbye. I'm leaving now, Mother."

"Diane. Wait." She stands in front of the closed bedroom door.

"I thought you were asleep."

"Here's money for the hotel. I don't know how much you have." "I have enough," pride says.

"Take it anyway. Call me tomorrow. We *must* talk, Diane." "I know."

"Good night, Diane."

*

Thought checking into a hotel: alone.

*

Thought checking out of the hotel: alone. Need to return Richard's call, but coffee first.

*

"I don't want to talk on the phone, Diane, about the house. Meet me this afternoon at three."

"Not at *that* house, Richard."

"I swear not to touch you. Bring someone if you don't trust me. I'll expect you." The bastard husband's continual control ends the call before I can answer.

*

Thought racing for a solution: Samantha won't judge me. What will I do if she refuses?

*

"Are you sure, Diane?"

"Richard doesn't know who you are. All our sessions were cash. I've been careful."

Her long silence must mean she won't come. "Why this visit, Diane?"

"I said this relates to our house. I don't want to be alone with him. You *know* how he is."

"I guess the police can't help without a restraining order you never filed."

With all her digs, my doctor might not be the friend she claims. My last resort dealing with Richard is the gun I've hidden in the car's spare tire compartment. One-shot for him and one for me.

"Are you still there, Diane?"

"You know I've never pressed charges. Sorry to bother you, Samantha."

"Wait. I told you I'd help you. My questions are normal. I'll meet you, two-thirty, at a coffee house on Bend and Appleton, a short distance from your house."

"*Thank you, Samantha.* I'll see you in two hours."

"I'm going as your friend. Richard mustn't know I'm your therapist. Don't ask me to explain now. Just trust me." "I *do* trust you."

∗

She's on time. I crave a drink, not knowing how it will all play out. "Hello, Diane. Want some tea or coffee? We have time. Your house is less than ten minutes away."

"No. I'm okay. I bet none of your other patients are in my situation." "I need a cup of coffee." She hunts for a seat. "Over there. Can I get you a sandwich? *Are* you eating?"

Can't she turn off the doctor's quizzing? I can't remember my last decent meal.

"Yes," I lie.

"Good." She taps an approval on my arm before ordering a cup to go.

∗

Thought of the minute: why did I agree to meet so close to the house? What if a neighbor should spot me? How can I be sure Richard hasn't been to the Club announcing our house is for sale because we're getting a divorce? It's over. Get over it. Soon you'll be gone, and nothing will matter.

∗

"You okay?" Samantha asks. "You appear jittery, looking around at the patrons."

"We might run into some people who know me."

"Do you think rich people in gated Bend Hill have coffee here? I'd think they're happier behind their million-dollar castles." She laughs, drinking her coffee in a plain brown paper cup. "Did you ever stop here?"

"No." I laugh. "You're right. Wealth sets you apart."

"Don't fret. Your time here isn't long." She looks at her watch. "Do you still have a key?"

I show her the house keys. Thirst for a stiff drink shakes my hands. It seems forever since I've driven home.

"Let's go."

"I'm here, Diane. The owner said, park my car in the back. We should take one car to keep your husband's suspicion down."

"Funny, you know her. I mean, you live on the other side of town."

Samantha takes a quick look back to the stunning redhead with skin as pale as white paint. "She and my sister were lovers. Let's go. Meet me by your car."

*

My curiosity spins about Annette. Samantha's abruptness shows this can't be the right timing for my reasonable questions. Whether I'm fond of Annette, Richard is next on the menu.

*

I still recall Julie Meyer's car passing me from my house's direction when I reached the hill's four-corner stop signs. Slow the vehicle; pull into the driveway behind his black convertible *Porsche*. The car he and Leah drove to Mother's. Leah and Richard go beyond my worst nightmare. What should I do?

*

"Did you hear me? Shall we go inside, Diane?"

"Yes," I answer with as much courage as a blind man crossing a busy street.

A wife, more of a stranger, decides against using her key. She rings the front doorbell.

The bastard opens the door, yet barring the entrance. "I'm Samantha," my ally introduces herself.

His sharp cut to me feels as if I've done something wrong.

"I didn't know you were bringing someone with you." He hunches a whatever-shrug. "You should've told me, Diane. Come in." He leads us into the formal dining room.

"It's a lovely room, Diane," Samantha comments.

His unusual quiet studying her movements stiffens my posture. "Have you been here before?" he asks while lighting a cigarette.

Step in between them before he grills her. "Samantha lives near my mother. You said I could bring someone."

"I see. Odd, in all this time, Diane never spoke your name.

Samantha, is it?"

"Yes," her coolness answers.

"I won't keep Diane too long. I had wanted a private conversation." Walking about waving his hands, Richard points out, "See, I've brought no one. Yes, I did say you *could* bring someone. *Didn't I?* Are you married?" He sidesteps me to give Samantha a flirtation grin.

"No," she answers straightforward.

Richard's aggressive laugh and towering height don't shake her.

"I can't believe real beauty is without a few lovers or an ex- husband?"

"I didn't say I'm lonely. I believe your question, 'are you married?' I gave you my answer."

"How novel finding a striking woman with a sense of humor saying the *right* words coming out a perfectly shaped mouth. Too bad Diane never had you over before now. Let's get on with my business."

Samantha's gentle hand on my shoulder settles what she knows by my pulled in lips is my ill at ease.

"Diane," he clears his voice and speaks rather formal, "I'm selling the house. Mother said she told you. I assume since we're never going to live here together that it's pointless maintaining it."

*

Thoughts of nothing left: he didn't mention needing the proceeds for Julie's hefty monthly payment. He didn't say why he has to sell the house. I want him to be fucking honest about why we're not living together. I want to demand an answer concerning Leah. I want to hold the gun I left in the car to his damn head and unload all the bullets into it. I collect my wits, keeping a stern poker face.

*

"When will you put the house on the market?"

"My agent, David Wilson, will contact you with the papers to sign. I've already approved them. Wait in the kitchen or outside, Samantha. I've some personal things to say that are none of your business."

"Diane, are you okay?"

"Of course she *is*," his voice rises laughing. "I don't know what my wife has been telling you."

"I'll be okay, Samantha." "Where's the kitchen, Diane?" He shows her the way.

"Fix a drink for us, Diane—for old time's sake. Let's sit in the sunroom. I believe your favorite room," his request, I count as his last one.

*

Thoughts of a final time: as bad as cravings hunger for a drink, the desire to share air with Richard lessens by the minute. The wife mixes a gin and tonic and hands it to him. She finishes her drink. They sit across from each other. The sun shines, but all she replays is the last time they sat in this room while their children slept as he raped and beat her.

*

"Your friend is pretty." He puffs down his cigarette. "What would you have in common with a much younger woman?" He rattles the ice in his glass before sipping.

I can't stand his voice. I look at my watch and wonder how long I will be there. "What do you want from me?"

"I'm lost, Diane. Would you believe turning back the clock to when we first met? I wish I'd just screwed you without the marriage bit. We're too different. I'm sorry for Julie, and many *other* things. I'm not a monster, just a frustrated husband." Fucking watery-eyed bastard plays for sympathy to take him back.

I loathe him. Now is my chance. "Richard, I want a divorce, to be happy, and I don't care about Julie, but I once did." Humiliation tears my heart. "I *gave* you my soul. I asked to be loved, which, if you did, I *never* felt it for a long time."

He can't look me in the face, long swallows of alcohol empty his glass; he fixes another drink and resumes his seat.

"I wanted a woman," he begins after lighting another cigarette, "not a girl, who knew nothing except how to keep the house and take my orders. You never asked to attend college. I admired your teenage ambition when you showed me those fashion sketches. Diane. I tested you. I hit you on purpose, the first couple times, to see what you would do. You took the blame for my supposed anger. You took my shit. It was easy to pull you from your dreams because they meant nothing. And with that, I lost respect for you."

Boiling frustration screams, "*I loved you, Richard.* Why was that not enough?"

"*Love,*" he mimics me, "*is never enough.* You ate up my shit. You took me hitting you and fucking around. No real woman puts up with that. The reason I never left Julie is that she demanded respect. When I wouldn't marry her, she left with a tab to pay for our kid until they're eighteen. You cried like a weak child. Why didn't you call me on the *Julie thing*, years ago? I would've given her up. All you are and have been to me is a pretty face. There's no substance for me with you. What will become of you without the handout my mother has offered?"

All I can do is dab those demoralized weak ass tears. "You know?" "Mother and Father told me the arrangement well before you knew.

My freedom is selling this house. I can do this for my happiness *and yours. Our home is just a mailbox address.*"

My dehydrated lips press together. The finicality can't link together a summation with a man I married twenty-eight years ago.

"Your rationale is glass peeling my skin, Richard. I hate you. I hate you. *I hate you.*"

"I'm a Fletcher. You know that. I want you to remove what you want today. There are boxes upstairs for your clothes. You can have the jewelry. Even though you told Mother you didn't want it. I will sell all the contents except for the art pieces."

I walk over to the bar and pour straight whiskey. Tears plaster my skin. Turning to the bastard husband, I'm more confident than anything that ever happened between us.

"I don't want a damn thing, Richard. No clothes. No jewelry." Mental relief ignites with removing my wedding rings and placing them on the table. "I'll sign all papers next week with the attorney and real estate agent."

I've not seen this vulnerable part of him in years. He slumps back after putting out his cigarette. The whiskey glass tilts out of his fingers. It falls onto the rug. His hand holds to his head. His mouth pulls into a quivering line. Those intoxicating eyes I fell in love with—discolored in desperation red can't be wiped because I have my own to dry. As we reach for each other, the last embrace feels as empty as this house.

*

Thought driving down Bend Hill: Samantha allows me the privilege of silence. I'm alone and afraid.

*

"Please let me come home, Mother. I want to talk to you."

"Camille is in labor, Diane. Alan's parents are on their way to pick me up."

"Can I come home soon? It's been several days now."

"I'll be here when you want to talk, Diane. I told Camille I got a voice mail. You were settling things with Richard."

Settling things—a joke. I've been hiding in this hole, unable to sleep or think straight.

"Who's watching their son, Michael?"

"A neighbor has come over. We'll talk later, Diane."

*

Thoughts on the way to Mother's: in a hotel for three days, binge drinking, failure as a mother and wife push me to contemplate suicide. Mother saved me. She said I'm welcome; I need another bottle of something. Need Helen's money. I need to talk to Mother and Samantha. I need to call Camille. Where is Ruby?

*

"Diane, wake up. It's nearly noon. I've given you a few days solitude by staying at Camille's—it's time you and I *had* a frank talk."

"I should've called Camille, but now I'm in no condition to see anyone. I know she hates me for abandoning her."

"She and Alan have a girl." Mother is happy, and for that, I sit up even with a hangover. "She's named Ester Christina Diane. Camille took my first name and your middle and first name in reverse. She's beautiful."

The light in the room cracks into my eyes. We both look at the empty bottle of wine. I don't care. I'm happy someone, my sister, still loves me.

"Get up. Take a shower. Come and talk to me. Don't forget to bring that empty bottle with you." She closes the door.

*

Thought in my mother's house: Richard's presence inhabits all that I am. Guilt hits hard, and my failed marriage is my fault; a hot shower can't cleanse my thoughts of you, Richard. I still love you. People will think I'm a fool admitting these feelings after a mess of our marriage. Leah conjures rage, antagonism, and heartache. Where to go from here? I'm sure Samantha will have her say.

*

"Good morning, Mother." "How are you, Diane?"

Her snippy greeting requires lots of black coffee. "I'm better with each day, Mother."

"How *much* did you drink? Why don't you stop drinking so much?" "Don't lecture me. I bought a bottle of cheap Merlot. I *needed* it."

A narrow squint observes my redder than red-puffy eyes and dark embedded circles, the second I sit with her.

"Despite Camille's precious moment, a curse follows my other daughter."

"I want to be honest with you, Mother."

The more her glum face sags, the more I wish my coffee was that cheap Merlot.

"A lot weighs in your face, and it's not a damn hangover," she agonizes, shaking her head.

"Life," I give a short reply to my cup.

"How did this shit happen? War rages between my cancer and your battles with Richard. We're alone now. *Divulge to me everything.*"

She's terminal. I can't tell it all, even if her life depended on it about Richard and Leah.

"Helen spoke the truth about Richard's affair," I open with what she knows.

Mother's arms locking across her chest won't make this confessional easy.

"Helen is a spiteful bitch. The stories I can tell you. Where *are* your rings, Diane?"

Acetic acid churns in my mouth. "Give me the truth, Diane." "Julie Meyers," I mumble.

"Didn't your detective give you all the details about Julie? Are you saying Richard has been with her all this damn time?"

Blink hard not to cry, and give a partial story, because she'll never find out about it all.

"They first met in Santa Barbara on our tenth wedding anniversary." "Are you *telling me* the son of a bitch has been seeing another woman for eighteen years? I thought maybe a few years. And you *never* told me. Why?"

"I don't know. The detective gave me what he had. I stopped the investigation five years ago. I didn't want to know anymore. I got a facelift, breast implants, and liposuction. I wanted Richard to love me. Richard confessed to me a couple of weeks ago, the length of their relationship."

"Get me the damn twelve-year-old Scotch from my bedroom closet's floor. It was your father's."

The daughter finds the bottle and opens it. She drinks from the bottle before serving her mother.

"How can you be so calm, Diane?" she presses after a few sips.

"I'm not," I show a bit of a smile. "Helen's money gives me freedom. I'm on my own. I'm not the first. Damn sure won't be the last."

Mother steadies the glass to her mouth. It breaks me watching sadness consume her. Silence for a few minutes speaks for us.

"You deserve much happiness, my daughter." She toasts her glass to me. "You have a good heart. You're a good mother. Do the girls know?"

"They suspect a change between Richard and me. I'll contact them."

"What's next?"

"I have an upcoming meeting with an attorney, Helen, and the real estate broker. I sign the papers for the house, the divorce, and finalize Helen's agreement."

"I'm going with you," she insists. "No," I'm adamant, "I'll be okay." "What are you going to do, Diane?"

"Can you write me a check for five hundred dollars for clothes and the beauty shop? I feel like used furniture."

She looks again at my finger.

"Where are your rings? You could've pawned them. I'll give you the money. I want to know."

I feel the free ring finger. The solitude of loneliness, hold my head down. "I gave them back to Richard," I answer. "I left everything from make-up to shoes to underwear, designer clothes, diamonds, and even the pictures of the girls. I'm not even asking for any money from our accounts. I'm completely naked. I'll give back the car and change my cell number when this is over."

Her voice wobbles. "Are you leaving?"

"I know you're ill, Mother. I want a new start. I promise to come back."

Her hands rest on mine; she nods, I cry, she cries, "I left you alone on purpose, no matter how hard your sister wanted to call you. Goddamn, Richard. I'll write you a check. Take me to my room. Have you told me *everything*?"

"Yes," I lie.

*

Thought to help my mother to bed until she falls asleep: how could I have disappointed her so much? Please forgive me, Mother.

*

"Camille, I'm so happy for you. How are you feeling?"

"Diane. When will I see you? Mom told you the name for my daughter?"

"You made Mother happy, naming the baby after her." "She has your name also."

"I'm sorry I've been absent, Camille. I'll fill you in later. I promise." "Tell me. Does Mother know about Richard?"

"Yes, and *more*. I need to leave now."

"You sound tired, Diane."

"Don't worry about me. Just have to finalize things with Richard."

"I want to help you—a new baby or not. *Please* call me." Her worried voice emphasizes my state. "I'm still your only sister, Diane."

*

Thought on the way to the most important meeting of my life: beware. These people are your enemy. You should've taken someone with you. Samantha? No. You've imposed too much. The next life will include many friends.

*

Helen makes ready to leave no sooner than I open the door. "This is my attorney, Calvin Colfax," Helen introduces us.

"Where are you going?" I'm confused. "I thought you were going to stay with me."

"This is your show, my dear. These professionals will answer all your questions. Goodbye, gentlemen. I'll expect your call, Calvin."

The two men stand to shake her hand.

She cuts to me without a spark of warmth from that perfect make-up face.

"Of course," he nods. "I'll be in touch."

"Goodbye, Mrs. Fletcher," they bid her farewell and then turn to me. Alone. Afraid. My dry mouth hungers for a drink.

"I'm David Wilson." Richard's real estate agent sounds more human than a hot-shot salesperson. "Please make yourself comfortable."

*

Thought of observation: both men watch my movements from sitting down to crossing my legs to folding my hands into my lap. They inspect and dissect as if they know my whole history. I believe, by their tailor-made suits, crisp white shirts, patterned silk ties, and those manicured nails, to precise haircuts—my attire of a drab black skirt and jacket, no stockings, black pumps, bare face, unpolished nails, and hair pushed into a bun, colors me a discarded woman with little than two cents to rub together. These men don't know my story, a wife bearing the last name of one of the wealthiest families in the country. They don't see the woman I was yesterday has died. They have no idea of the woman's power sitting before them. How funny, neither does her.

*

"Will Helen be rejoining us?" I ask to break the ice, knowing full well she's gone.

"No." The attorney, I detect now, has more of a British accent. "We have all the signatures from our clients. Only yours is needed. I will notarize."

They both sit opposite the soon-to-be-ex-wife.

Extreme nerves steal my words. "May I have a glass of water?"

"Of course." The real estate man steps toward a desk's refrigerator to retrieve me a bottle. "Did you have trouble finding the address?"

"This is one of the father-in-law's properties. I'm not expecting to see any of the Fletchers. Lloyd has avoided me for months as well as Richard's brothers."

*

I drink my water. It neutralizes the end soon to come.

"Shall we get started?" David now sounds not so warm and fuzzy as he readies a stack of papers in front of him. "I have these documents for your signature. Mr. Colfax will notarize your signature on the addendum stating you forfeit your claim on all proceeds of the sale. Also, Richard Fletcher pays all subsequent taxes."

*

Thought of separation: the attorney hands me a pen. He directs where to initial and sign. He explains details. I don't cry while he talks because my mind is elsewhere. Images are stained. I remember starting with the architect's house designs and the thrill of seeing our home complete. Its naked grandeur slowly filled with paintings like Monet, antique this and antique that, one of a kind this to one of a kind that. Unobstructed views from large rooms to host lavish dinner, birthday, and holiday parties, allowed me the opportunity to wear enviable designer clothes and jewels. Showcase gardens producing abundant bouquets, acreage with paths I walked to lose myself, the horses Sarah and I rode, and the incredible sunset views against the mountains. All is left behind, including my Tiffany wedding rings. The wife, who endured the fights, the sadness, and the loneliness, is no longer the wife. He is no longer the bastard husband; I am Diane; Richard is no one to me *anymore*.

*

"Thank you." David shuffles the documents in a neat pile, placing them in his briefcase. "My office will messenger your copies. We have the address."

"*Okay.*" My voice trails off. "He must know what I've given up. I was once happy there at 15117 Bend Road. Thank you, Mr. Wilson."

"You're a lady, I admire. Not many women would walk away from this. Take care of yourself, Mrs. Fletcher."

He exits the room after giving me that salesman tooth-grin and handshake.

*

A severe lawyer pulls three envelopes from his briefcase. He places one in my direction.

"Open this one first," he instructs.

My hands shake, unsealing a handwritten letter.

The lawyer's face is void of expression. "Take your time. Feel free to ask me questions," the lawyer says calmly, barely shifting his posture.

I release a solid breath after a long drink of water. Each word must be read and understood because of its composer.

*

Dear Diane, What can I say? Much? No. Nothing except to wish you well. You've reminded me always of a child lost in a big city. I think you've been out of your element with my son. When two people marry, it's either for love or money. The reality is money will keep a woman happy when love leaves. In your case, love vanished, and you clung to it, not enjoying the money at your footstep. I don't know when I'll see you again, as I've gone for a holiday, in England's Lake District, with my sister Doreen. Once you get settled and if you wish, contact my attorney to let me know where you are. In closing, my dear, remember you can't make anyone love you. Love yourself and find a bit of happiness. I leave you well. Helen.

*

Can you go on? Do you want some more water?" "No. Let's finish. *Please.*"

"Here's the second envelope."

I open it reading along with his explanation and using his draft.

*

My client, Mrs. Helen Fletcher's wealth, comes from her father's textile mills and manufacturing plants. For this opportunity, she will afford you the sum of one million dollars a year for twenty-eight years, being the duration of your marriage to her son, named Richard Francis Fletcher. Should my client pass away, the terms of this agreement will continue with honor. An account established in your name requires your signature. All documents are present. The first payment deposited as soon as you sign this document. My client, Mrs. Helen Fletcher, has taken care of all taxes on such a yearly settlement.

*

I can't say anything; I accept the last envelope, the words are legal enough, I read them as tears saturate my lashes; even without mascara, my eyes burn.

"This is the last envelope," he points, "the divorce papers."

Considering the meal served me. What's one more dish to the plate? I open the package. As I read the first lines, my breath stops.

"What does this mean? Tell me."

"My client, Mrs. Helen Fletcher, has a son, Richard Fletcher, who will grant you a divorce under these conditions. You relinquish all claims to his estate, assets, now, and until your death. You do so with full knowledge of his inheritance from his own, and his family will be divided equally to your daughters, Leah, Nina, and Sarah. The conditions of the divorce are the alienation of affection, sharp unresolved and unrecovered differences, and mental cruelty. Please note, if you don't sign these papers, you forfeit my client's settlement agreement. If you do sign, the divorce finalizes six months from today."

"Where is Richard?"

"My client is out of the country." "Is he in Sweden?"

The attorney turns to look out the window. "Mrs. Fletcher, I can't say. My objective is to have these papers signed so both you and he can get on with your lives," his formal matter-of-fact position does not bend. "Do you have any further questions?"

"Richard's wealth is far more than twenty-eight million dollars—his mother's money to me. He's a liar on the terms. He's an unfaithful husband, a wife-beater, and . . ." I'm an inch away from saying he committed incest, but can't say the words.

The attorney walks to me. "Will you sign the papers, Mrs. Fletcher?" He snarls, shoving the pen in my face.

"What choice do I have, Mr. Colfax?"

"Listen. I give this advice to you because I have a daughter. I won't say more except sign the papers. Get on with your life."

His wisdom doesn't soften or validate Richard's terms, no matter how large my bank account will be. Taking a simple pen, to sign on all the right lines below Helen's signature and Richard's name, is no better than committing suicide. All of who I erased with a notarized seal and stamp.

"Do you have any questions, Mrs. Fletcher?" *Please,* call me Diane. No," I answer. *"Shall we go, Diane?"*

"Yes," I sigh, either because of relief or sadness. It doesn't matter.

His posture straightens as we exit the office for the elevator. Mission accomplished. He looks at his pocket watch after pulling a plane ticket from his jacket pocket.

We reach the ground floor without conversation.

"Where do you live?" I ask, maybe to keep from being alone. A pause before speaking, "London is my home."

I begin crying for why I don't know.

"You're a nice woman. I can tell in your eyes. I'm a good judge of character, Diane. I'll tend to the bank documents. Show your identification to the manager, Mr. Andrew Monroe, for the final detail. One thing, *live your life*. All this will soon pass." He extends a handshake then hails a cab. "Good luck to you."

"You'll send the final divorce papers to me?"

"My card. Contact me in my London office for questions and updates on your residence."

"You think I'll leave?"

"Diane," he nods and smiles before entering the taxi, "the world awaits you."

*

Thought of unknown: attorney and real estate agent complete their business. What will you do with Helen's millions; you might as well be dirt poor - your talents are no bigger than a dot, you need Samantha's guidance!

*

"Mother, I'm okay. Stay with Camille. I'll see you when you come home."

"What about Richard, Diane?"

"We'll be divorced in six months. Our house goes up for sale this week."

"Diane. I'll come home."

"Stay with Camille. Don't worry about me. I'll order some take-out."

*

Thought of uncertainty: keeping close to the house. Not hungry. Make a salad and open one of the wines I bought. No friends to call. Where's Ruby? Maybe Samantha will talk for a few minutes. Am I imposing? No. She'll want to know about the details. Call her.

*

Samantha eases with chopsticks. It would've been better to talk on the phone.

"Have you been to this restaurant before, Diane?" "No. Richard doesn't trust the holes-in-the-wall."

"I see." She frowns. "Try instead of your fork. Chinese tastes better with them."

Clumsy fingers drop food. Little bits get eaten. Hear Richard, '*Use the damn fork, Diane. You're embarrassing yourself and me.*'

"My next life will be different," I joke using my fork. "Have some Sake." She pours.

Giving my apology swallows better with alcohol. "I shouldn't have brought you to my house. Richard is an asshole."

"I heard your whole conversation from the kitchen. It's as if Richard was deliberately bullying you because he knew I was in the house. He's a vicious man. I've been telling you this for years."

She's right. Suck up those pity tears. "I've ended it all." "All?" I hear her question.

She orders Sake when the server comes to the table. I'm glad because drinking to me has become more important than food. Without alcohol, insecure fear buries my confidence and courage.

Samantha's poker face pounds my depressed state of mind, which should be happy given a fresh-start opportunity.

Sake drizzles into my throat, and I begin not caring about her judgment. "I've met with Helen's attorney. She's allotted me a million dollars a year for twenty-eight years of marriage. I've signed all documents selling my house and forfeiting its proceeds. The end stands before me. I'm free and no one to answer to." I laugh in almost hysterics. "*I'm free. I'm free.*"

"You've told me about the money, which is generous, but then, rich people have options. Helen's clean conscience allows her a better sleep, given all her son put you through." Samantha stares, quite composed.

"It fucking *doesn't* matter. I made the best decision for *me*. Everyone can kiss my ass."

"How insulting can you be?" She drops her napkin onto the table. "If I didn't care about you as a friend, I wouldn't be here, Diane. Over five years, I've listened to how Richard beat you, cheated on you, and sexually and verbally abused you. Do I need to remind you of your numerous trips to a gynecologist because of Richard's love of couple swapping?"

I could scream. Why am I here? Leave. I don't need Samantha.

Helen's money can buy me another psyche doctor.

"Wait. You know I'm your friend, Diane. Talk to me. What about your divorce?"

Sit back down because you know she speaks the truth. Pour more Sake.

"You've admitted on more than one occasion patients who stay with men like Richard are damn fools. I sense by your unemotional stare, puckered lips, and condemning head shaking; I'm a neat pile of weakness."

Samantha turning away means I'm right.

I ask her, "Do you know why I chose to start seeing you?" "No," she says, looking put off.

"I came because a neighbor, one of my few confidants, said you gave her the strength to leave her husband after forty years of marriage. You see, this man beat her just because he could. Her name is Mary Brooks, lives now in Italy while Mr. Brooks's rots in jail for conspiracy to commit murder—hers. He hired a hitman."

A flinch of her eye means Samantha knows Mary.

I continue because she must know as the tears are real, "Seeing you don't have any children, I made this decision, and not one I wanted, because I did deserve consideration for giving birth and putting up with Richard's shit. I relinquished all claims to Richard's inheritance, money, and assets. His money goes to our daughters. Helen's offer and Richard's settlement to our children required my signature for the divorce."

"*What* the hell do you get after all this time with him, after all the hours and years that you spent in my office?"

I sit up and state with conviction, "Freedom . . . I get *freedom*. I don't care about his labels."

"What goddamn labels? Why didn't you have your attorney? You've missed for good a chance for revenge of what you suffered all those years with Richard."

I hear her angry tone and don't even mind a stiff index finger in my face.

I can swallow all indignations because, as the British attorney said, *'the world awaits.'* I can feel no shame as Samantha implies my stupidity for continuing to be the victim by not having my representation. I can do this because I died when Sarah told me about Richard and Leah.

I find humor with giggling. "Richard's review of my long-running wifely performance reads alienation of affection; acute irresolvable and unrecoverable differences, to mental cruelty, being my darling husband's reason for divorcing me."

"You're kidding? He's abused you right down to the end with cracker-jack box legal bullshit. I can produce our files showing what he did to you. Why didn't you have an attorney? You could've asked me. I would've given you a referral." Her questions are valid. Her being upset is understandable.

I observe Samantha sucking down her drink and wonder which one of us will not get over my divorce. I knew my rights and still chose Helen and Richard's cyanide pill. Picking at cold food is a waste of time. Even Sake doesn't drown Samantha's hard facts.

"Abused women aren't stupid. Entrapment, love, fear, and money are their weaknesses." Absolute frankness must make the woman across from me, who knew me, understand my position. "Whatever I got or didn't get doesn't matter. I will no longer be a soft landing for Richard's beatings, endure rape as if a piece of trash, or undergo public and private vile insults, and *these* are just the good parts of the marriage."

She must empathize because relaxing facial muscles and hands, and showing me a small smile, mean I've not lost her friendship.

"I've been through a lot myself," I hear Samantha opening up after she orders more Sake. "I told you my lover hospitalized me before I bought my house, the one you visited."

"Why are you sharing this with me again, Samantha?"

"Education has no border to abuse. I feel all your pain, as your friend. As your doctor, I wear another hat to push you onto a better path. I'm sorry if you think me a cruel bitch."

My face lightens, and I willingly hug her. "Thank you, Samantha, a friend for life. Know that I want to leave Denver. You once said you have a name for me."

"Are you heading to New York?" "My daughter lives there."

She reaches inside her bag. "Here's her card. Your life next time this year will be different in a good way. My contact can and will help you."

I read the card: '*Cleo Miller*', with just a phone number. "Who is she?"

"A trusted friend—her organization *Lost and Found* helps women repurpose their lives."

"Women like me?" "Yes"

"Maybe she can help Ruby, alone in New York." Her scowl replaces that happiness to help me. "What's wrong, Samantha?

"*Why* are you still hung up on that woman?" "I feel like she's in trouble."

Samantha plops her chopsticks into her ginger chicken and refills her Sake. Her frown is still apparent.

"What did I say wrong, Samantha?"

"I don't know where she is. Dr. Bishop diagnosed Ruby, a dangerous psychotic who needs regular medication," I told you that, Diane," Grabbing hold of my arm doesn't feel like friendship. "Why are you hung up on her?"

Determination answers, "Ruby and I had *abusive husbands*. Talking to her helps me know I'm not alone. She's no threat to me. I've no damn friends except trapped trophy wives and girlfriends of Richard's asshole buddies. None of these women I care about."

Samantha is unfazed at my dripping tears. Her eyes lack warmness. "Promise to stay away from Ruby. I'll *always* be your friend. Cleo will make sure you meet people."

I nod, which she endorses, by reciprocating feather taps to my fingers. Inside I'm clear. My decisions will be mind. I will try and locate Ruby.

"I guarantee Diane next year will be different in a good way." A laugh lightens the mood. "I'll stay in touch with you. We're beyond doctor and patient. Do you know what you'll do?"

"I've no idea. I need to settle a few things first. Decisions for the first time are my own. I want so much more than eating at a restaurant Richard would disapprove of."

*

Thought at the end of dinner: Samantha drives away. Why didn't I tell her about Leah and Richard?

*

"Are you sure, Diane?" Her voice chokes. "I must and need to leave Denver, Mother."

"Damn, Richard. Help me into the chair. Sit in front of me so I can at least look at you."

Fluff her pillows. She's clenching my arm. Prepare for a sermon she's to preach. "Are you comfortable?"

"Tell me *what's* going on, Diane, because I'm damn tired of asking." "I've explained about the divorce and selling the house, *and Helen's settlement.* I know you think me a fool."

"You had promise and wasted it on a man who, in the end, tossed you out like garbage. For once, think for your damn self, Diane. Leave, if you've decided. Hell, I'll soon be dead. But before going, you must force accountability down Richard's throat for all you're not telling me." "Helen's money, no matter how I feel about her, gives me freedom.

Yes, I've sold my soul."

"Why do you cry out Leah's name? I hear you late at night when I can't sleep."

I yank my arm away, rubbing the indentation Mother's hands left. "You're hurting me."

"*Tell me,*" she demands in that stern motherly tone I heard as a child. "Leah and I aren't close. We've argued over the silliest things recently," I lie with conviction. My lips can't repeat Sarah's story.

Her mouth twists into an unbreakable pout; I know the sign. She is quite angry with me.

"Even on my goddamn deathbed, you *can't* be honest. I'll be in my room until it's time to go to Camille's for dinner. I'm sick of you and all these damn secrets. I think best you leave as soon as you get your shit together."

Remain calm.

"I've got to tell the children about their father and me."

"Do you what you must, Diane," she yells, slamming the door behind her.

*

From the bedroom, Mother's temper curses me. She curses Richard.
She wants me out of her house.
My hands shake, dialing the first number.

*

"Stop crying, Sarah. Divorce happens every day."
"I hate Richard, Mum. I'll never call him father again."
Need a drink. Replaying Sarah's story is killing me, hiding its depraved secret from Mother, Camille, and Samantha. The subject needs changing.
"I will take care of this, Sarah. He'll never hurt you again."
The more she cries, two things are evident—I didn't protect my children, and I need a drink, bad.
"I'm seeing a therapist for a long while ever since I saw *them together*. There's nothing to do because they're adults. It's so damn immoral. I'm taking a semester off to reason my head around this shit. When did you say you're leaving Colorado?"
"I'm going to New York soon, a short plane ride to London. Sarah? Are you there?"
I know she's twisting the ends of her hair and rocking back and forth.
Need a cigarette and drink to divert damn ready tears.
"I understand if you need to take a break from school. I promise to visit you."
"*He's* taken care of my four-year tuition and into graduate school. I wasted a whole year and a half trying to be like Dad and Leah, fucking legal briefs. Leah calls me brainless for choosing what I love, English Literature. I want to teach. I'm not like her. If only you knew the things Leah is capable of."
"I'm aware of more than you think, Sarah."
She bursts out, "I'm the goddamn keeper as you, Mum, of bloody secrets."

"What are you talking about?"

Close your eyes, wishing this all away.

"Do you know he came here often? He stands different, Mum. A good child learns respect, fear, and to keep her mouth shut after your father beats you and threatens to cut you off. I know about another woman, Julie, I've met her. He said you and him had some fucking open marriage. He's a piss-ass liar. I never told you because of fear he'd hurt me. I've told you about him and Leah because I've made up my mind to kill him if he ever came near me again. I don't need his damn money. I'm smart enough for a full fellowship when I choose to go back to school."

I crumb into a ball on the floor. Sarah's voice penetrates like hot needles. "Don't tell me any more. I knew about Julie. Your father and I didn't have an open marriage. He cheated on me for eighteen years. *Why* didn't you ever tell me about him beating you? How can I protect my children when I'm in the dark?"

"Don't cry, Mum. I'm glad those snobby rich shits, the Fletchers, are history. Their noses are so far in the clouds that not even God is good enough. I promise none of them will ever hurt me."

Move off the subject. I need to calm Sarah and myself. Insomnia and migraines are our enemies. "So, you've withdrawn this semester?"

"I'm an assistant at a quaint bookstore. I'll be fine, Mum. By the way, I heard from Aunt Camille. I'm thrilled for her baby daughter. I'll never marry, though."

"Don't say that, Sarah. Therapy can help you. I've needed someone longer than I care to admit."

She weeps, the mother cries. They cry like babies. The mother is afraid to ask the real reason this one chose to live far away.

"I know all of us will be fine." She sounds not quite sure. "It's late here, Mum. I'm tired."

"Love is wonderful. Sarah. Don't judge them all by your father. And please don't hate Leah. Get some sleep. I'll be in touch. I love you."

"Good night, Mum." Her usual happy giggle sounds forced. "All looks better with a pink pill, a drink of whiskey, and a couch-talk to your neighborhood shrink, doesn't it, Mum? At least it does for me."

*

The immediate thought of failure: can the wallet picture of my girls with Santa be tainted? We were the center of each other's lives. We were family. What have I done to my daughters? Did Richard molest them all? Call Leah. Nerves unravel. We've not spoken since she visited with Mother.

*

"I've left two previous messages. I need to talk to you, Leah. *Please* call me."

*

"Hello, Nina. I know it's late. Do you have a few minutes?"

"Are you okay?" You sound groggy. Is this a good time? You seem half asleep."

"My new roomie had a party last night."

On top of everything else, Nina, with constant changing addresses, roommates, and jobs, needs my help. Breathe. Don't lecture.

"I'm living in a Village studio with Alexandria, a stage actress. Luckily, my cell number hasn't changed." Her giggles don't ease my worrying.

"Your father and I are getting a divorce, Nina. We're selling the house. I'm starting over in New York with an apartment for us. You won't have to worry anymore about a place to live."

She's quiet. Suppose she doesn't want me there? "Nina?"

"You're calm, and I'm not upset. How's that for life? Dad is a monster. Why do you think I came home only for Christmas Eve and left before New Year's? I'd hear you crying in the corner of the house. I've seen your marks. Fuck. I couldn't ask questions with him hovering, listening. I know his capabilities. What a fucking mess. I wanted you to leave as I did. Why did you stay?"

Her question requires truth. Can guilt separate it? "I loved your father. I stayed trying to make a home for you girls. Guilt gives me a first-class ticket to hell."

"Don't, Mom. I love you."

She didn't mention Richard abusing not just Leah. Fear of her answer stops me from asking.

"When are you coming, Mom?"

"I think in a week. There are things to do before leaving." "Have you spoken to Dad or Leah? Was Sarah relieved?"

"I'll take care of your father. Leah hasn't returned my calls. Sarah is glad."

"I *believe her,* Mom. Leah mirrors him thinking you're unintelligent. I've heard them say awful things. Couldn't you see how he favored her with excuses because she took an interest in his work?"

Swallow. Breathe. Brace yourself. "Did Richard *ever* touch you . . . or Sarah?"

"Dad is a monster, Mom. I protected Sarah and me. I don't *want* to talk about it."

Stop her temper. "Settle down, Nina. My divorce finalizes in six months. So much I didn't know in my own house due to Richard raging constant wars."

"I don't want to see the fucker. I don't want to see my twin, the shitty bitch, Leah."

Camille will be here soon. End this call.

"Nina, Camille expects your grandmother and me for dinner. I must wake her. Know I love you. Your father won't ever hurt you, children, again. I swear it. By the way, Camille had her baby, a daughter named Ester Christina Diane."

"Mom, let's talk later about the details of your trip and plans. I'll call Aunt Camille. I love you. Don't ever forget it. I don't lose sleep over my father and my sister."

*

Thought of concern: why won't Leah return my call? What if I can't bring back my girls as sisters again? Where is Ruby? Phone rings. Need a drink. I am not prepared.

*

"I want to talk, Diane. I didn't think it a good idea showing up at your mother's."

"*Sure,* Richard. We need this *last* conversation."

Bite down. Don't ask where Richard was. You know he was in Sweden as you were signing away your life.

"I have a buyer for the house." "So, I assume, Richard."

Close your eyes. Trace your life. Not out of high school but accept his first beating. Teenage virginity lost in his family's candle-lit, Telluride mountain chalet. Endless happiness flowed on your wedding day. Recall his happy tears after the birth of the twins. Wasted years dumped down the goddamn sewer.

"Diane, did you hear me? I wish you well. Do you have an investment advisor for Mother's liberal settlement? You're not good with numbers. I recommend Bill Moore's firm. I'll call him."

Ask for his help? I'd instead take a bullet to the head. Light a cigarette, and say what's on your mind.

"I'm sorry, Diane."

Now is your chance—bury him. Don't blink twice. "I don't need your damn help. You're *sorry?*"

"I *am* Diane."

"Sorry about your affair for most of our marriage, your bastard child, you beat me, *Leah,* and your control. The list goes on."

"All of it. Wait. *What do you mean, Leah?* I *never* touched her."

"I *never* said anything about you touching Leah. I've been harboring something inside me for weeks."

"What? You know all about Julie." "You've opened another door."

"What the fuck are you talking about, Diane?"

"Sarah confessed to seeing you and Leah kissing when you visited London."

"Diane—that is a lie. It's a fucking goddamn-damn-lie."

Stuttering reveals he's lying. I know sweat drips from his temples. Foul spit slobbers from his lips. Hands balled into fists ready for warm flesh—mine.

"You son-of-a-bitch, I know you fucked your daughter. Sarah wouldn't lie. It makes sense, a child growing into adulthood siding with you against me. An adult has to press charges. She won't, or she would've. I could kill you and gladly take a death sentence for what you did. Did you touch Nina and Sarah?"

"Leah *is my daughter*. You're accusing me of a despicable thing. Have you been spreading these lies about me? You'll pay if you have."

Light another cigarette.

"Your threats mean nothing. Divorce papers are signed and recorded. Tell your mother to stop my settlement. Don't. I'll go to an attorney with your daughters, report you to the bar, and I will make sure all of Colorado knows a fucking incest pervert lives among them. If you come near my children again, I'll take the gun you gave me and blow your damn head off. I promise you."

"I've done many things in my life, Diane, and I'm not proud of many. What you accuse me of isn't one of them."

"You, your bitch, and your bastard child can go to fucking hell. Goodbye, Richard."

*

Thought to descend into a dark place: if I don't believe Sarah's story, I'm a bad mother. If I believe Richard's story, I'm a fool. God, help me.

*

"Leah, this is your mother. Please call me."

Mother's knock interrupts another re-dial to Leah, whose avoidance disturbs and hurts.

"Camille is on her way. Get ready."

Humor slaps me hard, and it's not funny. Open the door. Mother leans against its frame. What has she heard and not heard? I won't tell if she doesn't ask. Not in the mood for another inquisition.

"I'm almost ready, Mother."

"Meet you in the living room, Diane. I have something to say."

*

"Are all the calls done, Diane? You looked frazzled." She knows me well, giving a subtly raised eyebrow. "I've not reached Leah."

"Did you speak with Richard?" she prods. "He called. We spoke. It's over."

Restrained words don't sit well. Mother's poker-face coyness has its history with me. Why doesn't she admit to eavesdropping?

"What are the details of the conversation with Richard? When do you leave?"

"I'm going to find a place, Mother. I'll be back soon." Her continual probing intensifies uneasiness. "*I see.*"

"I'd think you'd be happy for me with all I've been through with Richard. You're ill. I *hate* Denver. We're at a crossroads, and I got to see my girls. Try and understand."

Remorse swallows me. Mother is dying, and I'm abandoning her. I'm not only a bad mother, a stupid wife, but also a horrible daughter.

"Not to worry, Diane." A small smile finally finds her mouth. "Camille is here. I'm happy for you. Life carries on. Richard deserves everything he gets *in this life and the next.*"

Breathe before bringing up another taboo subject. "Have you changed your mind about treatment? I can help you."

Mother's iron face seals into a defiant head held high. "My decision remains."

Camille's footsteps are on the porch. "I'll let her in."

*

Thoughts of lost a family: why wouldn't Richard allow us to be more a part of my family? How can I explain paranoid control of checking my car's speedometer, listening to my phone calls, or forbidding visitors when he was home? Sneaking off to see Samantha, Mother, or Camille is a rich wife's prison.

*

"Why so quiet, Diane?" Alan, my protective brother-in-law, jumps into my thoughts.

All eyes fix on my mouth full of Camille's peach cobbler. More Merlot requires answering.

"I'll miss all of you," I cry out.

"We can't believe you're leaving, but then it's more than understandable." Alan appears quite sad. "New York is a big place. Where will you live?"

"Nina and I will share an apartment—after that, I'm not sure." "You need a plan, Diane." Mother forces my hand. "What is it?"

Keep calm. Force down a long drink.

"I'm not going sit and lunch at *21 and shop until I drop,* Mother." "Helen's settlement," Mother moves in, "is substantial beyond means. Why?"

Pour more wine. "I don't know, Mother."

Contempt colors her cheeks red. "The bitch knows her son made you miserable. It's *blood money.*"

"Helen is offering a million dollars a year for each of my marriage." More of the wine helps darken my family's gawking. "Truth is I'd give it all back to make my relationship work. I love Richard despite his faults." Honest-twisted admission forces down another long drink. "Will I ever be happy? Who the fuck knows? "

Camille's arms catch mine. "One day, you'll find happiness. *I know you're hurt.*"

Mother twists her mouth. I dread her next words.

"I'm only leaving to find a new home," I say to appease Mother. "I'll return."

"We'll take care of Mom. Don't worry, sis," Camille promises.

I feel more of an outsider as the evening ends with an armful of unspoken truths.

*

Thoughts of the family business: Mother won't speak to me without raw arguing. Camille doesn't need me. She got her family and Mother. Richard's rules of separating me from my family have become permanent non-existence. Having me around doesn't make a difference.

*

Camille and I walk to the end of her driveway, and I chuckle because even at this late stage, Richard's shadow is still with me.

"You know, Camille, my car is a Richard-purchase after a Christmas Eve fight. I can't shake that bastard."

"He'll soon be history. By the way, Diane, now that we're alone, what happened to *that* woman?" Camille brings up Julie's name while looking back toward the porch where Alan and Mother wait.

My attention isn't on Camille's question, but instead on Mother's slower walking, and significant energy, appetite, and weight loss. All signs point to death. Thoughts of Richard and Leah, Richard and Julie, the inevitable end of my marriage, and my uncertain future, no matter how worthy of robbing my sleep, today aren't necessary. "I'm worried about Mother, Camille."

"I'll watch over her. Get your life in order. Come back to us soon."

"She's stubborn, Camille. Mother refuses treatment."

"I have a solution. Roberta, a church member, holistic and cancer specialist, arrives back in the country after assisting *Doctors Without Borders*. We'll introduce Mom. Roberta can be persuasive."

"Good luck." I smile at my sister's initiative. "Mother can be a bitch at times, herself."

Our laughter brings a hug, one to me, not often enough. Alan calls out, "Camille, are you coming?"

"The other woman is Richard's mistress," my embarrassment rushes out.

Camille's wide-eyed shock is nothing to me because I've had a front-row seat.

"Tell me everything after you've moved. I need to get back. I'll pray for you, Diane."

"*Everything?*" I mimic thinking of my hidden treasures. "Yes. One day I'll tell you a real bedtime story."

*

One more phone call tonight.

"This is Diane Fletcher. Is Ruby home?"

"Ruby doesn't live here no more," her sister Patty yells back.

"How can I reach her? Is she in New York? I'm asking because I'm moving there."

"Last time we spoke, she was visiting her daughter in Boston. I don't have the address."

Breathe. Relax. Don't rush. Don't upset Patty, remember she's short on patience and would hang up if provoked. "Do you have a phone number for Ruby, *please*?"

"Wait. Shit. Nobody calls me."

Patience comes and goes until Patty comes back to the line. "Write this down."

Getting the number and address means one friend in a new city. I don't care what Samantha says. Ruby won't harm me.

"Thank you, Patty."

"Tell her I boxed up all her shit." "Goodbye, Patty. Good luck to you." A disconnect means *fuck-off.*

*

Thought of reinvention: who is this woman? Outdated French-roll cut into a headache-free pixie. Luggage, Mother's gift: both of them packed with new body-conscious clothes and lace underwear. Pulse bangs blood into her heart; she wipes happy-sad-tears. Insomnia passes, giving a full night's sleep; she turns forty-five on her next birthday, January will be the year *2000*. Is she ready? Can she forget everything leading to this moment? Apple red lipstick retrieved from a *Chanel* purse, the reminder of her past with *him* when the money ran like water. She's a new woman seeking no more trinkets from a man. She studies reflections of particular make-up concealing healing scars from his beating months ago. She'll survive, manicure and pedicure polished in perfect cherry blossom red feel liberating. *He hates* red polish—soft pink looks best. The refuge has been her mother's house since leaving *him*. *Independence* is a plane ride away.

*

"Thank you for taking the car to Richard's office."

"I don't mind," sweet Alan reassures me, "my dad can follow me over in the morning. We'll handle it for you, Diane."

Alan switches the radio to classical music; it's playing La Boheme, Richard's favorite. I chuckle. Even my last hours, he's still with me.

"Give the envelope, in the glove compartment, to the receptionist on the 24th floor. Inside are the car keys and the cell phone. I cleaned the car. I've disconnected the number."

"Odd, you would give him back the phone, Diane, having lived here all your life." Mother points out another fault.

"It's a clean cut off. Richard bought the phone and the car," I say quite aware of my intentions because I've had years to prepare for this exact second.

Mother's fingertips touch my knee.

"All your life is here, and now you're leaving," Mother says with a worrisome expression.

Torment chokes me, stretching my arms around her fragile shoulder bones.

"We'll take care of everything, Diane." Camille turns around from the front seat. "I'll miss you."

Regret carries its toll, ruining my make-up with its sobs.

"I'm sorry for my life being so fucked up. Kiss my niece and nephew. Take care of Mother. Forgive me for Richard." Camille sniffles, "It all appears final."

"Diane," Alan utters, I know this decision to divorce and leave home hasn't been easy. Richard is he's a man with his own set of rules. He wasn't one to invite me to your house. I felt like a fifth wheel at the Country Club. I'm not a rich golfer. My bank account levels from paycheck-to-paycheck. "

"Alan, Richard's family lives by judgment and control. They *are* the Fletchers."

"We don't blame you, sis. Richard wasn't part of our family's equation."

Camille's serious face looks at mine. I catch Alan's sad eyes through the rear-view mirror. Both of them reduce me to a small, nothing being Richard's wife.

"We've had our differences. Half of which I never meant to say to hurt you. I love you, a daughter. You look good." Mother's compliments mean more than she'll ever know as she plants a kiss on my cheeks. "New York is a good start. Nina needs you. Hell, I'd go with you if I could."

Mother's hands run through my hair. This faint gesture lifts my spirits on for a journey taking me away from my family. It's the first time in weeks we both laugh together. Her nod gives me what I've longed for—her approval.

"Those New York men don't stand a chance," Alan pokes in as we pull up to the airport passenger unloading lane.

He removes my luggage from the truck. I see him place them on the curb.

The lingering breaks my heart, but I can't open the door. "It's time, Diane," Mother gently nudges.

*

Father and I shoveling snow, Camille and I race up the steps from school, and Mother in the kitchen baking and cooking better than any restaurant to place on a dining table. We ate more meals than I can count. Memories so many not thought of until now.

*

"You don't want to miss the plan. You'll be okay. What are you thinking?" Mother jolts reality.

"Nothing," I whisper.

She steps out and opens the back door. Her hands reach for mine.

I stand before my mother and let honest tears flow. "Don't hate me. I'm sorry."

"My, Diane, I love you," she sobs back. "This *must* be your time."

A long sigh comes. I'm ready after dabbing my face and clearing my throat.

I give one more gigantic hug to Camille, joining us. I soak up her open kid grin, the one always melting my heart.

"Call me. I'm here for you, sis," are her last words. "Thank you, Alan." I mean it with a kiss to his cheek

"Take care of yourself, Diane. I'll keep prayers for you," he whispers back.

*

Waving goodbye carries me into an unknown dimension I'm neither prepared for nor want. Terrified is what I am. I want to turn back. I don't. Get through airport security. Go to the bathroom, freshen my make-up. Head to the bar. I've five hours to kill.

*

Thought of lost: boarding the plane. Samantha couldn't come; I never spoke to Leah. I didn't call Ruby. Wonder what *Richard* is doing? Wonder what I'll be doing a year from now?

*

Nina jumps around like a child on Christmas morning with an excited voice taking over the bag claim, "You're here with a haircut, making you look years younger. I love it. Today is the best day of my life, Mom," her teary voice whispers into my earlobe. "You're here. We're together. Everything is good."

Nerves about this mission eased after the tenth hug. I belong here.

"Your hair comes to your waist and is *quite* red, Nina."

She giggles and giggles, bringing out a grin or two from me. I won't miss Denver.

"I love my bangs," she rattles on while hailing a taxi. "The colorist chose chili pepper. I feel *super* sexy. My agency gets me tons of print work. There's a chance for me to do some work in Paris. We should go anyway and have Sarah meet us. I'm so glad you're here, Mom."

Catching my thoughts and breath is a juggling act between a hectic airport and Nina's full-blown energy and confidence. Maybe the daughter doesn't need looking after. Instead, it's her mother who needs a lifejacket.

"Where do you live, Nina?"

"I'm apartment sitting in lower Manhattan for a photographer and his partner. Did you sleep on the plane? First-class is a treat. Are you hungry? I bought some things, just in case."

We travel through traffic passing cars, buses, pedestrians, then one brownstone after another, putting a mental distance between Mother, Samantha, and Camille.

"Nina, I'm not hungry, but tired."

"We're almost there," she alerts into a tree-lined, older residential brick apartment neighborhood.

New York is front and center. Freedom without Richard's shadow tastes sweet. I can breathe, not hearing his voice as people are buzzing about the streets, or sitting for an afternoon lunch at a sidewalk bistro.

"I'm glad to be here, Nina," I say with full conviction.

*

Thoughts of feeling anew: my temporary home on the eighth floor overlooks tree branches. No open sky except sun streaks hitting the window. I slept well despite hearing the neighbor's music and them coming home all hours. Where's Nina?

*

"Nina?"

No answer. Wandering out into the practically empty-white-bare-walled apartment gives me concern about my child despite her display of independence.

She left a note taped to the bathroom door.

*

Mom, I had a sunrise photoshoot today for my portfolio. I'll be home around three. Make yourself at home or explore the neighborhood. I've told the manager you're staying here. Don't freak out if you see him, a thin, bald man with a white beard. Love Ya. N.

*

Thought here alone: call Mother and let her know I'm okay. Call Samantha. Call Ruby. Think about reaching Leah when you feel like it. Find the business card of Samantha's contact.

*

"I made it safe, Mother. Nina isn't here, sends her love."

"We're okay back here. It's still raining. Are you *happy,* Diane?"

A bare ring finger, ending divorce, stirs a blank. Smoking calms me. Happiness, as Samantha says, is about finding treasure. I'm not a good hunter, so my quest will be a long one.

"Are you happy?" she repeats.

"I hope one day, Mother. How's Camille?" I detect shortness in breathing.

"She and Alan took the kids to the doctor for checkups. Did you reach Leah? She called last night. I don't know your new phone number to give her."

Leah doesn't conjure up one single happy thought. *"I'll call her.* I don't have a phone yet. I'm using Nina's old phone."

"What are you going to do today?" Mother's question gives me no real purpose.

"I don't know . . . unpack, explore the neighborhood, and get a phone."

"Don't call Richard. Promise you'll make a clean break?" Her request sounds more of a demand.

"Why? It's over."

"He phoned here last night wanting to speak to you. I told him you left, he asked where. I told him I didn't know. Warn Nina not to call him."

"Mother, don't get upset. Nina or Sarah won't betray me. I'll *handle* Richard."

"Be careful of Leah, Diane. She's like Richard." "What do you mean? I haven't spoken to Leah."

"I'd like to rest, Diane. A mother knows her child. Need I say more? Call me tomorrow."

*

Thoughts of worry: will Richard dare come here? *What does* Mother know about Leah? Take a shower. Call Cleo Miller, Samantha's contact. Need to let Samantha know I'm okay. Why did I wait so long to leave him?

*

She speaks straight away, "Sam informed me about you, *but everything?*" She cackles, talking, "You will do that, I'm sure."

I cut to the chase. "I must find a home. I have the money."

"*Lost and Found, my underground* non-profit has connections throughout the city. I'm a sewer rat finding food and shelter for women in need here and there." She laughs. "I feel shit tastes better when swallowed with humor. You in shit, aren't you, Diane?"

"Is it possible to meet you today, Cleo?" "I have time. Where are you?"

Even this simple question shakes me. I don't know.

"I'm staying with my daughter, who is house-sitting. She's not here." "I'll hold. Find me *the* address, Diane."

I can't let the New York-don't-waste -my-time in her voice scare me.

Get over it. I need this woman's help. "Yes. Okay."

Finding where I belong isn't easy. I search through Nina's bedroom. Her historical neatness leaves no clues. A metal desk, one sofa, two folding chairs, a living room reveals nothing. Dig through kitchen drawers. Last resort plows through the trash. Bingo. A take-out delivery receipt shows my location.

Apologizing, "Sorry to keep you." I give the address.

I know where you are." She sounds relatively calm. "A tea house five blocks from you called *Tea for Two* will be perfect. Meet me at noon."

"Are you far?"

Her laughter resurfaces. "This is New York, land of cabs and subways. I'm fifteen minutes away. See you then, Diane."

*

Thought of wondering: what the hell am I doing? Mother is dying. A million dollars in Colorado could set me up better. Nina doesn't need me. Make a new start. Camille promises to help, get settled. The family is a quick plane ride away; Nina wants you to stay. Stepping into *Tea for Two* transports me to China. Servers dressed in traditional clothing. Private rooms, wooden floors, bamboo covered walls, paper-divider screens, low tables, embroidered cushions, walls display intricate ink sketches of its countryside. Bach's Sonata adds its absolute serenity. My date arrives on time.

*

"I'm Cleo," a radiant, statuesque woman with make-up-free, smooth chocolate skin, introduces herself. Her arms open wide as if we are long-lost friends.

"How did you know me?" I ask.

"Noon and no one else waits for a seat," she deducts with a wide grin.

Tripping over my confidence, comparing Cleo's looks to mine, I clutch my purse as if a scared tourist in an alley.

"*Pleased to meet you*," I say, exhaling.

Our hostess knows Cleo. They nod, and we walk to a private room of a low wooden table and rectangular tapestry pillows. She bows before leaving us.

I'm grateful for past yoga classes; sitting crossed-leg isn't a chore. Swallow pride and speak honesty to Samantha's connection, whose expressive doe-eyes watch my movements.

"Are you a tea drinker, Diane?"

My view over bamboo walls and paper doors reminding me of my last dinner with Samantha, who, in her way, would say, '*Relax*.'

"Not really, Denver is more of a coffee town."

"I like their *Tiger Eye Ginger*. Try it," she pushes in a Samantha way. "Our host will bring us a pot."

Forcing an agreement, I say, "Okay."

Even if vodka laced this tea, I'd still be on edge. Control over my decisions is something I vowed never to forfeit since Richard.

Compared to Cleo's closed-eyed quiet until our tea comes—the tourist fidgets. Unaware of my protocol to pour or not pour the tea, thinking her silence must be a test, I decide to break the ice and pour our drink.

"How do you know Samantha?"

Another pause permits her eyes to open slowly. "Sam and I attended Columbia," gentleness speaks. "Our friendship grew into a sisterhood. We've worked projects together—a student-suicide hotline, homeless shelters, even set up a halfway house in Brooklyn. She helped me financially when I divorced. From time to time, she sends me lost little kittens like *you*."

"Samantha is . . . *was* my therapist for years, Cleo." "Drink your tea, Diane."

She sips hers.

"It's good. Thank you."

"We all need a bit of therapy in our lives. Think about how long we live. Not all days or years are perfect dresses."

Her logic and wisdom, or maybe tea, weaken my barriers.

"Are you *prepared* to start all over, Diane?" Cleo's stark question hits me.

"Yes," I say with as much certainty as a stranger to New York can. "If I help, your *Ex* must remain that. I don't need or want to waste my time. I won't allow danger to others associated with me. Am I clear?" "I'm done with *him*." My answer, this second, feels sure. "What else can I say?"

"Alright, Diane, Sam said you are in dire straits. My intuition tells me to believe her."

"And me?" I push for her trust.

"Time will tell." She studies my hands, twisting one another. "Calm yourself. I *will* help you."

Sweat waits around my scalp. "What do you charge?"

"My fee, a life-changer, is simple. You pay one month's rent for *Lost and Found*—three thousand-four hundred dollars. Also, volunteer after you get settled. We need women helping women."

"I have the money. What will you do for me?"

Cleo squints, giving a wide grin. A slight laugh follows, repositioning her legs. Her silence as she drinks her tea breaks with calmness, "I like your style. You must've been through hell and back. I'll find you a safe place to live, my dear. Be your trusted friend. And most important," she touches my cheeks, "give you back dignity. I see he beat you."

Water seeps into my eyes. Cleo's hold won't let me turn away.

"We at *Lost and Found* have all been through the mill, hell, and much more." She unbuttons her blouse without flinching. Cleo lowers her shirt.

The black-lace bra doesn't draw my attention. I gasp. We share permanent cigarette burns, dotting our lower backs.

"The wrong man *can and will* kill you, Diane."

Yearning understanding for my weakness, I ask, "How did you leave?"

Pouring more tea, she hardens in a voice, grabbing all my attention, "It took me twenty-five years, three broken ribs, a fractured collar bone, and many unmentionable cases of abuse before escaping from a prominent Paris surgeon. I sold my wedding rings to come here. I prostituted on the streets and slept in rat-infested buildings. One day a man saw me in the rain with barely enough clothes to cover an ant. He became my guardian angel with substantial means. He paid for my divorce. We married. He sent me to Columbia University. His heart attack left me a wealthy woman." She laughs. "I did well for a woman born in Kansas of Cherokee, French, and slave ancestry."

I can't shake Richard's face. I wonder what he's doing.

"What are you thinking, Diane?" She taps my fingers. "Are you time traveling?"

"Just listening—trying to take it all in, Cleo. Why didn't you go home to Kansas?"

"I'm an only child. My parents and brother, killed in a car accident. Dad's insurance policy got me Paris." She looks with the same reflection I've experienced. "The city of lights almost killed me. You're a beautiful woman," giving an abrupt change of topic, "confidence will come. Believe me."

"I don't *ever* intend remarrying."

She shakes her head and flirts volumes of long curls.

"A love affair in the afternoon brings the most enjoyment." "How long did you live in Paris, Cleo?"

"I went there at eighteen to absorb life. I met Louis the week I landed. Lost my virginity with passionate love all summer." Her beam mirrored mine when first meeting Richard. "We married three days before Christmas. I'm forty-six. I read your thoughts. No children *because of his beatings*."

"Why did you stay?"

"Louis' family came from old money. What woman can say *no* to homes around the world, including a castle and vineyard in Bordeaux? What's *your* story?" She stops hers.

I clear my throat for words to dribble from my head to my mouth. "I met Richard as a teenager, to marry at eighteen into a wealthy Denver family. We have three daughters. Nina, a twin, lives with me here. Her twin Leah, an attorney, lives in Chicago. Sarah, my youngest, lives in Oxford. I never attended college. I got beat most of my marriage." Tears eat my makeup. "He's had an affair most of our marriage. She's pregnant. I gave up *everything* to gain my freedom *in six months*."

"Don't weep. Your heart and mind require clarity."

Wiping my face and giving a pitiful smile, I know she's right. "I have money to buy or rent a place for my daughter and me."

"A realtor associate can show you a clean, quiet, partially furnished one-bedroom rental near West 78th. A jewel neighborhood close to anywhere you want and have to be. The price per month is thirty-nine hundred. I suggest renting for a while."

'Independence comes with a price,' I think. "I want to see it. Can I do it today?"

"Good idea. Spaces go fast in New York. Rich sisters own the building, leasing through two agencies. Sadie Richman, my friend, comes from one of them. I'll call her."

*

Thought of new adventure: is it possible less than forty-eight hours ago, when my life lay in a ditch, one call can change everything? I hear the words, *'I'll bring her over.'* I'm ready.

*

"She'll see us in an hour."

"Do I have time to call Samantha?"

"Go ahead and call her. I want to say hello after you talk."

*

Samantha is ecstatic, "It's good to hear your voice. Have you met Cleo yet?"

"Yes. Hold on."

Two friends are carrying on, illuminating beliefs of what I could have with Ruby.

"I'm taking care of this one." Cleo winks. "We're on our way to look at an apartment in your old neighborhood. Sam wants to talk to you."

"Diane, this is your chance. I'll come and visit when you settle. Be brave, eat good food. And be happy. I have another appointment waiting. I'll be in touch."

"We're fortunate. Sam's friendship saves lives." Cleo gathers up her things. "We'll walk a bit before taking the subway over."

I crave knowing more about Cleo and Samantha, but walking outside kills our privacy.

*

Thought of being less: Cleo's coolness oozes sexuality. Past abuse is a ghost — head high. Hips sway an imagination of her being naked. Coy glances to the left to the right—aware of men and women's attention to her perfect, goddess, lovemaking body. I've lived in a cave with all my Denver status. No rich woman I know leaves. They stay for their husband's private jets, first-class European vacations, accounts with the best couture designers, jewels worth a fortune, the mansions, and of course, the money. Managing my bank account frightens me. Don't want to meet another man. I've been to New York many times with Richard. He took care of everything. How can I be fearless like Cleo or even Nina? I will. I have to.

*

"You're quiet," Cleo observes as we reach a corner.

"I'm taking it all in," I answer. "You see, I've been a homebody." "You won't be lonely. I know lots of people."

"It'll be nice to meet new people. My shell is full of cobwebs."

She giggles, "I love your outlook, Missy. Let's go on to the next adventure."

*

As the saying goes—be careful what you ask God to send you. A man stands next to me. We wait to cross the street. I sense his eyes crawling over me, forcing my shoulders to curl as if cold.

"Have a good day," is all he says, and then advances across the street.

*

"Well, well." Cleo channels a mischievous grin and a few nail taps on my arm.

I catch myself watching his shoulder-length, grey waves tied in a ponytail. He slips into a coffee house. I mull over, *'not a tea drinker.'*

"I'm not interested, Cleo. He's a stranger, probably a serial killer." Our straight faces crack up.

Temptation pulls me to peek inside the coffee house. He waves from the window seat; I pick up my pace.

"Cleo, slow down," I call out.

"So, you had your first lesson, Diane. I'm not saying fuck the next man you see. Don't act scared. New York is yours. You belong here." She grabs my arm so I can keep up. "We don't want to be late for the appointment. The subway is down these steps. Have you taken it before?"

"I've been here before with my ex-husband. I'm okay." "Good. Our ride won't take long."

*

Thought of protection: how can Nina live here? Don't feel safe. Even with an updated haircut, new clothes, and that *Chanel* handbag, I'm a hick. People look at me. Find my space. I can't go back to Denver. New York is home now.

*

A different atmosphere comes less than twenty minutes: residential rowhouses with brightly painted doors, potted plants, clean sidewalks, no crowd, or honking horns.

"Where are we, Cleo?" I wish this were the place she'd chosen. "We're near your *new* Upper East Side home. Holly Golightly's apartment is near you." "Who's that?"

"Honey, it's where Audrey Hepburn's character in *Breakfast at Tiffany's* lived."

"Still not sure of where the hell I am, Cleo, but I do remember the movie."

"Now, when you meet Sadie, the realtor, be completely honest when answering her questions."

"What prying question will I have to reveal?"

"We're here." Cleo doesn't answer except pointing to a white row house with a cobalt blue door and geraniums and daisies filling navy blue window boxes.

Don't trip up the stairs. Take a deep breath.

Cleo knocks. It opens to a cheerful woman showing a mouth full of teeth. "Hello, Diane." Her firm handshake sets the mood. "Hello, Sadie. Thank you for meeting me."

Sadie leads the way in a fashionable white suit and black pumps. "Let me show you the apartment."

*

Thought of new life: do all Cleo's friends have this *same* come-fuck-me-in-the-afternoon sash-shay? She presents for thirty-nine hundred dollars, a 600 square foot, one-bedroom, ebony wooded floor apartment on the second-floor-walk-up facing the street. White drowns everything: walls,

French window frames, baseboards, older appliances and cabinets, kitchen sink, toilet, claw-foot tub, linen curtains, subway backsplash, and floor tiles, and all knobs on the doors and cabinets. If valium were my go-to-pill, a years' supply would be required to live here.

*

"What do you think?" Cleo nudges my sides. Expectant eyes insist on an answer.

"I like it," I reply, knowing the fear of being on my own is kicking my butt. "It's beautiful, Sadie."

"I knew you would. I have a few questions. Do you have your checkbook with you? I can call the bank and verify your funds. Do you drink and smoke? Do you have a lover who will be living with you? Can you sign a three-year lease with six months in advance? Do you have children?"

I give away nervousness; the drilling makes me sway back and forth. Perspiration flushes my face, and my hands feel an uncomfortable cold.

"You're doing fine," Cleo says with an assuring nod.

My pathetic mind speaks, "I drink and need to stop smoking. I'm divorced from an abusive husband of twenty-eight years. My daughter Nina does print modeling and will live with me. She's my only relative here; I can give you a year's rent in advance. I have two other daughters, Leah's a Chicago attorney. Sarah is an Oxford student. My father is dead, and my mother has terminal cancer. I have one sister whose husband and two children live in Denver. I need a home more than I need a drink and a lover. Here are my bank statement and checkbook. *Please*, give me a chance."

Closure ends. Melodramatic tears won't stop.

"*Dear, I'll rent this apartment to you*," says a woman about Mother's age striding into the living room. "Write your check," she addresses me and offers a tissue.

Her white linen suit, Jackie Kennedy's big-style sunglasses, pearls, and a diamond ring and watch costing serious money—tosses Helen off the bus.

"Hello, Auntie," Sadie greets her, following up with cheek kiss. Cleo's wink indicates a good sign.

"Hello, Cleo. You've brought another *Lost and Found kitten?*" "Good to see you, Catherine." Cleo slides closer to me. "Her name is Diane Fletcher, *Sam's friend.*"

"I like this one, Auntie," Sadie approves. "She's flawed with honesty. Diane, this is my aunt, Catherine Moore, who, with my other two aunts, owns this building. My sister and I have the exclusive."

"Pleased to meet you, Miss Moore."

"Tell me," the old woman walks toward me, "how long has your mother had cancer?"

"Mother's first diagnosis was ten years ago. It went into remission for a long while. Now it's back."

She does something odd for a stranger, squeezing my hands together. Her uninvited actions touch my face's scars. Sensitive, searching eyes, examine with gentleness. I know shame doesn't belong.

"The rent is twenty-two hundred. I can afford to do it, and I desire to." Miss Moore's hands slide under my chin and tap my cheeks. "I have a doctor for those, my dear. Fill out the papers with my niece. Give your check. Move-in when you can. It's nice to meet you. I'll say a prayer for your mother."

"Thank you, Miss Moore," I say with more gratitude than winning the lottery.

With a flip handed goodbye, Catherine Moore struts out the door. "Angels are singing your song today, Diane," Cleo quietly comes undone with hearty laughter.

"Congratulations. You'll be happy here. Our neighborhood is safe. I know because my sister, aunts, and I live nearby."

Sadie hands me a pen and rental form.

I give two references—Samantha Rose and Cleo Miller, and my check.

*

Thoughts of immense freedom: new cell phone number. Papers signed. I wrote two checks without Richard's approval. Sadie got one, and Cleo received three month's rent for *Lost and Found*. She saved my life.

*

Nina's hysterical red-face giggles fill my heart with happiness—far from my relationship with Richard.

"What shall we do today, Mom? Why do you often look sad? We have a home together."

"I'm just trying to figure out the next step. We've moved in, unpacked, so now what?"

I release frustrations looking around a space smaller than my old kitchen.

Nina shrugs before I feel her kiss on my cheek.

"I love our black and white winter photographs of Central Park, and the thrift shop finds of a powder-blue cushion sofa bed for me, and two, second-hand green and yellow chairs. A coffee table for whatever and a big-enough-for-two-kitchen is our corner of the world, and fresh flowers and a claw-foot tub under a window overlooking trees. Most of all, your bedroom is free of *his* presence. You and I *are* home. We *choose* our next steps."

"You're right," I agree, sitting on our most comfortable sofa.

"You, Sarah, and I will be fine. I'm going for a run. Do you want to join me, Mom?"

"You didn't mention Leah."

"No," Nina's coarse stance shuts down the negotiation, "I'm not fucking interested. Why don't you get outside? Indian Summers are the best here. I'll be back later."

*

Thoughts of conclusion: roles switch from mother and daughter to woman to woman. Can I believe Nina when she said Richard never touched her? Time will reveal the truth if I listen and wait. Financial independence permits no leverage of control. *'Find your path,'* Samantha's, Mother's, and Camille's worlds scream inside my head.

*

"I want to come home next week."

No immediate answer. Mother's coughs agitate my guilt for leaving. "Did you hear me, Mother?"

"I'm at Camille's. They feel it best instead of me being home alone."

Anger begins heating. "Why didn't anyone tell me of this? Am I not a part of this family?"

"I don't answer to you, Diane. Come home if you want. Remember, you left because you hated Denver. You were worried about your children. You insisted on a new start. Our lives here don't *revolve* around you."

"I miss you all, Mother."

"*Is your honeymoon over?*" Mother's brazen slice pinches my nerves. "How are you feeling?"

"Some days are better than others. Today it's about four. Yesterday was five.

Camille's friend, a natural path, has me taking pills and juices. I go along to keep Camille and Alan off my back. In the end, I make up my mind."

Her anchored stubbornness salivates throughout my mouth for a whole bottle of anything.

"Let me take care of you. I can afford it. I miss and love you, Mother."

"Money isn't important to a dead woman. Your children need you more. By the way, Leah called here last night. She talked to Camille for quite a while. Have you spoken to your daughter?"

"*What* did you mean when you said, be careful of her?" "I can't remember, Diane."

"Can you try?"

"Here's something of interest," Mother's hoarse voice speaks. I want to quiet her, but curious about her news.

"What is it, Mother?"

"Leah's left her firm with an attorney. They're in Paris. Check with Richard, who, by the way, calls to check on me. Damn bastard told me years ago not to come to his house. Now he's my best friend. When you're dying, damn vultures hover ready to pluck your soul."

My love for you, Richard, is still there. New York isn't far enough. "I was wondering what you meant about me being careful of Leah?

I'll call her. I guess she's happy."

"I'm tired, Diane. You know your children as I know mine. Whatever I meant about Leah, hell, I can't think. I forgot to tell you, one of my neighbor's daughters will rent the house."

"Who is renting your house?" I ask, tasting more guilt for not being there.

"JoAnne Williams employed with some computer company. Call us when you can, Diane."

"I have my new cell number. See that Leah gets it." "What is it?"

Isolation rips me—a new number, a new city, a new home. I made a mistake; she doesn't want me to visit. Camille and I haven't spoken often.

"Goodbye, Mother." "Bye, Diane."

*

Thought of ticking reality after drinking almost a whole bottle of wine: the home *is* here. Mother's eventual death is her stopwatch, not mine. I must decide my fate without permission or guilt. Okay, to be selfish because Richard sucked up half my life. Why didn't I protect my children from him? Failures will carry me to my grave. Go for a walk. Directions to *Tea for Two* aren't tricky. You're not a scared tourist. You belong here.

*

I'm almost there. Rest my mind from thinking about Denver. Keep repeating, *'I can do this and more.'* Breeze strokes my bare legs and flies through my love-it-short hair. Emulate Cleo's strut. I belong here, at least I do *today*.

"Have a cup of coffee with me," an unknown man's voice separates itself from the passerby conversations heard around me.

I'm a guarded tourist again. His pace follows. Don't look at him. "No, thank you." My words spit out, aiming to focus on my destination two long blocks away.

"It's only coffee. I have a good memory. I saw you several weeks ago."

He has my attention. Oncoming traffic stops me. It's *him—grey-haired-ponytail-coffee- drinker*. I noticed him when first meeting Cleo at *Tea for Two*. His close up exposes a fall into my arms, a cowboy poster image for a Montana tourist billboard. I recall Richard's entrapping handsomeness. *'No, not again,'* warnings scream inside my head. Good. Traffic allows walking now. One block away to distance me from this hazel colored eyed temptation.

*

"Wait."

"What do you want?" I demand, forgetting Cleo's stride, now owning my usual tense walk.

His laughter leaves me unimpressed.

"I swear I'm not a thief, a murderer, or homeless. My name is Eric Montgomery. I live not far. I'm an attorney on sabbatical, so technically, an attorney on vacation."

He laughs again. Liberties step in front of my uninviting expression. "I'm sorry. Did I offend you?"

My guard tightens hands over my purse. "*What* do you want?" His answer gives an open hand pointing to my destination. "Have tea with me."

"No. I don't talk to strangers or attorneys. My ex-husband is an attorney."

Fool. Why did you bring up the ex-husband part? Walk away.

He's perplexed, scratching his head, and his small smile stays. "Still *holding* on to your mother's advice about not talking to strangers?"

He's determined to bother you. Don't scream, hide your fear, be polite.

"So, does that mean you won't have a cup of tea with me *because* I'm an attorney?" His hands wave into the air. "It's a beautiful day for two people who have time on a weekday. I'm not going to hurt you. I'm asking for some free time with you."

"I'm sorry. I can't. Thank you anyway." He shrugs. He turns away.

"*What about tea*? Will you have a cup of tea with me?" He's relentless coming back. "We're *right* here. It's not a date. We can pay for our own."

"Why?"

"*Because I'd like to.*" His voice slows to a gentle crawl. Confusion is killing me. What do I do?

"I'm not asking to sleep with you. I'd like to have a cup of tea. I think our generation feels more comfortable with conversation than texting, emails, and website dating."

I correct back, "I'm *not* dating you."

He returns, to my frown, a short laugh. "A date? It's only tea."

Without consent, my stranger plods along with me, reaching not mine, but now our destination. He opens the door. Forwardness indicating to a soon-to-be-ex-wife, he's a controlling polite little shit like Richard.

"Are you a tea drinker?" he asks, pondering his menu our server left. "I'm in New York to expand my life," my reason points out. "I'm learning to like it."

"Coffee opens my brain. I've never been in here since it opened a year ago." He skims a full room. "Business appears good."

*

We order. Green tea for my pickup. Lemongrass for me.

*

"My name is Diane," I announce for politeness while we wait for our drinks.

He stretches his hand across the table. "Pleased to meet you, Diane." Shaking hands doesn't break the ice. We've materialized into an old, non-talking, married couple filling space with silence until our tea comes, seeming in years, instead of a few minutes.

"Let the teas brew in their pots until the timer rings," the host instructs.

"How long will you be in New York, Diane?" his curiosity intrudes. "I moved from Denver."

"I was born in San Francisco, Diane. I have lived here since graduating from law school."

The timer rings.

He pours.

"Are you hungry? Shall I order jasmine rice, soybeans, and lettuce wraps?"

My stranger sounds gentlemanly compassionate. But this woman's past remains a constant thorn. All the men are nice until they close the doors. I say, "Sure," hating myself for leveraging an ounce of independence.

His cocked head studying my appearance, undressing me while sipping tea, is perhaps all in my imagination. An uncomfortable placement of thoughts won't let me eat much.

"I should leave. My daughter will be waiting."

"Is our lack of conversation because of disinterest, Diane?"

How dare he pin me into a corner? I won't and can't allow another man to take over. Get the hell away. Next time I choose the man I drink with for fucking afternoon tea.

"*What* do you want from me?" "Dinner."

"No."

"Why?"

"I don't want to."

"I think you do, Diane. I *know* I do."

"You don't know me."

"And you *don't* know me, Diane. Shall we have your daughter escort you?"

"You're an arrogant bastard. Do you always get your way?"

I gather with his sucked-in lip, he's thinking of some profound answer. If I'm fortunate, he'll leave.

"It's clear your New York expansion doesn't include a dinner with me. I *apologize*."

Richard's vocabulary avoided, *'I apologize.'* Can I not allow an exception? If not, I'll always be alone, and I could've just as well stayed in Denver.

"I'm sorry, Eric. Divorce leaves little room for imagination." "Do you know persistence won't allow me to give up?"

His question pushes me back into my seat. Half of me ready for some lame answer, and half of me wondering his angle.

I reel in, "What's your line?"

He smiles, and then it fades. My father beat my mother. My sister almost died from her husband's abuse. I can tell by the imprints on your neck, wrists, and cheeks someone beat you, your husband, by the way, your head lowers. I *don't* hit women. I'm separated. My wife lives on Long Island. She's an alcoholic and addicted to painkillers from a back injury years ago."

"Is she in a wheelchair?"

"No. My dear wife is a drunk who fell down the steps. She claims her pain never stops. We've been to doctors. The verdict—back spasms controlled with a mild dose of this and that. After a while, the mild dose becomes a lifetime habit."

"You're asking me to dinner because you feel sorry for me?"

"No. I feel a beautiful woman like you, whose husband beat her, deserves a dinner instead of an ass-kicking. There's no plan behind my invitation."

"I can't commit to anything, Eric. I've not been with anyone but my husband. I'm no good at date-chatter as you see, or accepting rare compliments and apologies."

"It's just dinner, Diane."

I harbor doubt, caution, and awkward loneliness for a preconceived disastrous evening.

"Where do you want to meet, Eric? Can we make it early? My last name is Fletcher."

"I own a little café in the Village. My mother runs it, and my sister is the chef.

It's called *A Piece of Heaven*."

"How ironic, because I've been searching for a piece of heaven since Richard and I met."

* "And this is how it started, Cleo."

*

Cleo's infectious laughter is a welcome change from my and Nina's arguments over Leah and Richard.

"I've been wondering why I hadn't seen you, Diane. I took a chance to come by. Sorry, we keep missing each other's messages. Honey, you're not a kitten anymore. I have a housewarming little something." She passes from her hand to mine a small wrapped gift. "Open it."

"You didn't have to."

"I wanted to, Diane, for your generous donation to *Lost and Found.* I gather you're doing well?"

"Yes, compared to where I was a month ago when I came here."

Pulling apart a white ribbon around its sapphire box ignites her giggles.

"Let's toast," she giggles, replenishing our champagne. "Cleo—a gold jeweled heart pin. Why?"

"They're from a woman, a diamond buyer, I've helped." A broad smile puffs her cheeks. "I use this connection whenever I need something special. Besides—every woman needs a little diamond heart protecting it from being broken." Taking the pin, Cleo opens its clasp to put it to my top. "See?" She opens her compact.

"Thank you, Cleo, for everything."

*

As Cleo chatters about men, sex, and almost anything else popping inside her head, my mind follows the outline of Eric's face. We meet for tea, coffee, dinner, and walks in Central Park. Time is quiet, relaxed, and enjoyable, hearing a man speak respectfully.

*

"*Where's Nina?*" Cleo interrupts my daydream. "You haven't mentioned your daughter's name."

"I'm not sure. How do you know Nina?" My mood changes gliding hands over the seat of the sofa, which is her bed.

"I came by a couple of weeks ago. Nina said you've been going for walks about the same time of day. We spoke a bit. She's striking."

Nina's absent. I can't speak of our rages over begging her to forgive her sister, Leah. "My daughter has friends," I slam the door to a shameful secret.

"We all have friends at some point or another. Odd, you don't know where she is."

Cleo's wisdom gives a raised eye to my stiff jaw and well-played poker face. No one will ever know my secrets. Changing the subject is the best. "When can I volunteer for *Lost and Found*?"

She must find my question amusing as she is barely able to contain her grin.

"Do you have time?"

"Yes, Cleo. My social life doesn't make headlines. Eric and I are friends, not lovers."

"You're evasive." I disapprove of her shaken finger as if I'm the child. "I'm not criticizing. You came here a wet mess. I check-up on all my ladies because I care and offer therapy groups, housing assistance, *as you know*, networking opportunities, and even employment connections. Sam knows my abilities quite well."

While she finishes her drink, she eyes a glimpse of one of my other secrets.

"You draw?"

My defensive claws come out. "Why?" In return, she throws a definite frown. "Why?" I ask this time more civil.

"I see the edge of a sketchbook on your coffee table. Your daughter didn't mention drawing was her hobby. Honey, I'm *not* your enemy."

"I'm sorry, Cleo," picking up the book, "I've not made many female friends. Richard chose who he wanted me associating with."

"Oh my God, Diane—you've got to be kidding me?"

I wipe away visible tears as soon as her hands rub my back.

"Men like Richard are evil. Let's not dwell on his ass. Tell me about you."

"I dabbled since my teens drawing women's fashion. Some I copied from magazines. Some are my own."

"Show me." Her interest sounds sincere.

It lightens my disposition, to reveal my original designs, filling up more than half the book. "As I said, they're a pastime hobby. I'm not good anymore."

"You know what you're good at, Diane, *tearing yourself down*. These *are* damn good. They're fabulous as worth thousands of dollars. I'd wear any of your formal designs. I have an important fundraiser in a month. Can you make this for me?" She points at an original design.

"Can I let you know?"

"Walk the way you want to, Diane. We'll talk soon."

*

Thoughts of indecision: curtains drawn in the middle of the day. Promise to design Cleo's gown fills me with depression, not joy. Terrible loneliness shovels a tear into my heart; Richard can't share my news. Home and marriage are gone. Accepting this new woman, I'm trying to ignore her true feelings of failure. Two of her daughters, Leah and Nina, have shut off communication. Sarah lives far. My mother offers no open hand to come home. Camille's family is her priority. I miss talking to Samantha. Where is Ruby? Unsure of Eric's intentions or mine. Continue later — intruder rings.

*

"This is Catherine Moore, Diane. Are you there?"

Breathe. Open the door. My politeness escorts Miss Moore up the steps to the apartment. After all, she gave me a place to live.

"It's nice to see you, Miss Moore."

Her heels mark a path to the sofa. She sits crossing well-paid for shoes. Removes a straw sun hat from a *Neiman Marcus* ad, and presents a face untouched by plastic surgery. Catherine's high-tea handbag, gloves, and perfectly fitting suit over nylons are capable of willing a curtsy.

"Can I offer you something to drink?"

"Do you have a nice glass of cold water, my dear?" "Yes."

225

"I assure you, Diane, my visit isn't to spy. I saw your curtains drawn on a sunny day and thought you might be ill." She sips her water. A believable honesty extends from her to me.

"I'm well, Miss Moore."

"Please call me Catherine. So you're making way for yourself here. I hope so."

"Yes. I'm trying, Catherine." Glimpsing toward my sketchbook, I decided to share my news. "Cleo wants me to design a dress for her. I need to figure out where I can put a machine and cutting table. Then buying material and supplies," I catch my grin for a chance, "but I can do it. I can."

Catherine puts down her glass. I can't read her eyes scanning through my drawings. Why did I show it? A slow study of each one takes on a critique I don't desire hearing for my amateur skills compared to her masterful coordinated, expensive clothes.

"You're talented." Simple words from a woman I don't know, but respect because I judge her to be fair and honest. "How is your mother?"

"She's managing."

"A pity about cancer—is she on chemo or radiation?"

I don't want to talk of Mother's stubbornness. It's best to lie, "She's on a break from radiation."

"What's your line, Diane? Are you a fashion designer?" "I'm trying to figure it out."

She sips her water. I sit — quiet settles around us without questions.

*

"What about your ex-husband? Did he do that to your face?" Her questions pop up in the sweetest old lady voice.

Remnant dark marks from Richard's temper drag my head down. "Please don't stare. I see the scars every day."

"Look at me, Diane." Sadness comes into her eyes. They remind me of my mother's. "Stupid men need no reason. Have you met the women in the building? They all have stories."

"I've said quick hellos, but nothing else."

"My sisters and I give safe passage to women like you. You see, my husband Stanley was a mean-wealthy drunk. Fortunately for me, his car rammed head-on into a tree. My sisters, Virginia, Nadine, and I chose old, nasty, but rich husbands. Our mother preached a woman can tolerate a rich man for all his weaknesses." A wink she gives me in between sips of water. "You see, men are cowards. Marrying young for money, especially to an old fart, ensures your security when he dies."

"You have it all worked out, don't you?" I say while pressing my chin, still hurting from Richard's fists.

She places the glass on the table, then dabs away drops of water from her mouth. "I've learned in my seventy-one years answers drop at your feet whenever you need them. Juliette Cloister lives above you. Get to know her. Her husband resides in prison for attempted murder. My *point is y*ou can't live here by yourself—New York *will* eat you alive."

"Alright," I agree.

"Now, I ask this of all the women I rent from me. How can I help you?"

"I don't know, Catherine. I have the means to take care of my daughter and me."

"Life asks you a question for a reason, Diane. I will give you the answer to which you can't see. I have friends who need fresh designs for this event or another. My ladies are rich who desire standout individuality."

As she flips again through my sketches, a child's excitement churns my belly. I get it. Catherine *is* my answer.

She approaches with her hand into mine. "*Now,* how can I help?" she asks again.

"Introduce me to these women." My answer this time comes without hesitation.

"Here," she hands a business card from her purse, "call her."

The white card with black embossed letters read *Juliette Cloister, Designer.*

"She lives above me. She's in a rush when her cab arrives. Our paths crossed maybe three times with a short wave-nod."

Catherine peeks at her watch. "I mustn't keep you. I apologize for disturbing you. I've enjoyed talking to you, Diane." She hands me another card. "Call me after you speak with Juliette, who, by the way, goes by Jules." She extends a handshake and her business card. "You'll find your path. Suffering has a way of straightening one's back."

"*Yes,*" giving gratitude, "thank you. I'll walk you out."

"No. No. I have another lady to see before I leave. Grace. Do you know her?"

I shake my head.

"Grace is from Nigeria. She moved in last week. Her husband is her business. I'll let her tell you."

We reach my door; I'm a little sad to conclude our talk. The company felt good. Miss Catherine is a Godsend, offering in-my-face-common sense.

"Thank you, Catherine. I'll call you. I appreciate any help you can offer."

"Good luck, Diane. New York is rooting for you."

*

Thoughts of freedom: my commitment. No one can do this *except* me. All my life wasted, struggling to tie unraveling knots. Let go.

*

"Eric, can I see you?" "Yes. I desire it, Diane."

"Meet me at the tea house?" "No."

"I'll send a cab for you. Come to my place."

Eric's-never-given-me-before-invitation unravels me. "Are you still there?" his seduction asks.

"Yes. So, we're not meeting at the normal place?"

"We can if you want instead. I'll meet you there in an hour." "Eric, I'm sorry I called. I have to speak to my daughter." "I'm here. Call your daughter. Handle what you need."

Hesitation taunts his invitation; I'm a fool. Nina isn't here. Eric is. "Send the cab for me."

*

I have to reach my daughter.

"Nina? Are you coming home tonight? Where are you?" "Hello, Mom. I'm in Maine."

"Maine? Why? I've not seen you for a week. Text messages don't cut it. You take off without a word. Are you still living here or not?"

"I am. One of my friends, Claudine, invited me to a retreat. I took her up on it. It's a spiritual purge from toxic food and *evil* habits."

Her hilarity irritates me. She's excluding me from us.

"Are you avoiding me, Nina? What are your plans for us?"

"I've been thinking much about Leah, you, Dad, and my life. Can we please talk when I come home in two more days?"

"We must talk when you come home. I love you, Nina. We must settle things. We *have* to."

"I love you, Mom. We'll sort out everything when I get back. Don't worry. Nothing can destroy you and me."

*

Thought of conclusion: past Central Park, Museum of Modern Art, or as we locals say, MoMa. We turn left. We turn right. Lost track of the turns and sways the taxi makes. My mind is on Richard. No other man has been attentive to me since we met as teenagers. A bare ring finger permits me to be where I am at this moment. I wish my heart gave its permission—cab parks under trees in front of well-kept brick apartment buildings. You must bury the past and Richard. New York, Eric, and better relationships with my daughters are now my future.

*

"We're here, Miss," Mr. Cabbie announces. "No, you don't owe me." He stops me from paying. "Your host already paid. Have a good evening."

The scared date slides out the back door when Mr. Cabbie opens it. He jogs down the brownstone steps. Eric's exuberant glow says it all.

I, on the other hand, hope for a stiff drink. "It's good to see you, Diane."

My put-on huge smiley face mirrors his. Endearing giddy laughter draws his arms around my waist to escort me up to the steps.

"I'm on the fifth floor. Thank God for an elevator. Right?" He jokes, noticing my initial shock gaping at the continual winding staircase.

Relaxation pushes through entering an elegant crystal chandelier-lit entry.

"This is nice, Eric."

His hands slide into mine as we move to pass a subdued yellow- painted foyer housing a rectangle marble table under a large glass vase with a floral arrangement seen at the Plaza Hotel. I take note, an espresso leather sofa, matching wing-back chairs, random gallery size, oil landscapes of the turn of the century New York, and a doorman, who tips his hat behind the mahogany lobby desk. Eric, my tea drinker, is class.

Our elevator reaches his open floor plan to a corner unit dimmed with candles and low lights. Piano jazz standards flow in the speakers. His culinary skills pull aromas from the open patio doors. Void of over-done furniture or bragging rights to auction art conveys an unpretentious man.

"This is lovely, Eric."

"Please make yourself at home. I hope you're hungry. I'm roasting rosemary chicken on the grill."

Stepping onto the patio behind him are potted plants and randomly placed seating arrangements of small wooden chairs and tables—my thoughts pound—'relax.'

"Follow me," he signals to the kitchen, "I've got a few things to prepare. I think you'll like this." He hands me a high stem glass placed on the counter.

"It's good," I respond, savoring a rustic red wine settling my gut. "We import it from Italy for our restaurant. How was your day, Diane? Are you glad you're here?"

My laugh sounds ill-placed as I place my glass on the counter. He looks confused.

"It's been a long time since a man cared to ask. You have it all together. I like you, Eric, but don't want to make love with you. I'm sorry. I should leave," I lay it all out, biting off my nose to spike my face.

Aware this could be one of my biggest mistakes, sizing up his sudden quiet disposition, I feel foolish and childish. How could I be so stupid knowing his presence means everything?

"Forgive me. I've not been with anyone but Richard. I'm no good at intimacy."

His bare feet approach. "Sit," he directs.

My shaking dreads an altercation as with the first time, and I won't let Richard touch me.

"Diane," softness speaks with bended knee until we're eye to eye. "I know your ex-husband hurt you. We've been talking for a few weeks. Your company *tonight or any other* isn't about me fucking you because the night expects it. Do you understand?"

Inward puzzlement allows me no answer.

"Here," he recovers my glass, "drink your wine. Listen to music. I'll be back after checking on dinner."

"Tell me about your wife." My immediate question shadows him. "*Why* this question now? Are you fishing for the conversation to kill this evening?"

"I'm sorry. Maybe dinner here wasn't a good idea. You know things about Richard. How did you get to this point?"

"My wife," he chooses his corner of the sofa, "sit down, Diane, please," pointing to my spot, not at all near him. "Stephanie is probably on her third bottle of champagne or second bottle of white wine, or sixth martini by now. We met when I interned with a New York Law firm, my uncle, a Municipal judge, recommended me for."

"Was she an attorney?"

"No," He shakes his head. "Stephanie's father, one of the richest land developers in the state, gave her everything on a diamond platter. She accompanied him to the building I worked each day. She spied me having coffee nearby. Our instant attraction led to marriage, the next Christmas Eve, thirty years ago. We have two sons whom I see infrequently."

"I shouldn't ask, Eric."

He doesn't seem to hear me. The story goes on. "My wife lives on Long Island involved with charity and board member events. I'm here. We meet once a month to discuss the relationship. The lunch includes *her, me, and her lover.*" Eric gets his drink from the counter. He slowly drinks, never taking his eyes off me. "*The lover and* my best friend since college roll things into a complicated nasty ball. He's there. I'm there. And Stephanie is in the middle."

"Why?" I must know.

"We were best men at each other's weddings. He and his wife are godparents to my oldest son. Years ago, when life had no consequence, we all were a part of the secret, Long Island community of couple swapping."

His wine disappears. He pours another.

"What are you saying, Eric—couple swapping?"

"It's true. I'm clean of any disease. I've made sure of it for the last ten years."

Wine isn't enough buffering this shit, our lives mirrored. We're two damaged people. I drink and pour myself another one before returning to my not-at-all-close-to him-spot on the sofa.

Watching his generous, happy mood drain into sad—why did I have to spoil our dinner? I had to ask. I had to know. What good is all this dead pain?

*

"I'm sorry, Eric, for bringing this up. You must think I'm a waste of your time?"

"I'm not ashamed to tell you because I want you to know all about me. I left that world for good over three years ago. Divorcing Stephanie hasn't been a priority *until now.*" He doesn't flinch at all. "It's the truth."

Thinking halts. Hearing '*until now*' are words I'm unprepared to hear. "What *do* you mean . . . until now?" My defenses are on fire. I mustn't listen as I did when I first met Richard. No matter what this one says.

"Don't look at me as if I'm crazy. You've captivated me, Diane. I miss you each time we part."

"What do you want from me? You don't *know* everything about me, Eric," a scared woman voice lets go.

Lingering frowns of hesitation are evident; his answer won't come easy. "The reason my sons refuse to have anything to do with me—is because Michael's, my eldest, girlfriend's parents, were involved in our couple swinging group. Discovery planted the blame on me. Both boys closed ranks. How could I tell them I joined to keep their mother from cheating on me? You see, when your husband's success keeps him in the city, the wife tends to get bored."

Sliding a little closer, I confess, "We all carry burdens. You aren't alone."

"You're still here after hearing my worst secrets. I value truthfulness with *you*—a woman I desire a relationship with."

Courage necessitates a mouthful of wine. Swallowing alcohol doesn't make it easier, exposing shameful personal information.

"You can trust me, Diane."

'I know, Eric,' I think, considering his raw confession and my secret making us two fallen creatures deserving each other.

"Richard beat me similar to a man. His affair, for most of our twenty-eight-year marriage, was with one woman, whose pregnancy massacred my love. I think about him *even right now;* he was my first. His sexual carnage included a female escort or another couple. I humiliated myself in ways I'll never speak of." "Is that all?"

I breathe a long sigh and let it all vomit. "My grown daughter saw Richard kissing as if his lover, her adult sister."

Admitting the taboo I've carried for many a week draws doubt I made the right choice as Eric stands walking about and shaking his head. If it ends tonight, I am better off than wasting my time.

"When did this happen, Diane? Tell me."

"I don't know when Richard first rapped our daughter. I only learned about this recently, which is why I left him. I could take his abuse and his affairs, all are horrible in themselves, but incest is the vilest sin." Reaching for the wine bottle ignites an old habit of drinking to forget.

"I'm flawed, Eric," I begin for my eager listener. I feel honesty sheds grotesque aged plaster. "Therapy has been for years—contemplated suicide more times than I can count. My children left home after high school graduation. I'm a coward terrified of my reasons for staying married. Richard's rules kept in a loveless house, five-hundred times the size of this apartment. Leaving Denver took all my strength. I left everything.

Some days I'm barely hanging on. I couldn't predict the next second being Richard's wife."

"I'm not leaving, Diane. I can help you with the legality surrounding Richard. I'm here and will *always* be here."

*

Thoughts of openness: Eric's fingers slip away my glass. His lips conquer mine. Tasting his passion intoxicates me. Without words, we cradle each other into his bedroom. Only the city lights are with us. I allow. I choose. He strips to my imperfect, scarred skin. I accept his lips, his tongue ravaging my body. In my hands, a part of him I wish pleasing becomes an obsession. Our movements are sweat and fulfilled, more than the first time with Richard, whom I still desire.

*

"Where have you been?" Nina's hands on her hips represent more of the mother. "I'm here for two days. No calls. Why? *What's his name?* I'm thinking about a man and not a woman. You're *not that liberated*. Also," she points out, "no overnight bag, a black pencil skirt, *my* white silk shirt, so, Mom, I'm assuming a dinner, then endless, *raw* sex." Her laughing and bear hug means two things. She's forgiven me for washing Leah's shit in her face. Two, humor can be had, even at my expense for her mother acting a hormonal teenager.

"We'll talk later. Eric Montgomery is his name," I tease wagging my finger."

"I do want all the details, Mom. Before I forget, you have three calls, Sarah, Camille, *and Leah.*"

Hearing Leah's name requires me to gather my wits. A glass of water loosens my throat.

"What did . . . *Leah,* want?"

"We didn't speak. Leah's message is like some Western Union Telegram: Landing in New York next Saturday-engaged-living in Paris, blah-blah-blah." Nina empties my water for a beer. "You're sweating, so drink, and fuck the worrying. I need a drink too. My twin is a piece of

234

shit. It's been months since I've seen or talked to her. I don't miss the thought."

"I can handle Leah. Let's not spoil it. Sit with me, Nina. I've much to say, and thinking about it all is a little scary and exciting."

"You sound serious, Mom."

I take a few more sips of beer and an even more giant gulp of air. "Over the past days, I've found a new life's balance."

Curiosity quiets Nina down into a chair.

"I've been offered a chance to create my designs."

"How, Mom?" Pride and enthusiasm ooze out the daughter's face. "Tell me."

"Our landlord, Catherine Moore, saw my design sketchbook while visiting me. She has many contacts, for example, upstairs neighbor Juliette Cloister, a fashion designer. I'm to call her. Maybe I can work for her. Who knows? Cleo also saw my book." My excited hands locate a page with turned a down corner. "She wants this one. My life can change, Nina."

Thumbing through my drawings brings me chills at what my life was in Denver, bouncing between nothing worth the next day.

Nina's happiness leaps into a wraparound embrace. "I'm happy for you, Mom. I'm sorry for my behavior. Forgive me. We both have good news."

"We do? What is your news?"

"I know you think, from Leah's label, I'm a professional student."

"Let's leave Leah out of this."

"Don't judge me." Nina bites her lip and then takes a long pause. "Tell me," I clutch her close. "I'm on your side."

"Well, my longtime photography hobby has landed me a paying job. Instead of print modeling, I've been learning behind the scenes of fashion photography as assistants to several in-demand photographers. I've placed an application with Parsons School of Design. *Please don't hate me, Mom.*"

What I do best—hold my children, and I do with this one. "Nina, two things are true. Leah is still my daughter and your sister. Second, I don't hate you. Finding your mark takes trial and error. I'll be here to help you."

My words don't cushion her continual crying. "I can't forgive her or Daddy. I know you want me to."

"Nina. Stop crying. I'm no longer with Richard. As for Leah, I *will* confront her. Concentrate on yourself. Let me worry about the rest. Okay?"

She sniffles as when she was a little girl, "I love you, Mom. Thank you."

"I love you too, Nina. Everything will work out. We're in New City, and all things are possible."

I received a big hug. "You're right, Mom. I'm going to shower. May I rest in your bed for a while? I'm not too hungry. Oh, by the way, I'm happy you found someone nice."

My first thought is to say *a friend*, but after the last two days, Eric is emotionally more than that, but am I ready?

"We met by chance at a place called *Tea for Two*."

"He was a pick-up, then?" Catching my daughter's wagging-finger-tease on her way to the bathroom is amusing.

"Nina, don't make fun of your old mother. I've been meeting Eric for a few weeks. I'm all new at this. The last few nights were the first time…"

She turns around, showing me a broad grin. "I knew it was something when you left the house at the same time during the day."

"We meet and talk. Eric is his name. I like him," I feel nervous explaining. "Stop it, Mom. Take it one day at a time. Enjoy the ride. Let me know when I'll meet the man who makes my mother happy."

She's right. Time will tell. Now make those calls while Nina is in the shower.

*

"Sarah, did I wake you? I forget the time difference."

"I'm awake reading. How are you doing, Mum? Nina says she happy you're her roommate."

"We're getting to know each other as friends, mother and daughter, and as two women."

"Nina is a wonderful sister. I can talk to her about anything, Mum." "How are you doing, Sarah? Have you talked to your grandmother?" "I'm doing well. I spoke to Grandmum a couple of days ago. I think that she'll live longer than we think. Her breathing is better."

"My mother is living life on her terms. I want to visit her soon, but the reason I called is to share my news."

"You sound quite upbeat. Tell me." "I've been sketching more each day."

"Mum, I'm happy. You know, I still have one of your drawings of me as a little girl. You have great promise, and New York will let you explore it all."

Sarah's giggling does my soul good. Our last time together was a crying festival, and now since I've left Denver, our conversations are happier.

"There's a chance I could work with fashion designer, Juliette Cloister, and Nina has enrolled in Parsons to study all fashion photography. Things on this end are shaping up." The reinvented mother beams, also thinking of Eric, as she outlines her lips as if it were his fingers.

"We're toasting life, Mum because I've re-enrolled into my school's spring term in English Literature. Don't be mad."

The mother listens. Her pride spreads over her face. "I want you to *find* your way, Sarah."

"Mum, I've landed a research library position through a professor, Abigail Lawson, a mentor I met first coming to Oxford. She thinks I'm brilliant. I want to teach and *never study law again*."

"I'm glad because I never thought of you wearing one of those white wigs."

We both find a laugh at that picture.

"I'm not like her or him," Sarah's darkness changes her voice. "Sarah, Nina is stepping out of the shower. Now isn't the time to discuss Leah and Richard, a bad topic also with Nina. Don't think about them. Concentrate on you. I'll call back soon. There was a need to share good fresh news, *and I wanted to hear your voice.*"

"Mum. We're family. I love you."

*

Thoughts of unforgiving: Leah's impending visit overshadows. Sermons are pleading Nina to forgive Leah; realism is a contradiction. Images absorb Richard's hands, slaughtering the wife. Accusations of her husband and daughter's incest leave harsh condemnation.

*

"Did you hear me, Mum?"

"I'm sorry, Sarah. My mind was somewhere else." "I'll book a flight from London to see your new flat." "Why don't you come next week? Leah will be here." A pause on both sides of the line isn't right.

"I *don't want* to see her. I've declined her Paris invitations. Who cares if she's engaged? Her depraved act has closed my heart to her and *him*."

"I can't force you, Sarah. Leah *is* your sister."

"Are you talking *that* shit again, Mom?" Nina's towel-wrapped around her body approaches. "Sarah and I don't want anything to do with Leah," tears welling, "I *hate her.* I'll be at a friend's during her visit."

My daughters squeeze me into a cube, and for this, I feel no matter what I do, my life will never be healthy.

"Mum? Mum? Are you still there?"

"She's here," Nina snares after snatching away my phone. "You and I need to stick together *against Leah and him.*"

Whatever Sarah responds, I can't hear with Nina's intentional whispering on another side of the room.

"Here," she slaps the cell into my hand. "Sarah wants to talk to you. I'm heading to a friend's in the Village. I won't be late." She disappears, slamming the bathroom door behind her.

"Please understand, Mum," Sarah's voice allows me no space, "I can't and won't talk to Leah."

"I *do*, Sarah."

Sarah's agony amplifies mine watching Nina's silent, quick nod goodbye out the living room door a mere few feet away. I see healing will take time.

"Sarah. I know you saw your father and Leah. Absolve Leah. Richard holds all blame."

"One day, you may get your wish, but not today," she bites back. "On a brighter note, Camille and I talk all the time."

"Then you know Mother has rented out her house and stays with Camille and Alan?"

"It's best, Mum, because Camille *is* there. I need to hang up now. It's rather later here. Let's look at the times I can come *after* Leah's gone."

"Good night, Sarah. We'll talk in a couple of days. I love you." "Love you too, Mum."

*

Thoughts of isolation: silence on the phone. Silence in the house. I can't reach Samantha. Cleo asks too many questions. Fear too much neediness will ruin my relationship with Eric. Mother's ill. I can't burden her. Camille's family is her priority. Ruby understands, but I can't find her. How did I find peace? The kitchen cabinet has a friend. A bottle of Scotch calls me.

*

"Who is it? I can't hear you."

"I'm your upstairs neighbor, Juliette Cloister. Can we speak?" Shit. Primp my hair. Throw water on my face. Pull my robe tight.

"I'll be there," says disinclination thinking a career might be fruitless. After all, Helen's million dollars settlement over the next twenty-eight years has set me up, "Coming."

Open the door to a polished woman about my height, with smooth, pale skin comparing to my flaws, and a straight jet-black neat long braid, to my blonde pixie matted mess. Her attire reads *Ralph Lauren*.

We say, "Hello."

'No way can I measure up to this,' I think to invite my guest to join me. "Please come in. It's good to meet you."

Black slim pants and a white shirt under a waist-length jacket fit her as if for a fashion runway. My dull-white terry-cloth robe shows like a second-hand store. Red-ballerina flats and an oversized black shoulder bag emulate a woman of exquisite taste.

"Please have a seat. Can I get you something to drink while I freshen up?"

"A glass of water would do," she answers politely, sitting straighter than straight.

Slip a piece of lemon into my just purchased Waterford glass shows I've class too. Hand her the glass, and set one down for me, also. Take a deep breath.

"I'll be right back."

Thumb through a closet full of black, more black, upon more black piled on black, speaks the color of New York women in my neighborhood. Select pants and a red silk blouse. Mouse-up my hair, tap on a hint of red lipstick and apply a light touch of camouflage make-up. It's my show time to an elegant, cross-legged woman wearing a *Cartier* watch, ballerina flats, and magazine cover barely-there make-up.

"Catherine said I should meet you," Juliette speaks firm. "I'm curious as to why."

Taken aback by her choice of words, I can see this one means business. My first impression must've set the tone.

"I draw . . . I mean sketch fashion. I have for a long while. Dreams of design left me long ago after I married out of high school. Divorce and a desire to start a new life landed me here. You've seen me with my daughter, no doubt."

Her eyes settle more into space ahead of her before I get a full look at her again.

"She's a pretty girl. Show me your compositions."

Breathe. Take control, don't shake as you hand Miss Perfect your book. "Here are my sketches."

What the hell is she thinking—slow-then-flipping fast-stop-then turning slow-then stopping at one page, then another, to closing the book? A sterile examination yanks me back to high school, waiting for the teacher's approval.

"They're nice. Some are original, yes?"

"Yes," I boast, "these are the ones. I have a commission to create this one for a woman who introduced me to Catherine."

"You do?"

"Have you met her, Cleo Miller?"

Juliette suddenly changes her expression into solemn. "She's quite a social networker with photographs in *Town and Country, New Yorker*, to name a few. *Lost and Found* received city recognition for raising money, helping women get on their feet. *I owe her much.* I won't ask you why you ended up here if you don't ask me."

Taking a seat next to her, "Agreed," I say as the fresh lemon water slithers down my throat.

"Diane," she opens into a brighter voice, "I've been searching for an assistant. Your original designs are French couture making love to old Hollywood Glamour."

I'm speechless on the edge of containing jubilant screams.

"Catherine is your fairy godmother. She has great intuition about people. I trust her and Cleo. They're right about you. I have a studio, although my talent isn't yours, Diane. We can complement each other."

Stomach knots. What's happening in less than twenty minutes?

"Am I working for you?" I ask, not caring what I do because I've never held a job before.

She laughs. I don't.

"Dear, I'm *offering* an equal partnership based on your sketches. I count one-hundred and sixty with your initials."

Tears trickle down.

An unexpected gesture shows Juliette removing tissues from her purse. She dabs my flushed face.

"How humble you are, Diane."

My childhood dreams shout, "Yes. Yes. Yes.".

"Come to my Soho loft tomorrow," she says, producing her card from that purse-envy bag. "If you think we are good, we'll draw up the paperwork."

"How can you be so sure?" I wonder, observing her calm, collected persona.

"I've been looking for a business partner with *your* talent. I've done alright on my own with custom-one of a kind design, yet a piece was missing." She continues with a bat of those very long natural eyelashes, "I also act on my intuition because your designs are unlike anything I've seen. I'm professionally-schooled; I can teach you what I know. I have one good pattern maker, Charles. The three of us will set the fashion scene on fire."

"Thank you, Juliette," I can barely catch my breath, "I will see you tomorrow. What time?"

"Come with me. I'll knock on your door at nine in the morning." "I'll be ready, Juliette."

*

"Didn't I satisfy you, Diane?"

"Yes, Eric, but I have another favor."

"You're in my bed. You can ask me anything, Diane." "First, let's make love, Eric. My request can wait."

Eric responds, sucking my earlobe. His hands are intent, spreading my legs in full view. His concentration vibrates fingers inside me until they are wet from my orgasm. I salivate licking Eric's wet fingers after he's had them inside me. I allow his hands to gently arch my back to accept his tongue on my erect nipples. The minutes crawl into long walks

"Now, what else do you need me to do?" Eric teases with a lush French kiss.

Heat sizzles from perpetual oral vagina feasting until my mind has no reason to think about anything else.

*

Thoughts of pleasurable pleasures: pulsing. Pushing, grinding uninhibited eroticism. Positions on our backs expose naked, panting, and sweating marathon runners. The mental question hits hard. — *Did you, Eric, learn these pleasures from couple swapping?'* I remain confident you did because my sexual appetite watching Richard's porn movies, inviting another woman or couple into our bed gives me all the tools for satisfaction.

*

"Before we commence to round ten," I gradually pull back from his next kiss, "I have a favor to ask. As I said, when I first got here, there's a real opportunity to design clothing."

It's hard to tell if the consuming perspiration is from nerves or sex. I think both.

"Can you draw up our contract?"

Did I not make myself clear? Eric scratches his head. "Give me a chance to explain, Eric, before you refuse."

"I have a couple of things to say, Diane. First of all, ask anything of me. How can I deny anything with you naked in my arms?"

I kiss him. "Thank you, Eric."

"Wait, before we fly to into sex-land again, who are these people?

Getting into a binding contract with strangers spells trouble." "I know. Remember, I was married to a lawyer, Eric."

"Touché," he grins, returning with a wet kiss into my mouth.

"She's Juliette Cloister," I announce. "You probably don't know her." Whatever I said, Eric rushes from the bed to the living room table where a *Times* newspaper is there for him to page through until stopping.

"Come here,"

My nudity doesn't matter next to his. "Is this the woman?"

"Yes. Juliette lives above me."

"I'll be damned. There's half a page about her upcoming collection. It seems she's the real deal. Look at this picture."

I don't recognize the two women with Juliette. I gasp reading their names in the captions. "One is the art director for the Metropolitan Museum and the other, Joanne Leaver, one of New York's richest socialites."

"Your neighbor won't be your neighbor too much longer with designing evening gowns for these types, Diane."

"I had no idea. Denver *isn't* New York."

Eric's hardy laugh accompanies one of his romantic movie kisses. "Yes, I'll write up the contract for you and Miss Juliette. I scored an *A* in business contract law 101."

'I love you' dangles on the tip of my mouth. Instead, I return Eric's kisses in bed during another intense lovemaking workout.

"What time is your meeting, Diane?"

"Juliette will knock on my apartment door tomorrow morning at nine."

He looks at the nightstand's clock. "Do you have to leave now?"

Thinking Nina won't be home until near dawn, or home at all, as is her way.

"No," I answer.

"Good."

Eric's beckoning body renders bliss until Mr. Cabbie comes past midnight.

*

A small light reflects from the window—Nina's home. "I beat you, Mom."

I get a daughter hug, and her pleasant mood settles us side-by-side on the sofa.

"Tell me about this man *who's* been sleeping with my mother."

"Is it obvious? I like him?"

"Mom, *are* you serious? Look at your hair, and your blouse is miss- buttoned."

We both notice my top and then burst into a roar.

"I told you his name, Eric Montgomery. We met perchance on my way to *Tea for Two*. Eric is an attorney," I reveal to her eye roll. "He's unlike your father."

"It's hard to find a perfect man, huh?" she kids. "So when do I meet *this,* Eric?"

"He'll be here in the morning, Nina. I have an appointment to meet our neighbor, Juliette, at her Soho working loft. She came over. Remember?"

"I love you, Mom. Take your chance at some happiness."

Richard's image holds tight. Forgetting the bastard ex-husband isn't easy.

"How was your evening, Nina?"

"Just friends Bill, Jessie, and Iris heard jazz in Harlem and ate dinner."

"We'll talk about *your happiness* later. I'm glad you're home, Nina. I do need to get some sleep for my meeting in the morning."

"Good night, Mom. I love you."

*

Thoughts of fulfillment: all is coming together. Richard would be proud. Why do I still care? Soon I'll return to Denver. Where are you, Ruby? Don't want Leah's visit. I wish I could see Samantha. Can I pull off designing clothes when I've never done anything before in my life? Eric. Eric. Eric.

*

"She's a Renaissance painting," Eric comments while we're walking down the outside steps.

"My children are different. Beauty connects them."

"None as beautiful as you are, Diane. You capture the seasons and the universe," Eric delivers a fiery good morning kiss as our cab pulls to the curb. "*I could love you*," he whispers.

We give the address; we hold hands. No words travel between us. Our about our age cab driver's slight nod seen through the rear-view mirror alleviates my embarrassment of Eric's open affections stroking my neck and kissing my hand.

"You're beautiful, Diane," he breathes life into my ear. "This is a good day."

I believe it, with him by my side and my sketches bound together on my lap.

*

Thoughts of home: if Eric says things to appease me, I don't care. If he makes love to me because I'm there, I don't care. Richard starved me for years. I must feed my soul — wet heat pulses between my legs. I don't care. Eric. Eric. Eric.

*

Thoughts are erasing home: instrumental harp music empties into speakers. Unexpected describe Juliette's loft of over massive unfinished plastered walls behind open metal shelves packed with spools of threads, boxes of buttons, zippers, and stacks upon stacks of magazines from A-Z. There are several commercial sewing machines, cutting tables, bolts of satins, silks, brocades, wools, and cotton piled and spread out over long, distressed wooden tables. White gauze curtains suspend on moveable rods hung from wooden beams sectioning off into work and eating areas. We follow into a room filled with oversized white, emerald, sapphire velvet sofas surrounded by wrought-iron tables saturated with poetry books, more fashion magazines, odd-shaped pottery with embellished stone, and glass vases holding occasional single red roses. All of this, a woman in a black silk robe, shows Eric and me, on tour, of my new career's office.

*

"Juliette will be here momentarily. Please have a seat. May I offer you a drink?" our guide asks. "My name is Gina," she introduces, "I work as a fitting model and secretary—if need be."

"No," we answer together.

Thrills collide with future uncertainty making it an effort not to fidget, taking it all in, and desperately wanting belonging.

After Gina leaves, I speak frankly, "Who would have thought that I'd have a fashion design studio, in an alley of once-abandoned warehouse buildings, now housing many of New York's prominent art galleries and restaurants? How different here is from my prison Denver-gated community, once home. Can I do this?"

"Imagination serves up adventures in many New York neighborhoods," Eric reminds me with a kiss to my hand. "Yes. You can do this, my dear."

Juliette calls into our space, "I'm sorry I'm late. I'm glad you got my note to leave ahead." Pushing back the curtain, she carries a bolt of red pepper silk. "This had my name on it for a design for a client. I'm Juliette Cloister," she introduces herself.

"Eric Montgomery," he replies, extending back her handshake.

"He is my attorney," I explain, "thinking if we decide, then Eric can draw up the papers."

"*I see.*" She takes him in, from head to his feet. "Good idea. I have an attorney, but he specializes in divorce." She presses a pinched lip while taking a seat opposite us. Toned bare calf muscles give me a small wonder if Eric's short glances would stay if I weren't here. His attention to me reinforces with a spontaneous kiss to my cheek.

"How endearing," Juliette remarks.

Catching myself, the object of this meeting pushes me back from Eric. "Your office, Juliette, is unexpected."

"I recognize your name and face from articles written," Eric adds. She leans into Eric. "*Then, your lady is in good hands.*"

He nods toward me. "I know."

An exchange between Juliette and me, I take as the first step to my new life. "I've brought my sketches."

Juliette's attention heightens the moment I set my sketchbook on top of magazines, placed on the table dividing us.

"What is your arrangement? Is there coffee?" Eric switches into lawyer mode.

"Bring some coffee, Gina," Juliette calls to our tour guide.

"The arrangement is this," Juliette starts as she reshuffles her crossing legs. "I've put in five-hundred thousand dollars. I need the same—for an equal partnership and serious investment. Can you do that?" she asks me without hesitation.

"*I can,*" I speak out before Eric can answer for me.

She turns to Eric, "I think Diane's talent is worth a fifty-fifty partnership. Have you seen her sketches?"

"Yes," he beams into my eyes. "So we are looking at a fifty-fifty split and ownership, Juliette?"

"I like to keep my life simple. Do you agree, Diane?" "I'm more than honored."

"Your ability to transport an idea from here," Juliette points to her heart, "and give it life is pure artistry. Coco Chanel and Edith Head had it and Diane, so do you."

I burst into tears, "I don't know what to say, except thank you."

Juliette's tightly wrapped arms reach around my shoulders stamps our agreement. "Welcome home," she tips her head and gives an enormous smile. "I can have the prelim-papers drawn up in a few days."

"Good." Juliette is satisfied. "I have ten commissions. We need to start as soon as the papers are signed. By the way, do you like the name, Cloister Fletcher? I think placing our names in alphabetical order brings a dynamic to our company and is the best way to keep logic in the business out of the drama department.

As I think of Richards and repeat the business name, confidence overcomes insecurity. I can do this. "I like it, Juliette. I do."

"Instead of coffee, this calls for champagne. Bring chilled champagne, Gina."

"I'm proud of you." Eric kisses my hand. "I'll help you with whatever you need."

"Drawing up these papers help," I respond with my kiss to his lips.

"Thank you, Eric, for the legal work. I have a Masters in Art from Vassar College, but the quid-pro of life escapes me." Juliette's enthusiasm rushes into her face. "I'm thrilled." She lifts her glass and toasts me, "To Diane Fletcher, a Denver unknown, now a New York lady of means, fashion, style, *and a knight named Eric.*"

*

Thoughts of revelations: we drink champagne. Gina and Juliette have animated laughter over a future international collection for wealthy clients, as they flip through my sketchbook. Eric tenderly strokes my neck. I want to call Richard. Why can't I let him go?

*

"Did you hear me, Diane?"

"I was thinking about my mother, Eric," a lie I hate to come out as comfortable as my kiss to his lips.

"I said I'm proud of you."

*

"We're happy, aren't we, Mom?" Nina repeats. "You've been busy these past few days going to your Soho office. We haven't seen each other, which is why I wanted us to walk in Central Park like we used to before Leah arrives tomorrow."

I lead, putting my arm through hers. I can't think of a time when I've been happier.

"This is a good place and time for me. Sarah arrives next week. All my girls *will* . . . are you going to be here when Leah visits?"

"*Maybe*," she mutters.

"I won't push you, Nina."

"Let's see how the first fifteen minutes go, Mom. Changing the subject, please, I can't believe you've hooked up with Juliette Cloister, whose designs stop traffic."

"The next time you go to a dinner party requiring a cocktail dress, let me know."

Our giddy laughs are something I've missed all those years living away from her.

"Are you seeing Eric tonight? I like him."

"Eric is special to me, Nina. I need you to understand that."

"Mom, I'm pleased you've found someone. Dad mistreated you and did the unthinkable. I hate him."

"I know," I mumble, giving little care about Richard because I'm finding myself.

Quiet continues as we stroll past many older couples, Richard's and my age.

I wonder two things. Is Richard with Julie? How long will Eric desire me?

"Let's order in," Nina suggests as we return to our starting point.

*

Thoughts of closeness: evening comes to an end with Chinese take-out. Nina sleeps in my bed. I need the living room to sketch Catherine Moore's evening dress for some event she's attending in a month. Samantha, where are you? Where's Ruby? What's Richard doing? Can't say the words, 'I love you' to Eric because Richard suffocates my mind too much. I left a message for Mother and Camille. I miss them. I think they'll be proud of me.

*

"Samantha, this is Diane. Call me when you can. I've news to share. I'm doing well." Next call.

"Cleo. Hello."

"How are you, Diane?"

"You sound sleepy? Did I wake you, Cleo?"

"I *have* company, honey. All divas have needs."

"I won't keep you except to tell you I've formed a company with another designer. Our Soho loft is where we work."

"Did you finally meet Jules? I mean, Juliette. Catherine Moore and I thought your two talents would be fabulous."

I laugh, complimenting, "You're quite the connector. Juliette and I have formed a partnership."

"This is New York, honey. I know where the Loft is. Why don't I come around in a few days, say Tuesday at two in the afternoon?"

"We'll see you then. Good night, Cleo." "How's your man, Diane?"

Squeezing my breasts as he does, salivates images of our last two full-throttle nights of lovemaking, bathing together, having our meals together, and me exiting his apartment for business meetings with Juliette. His door keys, on my key chain, prove we're past casual.

"*He's good*," I surrender.

"We'll talk, my dear," she whispers. Her bed-guest must be calling.

"Talk to you later, Cleo."

It's too late to call Mother or Camille. I'll catch them in the morning before Leah comes. Need to pull me together with a hard night-cap. The schedule hasn't allowed me to think about you, Leah. Now I have to.

*

"When will she be here?"

Nina wrinkles up her nose with a glass of wine—not yet ten in the morning. Not a good sign.

"You look fine. It's just Leah," I try hard, reassuring her and me. "*You don't have to be here, Nina.*"

My words are more meant for me as I watch the clock-watching me.

Leah's last voice mail says taxi arrives before eleven.

"Stop pacing, Mom." Nina offers her wine. "Drink, it'll loosen you up."

"Whatever happens, promise me you'll not say anything cheap. You won't pick a fight. I want us to be family."

My heart thumps perspiration onto my face. Dabbing my forehead shows an unintended weakness.

Nina reads me well, "*Leah isn't the parent—you are. I'll get your refreshments ready.*"

*

Thoughts of anxiety: today will either make or break my relationship with Leah. It's been months since last seeing her. I'm no longer begging her for anything. I got freedom; I'll extend a courtesy hand to forgive and heal. God give me the right words. The doorbell rings.

*

"She's here," Nina scoffs, "b*etter not piss me off.*"

"Don't start," I warn her answering the intercom. "Hello? Leah?" "It's me."

"I'll buzz you in. We're on the second floor." "I can read your name on the register."

"I'll walk down and get her. Set out our appetizers on the new silver cart."

"In my book, Leah is nobody special, Mom, but I do this for you."

"She's my daughter *and* your sister. We're family."

There's no time to address Nina's sour face. Because opening our apartment door, enthusiasm overcomes seeing Leah walk toward me. God help us.

*

"You made it, Leah." "Hello, Mother."

Breathe. Wrap your arms around Leah to prove you're glad she's here. Ignore her hard eye rolls. Ignore that she doesn't reciprocate.

"Home is down the hall," I say to a stranger beside me. *"Home, I guess for you . . . c*onsidering what you gave up."

"I'm happy, Leah, for the first time in years. Your sister is here."

I open the door to Nina's daggers. It's not even five minutes, and this visit smells like shit.

"Hello, Nina," Leah imparts a matching chill.

Nina lips the word, *bitch*, as Leah's three-inch heels strut pas her. "Where's your luggage?" Nina observes what I also see, a black shoulder bag and black leopard collar coat.

Leah sizes up our minimalist décor then turns to me. "I'm at the *Plaza.* Camille told me the both of you live in a one-bedroom. I find it *interesting."*

"Our sofa lets out into my bed. New York small apartments are about location and proximity to the subway. Ours is in a *most desirable neighborhood."*

"I *do* know the city, dear sister," Leah snaps back.

"Whatever, Leah," Nina's annoyance relocates into the kitchen, pulling together our food.

Defusing an escalating tension becomes a mother's priority.

I offer the chair. "Sit. You look good, Leah. Paris agrees with you." "Like *you*, Mother, I *am* happy."

Nina rejoins with glasses, a decent bottle of Bordeaux, cloth napkins, a plate of imported brie and blue cheeses, and slices of a baguette from *Michele's* Leah pours a full glass.

"You're not eating? You know Mom went through a lot of trouble," Nina questions Leah, who passes stares from me to the food. "Geez, like our food isn't good enough for you."

"You shouldn't have gone to any trouble. I'll have a little bit."

"Whatever," Nina answers as she pours herself a full glass and piles on cheese and bread. Shall we make a toast seeing you, Leah, after this long time?"

"Sure, let's make a toast to our little reunion," Leah sincerity sounds more mocking than anything else.

"You're engaged?" Nina cuts a mean once-over glance.

After patting her mouth, Leah, for the first time, smiles, flashing a large diamond solitaire. "He's CFO Lee Dubois, in France helping expand markets for his family's vinery. We met when I took on his family's bid to import here. The rest is history."

"*How nice,*" Nina spouts off, towering over Leah.

"Nina. Sit down," I demand, not liking Nina's lurching body movements.

"I won't, Mom. How can you tolerate Leah after *what* you know?" "Not now, Nina. *Please, stop,*" I order watching Leah's severe stare bounce between us.

"This was a bad idea. I'm leaving."

"Wait. Nina." I say in desperation, knowing her mind is out the door. "What the fuck," she fumes, looking at Leah watching with a malicious grin. Grabbing her jacket and keys off the counter, Nina faces her sister. "*I'm done with, Leah.*"

Nina slams the door. It echoes throughout the hallway—my heart breaks.

"Nina, *my dear, dear twin, is the ever drama queen,*" Leah unfazed ridicules.

Breathe. Say what's held inside for months. "Do you know why she's pissed, Leah?"

She does the eyes roll thing again and pouting from a mouth coated in blood-red lipstick. Legs cross red-bottom soled *D&G* shoes. Hands fold into a dress I saw in *Bloomingdales*. This visit isn't going to be easy.

"No. I've made an effort. I don't appreciate her *shitty* attitude." Sarcasm swings high. Breathe. Breathe. Breathe. You're the mother.

She's the daughter.

"You didn't ask how I'm doing, Leah."

"I suppose fine. You're divorcing Father." "What did Richard tell you?"

"Father's comment—the relationship ended." "He made no other remarks?"

"What *are* you digging at?"

She taunts, raising her eyebrow resembling Richard's intimidation.

Keep saying, *'You're the mother. She's the daughter.'*

"My marriage ended for many reasons."

She twists her mouth even more. "Your point is?"

I must move past me to the subject I've harbored for months. "I've formed a company with the designer, Juliette Cloister."

"So, your little drawing hobby pays off?" she smirks. Leah's defiance frightens me. She's as cold as Richard. "Look at me. Do you know why Nina is distant?" "Should I care?"

"Yes, you should because Sarah revealed a story when you three visited my mother."

"*What* the hell are you talking about?" she demands with a fingernail in my face. Leah's jester, I hate.

Grip her arm so she won't leave.

"You're hurting me, bitch. Let go of me."

Secrets rip out tear after tear until trembling overcomes my composure. "Sarah divulged you and your father kissing outside his London hotel room."

Silence pounds silence. A mother seeks answers, not her daughter's fits of anger. My child mimics my husband. Lunges ready to choke.

"You goddamn bitch," my daughter unhinges. One-two-three punches to my chest. Two severe slaps to my face. "*Let me tell you something, my dear fucked-up mother.*"

"*I'm your mother,*" I implore her to look into my face.

I'm sobbing and tasting blood running from my closing eye. I'm no match for her pulling me back, landing to my face a hard slap, then two more.

"I *have* the floor now. Do you *mind, Mother?*"

Protect yourself. Take your wine glass. If Leah attacks again—do what you must—deal later with the consequences. You will no longer be anyone's punching bag.

"You see, dear mother," she yells then downs two consecutive wines, "I need alcohol as you did all these years. We're both little fucking drunks."

Vomit wants out; my daughter throws wine in my face. She laughs, swallow hard. Take napkin. Wipe spit, wine, and blood. Don't show fear. The daughter's fists have control.

"Father calls you stupid, and a weak idiot, erasing his life with neediness. Why didn't you ever go to college instead of living off his money and pining after your children who'd leave one day? You're a lazy excuse for a mother." My daughter screams as if I'm deaf. I wish it true.

"I loved you all. Richard won't let me do anything except being his wife."

"Liar, liar," she fires back. "Father said your one-word answers at client dinners and *that* drinking embarrassed him. He offered to send you to college, but you refused.

Exhausted puzzlement adds to the pain. "This isn't true about college. I drank. My life was hell. I had to choose my words or get my ass kicked for choosing the wrong words, Leah."

"Father shared his frustrations. Our intelligence matched. I've been his confidant *for years*." She closes in with a half-grin. "*I have more, Mother. Do you want to hear it?*"

I weep into my hands. "*Go on, Leah.*"

Her cruel laughter drives me to the brink of smashing my glass into her face.

"You'll like this part, dear Mother. I'm fifteen. You take lovely Nina and Sarah for their ballet and violin lessons. Father takes me to the Club for lunch, celebrating my decision to study law. We got home late because he fucks me, taking my virginity in some hotel one hundred miles from home. *Nope. I didn't get pregnant.*"

She shoves me off the cliff. Shock dissolves into trembling terror, tasting drips of my vomit. I could cut her throat if I broke this wine glass, but why, when Richard is the fucking monster.

"I didn't know, Leah—I didn't know. *Why* didn't you tell me?" I wail. I've gone numb. "It's all true about Richard. *How could he?*"

"You knew. I know you did."

"No. I confronted your father before we decided to divorce. He lied. I didn't know, Leah. I swear. I could've saved you."

"*Save me?*" Leah chugs more wine, then laughs. "A fucking joke, when you couldn't save yourself. All women know when their mates are abusing their children. They choose to ignore it for security. Don't tell me its fear. Anyone can leave. You had big bucks, my dear mother." Leah's erratic sobbing-laughter echoes torment. But she won't let me touch her.

"I didn't know." "You did."

I take her slaps but still reach for her. "I love you, Leah. I love you." "Why did you argue with him? Did his family's position mean so goddamn much? He beat you. You stayed. I lost respect a long time ago. I put up with so much. You weren't there for me." Leah weeps as I've never seen, yet still refuses me. I wish she'd take a knife from the kitchen and stab me until she cried no more.

"Leah, please come here," I beg.

She distances more—twisting her hands together-uneven pacing in circles around the room. I doubt even Samantha can heal Leah's damage.

"Your comfort comes years late. Father's demons ruined my damn life. It's ironic and pathetic. Obsessed love comes when a father fucks his daughter."

Lacerations drop continual blood down my cheeks; the scenario playing is Richard and me all over again.

"Remember when you asked me to visit? I turned you down on purpose. I intentionally told Father—warning to tell you about him and me if he didn't stop you. I didn't want to see you, Mother. I blame you for my unhealthy addiction to my father. I hate you for sharing Father's bed because I'm his equal, not you."

All I can think about is the courage to consume those remaining sleeping pills.

"I left the firm after I became a partner. I called Father and told him if he ever came near me again, I'd kill him. You see, after *aborting* his child last year, my hell follows me around like a fucking shadow."

"Damn you, Richard," I scream. "You were pregnant with your father's child? Oh, God. Oh, God. No God. If you didn't want to talk to me, why didn't you reach out to your sisters, Leah? Your father is a criminal."

She walks toward me in a frantic outrage. I cover my face and head, feeling the same fear as I did with Richard. "Father is a bastard. I won't press charges to drag my name is the fucking sewer. My sisters *hate* me; I have no family. Camille gave me your address; I don't need her anymore; we've nothing in common. Grandmother will be dead soon. I said goodbye when I saw her. You and I are no more connected than strangers on the subway you take." She chuckles. *"I take that back. We do have something in common."*

Hearing her haunting laughter as she gathers her belongings after finishing her wine it terrifies me, her fixating into my face of mush.

"I owe you thanks for giving me birth. I owe you thanks for seeing I had the best education. I owe you thanks for my beauty. And I owe your weakness thanks because it made me strong and fucked-up. Goodbye, Mother. Don't ever contact me. I never want to look at you one more second of my life. I'll kill you. Are we clear?"

Leah's leaving is my life's indignation.

*

Thoughts of guilt: how could I have been a better parent and wife? Recorded in the mirror is your daughter's anger: black bruises about your cheeks, swelling over your left eye, swollen lips, and discoloration on your forehead. The mother breaks down. Why didn't you suspect a husband and daughter's voluntary closeness? Will admitting their persistent bullying weakening your self-worth validate withdrawing love for your daughter as it had long ago for your husband?

*

"I'm calling the police. Bitch canceled her reservations a week ago, according to the *Plaza's Manager. Where the fuck is she?"* Shift to another reality—Nina is standing in the bedroom's doorway, and her voice is driving crazy. "Leah is not getting away with this shit," Nina's yelling isn't what I need. "I found you on the floor. You need to go to emergency. *Why the fuck did she hurt you?"*

Remain calm.

"Bring the ice packs and my phone."

Her hands tremble the more she starts crying. "Mom, I'd never treat you like Leah and Daddy."

Take the truth to your grave. "Leah and I got into a fight about all the things she's been harboring."

"Was it about her and Daddy?"

"We had a long conversation about Richard. I don't want to talk about it now, Nina. I can't relive the words."

Nina edges inward, forcing a confrontation I don't want. "She *can't* blame you?"

"I don't want to talk about it now, Nina." "Don't you trust me?"

"I do, but for now, no more questions, please."

"I hate Leah, Mom," Nina discloses for the millionth time. "I'll make you some tea."

*

Thoughts of exhaustion: hearing Nina cry fries my desperation. How can I tell her? I need to talk to you, Samantha. It's been too long.

* "Hello, Camille. How's Mother?"

"We're all fine, Diane. You'll never guess who picked her up?" "I can't tell by your voice if I should be happy or upset. Tell me."

"Helen Fletcher. Over the past weeks, she's reaching out to Mom." "Why?"

"I don't know except a week after you left, she called with Leah's address. I remember you hadn't been able to reach Leah, so I gave it to her. Have you spoken to her?"

Rubbing my tongue throughout my mouth—Leah's scent is still fresh. "I saw her today."

"Did you? She loves France. Odd, she wants to stay in touch, or so she says. Anyway, about Mom, Helen invited her for lunch. I thought it was okay. You're not mad, are you, Diane?"

"No."

"How do you like designing? I'm all goose-bumps with your news. I saw one of Juliette's designs in an issue of *Vogue*. I don't know where I'd wear a ball gown."

Hearing Camille speak tastes like home, something I need because I've lost my soul to Leah and Richard's relationship.

"Diane, I said, Mom can't stop bragging about you." It hurts my jaw to smile.

"I love you, Camille. How are the kids and Alan?"

"Alan's a new school counselor. It's a goal he's been aspiring for several years. My kids keep me in shape, taking care of them. How do you like living with Nina?"

I lie, "She's fine," hearing Nina cry in the kitchen.

"I'd like to come and see you, Diane, one day." She sounds sad. "Mom can't make the flight, you know. She's taking homeopathic medicine, which is about all I can force down her throat."

"As soon as I'm able, Camille, I'm coming home."

"Do you want anything to eat? I'm heating the leftover Chinese food," Nina interrupts.

"Okay."

"Is that Nina?" Camille asks.

I know this isn't a good time because of what transpired with Leah. I lie again, "Your niece stepped out to get our take-out."

*

Thought of needs: my mind flutters between needing pills, to needing alcohol, to needing to hold my children, to need to make love to Eric. No. Eric mustn't see me. They'll be too many questions. Confusion strains my eyesight. I need you, Samantha. Why can't I let go of Richard?

*

"Diane, did you hear me? I'm proud of you. I'll make sure Mom calls you."

"Don't push her, sis. Say I called and will check back in a couple of days."

"Okay. By the way, Diane, there wasn't any need to send me a check for Mom. I didn't cash your five-thousand-dollar check."

"I want you to. I'm sending one every month. Helen's settlement makes *many* things possible."

"*Dear* old Helen, I admire her grace. Alan thinks she puts on airs.

Mom says, why not let the old bitch treat her considering *Richard.*"

I close my eyes and vividly see his face and wish it burned in acid. "I haven't spoken to him, Camille."

"I've lots of questions. They can wait until you come home. I need to go now, Diane. Alan is coming through the door. I'm sending you a hug and much love."

"Good night, Camille."

*

Thoughts of regret: Nina and I tiptoed around Leah's visit two days ago.

Glances slip, but words hold. I want to talk but not about Leah or Richard.

*

"We'll be fine once Sarah comes next week," Nina reminds me as we do the wash-the-dishes-pour-a-glass-of-wine thing. "I'll be glad to see her. Don't worry about me asking about you-know-who."

Brave a happy face. Nina can't tell Sarah about the fight. "How are the family at home and our grandmother?"

"Things are fine. I'm making a trip after I get a handle on what Juliette and I are designing."

"You're doing it, Mom." A smile helps wither Nina tears. "If you don't mind, I want to visit a friend for a bit. I won't be home late *unless you need me.* We also should get something for your face. I can get my hands on camera cosmetic make-up from a photographer I work with."

I answer, remembering Denver, *"I have plenty.* I'll be fine; I'm going to call Eric; ice packs are helping with the swelling. I'm a bit stuck with a black–eye." My laugh is more for me than Nina.

I allow her fingers to study my face. Her dismay requires nothing as her arm tightens around my waist. "I underestimate you, Mom," she whispers. "I love you."

* Breathe in, breathe out. Call Eric.

*

Thoughts of many mistakes: he touches me but not with his hands. We dance but not together. Usual compliments about my natural beauty void of make-up aren't spoken—judgmental leers over my hammered face—despite my fondness, whether we continue depends on him.

*

"Are you afraid?" He eases back.

"Talk to me, Eric."

"Why would you let your ex-husband come here? Where's Nina?" Now I understand. I need another drink.

"Do you want a glass of wine, Eric?" "I *want* answers."

Pour wine. Take a deep confessional breath to no push Eric out of your life, thinking you are not what he hoped.

"Nina left before you came. *Richard didn't do this,*" continuing as I drink with nothing to lose, "my *daughter Leah* did it. Don't ask me why. I can't rehash her words."

Repulsive shock hits hard. "I'll have that wine now." Hold back tears. Rejoin my reluctant guest.

"Can you tell me a little of *what* happened, Diane?" His touch opens my pent-up emotions.

Sobs are more for me than him out of desperation for someone to listen. Confession is killing me, but the guilt of Leah's entire story is locked, hidden, and buried within me. I do what I do best, telling a partial truth, "I've told you my daughter and my husband were seen together by her sister," I admit a disgusting topic again. Not even his caressing hands can make this story tolerable or halt volumes of guilt, drenching shame into my hands. "Leah blames me for Richard's abuse since she was fifteen."

"You're a good person, Diane. I told you she's the one who has to press charges. I will help you any way I can. I'll talk to her if you wish." "Leah said *all mothers know. Maybe* fear of Richard's relations, and, oh God, my hatred that their personalities, intelligence, interests, and ambitions matched line for line—could've made me ignore signs. Around them, I heard phrases *stupid, inferior, trophy wife.* Of all our children, Richard stood by Leah, rain or shine. Maybe I knew but didn't care?"

"You *would've* left him," Eric analyzes. *"Are you sure? You don't know me."*

"I do, Diane, because . . . *I love you.*" His fingers and lips touch each of Leah's marks.

"I love you, Eric." I close my eyes, pretending Richard and I never met. "You're still here, and all my shit doesn't matter?"

"I love you, Diane," I'm here and will be until you send me away."

*

Thought of exposure: I'll go to Hell because there's a *big if,* on what I knew and didn't, to stop Richard.

*

"Diane, I want to help you. Did you hear me?" My shoulder-to-cry- on brings me a glass of water. "I've finished your partnership paperwork. I have a doctor who can attend to your abrasions. I'll take you tomorrow."

"Sorry, I drifted off. Sleep is not my friend. Do you know a detective?"

"Why?"

My reason speaks, "I'm going to hire one to keep an eye on Leah just in case she needs me. One day I tell you every secret, but not today. I want to say I love you and imagine us happy." His hand takes mine. "What about Richard?"

"I'm done with him. I won't drag my child through court pressing charges.

My divorce will be final in a few months, Eric. I'm on my way to realizing my dreams. Men like Richard always get theirs."

"You and I will share everything from now on. I'm asking for a divorce, Diane. I desperately want to add to your happiness. Despite all you've been through with Leah, can you accept my news, and *our* future?"

"Eric. You don't mean it?"

Another long kiss proves me wrong.

"You made me long for you the moment I met you. Remember?"

I laugh. "Cleo and I were ready to cross the street after leaving *Tea for Two*. You stood next to me and said, *'Hello.'*"

"We were meant to meet, Diane." "We're two divorcees, Eric."

"It doesn't matter. Marry me next summer, Diane. I'll be divorced, and you'll also be. We'll go away to Europe. You're *the one* I should've married."

"Yes. I will," weeping as if this moment will disappear.

"I'll never hit you. I'll love you until I stop breathing, then I will wait for you in heaven. Following your dream has made me realize I'm happiest working at my mother and sister's restaurant—*A Piece of Heaven*."

"Are you leaving the law profession?" I wonder.

"I've asked the firm to buy me out. My heart is more with the restaurant. I think another chance with you has led me to life-changing choices. Do you understand?"

"*Yes, Eric.*"

I melt undoing my top, exposing myself.

Our time moves with love and obsession into my bed's open arms.

*

Thoughts of untied nerves: birthday is in three days. Much happens over the next two weeks: doctor visits healing Leah's anger beating. Cleo's ongoing gown changes need finishing partnership papers with Juliette require more details than realizing. Juliette and I don't judge each other's past. We'll talk when it's right, design decisions need finalizing for our next fall's debut collection. Plan grand opening Christmas soiree for *Cloister Fletcher Couture* in two months. Sarah's visit moves to next week.

When we're all together, tell the daughters about marriage plans. Eric erases Richard. Pay Nina's tuition for enrollment to Parsons. Reservations made to visit Mom and Camille. Meet with the detective about Leah. Return Richard's call.

*

"We agree about me living in their housing apartments close to the school?"

"Yes, Nina," my almost worry answers, "don't forget Saturday we'll be meeting at Eric's restaurant."

"Leah labels me a professional student taking general classes at NYU, then Columbia. I *hate* her. Some people take longer to decide on what they want."

I drift toward the coffee table covered with fashion magazines, sketches, and my cell phone recalling the last words Eric said to me this morning, *'I love you.'*

"Let's not bash Leah anymore. You're right. Life gives you what you want when you need it or something like that." Laughing more at my life than at Nina's, I offer my slant, "Find your way. I can help. Parsons will give you options."

"You like *him*. I can tell. You don't love him as you did, Dad."

"Your father is a sick person. I stayed out of fear, insecurity, and because I loved him. He destroyed our family. Secrets destroyed our family." Moving toward the window distracts tears. I'm tired of shedding.

"Dad still sends checks every September for school and living expenses. I guess he thinks I'm a professional student, too. Here," she hands me an opened envelope, "it's a check for twenty-thousand dollars."

"He got a good deal selling the house."

"It could be for a million. I'll *still* hate Richard, my ex-father." Hearing her voice shatter, I must help Nina move through this.

Holding my daughter close is my full plate, "Nina. Listen to me. Richard needs help. All you can do is pray for him. You must release this hatred, or you will never find love. If I can, then you can."

"I love you, Mom."

I hug her tighter. "My dear Nina, we'll be fine."

"I promised Alex to hang some pictures in his apartment."

"You like him. I *can* tell," I mimic Nina's teasing gestures colossal laugh. "When do I meet him?"

"I don't know. I care for Alex but haven't had sex. It's a friendship not demanding much."

"You'll figure it out, Nina."

"I think so, Mom. I'll be back not too late. Are you spending the night at Eric's?" she snickers.

"I want to."

Her kiss on my cheek makes me happy. "I like him. Have a good evening."

*

Thoughts of awareness: home. Alone. Joy has been a long time coming. I'm wearing my skin. No one will ever again strip it away. Get it over and return Richard's call after I check on Mother.

*

"How are you, Diane?"

"I'm coming home at the end of October."

Mother sounds much weaker. The answer is she's dying. Pretend she has years ahead. Close your eyes. Remember the day she took you and Camille ice skating, or the time she showed you how to bake your dad's favorite deep-dish apple pie.

"Camille says you've formed a company designing clothes for *high society*?"

"I did, with Juliette Cloister."

"Your sister showed me magazine pictures of her clothes. You've got talent. Don't ever doubt it because this Juliette would've passed you by."

"I'm making you a dress for Christmas."

"I hope not one of those ten-thousand-dollars dresses to be cremated in."

"God, Mother. Why do you talk as if you've one foot in the grave?

Camille says you're taking medication?"

"I take a pill here, a pill there. What damn difference does it make?" She does that stern, no-nonsense tone so well. "I'm entering stage-four cancer. Hair is going fast. Some days are good. Some are bad. I'm doing what I want as long as I want. Don't ask me again about some damn medication."

"I love you, Mother. I've so much to tell you. Camille says you're seeing Helen these days?"

"Shit. It's Helen's idea to get *acquainted*." Mother's laughter sounds normal if it wasn't for a cough. "She's attached herself to me as a damn puppy. It's a bit too late in the game. All the years you and that fool been married, I couldn't stand her upper-crust-British accent bullshit. Wealth with an absent husband whose affairs she accepts, grandchildren she doesn't see, and family secrets no one should ever tell, gives me cause to be dead sooner than later. I fill her life, so her conscience will be clear when I die. I don't care."

"*What* secrets, Mother?"

God make her tell me. Did Helen reveal anything about Richard and Leah?

"I'm tired now, Diane. Camille and Alan are over at his parents'. I'll tell them you phoned."

"Tell me . . . *what secrets?*"

"Diane, stop your whining. Secrets are good or bad. The Fletchers have many. We *all* do. I'm glad Richard is out of your life. Live your dreams. Don't waste two thoughts on Denver."

*

Thoughts of falling and gone: Mother's call ends before I want. Something's wrong. She shuts down. Nothing opens. I'd see her tomorrow if not for all these pending obligations.

*

"You're drunk, aren't you?" "I'm not."

He's lying. I can tell his words are slurring. "I called you three days ago, Diane."

"I'm busy, Richard. How did you get my cell number? None of my family would give it to you. Did Leah?"

He laughs in between sips of whatever. "Leah? No. I'm an attorney with endless resources. I know where you live and who you're fucking."

*

Thoughts of entrapment: I'll never be free. Why won't Richard leave me alone? I asked nothing from him.

*

"What do you want, Richard?"

"Take the damn chip off your shoulder. After all this time, why can't we be civil?"

Don't initiate anything. Be short with your answers to end the call. Don't give in to that Richard's stalking you bullshit. His hands are full with Julie.

"Richard, I'm fine. How are you?"

He laughs louder in a tone scaring me. He's miles away, or is he? "I'm moving to Sweden. My son will be born in a few months." "What about your practice?"

I hear more sips of whatever he's throwing down his throat.

"Dad asked me to take a break to tie up all the loose ends with us, the property, the marriage, and Julie. Damn bastard. I said, fuck it. Called Julie—*because I couldn't call you*—we'll see what happens."

All the time he's talking, I'm fixing a drink of the last Scotch I hid for emergencies. Our conversation is one of those priceless fucking emergencies.

"I *hope* you're happy, Richard, given the years you and Julie have been involved. No. You couldn't call me with your problems. Our marriage is over."

"Maybe you have a little backbone from me kicking your ass, Diane?"

"I had a lifetime of you beating the shit out of me to make me strong.

You've hurt our daughters and me enough."

"I loved our daughters. I'd never hurt them. You *know* that."

Get it out. Make the bastard tell you the truth about Leah. "Richard, did you ever touch Leah?"

"Bitch, I told you no. Why are you bent on slinging shit on me?" "Rage doesn't even come close to how I feel. I'm going to say this, and then I'll never talk to you again. If you stalk me, I don't care. If you kill me, I don't care. I will go to my grave with this. Leah told me when she was fifteen, that you molested her and have been raping her for years. You sick son-of-a-bitch. She told me she got pregnant last year with your fucking child."

"Diane, Leah is a damn bitch. She's a liar. If I did all she told you, Leah would have told you. She makes a fool out of you."

"Leah visited me two weeks ago and said the vilest things a child could say to their parent."

"Do you believe her, Diane? Answer me, bitch."

"Look at yourself in the mirror, Richard. You'll see my answer nailed to your soul. Whatever happiness you crave and desire, I hope you find it in hell."

"I'm not the sick animal, you think. I've always provided for you and our family."

Swallow hard. "And I'm not as dumb as you think. I will kill you if you come near Nina, Sarah, or Leah again, and they tell me. I mean every word. I'll kill you, Richard. I'll go to prison for the rest of my life if it means you'll never be able to hurt my daughters again. If I knew what you were doing, I would've seen you rot in jail, so you'd be some man's bitch being raped day in and day out."

"I'll never admit anything, Diane."

"I know. All those years, I loved you. Goodbye, Richard. Leave me alone. Don't ever call me again."

"Life is what you think you know, not what you expect. Goodbye, Diane."

*

Thoughts of my death: depression sharpens. Curse Richard until words are full inside my mouth. Cry until guilt bleeds my eyes red. God forgive Richard and me.

*

"Hello."

"Cleo here, Diane." "Yes."

"I called to tell you don't make any more changes to my gown.

What's up with you, honey?" "I'm fine, Cleo."

"You sound drunk. What happened? You need me. I'm always a cab away, girlfriend."

"I just had a phone call with Richard." "What happened? You want to talk?"

"It's done. One day saying his name won't bring horrible memories." "I can come over, Diane."

"I'm going to see Eric in a bit. I'll let Juliette know about your fitting."

"How's that going?"

"It's been a full two weeks with legal papers, finalizing our debut collection. The routine is reasonable; I get in about nine. My business partner comes in about nine-thirty. I like her; we'll see how long the honeymoon lasts. We agree. We complement each other's styles. It's an all-new me—working that is. I like it. I do."

"I tell all the women I help through *Lost and Found*, Diane, if you want to sing your song, open your mouth and sing about what you want to be and do. Honey, you're singing a damn opera."

Cleo's home-grown sense of humor can cut through life's bullshit. A few sniffles and a big smile pull me out of the dark.

"I still want to volunteer my time, Cleo."

"Honey, you're busy. Your check each month helps more than you know.

Some ladies I meet come to me in a terrible state with just the clothes on their back. Some come with children. My company's landlord raised the rent. I'm trying to buy a place."

Her statement gives me cause to be grateful for three unexpected gifts, Helen's settlement, a new career, and Eric.

"I'll make time to volunteer on Sunday or Saturday for coffee or a good conversation with a woman who lost her voice *like me. I know I can help her sing.*"

"I'm sure you can, honey. I look forward to your help."

Whispering Ruby's name forces a long drink down; one day, I'll find you, Ruby. I promise.

"Thank you, Cleo, for calling me." "You okay?"

"I *will be* because I'm singing my opera," I say, laughing at the thought of it because I can't carry a tune.

"I'll be at your studio in two days."

"Your gown is ready except for a pressing." "Good night, Diane."

*

Thoughts of captivity: keep on singing. One day Richard's memory won't hurt. Your life belongs to you.

*

"I have an early birthday present for you," he teases with hands behind him.

I move to the left. Eric turns to the right, moving about like a playful child.

"I give," pretend pout surrenders, "show me, Eric."

His hands reveal folded papers. His grin must mean good news. "My signed divorce papers—*I'll be free.*"

My reading catches the lines: *irreconcilable differences.* "She didn't fight you?" I ask with a slight panic.

"No. The papers were prepared months and months ago except the date. There's nothing to do. We had a prenup, my sons' Trust Fund, from their grandfather, pays for the college, I keep half our savings and investments, I keep my car and my apartment. She keeps the Long Island house. She won't fight me because of her lover and the mess I could make.

I walk away, and she gets to fuck who she wants to her heart's content, without fear, I'll barge in on them."

A soft landing into his sofa brings stillness thinking about marriage resolved with a quick signature.

"Is this what you want, Eric?"

His answer is ready with a locking kiss.

"I've loved you from the second I saw you. No one else comes *before you or after you*. I want to take my last breath in your arms, Diane. Marry me."

The legal papers tumble out of my hands onto the floor. I hold my lover's head between my palms. I know what I know. It feels—honest.

"I love you, Eric. I want to be your wife until the day I die."

"No one, Diane, *and I mean no one w*ill ever hurt you again. I make you that substantial promise."

*

Thoughts of calm: lovemaking falls into two categories: want and have to. Eric sleeps with my body inside his arms; I feel safe. I feel happy. I feel loved.

*

"I must leave soon," I remember. "Cleo is coming to the studio for her last fitting."

"No matter what our schedules, we'll have morning coffee," Eric greets me with a kiss showing me to the table with the roses he gave me last night.

My mind travels back to those Richard days when the beginning of the day started with an uncertain ending. Eric is no less handsome or accomplished. It's his quiet satisfaction, making my needs, and wants come first that dress him a better man.

"What are you thinking, Diane?"

"My thoughts are a joy to be here with you, Eric. We found each other, its one miracle in all the millions of people in this city."

"Love happens every second, Diane. Ours took one of those chance-seconds. I'll see you tonight?"

I blush to his fingers running through my hair. "I'll see you tonight."

*

Thoughts of contentment: how can a birthday be better? I recall loneliness because Richard was away on his business trip. Now I choose not wallowing in what I thought would be the rest of my life. Cleo has picked up her gown. Juliette and I narrow down the collection. My workspace consumes magazines, swatches of materials, charcoal sketches, and New York's skyline. All is perfect, knowing I'm in the place I should be. Juliette saunters gracefully, humming as her hair drapes long about her waist. She compares one sketch to another with precise calculation, setting aside the ones not cutting our collection. I'm okay with Juliette's decisions because this is just the beginning of a long line of learning experiences.

*

"Your choices are strong, Diane, for the collection. It's sexy and striking as if Coco Chanel is having dinner with Marilyn Monroe. Are you comfortable using red and black and white for winter?"

"I think winter needs a pop of drama. A woman's curves as in a coat I've designed should cover her from what she wants to hide." A snapshot of Richard's beatings about my arms conjures up a brilliant red coat I purchased in London that hid my marks, allowing me to forget. "A woman's coat gives the illusion everything in her life is perfect."

"I understand." Juliette ponders while putting my design on top of the new collection.

"Vibrant red and piercing white coats with collars pull up, and a button to the side will be one of our showpieces."

Her acceptance means more than she'll know. "Thank you, Juliette."

"Dine, let me tell you a tale. When my husband got jealous of my time drawing and collecting fabric and going to school, he showed me his love." A stark stare holds me. "His hands were cruel and vicious." She holds up her left hand. "He broke all my fingers except my thumb as a reminder he came first. He's in prison for putting out a hit on me."

The late sun doesn't warm the room.

"I can't have children. Winters bother my hands. Love is obsolete. Solitude brings me peace. I admire your affection for Eric, whose help with our partnerships is invaluable."

"You'll find someone," I try assuring.

"I want success more than love. I don't care to discuss our husbands ever, Diane. The negativity drowns and buries."

Agreement when we clink our cups of tea. Juliette will never know my hell. I won't ask more of hers.

*

"Happy birthday, Mum," Sarah wakes me up.

"Sorry, Mom, but you didn't have on your cell phone. She called me instead."

Opening my eyes from a late night of drinking with Eric doesn't matter because Sarah called and Nina's here.

"Sarah. Thank you. We're looking forward to seeing you."

"It's next week for sure," her energy runs through my veins, "and we'll all be together."

No mention of Leah. As if a part of our lives has died or never been born. Looking at the only picture on my dresser I kept from the Denver house is the three of them when they were barely teenagers on Christmas morning in front of the fireplace. *I'm sorry, Leah'* I breathe through Sarah's talking.

"Did you hear me, Mom?"

"Excuse me, Sarah. Nina's talking to me." "What is it, Nina?"

"There's a policeman on the intercom asking for you." Her apprehensive face worries me. "Sarah. I need to go. I'll call you back."

"Mum? What's wrong? Nina said something about a policeman?" "I have to go. I'll call you back, Sarah."

A tremendous itch overtakes my scalp; nerves stop concentration. Something has happened to Eric. I shake fearing and bracing for horrible news.

"Hello. Yes. Can I help you?"

"This is Officer Mitchell. We need to speak to you."

"What is it, Mom?" Nina huddles giving me no room to move. "*Why are the police here?*"

A knock on my door comes as I'm about to let in the policeman. It's my landlord, Catherine. "Diane. The police are here. What's wrong?"

Rattled, she pushes in, reaching for the chair. "I came wishing you a happy birthday and heard the police calling you. I identified myself as the owner of the building. Two officers, a man, and a woman want to speak with you. I let them in. They're waiting in the lobby." Catherine's massive worried look mixes with the perspiration sweat she wipes from her brow. "*Are you in trouble, Diane?*"

Her shocked voice needs calming. "Nina, please get Catherine a glass of water."

Baffled, I can't provide answers to two people gaping down my throat. Urgent assurance must be said to her before she pushes for more questions. "I'm not in trouble, Catherine," I promise. "I don't know what they want. I'll soon find out. Nina, stay here. Everything will be fine."

"Mom—I'll go. You're in a robe."

Pulling the robe tight and realizing I'm nude.

"I'll be right back, Catherine. Bring them up, Nina."

*

Thoughts of facts: I hear, but I am not sure maybe because I didn't want to after the word '*dead.*' Unconsciousness scatters its seeds, rooting itself inside me. Waking means acknowledging facts I can't bear to comprehend, keeping my eyes shut, drowning in numbness, hearing from the living room Nina's hysterics. Cleo, Eric, and Catherine comfort her. Juliette sits on the bed, rubbing my forehead. She calls my name. I open my eyes, blurred from what the police informed.

*

"Diane. Diane," Juliette's repeats, "I'm here for you. Drink this vodka. You've had a great shock."

At this moment—turning away from her, I wish I were someone else. Sour saliva dribbles. I've wet the bed. I don't care.

"Are the police still here?"

"They left after you fainted. I saw the police coming into your apartment, and I came down to see what the matter was. It's just awful." Juliette tries to stay calm, but her voice gives way to sobs. "Do you need me to call anyone?"

"Tell my daughter to come here. I must call Sarah." Juliette leaves.

Nina and Eric come in with Catherine and Cleo

"Nina. We have to call Sarah and Camille. I need to----."

"How could this happen, Mom?" Nina falls into Eric's arms. "Why?" I check my phone, and there are ten missed messages, all from Camille. I'm not good at this. What do I say?

"Eric, please take Nina out into the living room. I need to talk to my sister. Catherine, Cleo, Juliette, please stay."

*

Thoughts of despair: happy birthday to me. Three people are dead: Mother, Helen, and Richard. My mother's letter reads with blatant sobriety. Camille's voice shatters in our mother's own words in the letter she wrote.

Diane, I have six months of pain at best to live. It will be too late after reading this letter. My rationale is a straight arrow. I know what Richard did to Leah. I eavesdropped outside the bedroom door when you were staying with me. You asked if he molested her as you repeated what Sarah confessed about his and Leah's visit to London. I surmised he denied it. Call it my intuition as I begged you over and over to tell me what was on your mind. I knew your avoidance meant the most horrible thing a mother and wife can suspect of her husband. I want to think you never knew all these years. God forgive you if you did. I leave that between you and him.

Helen confirmed as much when she got drunk. You know how she could talk. Richard confessed to her years ago of what you accused him. She turned a blind eye because she loved her son and hoped he'd change. She encouraged him to get involved with Julie Meyers. It was her hope Richard would leave you and the girls. Richard's father or his brothers didn't know, or so she said. I don't trust the family. After I'm gone, you'll have to find out that truth. Her guilt, your settlement, was to wipe her conscience clean Calculated death is painless. I insisted Helen take us to Richard, who was removing some last items out of his and your house. I told her I wanted to say goodbye to him and see the place one last time. She drove me, unaware of my intentions. When we pulled into the driveway, I shot her in the temple. I feel nothing for my actions as she and I will meet again in Hell. My next planned steps are without a second thought. I rang the bell and shot Richard in the heart as soon as he opened it.

My own life dissolved, walking from one room to another, its beauty tainted from his abuse to you and his daughter. I saw no wonderful memories of birthdays, Christmas, or family visits. I heard you screaming because he was beating you. I stood in Leah's room and saw him on top of her as he took her youth. I made up my mind the last bullet would be the right thing to do.

Leah told me when she was ten, a wall divided the closeness between you and her. I'm sorry, Diane, for all I did as a failed mother. You have a chance to build a relationship with Leah. Try for her sake and yours. Her tough exterior is begging for love. I leave you. Know I'm better off dead than suffering from pain—as Richard and Helen are better off dead for their sins.

*

Thoughts of atonement: *first journal entry of 2000. Life has dealt me with many cards. Waiting for Eric, where we first had tea, is one of them. Eight months have passed since my birthday and the deaths of Mother, Richard, and Helen. Inquiry investigations, property, and Mother's WILL drag on. Samantha, my old shrink, has a new office in the Village. We are the same— doctor and patient. My assignment this week is to make a journal entry of what I feel. Ha! I hate this. Samantha is pregnant. Father undisclosed. I laugh. Motherhood is a bitch, so is being a sister. Camille and I don't talk much since Mother's funeral. Legal communication passes between our attorneys. Californian weather suits her family better and puts plenty of distance between us. She said Denver's beauty is gone since Mother died, and the winter is giving Alan arthritis. Camille blames me for Mother's death and for staying with Richard. How could I tell her the nightmares I had and lived? Leah, where are you? The detective said you left France and moved to Prague—alone. He promises a report soon. Sarah flourishes at Oxford with opportunities as a teaching assistant. My Nina takes pictures of the homeless and the gritty side of New York as she calls it. Her recent exhibit sold more than ten thousand dollars.*

*

Juliette and I are tearing up the fashion world. We will preview a spring collection in Paris, New York, and Milan. My investment is running like water. Cleo's non-profit, Lost and Found, was written about in the New York Times. And Eric . . . dear Eric, we marry in two months. I think about you, Richard, wishing your death, not on anyone. Samantha told me Lloyd, your father, died of a heart attack on Christmas Eve, and Jared Longview's heart gave out the next day. Julie Meyers sent me a picture of your son. Yes, for my atonement, I have become her friend.

*

My end of all I've been through is my beginning.